THE CHURCHGOER

ALSO BY PATRICK COLEMAN

Fire Season

THE CHURCHGOER

A Novel

PATRICK COLEMAN

NEW YORK • LONDON • TORONTO • SYDNEY • NEW DELHI • AUCKLAND

HARPER PERENNIAL

This is a work of fiction. Names, characters, places, and incidents are products of the author's imagination or are used fictitiously and are not to be construed as real. Any resemblance to actual events, locales, organizations, or persons, living or dead, is entirely coincidental.

HarperCollins books may be purchased for educational, business, or sales promotional use. For information, please email the Special Markets Department at SPsales@harpercollins.com.

FIRST EDITION

Designed by Jen Overstreet

Library of Congress Cataloging-in-Publication Data has been applied for.

ISBN 978-0-06-286410-9 (pbk.)

19 20 21 22 23 LSC 10 9 8 7 6 5 4 3 2 1

To my sister and brothers and our parents

And what remains when disbelief has gone?
Grass, weedy pavement, brambles, buttress, sky

A shape less recognisable each week,
A purpose more obscure. . . .

—Philip Larkin, "Church Going"

San Diego? One of the most beautiful harbors in the world and nothing in it but navy and a few fishing boats. At night it is fairyland. The swell is as gentle as an old lady singing hymns.

—Raymond Chandler, *The Long Goodbye*

THE CHURCHGOER

1.

WHEN I FIRST SAW CINDY LIU STANDING ON A STREET CORNER IN Oceanside, trying to thumb a ride out of town, I wondered why a young woman like her was hitchhiking, but I didn't think it was any great mystery—bad boyfriend, bad drugs, bad job, bad upbringing, bad decision making, bad luck, or maybe a misguided optimism, a romantic attraction to the sixties or some other brief bohemian flowering that rose up between the paving stones of greed or progress or those other more direct forms of bloodletting. A few facts between not-knowing and knowing, that's all. A puzzle. But this isn't about puzzles.

It was morning. The sky was mottled gray like a well-used rag. The day was threatening rain but only in that imprecise, Southern Californian way: the cloud cover could be fog off the sea, a marine layer set to burn off in the afternoon, or an honest-to-God rain cloud—a rare-enough prospect that most of us don't believe in them until the first drop hits our face. It was impossible to know whether the overcast would evaporate with the day or not. As the heavy traffic to the beach attested, everyone hoped—everyone demanded—that it would.

I'd gone to Angelo's for breakfast after an early morning surf at North Jetty. The floor and counters in Angelo's were red-and-white ceramic tile, or had been before the white had yellowed and the red browned. In the kitchen, visible beyond the counter, a loose piece of lettuce skittered on the griddle. A man wearing a red T-shirt and a white apron sang "Cocino dos hamburguesas en la mañana, yo cocino dos hamburguesas en la noche" to the steady slap and sizzle of flipped, flaring meats. It smelled like fry oil and oregano. I liked their self-serve coffeepot, something you don't see much anymore, one of those industrial ones with the brown-rimmed glass for regular. If asked for decaf, they'd send you down the block and question your dignity as you left, as was only right.

I ordered a breakfast burrito and coffee, filled the chipped mug, and made my way to a window booth that looked out over Pacific Coast Highway. On my way in I'd noticed the woman across the street, and she was still there by the pitched roof of the Wienerschnitzel. Between us was stalled traffic heading in both directions, one hers and the other not. Behind her, the ketchup-and-mustard umbrellas looked like a clutch of cocktails abandoned by a party of friends. I didn't know what that made her. Stray olive, maybe. She wore a yellow T-shirt and cutoffs, and her hair was short and black. A cardboard sign I couldn't read was wedged into her hip.

There's a person with a cardboard sign for every block of Coast Highway, but that was especially true here, by the freeway on-ramp and off-ramp. People were always coming and going from downtown Oceanside. It was the first southbound pit stop after the long, dusty expanse of the Camp Pendleton Marine Base, a place for those new recruits to let off steam, the most directly accessible beach on which the inland invasion from Temecula, Murrieta, and Hemet could mount their temporary assault, an easy town to hop a train (in one of the cars or on one) and ride south toward the border or north to Los Angeles. It was a good place to get a tattoo, if you didn't care about spelling or aesthetics. A good place to find a motel that charged by the hour. Or it was one of the places where you lived if you worked in San Diego and couldn't afford other options. It wasn't a place many people stayed if they could help it. I liked that about it. Maybe *like* is too strong a word. Anyway, I was one of those broke people, in more ways than one. So a hitchhiker with a sign taking in some lungfuls of exhaust and the tepid, sickly smell of hot-dog water was unremarkable enough. She was attractive, though, and I wasn't against looking.

The voice of the Greek woman behind the counter called out that my order was ready. The way she said it, without a pause, made it sound like my first name was the food I was about to eat: "Breakfast burrito Mark. Breakfast burrito Mark." It made me glad I hadn't ordered Tony's Special.

I got up, took my tray, and snagged a napkin and a bottle of Tapatío on my way back to the booth. Across the street, the woman tapped the sign against her calf. She was probably twenty-two or so, I guessed. I peeled back the paper on my burrito, took two shallow bites, and filled the hole with hot sauce. A car full of young men pulled off in front of her, and she leaned into the passenger window. With the red sedan in the way, I couldn't see much until it lurched back into the traffic, which was suddenly moving again. There she was, in the flashes between the passing cars, a fountain drink exploded at her feet, raising a middle finger to taillights. She craned her back, lifting the bird on high to make sure they saw it, and said some words that I couldn't hear but that were, in a more elemental way, intelligible enough.

She took a black hoodie from her backpack and wiped at her

feet. She kicked the cup away, cursed some more, cleaned her kicking foot again, and lost her balance, falling onto one hip and flinging an arm up as overcompensating counterbalance. She talked to herself, seated on the concrete, stuffing the hoodie back in her bag. The traffic ground to a halt once more, and she vanished behind one of the beach-bound cars. Bad drugs or bad booze, I decided. Poor kid. I went back to my food.

Lost to my thoughts, meager as they were, and the bundle of grease and chilies I was eating, I hadn't noticed the young woman cross the street until she came through the door to Angelo's. The counter was unmanned, and she propped one arm against it and pivoted, swinging her hips back and forth. I tried not to look—women can feel old eyes on them, and I didn't like being reminded of what I'd become—but then I would come to, wondering something not exactly ineffable about the frayed denim of her cutoffs. I poured more Tapatío on my burrito and bit.

She dropped her backpack on the ground and gave it a swift kick. Her worn T-shirt was more a vague impression of yellow over a black bra. Scowling at the menu, she mouthed the different options, squinted at off-putting items, debated her possibilities for an audience of one. She reminded me of someone, but I couldn't place it. I had a feeling she was never not conscious of being watched. Little did I know.

It's hard not to think of her as I would later: hair dyed, living under a different name. Those two versions of her phase in and out of each other, like the picture on my garbage television. It's hard not to wonder about the negative space between them, the lines of static, to ask what was real there. Everything else is a puzzle. That's the mystery.

2.

THE GREEK WOMAN EMERGED FROM THE KITCHEN TO ATTEND TO THE customer. There was a bit of back-and-forth that I wasn't trying to hear, but then a pleading note emerged in the younger woman's voice. The woman behind the counter had her hands up, saying, "I can't, I can't."

The hitchhiker gestured with her open wallet. "I had money—I don't—someone must have swiped it," she said. "I'm just trying to get a little something to eat. Please."

Then it came back, an impression from what felt like another life: Hannah Trout, one of the small-group leaders from the church I had led, and the way she would move from social circle to social circle, a kind word here, a prompting question there, a little shared anecdote about how prayer had helped her settle on her summer plans or pursue musical theater. And the look she'd given me when I'd taken her aside and questioned whether she was acting out of love for God or for the admiration of her peers. "I don't know what you're talking about," she had said, looking at me in horror. I asked her if she was too focused on trying to perform for everyone in this perfect way, said that I wondered if she knew the envy it was creating in the other girls, how it was seen as flirting with the boys, how she might be putting personal motivations ahead of God's. "What would you do," I had asked her, "if no one was watching? Only God." Her expression went cold, tears just held in reserve. "I was wrong," she said. "*You* don't know what you are talking about. There's always someone watching." Then she left, found another leader to work with. I know what she meant now, the impossible contortionist act asked of young evangelical women. But this was toward the end of my pastoral career. A precursor, a warning sign, a kind of imprecation. Before everything went dark.

"No, I just can't," the Greek woman said again to the hitchhiker. I hated these memories, their insidious tentacles, and forced them down someplace deep and dark. Memories never did any good. I needed them as much as watered-down Tabasco.

The hitchhiker needed a burger, didn't have the cash. Fine. Her legs were thin and pale, I could see plainly. She probably could use the calories. The cardboard sign rested against the white backpack she'd set below the counter. In a blocky but still somehow fanciful hand were the words SEATTLE? TAKE ME. GOING NORTH? TAKE ME.

I'd like to say it wasn't the Wienerschnitzel-strength whiff of suggestiveness that got me to my feet. That wasn't all of it, of course. *Caritas* and *cupiditas*, charity and cupidity, make nasty but satisfied bedmates all the time. There's a lot going on inside a person in a given moment, but I hadn't made a habit of helping people for a long time, and there was plenty down in there to be suspicious of, along with the one or two better impulses that had adapted to the lack of light and air, like a couple ghost crabs warming their claws on a deep-sea thermal vent. Maybe it was that memory of Hannah, the servant-leader, the look on her face, a history of disappointment there, working under the surface of my mind. It was my first mistake.

I stood and walked toward the counter, trying to keep my gait slow, disinterested. I knew how to approach someone like this. When I was halfway there, I called out, "I need a little guac, Cass." Cass, the Greek woman behind the counter, told me without a glance to hold on a minute. Then she told the girl she was out of luck. I studied the menu board, pretended I hadn't a clue what they were talking about.

"I'm not normally like this," the hitchhiker said. In the slight shift in how her voice projected—a little bump in decibels and a new clarity in the sandpapered tone—I knew she'd turned and was speaking toward me, that her words were making a more direct route to my ear.

"Huh?" I said, looking at her and then back to Cass. "Sorry, Cass, can you just give me the guac and I'll come back and pay later? My hash browns are turning to asphalt over there." The woman behind the counter mustered a look of complete disinterest, which was a step up from her usual expression of couldn't-give-a-rat's-ass.

In my peripheral vision, the hitchhiker turned her body to face me more fully. She was making no secret of looking at me, was waiting for me to turn. I could see what was happening. She'd made a mark. It was like watching a tiger hunt meat in the zoo, which made me both the meat and the keeper with the meat on his fishing pole. I turned.

"Hey, I'm sorry, man," she said. There was a jangliness to how she spoke. Up close she was pretty, young. There was a scatter of freckles across her nose, and her features made me think she was part Chinese, maybe. Her hair was swept across her forehead. It was dark and smooth, save the cowlick in the back that almost made her look like a hungover teenage boy but not quite. "I don't know what happened," she said, "but I must have got robbed. I had money and it's gone. Can you believe it?"

I shrugged. "Easy enough to believe in an empty wallet in Oceanside."

She was turning on the ball of her hand so that her elbow kinked out, and she let her head fall to the side just a fraction, not quite doing the sad, cute ingenue thing but doing just enough to suggest the idea. She was good. "I guess you're right. I was just trying to get a little bite to eat, you know?" She laughed but didn't drop that note of sadness. It might have been phony, but she looked so pitiful doing it, it didn't matter.

"And what," I said to Cass, "you can't spare one of those B-grade frozen Frisbees you've got in the back?"

Cass looked about as moved as the Rock of Gibraltar. "Now it's one, then it's twenty. So many bums around here, and if people start figuring out we're a soup kitchen—"

"Burger kitchen," I said.

"Whatever kitchen, free kitchen," she said. "Then we got a problem."

"If it'll move this show along faster," I said, reaching for my wallet, "let me pay for the thing."

"Oh, you don't need to do that," the hitchhiker said, but her voice was as thin as spider's silk and as sincere as a celebrity's lavender marriage. I just made a noise and passed some money over. She folded her arms and smiled sweetly. "Man, that's incredible. You don't meet enough people like you, you know? Any way I can get a Coke, too? I'm thirsty as hell."

I nodded and gave Cass some more money. "Never understood that one. 'Thirsty as hell.' I'd be thirsty *in* hell."

Maybe it was that I'd already paid, maybe it was the joke, but the girl picked up her bag and backed away, and the ingenue vanished.

Those sad eyes turned opaque, the way shop windows late in the day become mirrors reflecting Main Street. She looked like any teenager now. "Yeah. Good point. Thanks, man," she said tonelessly. She took her cup and made to go around me. Beneath the scent of cigarettes that wafted off her, I caught a slight sour note of alcohol. I'm always proud when I can sniff out my own kind.

"Being thirsty in hell," she said as she passed, "is a little like achieving nirvana and then having to go to the bathroom, isn't it?" She punctuated the comment with a brief, indescribable noise and kept walking.

Cass gave me my guacamole and change. I passed the hitchhiker at the soda dispenser. "If you want someone to bore you, I'm sitting over there," I said, pointing.

Most of the charm was already shaken out of her disposition. She said "Uh-huh" tonelessly. Then there was a terse smile, a quick glance that was more at my feet. "Thanks again."

But I hadn't stopped, was still walking back to my seat like I didn't even care to hear her reply. I didn't like these kinds of theatrics. They felt cheap, like a bargain suit off the rack, and I'd worn that costume too often in my old life to enjoy its feel on my shoulders. But I didn't know another way, and all interactions are more or less a self-gratifying manipulation anyway. Maybe I was bored. Obviously a little hard up. But she seemed like a girl who needed a hand, and deep in my brain some coming together of boredom and desire found a route into the memories of what it felt like to actually give one. It wasn't much, but it was enough to get me to trot out this cheap routine. Maybe she needed help, it was possible, though I admitted to myself how unsure of my own motives I was and always am. I thought of my younger self, never once skeptical of what he wanted and why. It made me shudder, that stranger.

A few minutes later, the girl was tossing her things across from me in the booth. She slouched into the seat and leaned back, head tilted down slightly, watching me with a gaze that had a canine quality—not the alpha but not willing to be kicked—cautious, paying a cautious attention. She was waiting for me to reveal myself as some kind of asshole, like she'd just sat through the trailers for three movies about assholes and now the animated studio logo for the feature was fading to black. There might have been a sullen smirk tucked into her mouth. I didn't know whether to tell her she was beautiful or call her parents to come pick her up.

"Are you a creep?" she asked.

"Excuse me?"

"You buy a girl a burger. Maybe you're a do-gooder, maybe you're a creep. I don't want to sit here with a creep. So which is it?"

"Not a creep. Not really a do-gooder either. I'm nothing."

"Nobody's nothing."

"You can get pretty close."

"Not without a lot of help."

She seemed to know something about it. I stewed on that for a minute.

"So," I said. "Seattle, eh?"

She looked startled a moment but then glanced at her sign and covered it well. "Yup. Seattle. So?"

I wiped my hands on a paper napkin. "What's in Seattle?"

She leaned forward on her elbows, hands pressed together against one cheek in a gesture of sloppy prayer. "The Space Needle."

There's cute, and then there's cute. This was definitely cute. She was looking to be irksome, and it irked me.

"Vegas has one of those, too," I said, feeling my blood rise unreasonably and not quite finding a way to back it down, "and there's about ten assholes on this block alone who'd leave their standing game of pocket pool to take you."

"I can see your hands."

"I hate Vegas," I said. I lifted my palms from the table, showed them, and went back to work on my burrito. I was going to ignore her now.

Cass's voice called out, "Crazy girl hamburger. Crazy girl hamburger."

When the hitchhiker came back with her plastic tray, she seemed different for the fourth time already. She moved bouncily. She had an affable air, like she was eating food with an old friend. She was trying to decide who best to be with me. It was manipulative, sure. A means to an end, no doubt. But also revealing of a need, like track marks on a forearm.

"I'm not trying to be a dick," she said as she peeled the wrapper from her burger and bit a glob of American cheese from the wax paper. "I'm really not. It's just been . . . man. A shit day." She sucked down on her soda and waved her hand at her hamburger. "But this. This looks magical. After a day like today, goddamn. You know, the world is full of shitty people saying shitty things."

"That's as good a description of the world as any," I said, and meant it. Most people who say things like that implicitly exclude themselves. I didn't. I wasn't sure where she'd put herself yet.

"Really, though. What's in Seattle? Let me guess, music career?"

"Now you're being a dick."

"That's a compliment. You look kind of punk rock."

"Punk is a sales pitch. I'm just done with this whole place. California."

"What's the plan up there?"

"Go plaid. Drink coffee. I don't know, throw fish or whatever the fuck people anywhere else than here do for day jobs."

"You can just say you're going to art school."

She laughed. "Fine. Film school. I'm not in, but I want to go to this place up there. I heard about it from a friend. It sounds amazing."

She took a few bites and stared out the window. I could almost see her trying to frame a view of herself standing out there twenty minutes before—establishing shot of young woman skipping town—and the kind of coming-of-age story that might start with.

"What's your name?" she asked while she ate.

"Mark Haines," I said.

"I'm Cindy," she said. "Cindy Liu. No jokes, okay?"

"Jokes?"

"You know. Dr. Seuss. *How the Grinch Stole Christmas*. The cartoon with the music? What can you do."

"No jokes," I said. That antennaed little Who from Whoville flashed through my mind, and then—there was, dimly, a child crying by a cradled telephone. The ruffles on her pajamas. My insides slipped a clutch. I felt something like thirst in my jawbone. An invisible hand reached out from my amygdala and smacked my cortex around.

There was a little too much rage in my voice when I said, "No matter how you rhyme it, Dr. Seuss was just another rich fuck from La Jolla who stepped out on his wife and didn't look back after she swallowed a bottleful of barbiturates. His books are garbage, too. Rhyming a generation's brains into insipidity."

Cindy looked a little appalled and a little amused, maybe at the story or maybe at me, I didn't know. "He wrote books?"

I must have made a face.

"Kidding," she said. "'Would you, could you, in a box? Could you, would you, with a fox?' You can't shake that shit out of your brain if you wanted to. Gets in early and it's stuck for life." That backed me off a little, but I could still sense my thoughts feeling around the edges of memories before some shred of self-protective rage chased them off.

"As far as rhyming goes," I said, "I'll start and stop with 'They fuck you up, your mum and dad. They may not mean to, but they do. They fill you with the faults they had and add some extra, just for you.'"

Cindy smiled thinly. "Good one, Doc." Maybe she thought she could glimpse an angle in what I'd said, old guy ingratiating himself to young girl with parent issues. But she left it alone, smiled, and then ate the burger in quick, eager bites.

I looked at the window. It had begun to rain. In the traffic a van packed with bobbing heads rocked on its shock absorbers. You'd think their beach day would be ruined, but now the out-of-towners would have the chance to play in the bubbly brown torrents of runoff where the right mouthful of water could mean diarrhea for a few days, or hep C. The shit stream gave them an excuse to stay out of the ocean, afraid as most people are of that less manageable body of water.

"Ahem," Cindy said, being downright polite with a sweet smile. "I wasn't kidding."

"What?" I asked.

"That whole *fa-roo, fa-roo* bit."

I guess I had been humming. "Oh, sorry," I said. "Watch out. The unconscious mind at work."

We talked idly while Cindy finished up—about the weather, the crowds, how hitchhiking wasn't what it used to be. She asked me how much better it had been in the 1960s. That stung. I could tell she was still hungry and bought her some french fries. She asked me if I was always this decent.

"Not always," I said, then heard how that sounded a little menacing and amended it: "I don't make a rule of anything beyond being just decent enough."

"Decent enough," she said, "is about as decent as I can handle anyway."

I nodded.

"Well," she said, bowing her head slightly, "thank you. I appreciate the food. I guess I was hungrier than I expected." A mannered, almost aristocratic note had entered her voice. Her enunciation shifted a degree to suggest more of an education than she would have owned up to, and her posture became more poised, her neck elongated. It was like watching a musician switch instruments during a single song. I wondered who she was, beneath all these selves she ran scales on. "You've done your good deed," she said. "You're decent enough for today. Commit your other crimes with a clean conscience."

I smiled. She was flirting. It wasn't often I got flirted with, and it flattered me. It probably had less to do with me and more to do with the food, but I didn't want to get caught up in that. I found myself looking a little too long at the freckles under her eyes.

"So," I said, shuffling out of the booth, "it's up in the air, but I might be going up to Oregon sometime in the next couple weeks. I could call you if it's going to happen. Not quite Seattle, but it'd get you closer to the Space Needle than Oceanside."

All the willful charm dropped, and she appraised me openly. The look presumed I was despicable, like she knew the different makes and models of despicable and she was cross-referencing my condition—my engine rattles, my dings—with some tragic internal *Kelley Blue Book*. I saw the tone was wrong. What I'd said was convenient like a lie, persuasive like an untruth.

Cindy tugged the hoodie from her bag and slipped it on, soda stains and all. "I'll be around town unless I find a ride sooner. Find me if shit comes together."

It was a dismissal, and I felt dismissed. I was back to feeling like someone to be suspicious of, some kind of creep. Her look had made me feel like that, though I wouldn't hold it against her. It was close enough to the look I gave myself most mornings. Still, I didn't like it coming from others.

I threw away our trash, including my untouched cup of guacamole, and we both left Angelo's.

Outside the light rain on concrete sounded like the hiss of a punctured tire. I asked Cindy if she was going back out to the corner with her sign.

"Rain out," she said. "I'm calling it a day."

In the oversized sweater she looked like a girl again. I could feel it in how my body relaxed.

"Peace, old man," she said in a way that wasn't exactly unkind, and then she walked off down PCH, and I went home. I didn't think I'd see her again. How wrong I was, like I always am.

3.

THE FIRST TIME WAS ABOUT A YEAR LATER. WE HAD TRADED A GOOD OLD boy for a cowboy in the White House, though that hadn't come to much yet. Otherwise, my life had drifted along, unchanged. That wasn't true. Time passed by uneasily, a week, a month, another month. What made it uneasy I couldn't figure out. Nothing had changed. Everything was exactly the same. The waves were different each day, but it was always the usual me paddling the board, and that was as far as my obligations could extend. But something was unsettled, in some minor way, like having the first onset of Parkinson's manifest as a trembling gallbladder, a deep and obscure interior twitch. I tried not to think about it and was succeeding.

The summer was in full blush again, the marine layer burned off by seven in the morning, fully cremated by eight, and buried at sea in time for brunch, leaving only heat and anything you could do to escape the heat. It was the only time of the year I surfed later than predawn, despite having to deal with the crowds. It was the only way worth its salt to stay cool. Paying an asshole tax was justified, if only barely.

I was threading my way through a pack of skaters, chain-smoking and catcalling from where the ramp from the pier came down to beach level, when Cindy called out from behind one of the pylons.

"Hey, old man," she said, grinning. "Did you ever go to Oregon?"

Being addressed in public—in any way, really—was out of the ordinary. I felt caged, seen. But I gave a wave, walked over anyway, not wanting to look rattled by a greeting, and told her no—still thinking about going, someday.

"Ah, that's too bad," she said. By then I was a few feet from her. She looked rougher than at Angelo's. The white V-neck had dirt patches up the back. Her hair was greasy. There was a new tattoo on her left shoulder, but the parts that emerged from her sleeve just looked like a splotch of spilled ink. I could have sworn there was a bruise on her forehead, painted over by concealer.

"What about Seattle? Too much grunge and coffee have you running back south?"

She smirked. "Seems like you and I both have a problem with follow-through. I'm ready to get the fuck out of here, though. For real this time."

I nodded. This time was different—that old line.

"It's nice," she said, pointing to the board I held under one arm. "Always rode a single-fin?"

"No," I said. I turned the green board over to look at the eight-inch fin on the tail. "But I like the feel of it. Slow and steady."

"Take me out."

"Excuse me?"

"In the water," she said, scoffing at my confusion. "I used to know dudes who wanted me to watch them surf, but no one's ever given me a lesson, and I've got jack shit going on today."

"What happened to getting out of town?"

"I'm working on it, but everyone needs a day off." To go by looks,

I would say it was more something else that was working on her. But it didn't cost me anything to say yes. That's what I told myself at the time.

She changed into a bathing suit—she kept it in that backpack—and came back. It wasn't much of a surf lesson: a half hour of her paddling face-first into white water, getting knocked off the board, scrambling back on, not catching waves. She called it off, obviously frustrated with the way the ocean continually surprised her, catching her from unsuspected angles, welling up when it seemed there was a moment of calm.

We went to the shore and I took the board from her. She looked lanky in the bikini she said she'd picked up for cheap from the tourist-trap gift shop, and she shivered as the water evaporated off her skin, rubbed red on the elbows, thighs, and belly from the friction of the wax.

"You did good," I said. "It was a good start."

"It was a good nothing," she said. "I know enough ways to get hassled already. I don't need another one as a hobby."

I tried to explain that it takes a long time to learn, that with a sport like running, if you run for two hours you're running for two hours, but a two-hour surf session might only mean actually riding waves for ten minutes, and that's if you know what you're doing. It didn't matter. She was done. Not unappreciative but more interested in warming up on the sand than getting into the ocean again. Everything I said made me feel like a burnout turned Little League coach. I didn't need that, as close to bone as it was, so I went back out.

The surf was small, but the sun was bright, the sky so blue it edged into ultraviolet. In the last few weeks the water had warmed that crucial degree or two. No wetsuit needed, and the feel of floating on my longboard a hundred feet from the pier, wearing only trunks, registered in a new way. I was aware of the salt water evaporating on my shoulders, the bead of it forming, then running from my hair down the right side of my nose and into my mouth, the vapor of sea becoming air rising up all around me to become clouds—clouds that travel the skies, that would form storms whose wind would send waves from distant corners of the Pacific to break where I floated. Sometimes a good water temperature can get you thinking like that. The last time it had happened to me, I was fourteen and preoccupied with asking God's forgiveness for what I'd been doing to the socks.

About twelve people were out: a few middle-aged men, an old woman, the rest teenagers. Looking south through the pylons, I could see the swarms of people who came to Oceanside in the summertime to turn the beach into the longest ashtray in the world. Cop cars bracketed the backside of the crumbling beachfront amphitheater. Dirty fires stoked with nonflammable substances sent up gray smoke signals. There were a thousand little shadowy bodies wading into the ocean, looking like a colony of misguided ants floating in a cluster at the edge of a puddle. On the sky-blue tower, a couple lifeguards in red swimsuits compared tan lines and tips for easy body-hair removal. Usually I stayed away except for dawn sessions to avoid the rankling presence of all these people, but they didn't bother me as much today. Instead of calling them the garbage of humanity, I thought of them only as stupid assholes, which was some kind of improvement.

Soon the crowd in the water changed. The teenagers headed to shore to eat burritos and catch seagulls in beach towels and throw fireworks at the rec center and cruise for girls who might fall for the insouciant, rat-haired surfer style. The usual things. They were replaced by a group of men in their thirties. It was like watching a time-lapse video. These guys were all heavy to near-obese, all too tan for their own good. A couple had some bastardized version of dreadlocks: short, thin ones sticking out in odd directions or tied up vertically in a style Pebbles Flintstone would have admired. One had a massive afro and was paddling carefully, trying to avoid having to duck-dive under a wave, probably not wanting to have to hit the salon for another perm. I knew the type: white guys who lived three to a room, some in the small pink houses between the pier and South Jetty, fancied themselves free spirits, drank too much beer, smoked too much pot, spoke too loudly, and surfed too poorly. They weren't the worst company, but I wouldn't hurt for losing it. After a half hour of watching them try to stand up on waves they hadn't caught, I was enjoying myself more.

One of them paddled out near me. He had a shaved head and a tattoo arching across his beer gut that read BARREL. He kept smiling in my direction. After five minutes of this flirtation, I smiled back. "Nice day."

The guy grinned and nodded.

I scratched my head. "I wish the waves had a little more push, but it's hard to beat trunkable water."

The guy raised his eyebrows like I'd said something profound and kept grinning and staring.

"Sorry, my mistake," I said. "You must be deaf, right? How about sign language?" I made a peace sign with my left hand and a special kind of bird with my right. A little flash of anger was all I ever needed. There's a kind of clarity to feeling that way. Maybe I wasn't touching some Eternal All anymore, or seeing the world in a grain of sand and a bead of salt water, but in the moment this felt better. I was feeling my limitations, and his limitations, and rubbing up against humankind's ability to make life an ineluctably large pain in the ass for others—the sad, gorillan mass of this humanity hurtling toward an unsatisfying and unceremonious end. But the guy was implacable. He just kept smiling. It baffled me into feeling a little less on edge.

Then he muttered something and started paddling in. "Later, man!" he called back.

I looked toward the beach and saw his friends all standing around in ankle-deep water. Then I noticed someone standing next to Cindy. It was one of the people from their group, the skinny one with the bleached orange, misshapen 'fro that made his entire head look like a goiter on a person from a *National Geographic*. He stood over Cindy, close to her. He was holding his shortboard and rocking a little, side to side. She was turned over partway and held her shirt, which she must have been lying on, up to her chest. She didn't look happy to be talking to him.

But then he walked away. Cindy watched until he was gone. A minute or two later, she lay down again. I tried to let it go and keep surfing, but the next wave I caught I rode all the way to the shore.

I walked up the beach to where she was lying on her stomach, reading. Sand clung to the upturned soles of her bare feet. Her hair had dried stiff and mussy, bits of salty white rime visible on the black of it. She looked like she was absorbed in what she was reading. I waited a full five minutes without her noticing, and the page didn't turn.

"I'm heading out," I said, too loudly.

The muscles in her back twitched. She turned over, not bothering to hold up the shirt, and gave me a hard stare. "You scared me."

I pretended to laugh, but I was watching her carefully. "Sorry."

"Yeah," she said. "I was ready ages ago." It sounded like something my grandmother would have said, and I almost called her on it. She started throwing things into her backpack hurriedly. I glanced at the title of the book she was reading and was surprised to see *Jane Eyre*. I'd have guessed *High Times*, or Plath.

"Don't feel too poor, obscure, plain, and little," I said.

It was the wrong thing to say, and she didn't even look at me when she told me to fuck off.

"Who was that curly-haired Rochester you were talking to?"

She was on her feet now, pulling a pair of khaki shorts up her legs. She paused with them halfway settled upon her hips, chewed her lip, realized she was chewing her lip, stopped, seemed to swallow, all in the space of a second or two. "No. He's nothing like that. As far from that as a subhuman can get."

"Was he bothering you?"

"Not really. He's just a guy from a while back, a jackass. One of those friend-of-a-friend situations gone wrong."

"So he wasn't hassling you?" I didn't know why I kept pushing at it. Just a feeling. If I'd thought hard about it, I would have recognized it as the feeling I used to get when, twenty years or another lifetime ago, I would be talking to a teenage girl, hearing her struggles and requests for prayers, nothing shocking or out of the ordinary, and in a moment, as if from out of the air itself, I knew something had happened with a boyfriend, that he'd been pressuring her, that it had just happened, that they'd gone too far. Then came a queasy kind of pleasure, the kind a doctor must feel at the sight of a body broken in a car wreck that she knows she can fix. But what I did wasn't fixing. It was discovering the injured person and then administering a kind of spiritual waterboarding. Follow-up treatment was the routine management of the resulting Stockholm syndrome.

Cindy buttoned her shorts, then rubbed her face and hair, hiding behind her hands. "He's a fucker but he's harmless, really."

"Someone should tell him to get that tumor of a head looked at."

She mussed her hair again, sending tiny flakes of salt floating around her face. With her arms over her head, her breasts made a set of parentheses where they met her armpits. As she brushed away the sand she found there, she said, "Protective rage. That's a new one." She raised her eyes to mine.

I was instantly rendered sheepish. "I'd just noticed. That's all."

"It's fine," she said. "It's even a little cute." She was teasing me, and I felt for a moment fifteen years old and clueless. "I don't think I'll have to deal with him again," she said, "so don't worry. No threat."

"Okay," I said, feeling false and insultingly paternalistic but also caught out, known for the part of me that was attracted to her, too.

"Ready to leave this hellhole of tourists and crackheads?" she asked, stooping for her bag.

"Yes," I said stiffly, now defensive.

She kidded me: "Aw. My protector."

"Where are you headed?" I asked as we walked up the stairs to the parking lot.

She stopped, so I followed suit. "Not sure," she said.

"I can give you a ride home," I offered. "I'm just a few blocks away."

She bit her lip and rocked back and forth on her heels. Her lip went white where the teeth pinched. A moment later, she said, "I, uh, I don't really have a place right now."

My gut cinched. It was like I'd swallowed lead weights. I'd bought her a burger a year ago, sure. But that was more a hazy memory than an ongoing habit of mine. The surf lesson had caught me off guard, but I'd gone with it, I don't know why. Maybe I do. That complicated dance, *caritas* and *cupiditas*, fluttering on the screen door like two lovesick moths. But knowing she didn't have a home to go back to now, and knowing what would come next, was all the reminder I needed of why I'd spent the last fifteen years avoiding—well, everyone and everything.

She watched me with half-lowered eyes, waiting to see if I would take up the thread. I did, against my better judgment.

"What do you mean you don't have a place?"

The response came fast. "Things fell through. Guy troubles. You know the drill."

"So back to your parents, then?"

"Ah, not them," she said in a tempered, brittle tone. "They're where they are, and my last living situation crapped out is all."

"Then where are you staying?"

She said, "That's what I was going to ask you."

My first response was dread. She rocked onto her toes toward me.

"I don't think that's a good idea," I said.

"What, your girlfriend wouldn't like it? Who's she?"

"No girlfriend," I said. There were plenty of reasons it wasn't a great idea—I didn't know her, she didn't know me—but I couldn't get one to come out of my mouth.

On the other side of the pier, two bikers fired up their choppers with a bang and rip. Cindy flinched and looked for the source of the sound. She tried to pretend she hadn't, but her neck flushed red and her breathing had changed. She was having trouble calming back down, and it showed.

She took a breath and smirked at me. "What," she said, "you're afraid of *me*? Fuck off. As the girl, I'm the one taking the risk in this situation. But you don't seem so bad. Let me just crash a day or two?"

She'd made a mark out of me, but that was fine. That was my name, and I was only in for a combo meal and a surf lesson at this point. Not that I took her for a true con artist. She was working her situation, with a good deal of caution and very little shame. She had reasons, I was sure. I could tell she hadn't always done this, but something in her life had turned over on her. I knew how that could go. How if it was bad enough, you might start to see how everything was a construct—an imaginary scaffold, allowing you to climb ten stories high but with no real bars to reach for once you started to fall—and so make your life close to the ground. How you might feel like you have more moves to make there, more control. I'd spent some time there before I saw its flaws and went further, subterranean.

Now she was angling for a place to stay. Who knew what else, down the line. I didn't like it but wasn't alarmed. Maybe that should have been the alarm, that I was letting myself entertain the idea, any idea.

"I'm used to my privacy," I said weakly.

"I'll stay out of the way," she said, her voice slipping into a soft, girlish tone without trouble. A memory of my daughter, Aracely, using the same tone crawled up my back like a case of sudden-onset scoliosis, left me feeling weaker, more hunched. I had been working out a tough bit of translation from the Koine Greek as part of a talk I was giving, long since lost in the oblivion of the past, and she came in to ask if she could just sit behind me and play with her small, blue train, she wouldn't even make a sound. I'd been struggling to keep all the theological implications of the passage clear and in context, struggling not to lose each shade of meaning in that strange alphabet. She wouldn't interrupt me, she promised. But of course—how could she help it—she had. I'd gotten angry then, my brain got ahead of me, and I didn't handle it well. Suffice it to say I was buying a new blue train the next day. Aracely never played with it again.

And here was this other girl, this young woman, and she was in a tough place, and she didn't seem like a psychopath, was even kind of beautiful, and she needed a hand, and what the hell did I have going on? What, even in terms of possessions, could she steal or destroy that I would miss? It wasn't the best idea, but I wasn't making many decisions with words like *best* or even *good* in mind—no words, in fact, but more the throaty sound a person makes when shrugging, a croak of resignation. I made the sound now.

"Come on," I said. "We'll try it, but if it's off, it's off. A couple days. That's it. Okay?"

I turned away and walked to my truck, not wanting to see the look on her face, not wanting to read anything into her reaction, not wanting anything she could do or say to call up any more memories, unbidden. I was afraid of them, and so afraid of her, but still I said yes. Why? Fear and memory, desire and self-sabotage. Maybe, only slightly possible, something like intuition, an intelligence that ran deeper than logic. It was hard to know at the time, and even harder to say, looking back. Like everything else.

4.

WE WALKED TO MY TRUCK, A LITTLE BEATER WITH A WHITE SHELL.

"A little on the nose, eh?" Cindy said, pointing to the sticker on the back window. It had AMBIVALENT printed over the Statue of Liberty in duotone red and blue. I shrugged off the comment, though I should have paid more attention to how quickly she'd drawn a bead on me. I'd been called ambivalent often enough, by everyone from my ex-wife to the guy taking my order in the Robertito's drive-thru. There was always an intended dig in it, an insult, but I failed to see what was wrong with it—took a certain pride in it, in fact. People with certainties were the problem.

When I got in the truck, the wave of scent hit me. It smelled like mildew and rotten seaweed worse than the Tokyo city dump—a good reminder to get the towel I'd been using all week out of the cab.

Cindy followed and stood at the passenger door. "Get in," I said.

"Sure," she said, voice muffled through the glass. She didn't move a muscle other than to raise an eyebrow. Maybe I wasn't the only ambivalent one.

"Well then," I said. "What's your call?"

"You said you were a decent guy," she said, and didn't move. Had I done something wrong? Had she caught me looking at her the wrong way on the beach? She eyed me with that cool, appraising expression again. There was a hint of warmth this time, a degree or two, maybe. She waved her hand theatrically at the door handle and let herself smile, and it was the kind of smile a person couldn't help but be pleased by. "Aren't you going to open the door for me?"

I grunted, annoyed, amused, and leaned across the gearshift to pull the handle.

After she got over hassling me about the smell, we both fell quiet. Heading down the road, having committed to this plan, there was a new tension in the air. I wasn't sure what to say next, and Cindy wasn't offering anything up, so we stayed silent.

On either side of us passed stereo shops and barber shops and sandwich shops with tiny sidewalk patios, the public library's stark white and blue facade and oversized square fountains. We crossed Mission Avenue and the specter of the newly built movie theater—the first part of a proposed "downtown revitalization program" that included five-star accommodations (that would maybe rank three when they opened), fine dining (which meant fish that wasn't breaded and served with french fries), and time-shares (scam opportunities)—in a place forever slouching around in the shadow of Camp Pendleton.

It was those fresh-faced jarheads, with weekend cash in their pockets and nothing good to spend it on, who would keep the used-car lots and seedy strip clubs and night spots humming, places where every other Thursday a Kentucky farm boy got knifed by a hood from the valley or vice versa, places where it was easier to find the rocks you smoke than the ones made of earth and shell. The chamber of commerce whipped up something like this every now and then, and the results never failed to disappoint, which was fine by me.

For a minute or two, Cindy's fingers drummed out emergency Morse code on the armrest. I knew what it meant. Then Cindy asked if she could smoke. I said, "Of course," and she held out a pack of clove cigarettes to me.

"No thanks. Quit a couple years back."

"Oh," she said, hesitating momentarily as she held the lighter up to the long black cigarette but then lighting it anyway. "I can wait. I don't need to." She inhaled hard, blew smoke out the window, and sank with a little more comfort into the corner between the seat and the door.

"It's fine. I still enjoy a little secondhand."

"Makes it sound like you have a watch fetish."

I turned left on Michigan, off the main drag and into a neighborhood of small old houses, fenced yards, and barred windows, and pulled the truck in at my place. It was a two-bedroom house a few blocks east of PCH, built in the thirties, last properly maintained around V-J Day. The paint was ashy green, and a monstrous bougainvillea grew up one wall, where the wind set it to tapping against a window. On the border of the yard, I shared a sycamore with the neighbor. The dead, yellow grass was all mine.

I headed up the walk and unlocked the front door where the smell of the ocean from the west and the freeway's collective exhaust from the east met at my doorstep. Cindy came along after she finished riffling through her backpack in the truck.

Just inside, I kicked off my sandals. I couldn't help but give the living room a once-over for anything embarrassing, which was like a porn star asking his prayer-warrior mom if his latest feature had any parts in it that made her uncomfortable. A wobbly metal doctor's tray held a very small, very old TV against one wall. Next to it was a sagging particleboard bookcase gone yellow with *National Geographics*, like the whole thing had been lifted straight out of the DAV thrift store, which had in turn gotten it from the death room of a ninety-eight-year-old recluse. I'd personalized it a bit, put a radio and a tiny, fuzzy cactus on top. That made me feel better now. The couch opposite the TV was forest green worn down to lime near each armrest.

Down the hall was an office and a bedroom, but she wasn't going that way. The living room opened up on one side into the kitchen, and I went there. Cindy followed, a neutral expression on her face as she weighed the items in the house as if they were words, feeling the connotations come together into a singular expression of the disrepair of my life. Or maybe I was projecting that onto her out of habit. I didn't ask, didn't want to know.

Instead, I opened a bag of coffee, the smell of which calmed me. I asked if she drank coffee, and she said of course she drank coffee, so I put a pot on. She sat at the small enamel kitchen table.

"Make yourself at home," I said. "I'll be right back." I went out to the truck, took the nine-foot board and wetsuit still dripping from my early morning session from the bed and the ratty stink of a towel from the cab, and walked through the side gate into the backyard. The yard was small, with a stunted palm in one corner and a square concrete pad under a rotting wood pergola. I lay the board on the concrete, hosed off the wetsuit and towel, and dangled them from slats overhead.

I went back in through the sliding glass door to the kitchen. Cindy had gone through my mail and was reading a catalog—reading at this point in history meaning to flip through a series of pictures and price tags.

The coffee was done, so I poured two cups, gave her one, and asked her where she was from.

She took a sip. "This coffee is intense. The good stuff. You might have trouble getting me out of here."

She watched me, smacking her lips like a woman in a Folgers commercial, waiting for me to remember my line, but that didn't stop me from finding her evasion irritating. I didn't say anything until she got the hint that it was my only question, that I'd just stare now.

"In the city. *Originally*," she said with a derisive edge. "But that was a long time ago. The last place wasn't too far from here. *That* place, whew. A dump, compared to this one."

"That's saying something," I said.

She tucked her head in embarrassment. "Oh, no. That's not what I meant."

I gestured my thumb toward the living room. "I don't get a lot of guests, and I've stopped trying to impress myself."

"Don't think twice about it," she said. "I'm not looking to be impressed."

Her fingers drummed out a slower rhythm than before, more a leisurely bossa nova. The other arm stretched out along the chair back, limp at the wrist. She held her chin up, taking a good full look back into my eyes. She was trying to be somebody's darling, but it was all a little much. She'd only taken a sip of coffee, but her energy had shifted again. I wondered what was in that backpack and how much of it she'd had while I'd been outside.

"Oceanside is sketchy, though," she said. "Why do you live in such a sketchy place?"

"You come for the beach. But it's the people who offer a hit off the crack pipe if you'll let them smoke it in your car that get you to stay."

"Oh, you know Bruce, too?"

I smiled. She was quick. "Why are you here?"

"I've been bouncing around. My South O family got weird."

"Oh, so your family moved here?"

"Ha, no, God. This guy and his two kids. Said I was like their aunt, but he just wanted free child care. Who knows what else. Well, I mean. It's not hard to know."

"Sounds like a winner."

"You should have seen the jarhead before that. Kinda fun to stay on base, though. Trip to walk around at night, all these killing machines everywhere. You feel like you're doing something important—like everything's a movie—even if you're just drinking Pabst and watching *The Matrix* a hundred fucking times."

I laughed. "What happened with him?"

"Let's just say there's a red pill, a blue pill, and then there's weed and Doritos. He was really into Doritos. So much for the brave and the few."

There was a lull then, enough time for the feeling of this all being a serious mistake to fill the air like smoke.

"What's the plan now?" Cindy asked uncomfortably.

"No plan for me," I said, swallowing the black coffee in big slugs. The twitching, dry need in my stomach began to go slack. The hum in my nerves went quiet. "I work nights, and I haven't slept since five o'clock yesterday. Before I go back tonight, I have to get some rest."

She motioned at the mug in my hand. "But you're drinking coffee."

I made a noise. "That's what works for me. Strange nerves." In truth, with the fresh caffeine running through my system, this was the most tired and calm I'd felt in hours.

"What's your gig?"

"Security."

"Rent-a-cop?"

"More like paid book reader, sometime walker, and occasional flashlight waver." I went to refill my empty cup and offered her another by pointing at the pot. She shook her head, waved her hand over the top of her still-full mug like a blackjack player committing to stay.

She pushed her chair back with a grinding sound—the kitchen

floor was covered in a fine dusting of sand—and made like she was brushing crumbs off her knees. "Shit, man. Sounds like a thrill."

I spoke facing into the cabinets while I replaced the pot. "I tried that 'living for work' thing. You know, instead of 'working to live.'"

"And?"

"At least this is clean. I don't hurt anyone. I protect things no one wants to steal. I get the mornings free to go surfing before all the goons arrive. I get to sleep early. It's nothing terrible."

She'd slouched in her chair and folded her arms. "I'm not one to judge," she said, making a Vanna White wave along the length of her body, "not when I'm, well, as you can see. But you don't have much of a fire lit under you, do you?"

I winced inwardly. Outwardly, I tried to cover it with a sleepy smile. It must have looked off, because Cindy frowned. That had been my father's phrase. My boy, he'd say, with the fire of God lit under him. Back when I'd been in love with the Lord and everyone else through Him. When I was the fresh, lily-white face of a rising church's youth program. Before my sister, Ellen, died, before God—the tricky one, the mean and silent one, the one conjured by a sand-blown heap of Greek and Aramaic letters written and rewritten by how many hands, hands that had grasped and clutched, thieved and hit, groped and fucked, caressed and pulled away—before that God had become inscrutable, insensate, absurd. That fire was transmuted by doubt into something else. Something that led me to resent other people's love and the way they continued to find something in prayer, that led me to drink, led me to tell my wife and daughter that I had nothing to celebrate, that none of us did, before a display of unopened presents and a birthday cake with my name scrawled on it in a five-year-old's hand—that led me into another blackout across several days, a limbo of losing myself. Having a fire lit under me was the last thing I'd ever needed.

"Extinguished," I said.

We looked at each other a moment. I thought I recognized something there, recognized her recognizing it in me. An intensity. A need to account. A failure to do so. She'd grown stiff and uncertain, was eyeing me in a different way—not just sizing up my usefulness or wondering to what degree she would laugh at the memory of me, this odd old man she'd crossed paths with, once she'd moved on. There was some glimmer of hope in that look, and a lot of loneliness. Then she leaned forward, cradling an invisible nozzle in her hand, and made the sound of fire-retardant foam streaming out toward me.

"Alright, alright," I said, waving the imaginary spray from my face. She stopped.

"Nah, I'm just playing," she said. "It's all fine. 'Working to live'—isn't that everybody? At least, I don't see anybody playing at it." Her laugh was bitter, a little condescending. I recognized that, too.

I nodded, finished the coffee, and rinsed my cup in the sink. "Okay, then," I said, feeling exhaustion stretch itself out in my limbs. "I have to catch some sleep. Help yourself to anything in the fridge. Try the TV at your own risk. Don't run off with all my stuff. You're not going to run off with my stuff, right?"

She raised a hand like a Boy Scout. "Swear to God," she said.

"No, not Him." I hadn't said it meanly, but something must have come through in my tone. Cindy looked at me in confusion, a bit of that wary-dog look returning. "To me," I said. "I'm the one paying attention."

5.

HUNGRY AND BORED, I CAME BACK IN THE PREDAWN DARK AFTER wandering the sodium-lit corridors of the industrial complex I patrolled. The other guy I worked with had called in sick, and I avoided chatting with the subs. The house lights were out, so I put the key in the door silently, lifted on the knob, pushing in toward the jamb to ease the creak, and went into the living room. I expected Cindy to be sleeping on the couch, but I could sense in the darkness filling the room that no one was on it. That meant she had gone, maybe with an armful of my things, or that she was in my bed. One prospect was more uncomfortable than the other. Parts of me fought to decide which. I moved down the hallway, opened the bedroom door, and flipped on the lights. The bed was empty, the comforter as flat as the surf at La Jolla Shores in the summertime.

Every room was devoid of signs of her. With the sense of emptiness came sadness. I didn't know what kind of sad this was, but like all sadnesses it was complicated.

Like all sadnesses, too, it was best dealt with by dulling the senses through gustatory self-hatred, but all I had were three frozen pizzas. I put one in the oven and then heard the sound on the patio. I couldn't place it and stayed motionless to hear it more clearly: a muffled cough. The glare on the glass was too thick; I couldn't see through it. I opened the door and stepped out, not knowing exactly what I'd find until my eyes dilated and my body recalibrated to the sudden lack of light.

"He returns," a voice said from the dark. "You do work the late shift, damn." It was Cindy. Her voice had a rough-sanded quality, and there was a smell of clove cigarettes and the lower, swampier stink of burned tobacco brewing in still water. Her form was still black on just lighter black.

"I thought you were a burglar."

"A pretty shitty burglar," she said. "But I couldn't get these chairs over the fence, and then they were just so damn comfortable. Maybe that's something you should try at your job: make things so awesome that robbers just don't want to leave." She laughed a little too hard at her own joke, and something glass clinked.

The backyard brightened as my eyes adjusted. The patio came into being, a series of nearly indistinguishable deep grays delineating the darker forms of the table and chairs, the lighter forms of concrete and skin—long, slender arms and bare calf where a pant leg of gray sweats had ridden up. There was a case of beer at her feet and one of my coffee mugs on the ground next to her that she ashed into.

"I'll see if we can swing pinball machines in all the buildings and let you know."

"And if you don't put quarters out, you could even make a little money on it in the bargain." She took a pull from the beer and waved her cigarette at the case. "Take one, sit down, relax."

I walked over and took one from the box. I should have said I was sober, that I had been for years, but I didn't. Instead, I sat in one of the other chairs and twisted off the cap. The bottle was sweating, a nauseating not quite cold. It felt weighty in my hand, and the bready scent fired off something in my olfactory bulb that cinched my gut. I focused on the sensation of my hand warming the glass where I held it. That would help keep me from taking a drink—focusing on the hand and asking why it had decided it was a good idea to hold this, to pretend to a self. Cindy looked happy to have company. Bad hand, I thought. Bad rest of me.

"So who'd you con out of the free beer?" I asked.

Cindy giggled in a guilty, pleased way. "Yeah, sorry. I have money. I don't normally go home with a guy I'd scammed lunch off of."

I nodded, not angry but more thinking about the beer going tepid in the bottle I held, the skunky flavor of it. My hand felt clammy. I tapped the bottle against the edge of the table. "Don't go rushing for your wallet," I said.

"I'll get you back," she said, stretching her legs across the table in my direction. I could make out the follicles on her calf. "Tomorrow or something. I swear. Maybe it should be a burger and fries. You know, quid pro quo, an eye for an eye, all that bullshit."

"Maybe we should think about breakfast first," I said.

"Mm, breakfast. Yes. I'm definitely going to need some breakfast here soon." She reached her arms above her head and arched backward over the chair until I thought she might tip over. The pale, sand-colored band of her stomach showed in the dim light. "Did you know you only get PBS on that junker of a television in there? All night, animals eating animals, stiff hosts who've lost the ability to modulate their voices, and the fucking British. Christ."

She was being charming. She knew she was being charming, was working that angle again. It made sense. She was good at it. But sometimes it made her seem like a drunk socialite trying to flirt her way out of a DUI arrest—like the rest of us were only so real. There was too much need in it, a touch of the desperate. But if I was being honest, that was the part that had me curious, more than the rest.

"And speaking of Christ," she continued, "why've you been playing the fool?" I thought of my soft-shoe in Angelo's when I first met her, the small steps to build trust and get someone to accept help, which I could enact as if by muscle memory, the bottle in the sober alcoholic's hand. But when she said, "Why didn't you tell me you were a thumper?" I was confused and a little relieved to avoid confronting those other things.

She didn't wait for me to respond, still playing out this routine she must have been running to herself while waiting for me to return. "I thought you might have been, with that joke about hell. But when you didn't try to trade a joke and a burger for a new convert in your strip-mall pews, I figured I was being paranoid. Those books you've got, though! Systematic theology, the 'historic' Jesus, pastoral care and counseling, and sin and this, sin and that. . . . Christ, man. You're the full-fledged, real-deal Bible thumper, aren't you?"

I almost took a swig from the beer without thinking about it but caught myself. "I thought I could trust you with my things." The books were in the back room. She must have been snooping around.

"I didn't take any," she said. Her voice was so loud I was worried about waking the neighbors. "Why would I want to? Lies and guilt trips is all that is. Besides, you never said anything about not *looking* at your stuff. Even that I could only do for so long. Just don't try to Greg Laurie me, okay?"

She seemed to know something about it, if Greg Laurie could be a verb in her vocabulary. Still, I didn't like her imagining me mounting a one-man, run-down Harvest Crusade out of my kitchen. "I'm nothing like that," I said. "I barely believe in breakfast, and those are old books. Haven't read them in fifteen, maybe twenty years."

"It's cool," she said. "Let your freak flag fly. I used to be a Jesus freak, too, so I get it. But just don't come at me with it. I'd be gone in a minute. I'd rather sleep in a ditch."

"I don't believe in anything. I have nothing to push. I'm re-formed, as they say." Unformed was a better phrasing of it: to have removed all traces of that structure that my parents had poured my childhood being into, the tower I'd built up from that poor, sand-soft foundation.

"Why keep the books?" she asked. "I would have made a bonfire from them and roasted marshmallows over the embers." She smacked the table with a palm for emphasis, and the inset glass rattled gratingly in the frame. It was getting broad, her reaction, and it made me want to go small—but I didn't think it was insincere.

"Sentimental reasons." I considered leaving it at that but figured it didn't matter—she'd already found the books. "I used to be a pastor. This is a long time ago. And when I gave it all up, God and the job, I said goodbye to a lot of people. A lot of the books were gifts. Some from my parents. They're dead." Now that I'd started, I wanted to try to explain more: how the books had lost their luster and meaning, but the shell of them had retained some magic of the gifting, of the gift giver. But I couldn't work it out in words just then.

"Ah. Sorry?" she tried out, unsure of whether my parents' being dead was a bad or good thing. She picked some felt off her pants. I realized I was clanging the bottle against the table a little too loudly, a little too frequently now. The neighbors really were going to squawk if we kept this up.

"What brand were you?" she asked in a softer, more intimate tone, as if she'd read my mind.

"I'm sorry?"

"Sect, denomination, flavor. You know."

"Pretty fundamentalist," I said. "Bible based. Literalist. Conservative. Two degrees away from bombing abortion clinics. We called it love." Even I had my stock phrases and scripted responses, a series of words that didn't quite touch on who I had been.

"Love. Right." She worked her fingernail under the label on her beer bottle and began peeling it from the glass.

I asked her if she knew something about that kind of love.

"Masturbation," she said. "The rub-up of hypocrites. That's what I know about it. A big show of caring, which'll go on and on until it actually costs them something."

There was some turmoil in her. I could recognize it like déjà vu, could feel it more in my chest than in my head. She wasn't like the young people I'd counseled, the ones who struggled with doubt, with anger, with the unreasonable terms of their families and lives. Those people I'd tried to make see how they were still arguing with God, even when they turned away from Him. But with her, it was different. Maybe she was closer to me, not angry at God for anything He'd done or ordained but angry at Him for being a ghost, a figment, an illusion—angry at the minds of some indefinite number of prior selves who had been fooled by the movement always on the edge of vision, the feeling of being watched that never went away, that sense of a presence who granted the deepest wish: never to be alone.

"Hm," I said. "What was your brand?"

"No special name. Pretty evangelical. The place was called Canaan Hills, if that's any indication."

"Sounds like a housing development."

"Big rock-band worship services, mission trips and prayer retreats every few weeks, the whole shit show. It's like living in Disneyland when you're young."

"What happened?"

"I stopped being young," she said. "You figure out there's a guy inside the Mickey suit. He's a dick. He's pulling down Ariel's Lycra tail to fuck her in the mop closet on Tuesdays. He's getting blown by Prince Eric in Monstro the whale's mouth on Wednesdays. The Queen of Hearts is a full-blown racist. Goofy's a dog, which means he doesn't have a soul and is going to hell. So there's that. And the food just makes you fat and sick and broke."

I let her see my smile at that. It was shtick, a script she'd learned to slip into conversation as a spontaneous and charming rant. Who was I to judge? But also, who was I to pass up a chance? The rote patter showed she'd told this before, and the pleasure she took in it wasn't just about getting a laugh. No, she relished talking this way, which meant it wasn't too long ago that she would have registered saying these things as blasphemy. There was still enough rebellion there, a turning away that she wanted someone or some idea of something to see and be dismayed by. Talking about Disneyland was pure Californian. That's all we can do. It's our foundational experience. The first time I saw fireflies I couldn't stop thinking it was nearly as good as seeing their twinkle-light cousins while knocking down the lazy river on the Pirates of the Caribbean. But the rant also showed her youth, which was something I kept losing track of with her leg stretched out before me.

I said "hm" again.

"What did it for you?"

"That's between me and the God that doesn't exist," I said. It was her turn to laugh. She didn't. Maybe she smiled. I couldn't tell.

A light offshore wind began to blow, filling the silence with the tittering of dry leaves in the trees. I didn't want to talk about the dark days, days when I drank in hopes of dying. When I regained something like consciousness in the middle of shouting at my wife or throwing every article of clothing my family owned out the window of our second-story apartment. I didn't talk about how, for the longest time after, I'd missed believing, felt it pulsing sometimes like a phantom limb working its way around the inside of my rib cage.

Her stomach growled, and I remembered the pizza in the oven. "Let me get you something to eat," I said, and went inside. It wasn't quite done, so I waited in there a couple minutes, still holding the beer bottle in a kind of death grip. Then I poured it down the sink and watched a thousand bubbles foam and sputter and slide into the drain.

I went back out with two plates and four slices. Cindy had pulled her heels up, wedged her legs against the edge of the table, and fallen asleep with her head on her knees. If she wasn't a child, I didn't know what was.

So I set the plates on the table and moved to lift her, putting an arm behind her back and the other under her knees. As soon as I touched her, her body scrabbled upright. One arm caught me, hard, on the head, and I stepped back quickly, holding my hands up.

"I was just bringing you inside," I said.

She wasn't looking at me. I didn't know where she was looking. Her breathing was deep and fast. She began slowing it by force of will. "Okay," she said. She was holding the arms of the chair like the ground had just shifted sideways.

"You fell asleep," I said. "I thought you'd want to sleep on the couch."

She kept looking right through me. "Okay," she said again. "It's okay. I believe you."

"Sorry. Look, take my bed tonight. I can do the couch."

"No," she said. "No, the couch is fine."

"Really—"

"The couch is fucking fine," she said more forcefully.

I felt thrown back into myself. I was trying to be kind, wasn't I? I'd felt some fatherly affection there for a moment. And it had come across wrong, she'd taken it differently, and I felt lecherous, predatory. I had to admit—that was my phrase of choice, the habit of forcible admission, the practice of not letting an ill-fitted stone of thought go unturned, never wanting to forget the worms beneath—that since I'd met her I'd been thinking about sleeping with her. She was beautiful and lonely, and I was lonely, too, it turned out. I hadn't intended to act on the impulse. Or, I had to admit, only would have if she made some definitive first move. But her reaction resonated with the buried intention, and I felt caught, accused, guilty.

"I'm sorry," I said.

Her gaze shifted. She was seeing me now. But she also looked lost—truly lost—for the first time since I'd met her. "No," she said. "It's fine. You were just being nice." She looked away and stood up.

"Decent enough," I said. "That's all."

"That's right." She turned to me. Her breathing was normal again. She seemed as hermetic and self-contained as an old-world maître d'. "I'm just tired. I need to sleep. I'm very, very tired."

I nodded and stepped back. Whatever she was strung together with was wound tighter than I could have guessed.

She went for the sliding glass door. The night was doing its slow vanishing trick into morning. Light from the east began touching the house, the things in the yard, our clothes and skin. Cindy waited by the door. The look on her face was new and disconsolate. Her cheeks were flushed. Light reached our feet. Color returned to all the gray things again.

6.

WE DIDN'T SEE EACH OTHER THAT DAY. I LEFT EARLY, AND WHEN I CAME back to get ready for work, she'd taken herself off, doing who knows what.

By one in the morning, I was in a batting cage, taking warm-up swings. Mike Padilla came from the front desk with a wide smile and a jingling handful of steel tokens. Mike was a big man, with a bruiser's walk and the facial features of a well-fed chipmunk.

"Alright, man," he said. "Best round out of five buys breakfast."

This was something we did every once in a while, to pass the time. It was either this or listening to Mike tell war stories of his time in the Merchant Marines in which all the skirmishes were with prostitutes or pimps in distant countries. I preferred taking swings at the machine pitches. Fewer curveballs.

The batting cages were in the sleepy industrial complex I patrolled, the kind that seemed to have metastasized right out of the chaparral hills of inland Carlsbad. The buildings were long, low boxes of white stucco—were any industrial complex anywhere in

Southern California. Only the small signs on glass doors differentiated them, and the changing of these marked out time: Max's Tool and Die became Trudy's Candles; Just Closets become a Vietnamese goods importer with a name I couldn't read; ABC Reupholstery became my favorite, Jack's Exhaust and Muffler. Father Time was a vinyl installer with a new set of letters and a putty knife. All around the complex someone had planted stunted palm trees and beach grass. When I'd started here, it looked ironic. Then maybe sad. A little desperate. But after a time, it regained a kind of beauty that testified to the lengths humans will go to in order to keep a place at the lowest threshold of livable.

I put my palm out and Mike gave me a token. "You better focus," he said. "I like a big breakfast, and I know how much you make an hour."

"Trust me," I said, nodding toward Mike's gut, "everyone knows you like a big breakfast."

Mike stepped out of the cage, clanging the door shut behind him. "Same way everyone knows you like a big cock in your mouth every now and then."

I ignored him and dropped the token into the box attached to the fence.

We were about three rounds in when the radios crackled. It was Esmeralda, the night dispatch for the security firm. "Mark," she said. "You've got a call."

I took the radio from my belt. "I'm in the middle of rounds. Can I call them back?"

"It's your ex-wife," Esme said. "Sounds urgent. I say stop dicking around with Mike and go take it in the office. I'll have her call there in five." Mike rattled the fence behind me and dragged his thumb across his throat. I gave him the finger, but I was thinking about the voicemail I'd left my daughter a couple days back. Aracely lived in

Eugene, had for the last fifteen years since things between me and her mother ended. Fifteen years of being far away, and then a little more arithmetic: six years since Aracely had begun refusing to see me at all. A dismal paternal sum. She wouldn't even talk to me on the phone, not that I'd been the best at making those calls in the first place. I'd been trying again since she found out she was pregnant, and then again when the father found out he wasn't the father and bolted. She'd had the kid a year ago. A boy. Gabriela, my ex, had sent me a photo of him—he looked, the way all newborns do, like a disgruntled member of the California Raisins—but even that pissed off Aracely. She didn't want me to see him, wouldn't even tell me his name. Then again, maybe I shouldn't have been leaving her the voicemails I'd been leaving. Maybe I shouldn't have done a lot of things.

So I knew Gabby wasn't calling to catch up.

"Thanks, Esme. I'll head over."

Mike opened the cage and took the bat from me. "Run along, Marky. Don't want to keep her waiting. I'll practice while you screw up your rhythm. I want to work up a big appetite."

I headed over to the office, thinking about how I had tried once to get Gabriela to lobby on my behalf. I'll come up, I said, just to see the kid who'd made me a grandfather before the age of fifty. I wanted to, I said, but "want" wasn't the exact right word. I felt some obligation, felt I *should* want to, that this was something I might wake up to—in ten years or fifty—and regret having let pass. It set me on edge, that confusion. I didn't like thinking about it. Besides, Gabby only had to list a handful of the reasons Aracely was against seeing me, the things I'd done and said over the years, and I lost it. It was bait and I knew it was bait, a test to see if I could behave, to see if I could be something other than the asshole I was, but it didn't stop me, and I failed, like I always fail, like I always knew I'd fail.

The office was essentially a closet in an odd, unused corner of one of the buildings. There was a desk, a mini-fridge, a microwave, and a john in there. Above the desk was an array of video monitors; someone off-site monitored them semiconstantly, but when Mike and I weren't making rounds or wasting time, one of us was in here. It was a good, quiet place to read.

I sat in the chair and waited for the phone to ring, whistling to keep the silence at bay. I tried to remember being married. I know I'd made Gabby tea every morning, that we would make love on weekend afternoons before Aracely was born. Though the memories were in my mind, they weren't mine, I wasn't in them. They were someone else's. It was as if the blackout years had divided me into two men, and one had died while the other—the weaker, smaller, cruder man—survived. I'd been a youth pastor once, a role model, a husband, a father. Now I didn't even like cutting my own grass.

But I felt no preference for the person in those memories, no desire to get back to that place. I felt little preference for anything. Gabby had mourned me like I had died, and that was good and right. But we had found our way back to something like affection—not love, exactly, but a mutual care. And that was good, too. Different, but good.

Then the phone rang, and I answered, and Gabby began by asking if I was trying to make sure Aracely hated me for good. Her voice was low, with a Mexican accent that had blended further and further over the years into the clear, cool water of West Coast Americanese.

My blood came up quickly, but I tried to keep calm. Sometimes I do try. "Hi, Gabby," I said. "How've you been?"

"She's going to cut you out forever. That hasn't happened yet, as much as you may think it has, but keep it up. Keep pushing."

"I just wanted to call and wish little what's-his-name happy birthday. Can't a grandpa wish his favorite little anonymous grandson another good year of whatever the hell he's into besides rubber nipples and having his ass cleaned?" That ended my trying phase. I felt my limbic system ripple at the deep pleasure of anger as it rose up in me. It was better than drinking, was what I went to drinking for anyway. Now that I didn't do that anymore, it was like taking a vacation from sobriety.

"You're an idiot, you know that?" she said.

"Sure, of course I know that. Better than being a sadist. I've been asking to come up for how long? I've been trying to be interested. But she's a stone wall. I think she likes hurting me."

"How could you say that?" Her performance of anger gave way to a more genuine kind, I could tell. That made me happy. Now we were getting somewhere. "She's your *daughter*, you ass. She's no sadist. And your version of trying is worse than not trying at all, which makes me wonder sometimes."

"Wonder what?"

"Wonder what it is you actually want." She was no fool.

"Well, I wonder what she is, if she isn't a sadist. A tease?"

Gabby's sigh overloaded the mic on her phone and made the speaker at my ear crackle. "Stop talking," she said. I heard her take a breath. "If you say a word, you won't hear from me again for a long, long time." She let the silence linger. She was calming herself, or she was testing me. Maybe both. I managed to keep my mouth shut. "We're going to pretend I hung up on you. For being completely out of line. We'll pretend I did that, and that after a time you knew you were just getting defensive because you were hurt, and you're not much more than a dumb animal. Actually, you're a bit less than that."

I started to say something, but she cut me off. "Not a word, Mark. I mean it. We're going to pretend I hung up on you, and I thought about it, and you thought about it, and when I called back you apologized, right out of the gates. Okay? Let's save the time. And after all that, that's when I'd tell you that Aracely isn't a sadist, or any other thing you want to call her. She's terrified. And confused. She's got a baby and no father for that baby. She's a parent now. And her dad, one of the two people who could have taught her what it meant to be a parent, he went crazy on her when she was little."

I felt myself react, but there was no anger now. It was the feeling the truth can sometimes inflict, of making you feel immediately and powerfully shorter.

"Her dad had a breakdown and then wasn't around anymore. And she's wondering if she could do the same thing, if she's got that inside her or something else. I know she won't, but she doesn't, and the thought of you coming around scares her. She's afraid, and she's sure as hell afraid of you. For being that father. For being a big unknown to her, a total mystery. And you've got to accept that, accept what you mean to her. You're everything bad she's afraid she's capable of. Do you understand me?"

She continued without much of a pause. "No, don't answer that question. If you don't understand me, think about it some more. Think about it until you get it. And stop pushing, Mark. Be easy on her. Let me talk to her, and for God's sake, stop making it worse with these messages."

For a long time, I didn't know if I was breathing. A movement on the security monitors caught my eye, but when I turned to study them the various interiors were full of nothing, a big emptiness. I felt doubtful, paranoid, twitchy. Sometimes I would get ahead of myself, ahead of the actual me that in another era I might have called a soul. My brain, starved and sick of its own company, steeped in hormonal tides—flows of epinephrine and norepinephrine and cortisol, ebbing waves of serotonin—would act up, emotional hardwiring would overheat, and I'd find myself acting in ways I knew I shouldn't. A different version of an older craving, a deeper want. The message on the kid's birthday was on one of those days. Gabby was giving me a chance to overtake it.

This wasn't the Gabby I'd married. She'd been sweet and nurturing and joyful with the promise of what I seemed to present to her—a gift without a hint of anything her future daughter would fear becoming. No, Gabby had seen in me a life in joyful service to our God, and she'd trusted me as she'd trusted Him: to do what was best, what was good for her. Misplaced faith.

That simple idea of service was gone in her now, replaced by a willfulness about providing for herself and protecting her child. I admired that about her, even when it was directed at me.

"I think you're right," I finally said.

"I didn't say you could talk yet."

I swore something moved on one of the monitors again, the one at top right for the fabrication shop, but there was nothing there.

"I'm still angry," Gabby said, "so I'm going to hang up soon. You be patient, okay? Stop leaving voicemails. And ask yourself: Why do you want to see this baby? Is it for his sake? For Aracely's? Or for you?"

I was distracted now, watching the screen, but I still thought to ask, "Can you at least tell me the kid's name?"

"No," she said, and the line went dead.

I sat there a few minutes, trying to let my mind go limp and to look instead at the screens with no thought about them. I hadn't seen anything else move. My mind was probably playing tricks on me, that old pattern hound, but I needed to do something, so I radioed Mike and told him I was going to pass through the shop on my way back to the batting cages.

7.

OUTSIDE THE OFFICE, THE FLAT-FACED BUILDINGS AND CORRUGATED METAL doors looked earthy in the sodium light, like adobe. The night air was quiet and dry. When I reached the fabrication shop, I shook out the right key and held my heavy flashlight in the other hand.

I'd never gotten a firearm permit—not interested in guns, in any shortcut to power—and so I always had these lower-paying gigs where the owners didn't care enough or have enough money to spring for more expensive security. If there was trouble, I could call the police or swing at it with the rear end of my Maglite. My shoes were decent for running.

I opened the door and stepped inside. It was still, as quiet as the bottom of the ocean, but something told me to leave the lights off. I walked softly, past the dim chaos of the reception desk, through a door, and toward the shop itself. My eyes began to adjust to the darkness. I'd been in the place before, part of normal rounds. One wall was lined with toolboxes and hand-labeled cabinets. There was space by the back roll-up door to bring in Harleys. The bulk of the floor was packed with heavy iron and steel machinery, things for grinding, for filing, for lathing aluminum, for welding.

As I came into the main room, I heard the soft steps of rubber soles in the dark.

What I did next was exactly how I'd always imagined I'd respond to a break-in: I hid. I dropped behind a rolling toolbox and turned down the volume of my radio. I heard what sounded like a few sets of feet. To go by the step-slap pattern they made, someone was wearing sandals. Sandals on a burglary didn't make sense. Maybe the shop owner was doing some late-night work. He hadn't called it in. And had forgotten to turn on the lights, too. I tried to tell myself that, but it wasn't convincing. The silence was shattered by the heavy screech of iron on concrete. There was audible breathing as they pushed something in the dark.

It was time to run away. One flashlight against three or more people wasn't something I was ready for. I crouched and backed my way out in the dark toward the door to reception. My shoes scuffed on something grainy on the concrete, some sand or abrasive powder, but with all the noise I didn't think they'd hear.

I got the door open, backed into reception, shut it as noiselessly as possible, and turned around into a lanky figure in a trucker cap swinging something hard at my head. Then I went down and got a front-row look at his enormous white sneakers shuffling toward me like twin Zambonis before things went dark.

I had dreams of being an airline pilot and trysting with flight attendants in the cockpit. The sleep was deep. That the dreams were punning was always a sign of that. I woke to the sound of giggling. It was my own. It took me a minute to tell myself to knock it off. At first I didn't listen, but then I did.

It began to dawn on me that I was in an office. There were office things, it seemed to me. Oh, that's a crumbling, veneered particleboard desk, I thought to myself. A computer that looked like it might still take 5¼-inch floppy disks. A calendar on the wall with a Gil Elvgren pinup girl above the dates, looking for all the world like she wanted to have sex with her vacuum cleaner as much as the vacuum wanted to have sex with her. No wonder I was confused.

I got up to try the door. The inside of my head crackled like someone was frying a pan of bacon in there, globules of hot fat splattering the insides of my eyes with bright flashes. The door handle turned, but when I pulled there was the sound of chain jingling taut and it gave only a half inch.

Dimly I remembered getting hit, falling to the floor, the shoes, the hat. I pressed the side of my head where the bat had connected. It was tender about a palm's length behind my temple and swollen. Luckily the guy didn't get as much batting cage practice as I did: a few inches forward could have done a lot more damage.

I felt for my radio, but it was gone. Of course. I still had my wallet, though. It was too bad I'd never owned a cell phone. That would have been handy. I cracked the door and began shouting. Hopefully Mike wasn't still in the cages, swinging away at that groaning automaton that threw him pitches where he couldn't hear me.

It wasn't until the next morning that I was found. I'd given up on the shouting, suddenly exhausted, and went to sleep on the floor. I woke to the sound of the roll-up door being opened. There were muffled voices for a while, no words I could discern, but they were alarmed. I woke myself up the rest of the way and yelled through the cracked door for someone to get me out. Things got quiet, and it was another five minutes before anyone came. It wasn't one of the machinists, though, or the owner of the shop. It was a police officer. He peered at me from a distance through the cracked door, went away to radio something, and came back with two other cops.

Eventually they got me out. Then came all the questions. First it was one cop, while I sat in the back of an ambulance getting my head examined not for the first time in my life. Then it was a man and woman taking turns with questions. They took me to the security office, showed me the tape of myself going into the machine shop. I was disappointed to see how ungainly I moved, a man well on his way to old.

Every time I tried to ask a question, they stonewalled me. When I got passed off to a fourth person, a detective this time, I asked where Mike was. "Why didn't he find me before you guys?"

The detective, midthirties maybe, in a blue dress shirt with the cuffs turned up, khaki pants, and work boots—he could have been in a Dockers ad—looked me in the eye. "You really don't know why this whole thing is up and running?" I looked around: Ten or fifteen officers and others in official-looking civilian clothes walked this way and that, talking to one another quietly. None of the other shops I could see were open. The only cars were police vehicles, an evidence truck, others I didn't recognize. "All this doesn't happen for a simple B&E, and besides, the owner says nothing's missing."

I watched the detective, still confused but already knowing I wasn't up for what he would say next. He seemed to register the change in me and looked down at his notebook, but he said it anyway. "Michael Padilla is dead. He was killed last night, in the back of that shop."

8.

THE NEWS DIDN'T SINK IN RIGHT AWAY. MAYBE IT STILL HASN'T. IT NEVER does, not really. Loss only becomes the injury you don't remember ever not having, until someone asks how you got your limp and for a second you think, What limp? But at that moment it was incomprehensible. Mike was killed while I lolled unconscious a few feet away. How had he so radically changed, so suddenly, from being to not-being? How had I been given the gift of a straightforward concussion? I had trouble coming to grips with how they changed the name of Hill Street to Coast Highway.

And there were the questions I'd been asked for the last forty-five minutes. Too many of them now seemed like ways to probe my relative sanity. The detective/Dockers pitchman named Harper told me I was free to go and, with his eyes and the suspicion in the grip of his handshake, that they weren't sure about me. Of course they weren't. I wasn't sure about me. It was my most basic trait, the one thing I could truly trust in myself. It wasn't unjustified. There were reasons I should be skeptical of myself—reasons the police, without a doubt, had read in the tabloid of my official record.

But still they sent me home. All I could think while I drove was, Mike is dead, Mike is dead. Just the words. It didn't feel like he was dead. It felt like he was somewhere, over those hills to the east, a few miles into the past—not here with me but *somewhere*, still somewhere real. What feelings feel is a joke. It's always just the past, always just yourself. Feelings don't know dick. Still, my feelings expected to sit across from him in a diner booth and taste some bacon and hear his endlessly crude jokes, but no.

The details were still unclear to Harper, and he didn't reveal much. Mike's body was found wrapped up in a tarp, in a corner of the shop. He'd been shot in the chest and then bled to death, no doubt quickly. It looked like Mike came in through the front door; no signs of forced entry there or at the roll-up door in back. They thought there was a struggle. I must have looked like a potential partner in that. The story I told about the burglars didn't make much sense if nothing had been stolen.

I found myself doubting my own story, too, but no, there were at least three or four people in the shop. Mike must have come after I'd been coldcocked, must not have run the way I'd done. And someone killed him for that. Mike was killed, Mike was killed, I reminded myself, saying this a few times. Then a feeling came over me that made more sense: a kind of despair at not knowing what lay at the center of his last few minutes. It settled hard into my stomach, this maw of unintelligibility, of unknowledge. It was familiar, a despair I'd worked over before.

I was exhausted, distraught, and hungry, but every thought of food reminded me of our bet—loser buys breakfast—and only sent me deeper into myself. He was just a guy I worked with. We didn't hang out, didn't go surfing or fishing, didn't talk about much beyond bullshit meant to kill hours before escaping back into our respective lives. But, I had to admit, he was the person I'd seen most often, most regularly, in the last ten years of my life. Still nearly a stranger, but not nearly enough. It had been a mistake, I saw, to let someone get even that close. I simmered with hatred at having made that mistake—hatred for myself, hatred for the grief I now felt. It wasn't grief for Mike, not only for Mike—a wide-open expanse of it, lurking at all times beneath the veneer of the world.

I went home and climbed into bed still wearing my uniform. Mike was dead, Mike was dead, and I was washed out: exhausted, numbed, gray.

I woke up to pitch black. The clock said 2 a.m. I got a drink from the kitchen. That's when I noticed that Cindy was gone.

I went from room to room: all her things packed up, none of my own taken. Only a single sheet of paper left on the back coffee table, something I hadn't noticed the night before. On it was a cartoon of two pocket watches in bed, covers around their middles. One held a cigarette, smiling. It had a thought bubble puffing out of its head: "Oh yeah, I like a little secondhand." The other looked disappointed and was saying, "Next time, come on my face." I flipped the paper. Here was a rough sketch of hands—hers, I thought—with every line and crease rendered in spidery blue ballpoint ink and a bandage drawn vertically across the palm. In script below the drawing, neater and more playful than I'd expected, it said: *Fate Line Plastic Surgery: Buy One Get One Free Special. Financing Available—and Definitely in Your Future!* She didn't have a bad eye, and her line was strong.

I was sure that I'd never see her again. This was the way of the world. Things arrive and pass away. Wanting or not wanting it doesn't change a thing. I felt sadder than I had any right to feel, a weak and regretful sadness. She must have found a quicker way to Seattle, a quicker way to someplace better than here. I thought about the night on the patio, felt like I'd let her down, that I'd fucked up, that I should be ashamed. But she would have to take her place at the end of a long line of people I had disappointed. This was how things went.

I put my surfboard in the truck and drove down to the pier and paddled out into the dark water. The glow from the lamps lining the pier sent an incomplete light onto the surface of the ocean. I splashed water on my face and felt the swells rock me as they passed. The current took me farther north, away from the pier lights. It got darker, and the clouds revealed very few stars. The only company was a band of mauve sand at my back and the rushing sound of the waves I couldn't bring myself to catch, crashing behind me and dissipating into the shoreline. I splashed my face with the salt water. I poured water over my face again and again.

9.

WHEN I GOT BACK HOME, THERE WERE THREE MESSAGES FROM THE security firm: two from a receptionist telling me the boss wanted to see me before my shift that night and one from the man himself. I called back and said I'd come by at four o'clock. But I didn't want any corporate sympathy. I wanted to be left alone.

After I waited out the clock, I drove over to the office in Vista. North County Security occupied a building that looked like something a personal injury lawyer would have loved in the 1980s, all red marble and tinted glass and chintzy brass accents. Inside it wasn't much better. The waiting room was furnished with the glass coffee tables and salmon-upholstered oak chairs of a thrice-divorced family therapist.

There was a little reception window in the far wall, next to a closed door. I gave my name to the receptionist. She was new and young and her pained expression showed how hard she was trying to imagine her way into crying. "Can I get you anything?" she asked. "Cup of coffee? I think we have some donuts in the back."

If I asked, she might have rubbed my back and let me cry into her pencil skirt, but instead I said, "Can you get this fucking appointment over and done with?"

She flushed. "Um . . . no. No, I'm sorry."

"Then I'm super." I grinned toothily, turned, and went to one of the hideous chairs to wait this out. She typed very, very loudly.

A few minutes later she called out in a voice that had as much emotion as a self-flushing toilet: "Mr. Watt and Mr. Gustafsson are ready to see you. Third door on the right." I knew Watt's office was third from the right, but I didn't know any Gustafsson. A buzz filled the quiet room and I went through the newly unlocked door.

There was a time I would have wanted that receptionist to revere me. That was part of the high of preaching: who it asked me to imagine myself to be, as others saw me. Charming, wise, pacing a stage like a biblical panther in semicasual wear. Cutting through the noise of modern life. Possessing a transformative truth. Seeing their compromised, convicted hearts like hotel stains under blacklight, but seeing with compassion, and with a way out: just hand over your life. Now that person sounded like a cross between QVC spokesman and bank robber who did too much shoplifting at the Gap. But once I would have done or said almost anything to believe myself admired by a young woman like this.

Before I headed to Watt's office, I backed up and said to the receptionist, "Look, hey, I'm sorry. Okay? I'm an asshole, I know." She shook her head as if to say I wasn't, as if she had any idea who I was. "No. I am. You're just being nice," I went on, "which is nice and all that, and it's not your fault that I can't handle nice. I'm not built for it. It's all a little too much on a good day—and I've been having a really bad day, which I know you know about. But I just wanted you to know that I know I'm being a dick, even if I can't stop myself, and it's not fair to take it out on you. Okay?" I asked, not really expecting an answer, riding along a certain kind of mania. "I'm horrible. You're fine. Trust me."

By the time I was finished, I was leaning on the little shelf of the reception window, and the receptionist was leaning away from me as far as she possibly could. Her expression was a mixture of disgust and fear, like she'd just been startled by a desperate, emotionally starved, and uncomfortably viscuous insect. Even in apology, I had a terrible way of putting people at ease.

I headed into the hallway. Esmeralda, the night dispatcher, caught me as I turned a corner. She was wearing jeans and a magenta blouse, fake turquoise on some fishing line around her neck. The whites of her eyes were a solid red tide. Before I could say or do anything, she had her arms around me. "Jesus Christ, Haines. I'm so sorry," she said.

I fought the urge to push her off me and walk away without a word. "Right," I said. She smelled of vanilla hand cream and cumin. She was a tall woman, so I had a wave of dark hair in my face until she let me go, which felt like a long time. My shoulder was wet where she'd rested her head.

"I can't even believe this kind of thing could happen, and happen to Mike. I talked to Darcy. She's devastated." She patted around her eyeliner with her fingertips.

"Darcy?"

"His wife," she said. She seemed to hold back then, to be waiting for me to do something to comfort her now. There were any of a half-dozen platitudes I could offer. But instead, I thought about wives and how Mike had never once talked about his, had never said her name. I tasted acid in my throat, which tasted like whiskey, and some deep rage came up to keep that desire at bay. I was pathetic, a drunk, a disaster. I hated pathetics, drunks, and disasters. The hatred was the only thing that kept me at all better.

"Esme," I said tightly. "I have to see Watt."

Esme opened her mouth to say something but then didn't.

I couldn't bring myself to say anything else. It wasn't me being an asshole. If I said anything, I didn't know what would happen after, and I couldn't open that door. I tried to apologize with my eyes for not offering more. She must have understood because as I walked away she said to my back, "I'll let you know when the funeral is. Maybe we can go together." I should have turned back to say yes, that was kind of her, that was a good idea. But the version of me who followed up on all my "shoulds" would be a thousand years old by now and ground to a bloody pulp under the weight of other people. So I kept walking.

The third door on the right was open and from inside came polite laughter. I knocked on the jamb. The laughter ended and was replaced with an overattentive silence, which is no kind of silence at all. It chafed. I entered the room, which was as sparsely decorated as a monk's cloister, though it stank of cigar smoke, decomposing particleboard, and a drunk man's sweat—which is to say, it smelled better than it looked. The two men in the room wore suits. My own uniform made me feel cheap, and I found some more anger there I could use.

"Hey, Watt," I said, eager to break the water of the pregnant silence.

"Mark, come on in, come have a seat," Watt said. He sat behind his desk, a scotch flush glowing warmly through an unkempt red beard and his wheedling kindness.

The man I took to be Gustafsson sat across from Watt with his back to me. I could tell by the cut of his hair and the shoulders of his suit jacket that he was well-off. Then he stood and turned around, and I realized I'd underestimated him. He was tall and tanned and very fit. His shirt was open two buttons from the neck, and a heavy silver watch adorned his left wrist. He had that profound, Germanic self-confidence—that special shine in the eye—that borders on glimmering idiocy. Watt stood up behind him, shifting uncomfortably.

I went directly for him. "We haven't met," I said to the stranger. "Are we switching health plans again?"

The corners of his mouth quirked in an almost smile. "No, of course we haven't met," Gustafsson said, "though it seems like we might have at some point." He paused and looked at the details of my uniform. I knew what he was doing, but I let him. I knew it because I'd done it myself. Next he'd shake my hand firmly, making sure to turn his grip just enough above my own, while holding my shoulder with his other hand. But knowing doesn't always help, and when he did what I expected he loomed larger for a moment, became taller, more dominant.

"I'm Tom Gustafsson. I'm the owner of Carlsbad Palms North. Since you've been guarding my buildings, I suppose it would have been good for us to meet at some point or another. That's what I meant before."

Watt pointed again to the chair. "Sit down, Haines. We wanted to—"

Gustafsson cut in, but he did it so gently that Watt was more pleased than annoyed at being left out of the dance. "We wanted, first and foremost," Gustafsson said, "to see that you were okay." He brought his hands together in a triangle at his chest. "Both physically and otherwise. What's happened is a shock and a loss for all of us, and I'm sure all the more for you."

I didn't like Gustafsson's thin, grim smile, the forced empathetic charm of it. "I'm fine," I said, "physically and in all the other ways that matter." The more I looked at him the less I liked: his cheese-cutting little nose, his wide-set and credulous eyes, his puppetlike mouth, his cutie-pie chin with its little dimple. He had a face marinated in a mother's kisses.

"My head's sore," I said, "and I'm a little shaken up, but nothing I can't deal with. If that's first and foremost, what's next?"

Watt dropped himself into his chair, which let out the embarrassed sigh of a wife who has caught her husband jerking off in the den again. "Why don't we all sit?" he repeated, as if that was all he could say. Sit. Stay. Shake.

"I'm tired," I said. "I'm a little bit frayed. I don't feel like sitting. Not right now. I feel like getting to my shift, if you don't mind."

Watt looked somewhat helplessly to Gustafsson for direction. Gustafsson, for his part, never relinquished that flat, corporate semi-smile. He made it seem appropriate, even though we were talking around someone who'd just bled to death after a bullet to the chest. He nodded at me as if agreeing to what I'd said, glanced at Watt, and folded his arms. "I can understand that," he said. "I really can, Mark. And I admire it in a person. Fortitude. Perseverance. That's good stuff. But to be perfectly frank, what I have trouble with is how insecure my complex has turned out to be."

I started to defend myself, but he stopped me with an upturned palm.

"I'm interested in what you have to say, but let me finish." His volume rolled up a decibel or two, and his tone became firmer. Every word he said was beautifully orchestrated, performed with a perfect ear for pitch. "Is that okay with you?" When I said nothing, he went on. "My tenants pay a premium for location and for the reputation my properties have: for high-end amenities, impeccable maintenance, and yes, for their security. The businesspeople I lease to, these places are their lives. They have expensive equipment and inventory there, sometimes a life savings' worth. They host clients, and for the government contractors, the work they do is subject to high-level clearances." Here he meant the missile designers, the drone aircraft R&D facilities, and all the rest of the military industries drawn to San Diego by the naval base. Every fourth person in the county got their pay from the military in one form or another.

"I've already spoken with several tenants this morning about what happened. I'm not blaming you, of course, and may Michael's soul find peace, but"—he took a step toward me very deliberately and stooped his tanned head a little lower to look me in the eye—"I am forced to say that I expect North County Security to accept responsibility for breaches of that security and to take the steps necessary to assure my tenants that it will not happen again.

"We've been talking," Gustafsson said, and pointed back and forth between him and Watt. For his part, Watt looked like he'd just shit the bed and wasn't sure if anyone had noticed yet. "I know North County Security doesn't want to lose my business, and we've had a good record so far. But something needs to be done to account for this. I need to offer my tenants something concrete to keep them feeling secure in their choice to lease my properties. What I'm saying is that Mr. Watt and I have agreed that he will step up a certain degree of armed security at several of my complexes, at a reduced rate, and that you won't be guarding at any of my buildings in the future."

He held up both hands as if I were about to start pawing at his pant legs. "It's not personal, and that's why I came here myself. To tell you, man to man, that I'm truly sorry about Michael and that I'm working with the police to make sure his killer is brought to justice. But I am also sorry that we need to part ways like this—for the peace of mind of my tenants, truly. I wish you nothing but the best."

"Is that it?" I asked. I'd kept quiet for the duration of his speech, like a good boy. I do try sometimes.

"I'm sorry it has to be like this," Gustafsson said, "but yes."

"And Watt," I said, "let me guess. There's no other work for me either?"

Watt's scotch tan deepened a shade or two. He was nearly purple, hypoxic. "Everything's full. As soon as something opens up, you're at the top of the list, but . . ."

"Right," I said. Watt feigned surprise at a smudge on his desk and began working at it with his sleeve. Gustafsson had his hands in his pockets and was rocking slightly heel-to-toe, looking like a president who has toured the disaster area—the same dress, the same forced folksy speech—and was glad to be re-boarding Air Force One where his in-flight vodka tonic was waiting. I breathed deeply, which did nothing, and felt the tenuous membrane between anger and despair running through my insides flex and shift.

"Someone is dead. I've got a concussion. And already you're onto public relations and maintaining profit streams. Cold-hearted bastards."

"It's not personal," Gustafsson said.

"Not for you," I said. "You've got the luxury."

Watt whined, "Come on, Mark. You know the position I'm in."

"Go to hell," I said. "And you," I said turning to Gustafsson, "are a slick and talented motherfucker." I jabbed a finger at him but stopped short of poking his chest. "But that doesn't change the fact that you're still fucking your mother."

Gustafsson put his head down and took it. When he looked up, his lips were pursed, and he wore an expression of charitable tolerance on his asinine face.

Watt pleaded, "It's just business. I'll make some calls, I'll write a letter of rec. You'll land on your feet."

I had another of those moments where I get ahead of my brain. "I hope this lands on your feet," I said and pushed a Tony Gwynn paperweight across the desk. Instead, it landed on Watt's lap and he grimaced painfully. With my arm already across the desk, I decided to sweep it sideways, spilling a mug of pens and dragging a computer monitor to the floor where it bounced once, hard. "It's just business, guys. You understand." I was looking for something else to knock over when Gustafsson grabbed me by the elbows and pinned down my arms. He was strong. I couldn't free myself.

"I think this is over," he said coolly. The door opened and a security guard half my age asked what was wrong. Watt had tripped the alert button under his desk, the prick.

"Right," I said. I tried to wrench myself free again, but Gustafsson's gorilla palms jerked my arms back into place and gripped me tighter.

"You're leaving now, yes?" he said.

"Yeah, I'm leaving."

"And I'm not going to see you at Palms North, yes? Or anywhere else, for that matter?"

"Well, I was thinking of doing some pro bono patrols, but on second thought, maybe I won't."

"Don't try to get smart," Gustafsson said, sounding like a sitcom version of a father. "I can't wait that long. I better not see you. Given this outburst, I trust you even less than I did this morning."

Watt stood and came around, visibly upset by what was transpiring in his office. "Just leave, Haines," he pleaded. "Give me your keys and go. You can bring the uniform by some other time. I'm not sending you out of here in your underwear."

"What a noble gesture." I barely looked his way. All my rage had taken Gustafsson as its target now, and I was studying his face for the best place to hit it, if I ever got the chance. "Silverback here needs to let me go." Right in the goddamn left eye, I decided. The asshole already had a depth perception problem, and it seemed like a good idea to make it a physical one, too.

Gustafsson gripped hard enough to leave bruises and then released me. "Thanks for justifying this decision," he said with snide self-assurance. "It wasn't an easy one to make, but I feel much better about living with it now that I've gotten to know you."

I took the ring of keys from my belt and tossed them onto Watt's desk. They clanged and slid off onto the floor. I turned to the boy security guard behind me. The only thing he'd done to help was perspire. His endless forehead glistened like a strip of fresh flypaper. "Come on, Opie, you can walk me to my car."

I didn't see Esmeralda on the way out, thankfully, and the young receptionist looked at me with confirmed suspicion. I walked out of the building with purpose, got in my truck, and drove away. By then I'd caught up with my brain and was reviewing the tapes, issuing harshly worded notes to the starring prima donna. Half a mile down the road I stopped and watched my hands shake and wondered, What next, what next. Then I drove the rest of the way home.

10.

THERE WAS A NEW MESSAGE WAITING ON THE MACHINE. IT WAS Harper, the detective, asking me to call. He had a few questions about what I'd seen before I was knocked out, so I did. Nothing I said made him go, "Aha." When he was done, I asked if there was any new information.

"Can't say much at this time," he said tersely. "There was a struggle, and there was blood at the scene that wasn't Mike's." He paused and then said pointedly, "Wasn't yours either."

So it wasn't just me being paranoid: I'd been a possible suspect.

I should have felt relieved now, but I was sore and bitter. Not at Harper so much as at myself. How I must have come across, when they found me, and then what they'd learned when they pulled my records. I imagined what was written there, the notes on drunk tank stays and disorderly conduct arrests, the investigation of complaints of domestic disturbance, and a passage that must have said something like: *March 15, 1985. Man found partially conscious upon arrival. Signs of intoxication—alcohol and prescription morphine tablets. Vomit on the couch, a bottle's worth of ibuprofen, assorted prescription drugs. Girl, approximately five, found in the bedroom, from where she'd dialed 911.* I was as close to the edge of death as I'd ever been but somehow the sight of Aracely on the floor, seated next to a phone placed carefully back in its cradle, made it through my dimmed senses and was etched permanently on the deeper surfaces of my brain. The pastel rainbow pattern of her pajamas, the ruffles around the hem of her shorts. Her tousled hair. The bottom of one small foot. I remember nothing of a day or two on either side of that, except this one image, which was never far from being recollected. More than anything else, though, I tried to avoid it. As soon as I got out of the psychiatric hospital, that's when I left for good.

But these cops found my coworker shot, and then they'd read a dissertation about me, and for a while they considered me capable of murder. It unsettled me. I didn't need it. Not after playing air hockey on Watt's desk. Not after another reminder that I couldn't be certain of what things I was capable. I didn't like that the cops had this story for me that included killing a man. It wasn't my story, but it built on parts of it that I couldn't deny. A true cynic starts at home, as they say—they being me. I could let that story dominate if I wasn't careful. I'm always careful but I don't always succeed, and sometimes a story is stronger than a person. Especially a story someone tells about you. Especially if others agree on it.

That was why leaving Gabby had been for the best. I couldn't look at her without seeing myself as she saw me—or if not how she saw me, then how I saw myself through her, how I read myself as she would narrate me: the disaster, the wounder, the betrayer, the unprodigal. I couldn't escape it, not then. And Aracely wouldn't talk to me, wouldn't see me—she had a story for me, too. I didn't want to think about that either.

So after talking to Harper, I went straight to the ocean and let the waves pummel me. Later, I rode a few. Some long, fast glides on a smooth surface and I felt at home in my skin again, empty in my skin, existing only at the level of my skin. As unreflective as the sea on an overcast night.

11.

THE NEXT FEW DAYS I LOST TOUCH, DRIFTED AIMLESSLY FROM HOME TO beach to dive restaurant to home again. I slept a lot. I knew I should make plans. I knew that for my own sanity. But when I tried, I thought about planning to get breakfast with Mike or the long-deferred plans to see Aracely, and then I'd go get carne asada fries and eat them on one of the jetties and fish for a couple hours with no bait on the line. Mike owed me breakfast, so I skipped that meal. It felt like the least I could do. It never occurred to me at the time, but Cindy owed me a breakfast, too.

Gabby had tried to reach me at work and someone, probably Esme, had given her the news. She caught me at home.

"I heard you lost your job," she said.

"Something like that."

She clicked her tongue and stalled. Her voice was too gentle. I didn't trust it. "I heard about the person you work with. Dear God."

"It's too late to start that prayer."

"That's not what I meant," Gabby said, "and you know it. And besides, you know it never is." Another pause. Her uncertainty made me want to hang up now. "Are you okay?"

"I'm always okay, Gabby. Like a rock."

I could hear her smirk when she said, "Like a lump." It was a relief, that.

"Like a whatever. Lumpier every year."

"Is there anything I can do?" she asked.

I thought about it, which is to say I waited a moment before telling her no. Then I added, "But thanks for asking. That's not nothing."

After we hung up, I thought about how kind she'd been, and the tenor of our last conversation. There was a while after I had stopped believing when her kindness had been mean: organizing groups to pray for my soul, for God to inspire me with shame and humility. She'd sworn it was all in my best interest, but it had another's at heart; it was about me, but I was the third party. Her sanctity meant no step to where I'd moved, no sympathy. That had been part of the decline, the drinking, the despair: the sudden loneliness of being without God and, in losing that, losing everyone else who mattered. But time had changed Gabby. She admitted that she still prayed for me and hoped I'd find my way back into the fold, but she was open to me as I was. It baffled me to think of how affection and care and hope and commitment could work independently, and so often at odds with one another.

On the third day, I went down to South Jetty. A lifted Ford truck with a few teenagers standing in the bed blitzed across the speed bumps near me in the parking lot, kids bucking and trying to hold on. It looked like a gag from an old *On the Road* movie, if Bob Hope and Bing Crosby were shirtless teenagers in matching long black shorts, dark and enormous glasses, and flat-billed hats. A sticker across the back window featured a Gothic sketch of a skeletal Jesus on a cross, flesh peeling away from His bones, and above it, the words HARD CORPS RANGERS.

When I came in from the surf session, the air had been let out of my tires, and I blamed those kids, though the only reason I had was that they looked like assholes.

While I waited for a tow truck to come—a long wait in summer, busy as they are with junkers overheating on the highways—I went for something to eat. Tucked along the inside of the harbor was a row of restaurants and shops near a small lighthouse. It was a tourist lighthouse, there to sell jewelry made from old coins and spoons, too small and poorly placed to serve as any kind of useful warning.

I skipped the crab shack with the dancing waiters and the rockabilly lobsters-and-tacos spectacle and got fish and chips from the tiny shop that might as well have been called the Fish and Chips Place. I took it back to the jetty and ate sitting on the rail that divided the parking lot from the steep decline into the river mouth of the San Luis Rey, where it fed into the sea.

The surf was transitioning from the low tide, glossy waves of the morning to the wind-chopped, high-tide shore break of the afternoon. It was one of the best versions of the break on the north side of the jetty: punchy, quick, unpredictable. I considered going back out after the meal, but then I might miss the tow truck, and I didn't want fish and chips for dinner, too.

A line of pelicans rode above the surface of a small band of swell and disappeared behind the rocks of the jetty. When I found them again on the other side, I spotted a group of men climbing down the rocks, struggling to balance with surfboards in their arms. One was my bald-headed friend from the pier with the BARREL tattoo. Another was the guy with the orange afro, the goiter-headed kid. They paddled out on the south side of the jetty, where the waves were mellower but altogether worse, and I walked onto the rocks to watch them. They surfed terribly. Every time one of them stood up, his feet were in a different position: wide apart in the pose of a stretching PE teacher, both together at the tail, too far to the right side of the board or to the left. How many times I watched one foot slip from the board entirely I can't even say. They seemed like they were having fun, but they looked high enough to make having a vasectomy fun. I was being reductive; they depressed me on an existential level. But being reductive wasn't something I had a problem with. And it wasn't clear to me yet, but that wasn't why I was watching them.

The tow truck came. The driver, a thin woman with a thin mouth ringed in tiny smoker's wrinkles, maybe sixty years old, saw the tires and asked, "Whose wife you fuck, honey?"

I paid her, she inflated the tires, and I waited for the guys to come in from the ocean.

They did eventually, walking to the free parking lot on the other side of the train tracks. I followed at a distance and then went and futzed with my truck and watched. They changed into street clothes, and I debated just walking up to Goiter and asking if he'd seen Cindy. Instead, I waited a little longer.

Soon they locked up their cars and walked back under the train tracks. They went over to the shops by the harbor and crowded into Jimbo's Bar and Grill.

Jimbo's was more a bar than a grill. Though, to be fair, it was also less bar than liquor store that let you drink on the premises. It had originally been a tchotchke shop about the size of a dining room, hawking T-shirts with airbrushed bikini bodies on them, but that had failed—not enough tourists. Booze for the boat-dwelling and beach-loitering crowd was unsurprisingly better suited. There were two small tables on the sidewalk out front, boxed in by a thin wrought-iron fence and laced with chain looping them together and to the wall at all hours; people in Oceanside don't wait until the middle of the night to make off with things like patio furniture. There were always three or four salty-looking men or women sitting out there, smoking Pall Malls, pinching them off half-smoked and tucking them behind their ears—people who lived on boats that never left their moorings and who often weren't as lucky as their boats.

As I walked up, I recognized one of the boat dwellers from the bait dock. Last time I'd been there I overheard him talking about his wife's lung disease. A dirty yellow mustache hung from his sun-ravaged brown face, a cigarette jammed in his mouth like it was the only twig jutting out of a cliff—a twig he was dangling from. No wife with him today. None for the rest of his days either, most likely. There was a dark weight always waiting to sink you in that grief, no resolution, like sailing a dinghy in a storm with an anchor tied to your back. I felt it pull, then put it out of my mind.

Then there was a shout from down the sidewalk, and it was her, in bathing suit and sarong, yelling to him, "Where'd you put the motherfucking dock key?" and smoking with a carton of Marlboro reds tucked under one gooseflesh but very alive armpit.

Inside Jimbo's the air was cooled by large fans. The floor was linoleum in the style of oak. The ceiling was standard-issue industrial. A handful of dollar store grass skirts had been cut apart and pinned around the walls about the height of a chair rail. Glasses were racked in their sea-foam plastic cubes behind the bar. Because they had only one rack, empties went back in next to clean ones until the rack got filled, and sometimes you got a glass with fresh lipstick on it. A few mirrored beer ads were nailed up carelessly. The rest of the room comprised four small tables, sixteen cheap wood chairs, a painting of a slutty hula girl, and a karaoke machine on a stool in the back corner. It smelled like dish soap and fish guts. The harbor cleaning station was just around the corner.

The guys from the water took up two of the tables. There was a pitcher of thin beer at the center of each table and, miraculously, since they'd come in only a few minutes before I did, there were already greasy burgers on plates before them. Happy hour. Regulars.

I took the last empty stool at the bar and ordered a soda and some fries, even though I wasn't hungry and don't like sweet drinks. When the food came, I set about dispatching it as slowly as possible, avoiding a conversation with the bartender who danced around behind the counter like he was hungry for one. I was waiting for the guys to get a bit more of that beer in them. About thirty minutes later, the bartender was telling me that global warming was horseshit.

"Well," I said, "livestock methane is the bigger problem, so it's more cow shit than horseshit."

"My dad was a scientist, and he knew this was all a racket to scare people into buying into a whole heap of nonsense."

"What kind of scientist?" I asked.

"Geologist."

"Probably petroleum geologist, then, or friends with them. Your dad was a sucker, a back-pocket guy."

The bartender threw his dishrag on the ground. He looked like he might tackle me from across the bar, and a few long seconds passed away. "I'm a businessman," he said, like it was a mantra. "For both of our sakes, we should talk about something else."

"You're a what?" I asked, giving the room a wave. Besides the guys from the water, who were trying to turn on the karaoke machine, there was only one woman in the place, reading tea leaves in the bottom of her glass of Southern Comfort. While I mock-presented the room, the guy with the BARREL tattoo made eye contact with me and shook his head in an exaggerated warning.

"I'm a businessman," the bartender said again. Then he got it and added: "What the hell."

"Not another word," I said. "I promise. Just a pitcher for my friends over there." The grass skirts flapped from the air moving through the open front door. The bartender picked up his rag from the ground and wiped out a plastic pitcher, shaking his head and talking to himself.

I walked over with the pitcher. The smell of it alone sent my insides sailing. The bald guy with the tattoo perked up when he saw the pale yellow beer and said hello. "I remember you from the pier, man," he said. "I never would have pegged you for a Jimbo's guy."

"I hope you don't peg me at all," I said.

We exchanged names. His was Anthony, which somehow made sense. We talked about how the waves were, and other breaks up and down the coast, from Black's to Terra Mar to Old Man's. The other guys drifted back from the karaoke machine, saying it was fucked. They sounded really broken up about it. I had trouble following their conversation. Maybe it was because they were sauced, but they also had a private language of "likes" and "dudes," acquired catchphrases and neologisms in put-on Spicoli accents. It was disorienting and a little frightening, like taking a beating in some rough verbal shore break. Or like gnarly, sucking-out pockets smacking right on the rockflops and schflitting your barney skull open, bra, as they would have put it.

Sometime during all this I heard the opening burbles of a synthesized, stripped-down version of Eddie Money's "Take Me Home Tonight." A midrange, squeaky voice sang along, switching to falsetto for the female parts. It was the goiter kid, looking for all the world like he had a giant clown nose pulled over his head. His eyes were shut. His throat undulated, and he worked hard to hit the right notes. He was trying. It was cute but pitiable, like a toddler strapped into tap shoes.

After the song ended, he set the microphone on the stool and wandered over. Anthony introduced him to me, calling him Shaw because, as was made immediately apparent, of a persistent lisp.

"It'sh good to meet shew," he said, shaking my hand. We chatted a minute, and I offered him a pour from the pitcher. I poured myself a half glass, too, because not having one would send the wrong message. More talking doesn't always lead to more trust, but sharing a drink, I knew from enough direct experience, could get someone talking.

"Hey," I started in, "you know a friend of mine, I think."

"Oh, yeah?" Shaw said. "Who? Besides these circle jerksh."

"Right," I said, with a little fake laugh. "No, her name's Cindy."

Shaw had a thin line of foam clinging to the balding caterpillar he called a mustache. He made a puzzled face and didn't say anything for a minute. You could almost see his eyes flipping slowly through index cards of former friends. "I don't shink I know anybody named Cindy," he finally said.

He didn't seem like he was lying, but I decided to push a little further. "Sure you do. You guys talked on the beach, north side of the pier. Flat, hot day. A week ago, maybe."

"You sure?"

"Yeah, I'm sure. I took her out for a surf lesson. Then she was reading on the beach, and I was out in the water with you guys. That's where I first met Anthony. And when you went in, you two talked for a while."

A light went on behind Shaw's eyes. It was dim and oddly colored, chartreuse maybe. "Oh, I remember the girl. I get chillsh just shinking about her. She's a piecsh. She's a four-piecsh shpecial."

My heart slipped in my body, like it was the last colored square twisting into place on a Rubik's Cube. I was worried about her. About where she had gone. The fact became clear to me, in a way it hadn't been before, that I wanted to know she was okay. Maybe it was the mess of the last few days, the mess of my heart and the shoddy wiring in my head, but it didn't send up a warning flare, this unfamiliar feeling: care.

Maybe I was too eager when I asked if he'd seen her since.

Shaw gave me a sly look with one pinched eye. It was a suspicious, you-dog-you look, as given by a dog. "You? And her? You're kidding me, man. And now she's not anshwering your telegramsh? Hate to break it to you, brother, but you're part of a big club there."

My throat was so hot and dry I almost took a swig of beer without thinking. I forced a laugh and patted Shaw on the back and then gripped him around the shoulder hard. "How'd you know Cindy, man?"

"That'sh not her name."

"What do you mean?"

"What I shaid. That'sh not her name. It'sh Emily. And thanksh for the hug, bra, but you can—"

"Emily?" I said. "Emily what?" Inside me the Rubik's Cube was being twisted at random by an unseen hand, and I felt a little nauseated.

"Emily who-fucking-knowsh, man. Shounds like she was working you. Shtill have your wallet?"

I didn't want to believe him, wanted to believe she'd given him a fake name. But mentally I felt for my back pocket, so it's not that I thought she was a saint. I asked Shaw how he knew her.

"I was going to ashk you the shame shing, old-timer."

My hand found the back of his neck and grabbed it hard. Maybe I shook him a little, too. I knew what I was doing. I was getting ahead of my brain a little, felt bad about being another bully in Shaw's sad life, and did it anyway. "It's a long story," I said, "and besides, I asked first."

The kid's shoulders tensed up the longer I held his neck. "Maybe mine's a long shtory, too. Come on, that really hurtsh."

"That's okay, man," I said with a little bite in my voice. "We're storytelling creatures. Where'd you know her from?"

"Chrisht, get your faggoty fucking handsh off me, grandpa," Shaw said with a squeaky whine that made him sound like a tantruming dolphin. One of his buddies looked over at the sound. I let go of the back of his neck.

"It's important," I found myself saying plainly. I wasn't sure why yet, but somewhere during the last hour it had become true. I said it was important because it was, and it was the first sincere thing I'd said all day, probably longer. Maybe a lot longer. Knowing what had happened to Cindy or Emily or whatever her name was had become imperative.

Shaw softened, straightening out the short-sleeved plaid shirt on his shoulders. "Look, man. I knew her through a guy we used to party with a waysh back. When I shaw her at the beach, it'd been a little while, and I shought I could get her number. Can't blame a guy for trying. That'sh bullshit, unless you're her dad or shomeshing."

"I'm not her dad," I said, feeling an odd urge to punch the kid and then buy him a self-help book. "So she was just some girl you met at a party once?"

"Naw," Shaw said, lighting up, "we used to go out to dude's houshe all the time. Crazy partiesh, man. Everyshing you'd want, right there." He got a little sheepish, looked down, shook his head. "To be honesht, it was freaky shit. I like a good time, but fuck. Horshe, cryshtal, and shome real shketch fuckersh. Kinda fun at firsht, but then it shtarted getting real weird."

It was easy enough to place Cindy/Emily in a place like that. It wasn't a surprise, but still my stomach clenched slightly in a kind of protective anxiety. "How weird?" I asked.

Shaw ducked his head, and we looked at each other for a minute. Then he shook off the eye contact and said, "I don't know why I'm telling you all thish, becaushe you're a dill. But damn that shit was fucked. Chick Emily? She was real cool to me when we firsht shtarted going out to the partiesh. Real friendly, ashking queshtions, getting drinksh. But she was alwaysh way faded. All the time. She sheemed to live at dude's house. He was dealing and maybe making, I don't know. Longer we shpent there, the more I shtarted sheeing all these guysh—weird guysh, shometimes looking like crackheads and shometimes just like golfer dudes in polo shirtsh—and they were all taking her into the back room, or maybe she was taking shem, or who knowsh when everyone'sh that fucked up. But that guy Sammy, it wash his place, and he watched it all go down in this creepy fucking way, I don't know. It was bad vibesh, man. I shtopped going. Too crazy."

My heart wasn't beating. My brain was a dull buzz. All I could feel was a dark, deep, endless angry blackness that was the inside of my body. "Sammy who?" I managed to ask.

"When I shaw Emily at the beach," he said, still lost in the story in his head, "I wanted to get her number, yeah, but maybe I jusht wanted to shee if she was okay. She hadn't been there the last couple times we went."

"*Shaw* her at the beach?" I said meanly. Meanness was the only way I could get myself to speak at full volume. "How long ago did you *shtop* going there, Shaw?" Shaw lowered his head farther, which didn't seem possible, and his eyes went from his left shoe to his right, back and forth. He looked awfully sad, and I felt cheap.

"A few months ago."

"And Emily was still there?"

"Yeah," he said sullenly.

I asked again, "What was this Sammy guy's name?"

Shaw took a minute to respond, and when he did his voice was so quiet I had to ask a third time. "Sammy Ray," he said. I almost asked to hear it once more, still disbelieving, but the kid spoke up: "Sammy Ray Gans. The partiesh were at his houshe out in bumfuck

Ramona." Shaw kept leering at his footwear sulkily. Then he said he needed to piss and ran off. I stood by myself, rocking on my legs like a prizefighter whose bell was so rung it had cracked, broken in two, and been melted down and remolded into a few thousand loose brass tacks.

Cindy was Cindy or Emily or some other name neither Shaw nor I knew. But Sammy was a specific, was attached to something solid: Sammy Ray Gans. I hadn't heard the name in fifteen years. He was something of a friend, in a previous life. Just thinking about him seemed to push at the edges of my being, like I was surrounded by a curtain of thick, dark cloth and the shapes of two hands, ten fingers, pressed in from the outside, displacing material. It made the space inside smaller but, in its suggestion of an outside, opened up onto something like the rest of the world.

12.

THE REST OF THE WORLD HAD ALWAYS BEEN THERE, OF COURSE. IT DOESN'T vanish when you blink—and whenever I did, it wasn't the annihilation of the known universe I saw but the face of the person I needed to call to find Sammy.

A couple months before, I had ended up chasing decent waves farther south than I usually ventured. I wound up in Cardiff, at a break called Seaside. The beach was state owned. The houses along the bluff above, which were stabbed into the cliffside like elaborately inedible decorations on a cake, clearly were not. But the swell was hitting the break just right. The waves were slightly overhead and powerful, yet the reef created a channel that made the paddle out less of a struggle. A set came through, six waves each barreling into a stiff shoulder to the right and peeling away like an expertly undone orange to the left. It was early, so the parking lot was mostly empty with fifteen cars in it. Which was good, relatively speaking.

While I paddled out, a thick fog rolled in. Sitting near the peak of the break, I couldn't see the shore. I caught a few waves over the next hour. I floated mostly. More people arrived, emerging from the mist. Then the fog burned off and a pack of twelve teenagers on shortboards paddled out, eyes less on the waves and more on their arm muscles as they flexed and stroked. They took turns shouting "Jesus! Je*sus*! *Jee*-sus!" like He was a favorite WWF wrestler.

Their tone wasn't mocking. They looked so proud and so confident, possessed by idiotic enthusiasm like they were cheering on number 3 in the piglet races at the fairgrounds. I paddled farther south, even though the next peak wasn't breaking as well. I didn't want that kind of company.

From that position I watched an older man on a longboard paddle through the group and then out a bit farther. He turned and joked with them. He looked familiar, but I couldn't place him at that distance. I didn't like being around familiar people, even people who only seemed familiar. I didn't trust them. Strangers, at least, were honest.

A solid set came through, and the man caught the second wave. He let one of the kids take the left, which was the better wave, and he took the right, not stalling near the lip to set up a nose ride but pumping impatiently up and down, the front three feet of board slapping like a kid's foam pool noodle. It was energetic, graceless surfing, and it carried him south. So when he paddled back out, he did so right near me. I recognized him immediately.

"Hey, Mark," the man said breezily, as if running into a racquetball buddy after a few missed matches at a gym. "Long time." He had a fat face for someone with such a merely pudgy body. His nose was streaked haphazardly with zinc oxide. He wore a blue long-sleeved rash guard and green paisley trunks and was shivering, just a little. His breasts quivered underneath the Lycra.

"Andy," I said. "Happy to see you've taken up sponsoring a group of young felons." I waved toward the kids.

"Those ones?" he said. "Good kids. I mean, they're all good kids, right?"

"Well." I was thinking about what he must have been like as a child. My best guess: mocker of the dyslexic and lord of the porn stash by the train tracks.

His expression went to one of deep concern: the furrowed brows, the puckered mouth and hound eyes of the contrived empath. "How about you? Have you been well? It's been so long since we've seen you." There was a sneer somewhere in those fat, stupid lips.

I said I couldn't be better and scanned the horizon. A small swell appeared on the surface of the ocean, but it wasn't enough to turn into a wave I could catch to escape Andy. I chopped at the water and asked, "How's my old job?"

Andy cracked his neck. "The community continues to grow. It's a blessing, a true blessing, to know these young people and be a force of good in their lives. But you know what I'm talking about. You made it all possible."

"Glad I could help," I said.

"Don't get me wrong," Andy said. "What you went through was awful. I don't mean that. First your sister, then . . ."

"It wasn't a day at Legoland," I said. "Sleepovers in the psych hospital are close, though. Lots of craft time. Does wonders for your perspective, and I still know people there. I could put in a good word."

He looked at me like I was pitiful and soulless. I gave him a look intended to say, Well, who isn't?

After a deliberate pause, he said, "You should be happy to know that the community thrives. Over twelve hundred parishioners now. Our outreach programs are doing wonders for Encinitas."

Encinitas wasn't exactly desperate for renewal. It was a wealthy coastal enclave with a self-absorbed, yogic bent. Its Self-Realization Fellowship, white stucco and golden mushroom domes on expansive bluff-side grounds, had given the break Swami's its name. Paramahansa Yogananda wrote his *Autobiography of a Yogi* there, which was responsible for doing something ineffable to George Harrison and Steve Jobs—enough of a reason to avoid it, even if it wasn't just a new flavor of exotic, miracle-greased masturbation for well-off and vaguely questing Americans in search of another way to have their cake and give their parents' Father Carnohan the finger, too. Cardiff-by-the-Sea, where we were, was technically part of Encinitas and had cloyingly cute Anglophilic street names, as if restaging some colonial standoff with its Indic neighbor. But of course both parts of town were overpopulated with the white and the wealthy.

"Tending to the sick and needy," I said. "Good to hear. I thought I'd heard there was an *E. coli* outbreak in Trader Joe's organic cantaloupe."

"Right," Andy said, seemingly bemused. "The Lord is good, and we minister where He leads us. And I don't need to remind you that you didn't exactly choose to start a mission in Tijuana."

"Look," I said, trying to bore a telepathic hole into his glossy, pug-like forehead, though I wouldn't have turned down a material one either. "You know I don't go in for God anymore. I know you know. Cut the shit, Andy."

"What do you mean?"

"Stop baiting me."

Andy looked genuinely stricken. "I wasn't trying to bait you. I'm sorry. Just trying to show you some concern. I didn't imagine you were getting much these days, at least from people who really knew you."

"You know dick," I said.

"Fine, fine. You know we're not into pressuring people at New Hope." He looked down at his hands, knocked them against the fiberglass of his board.

I was just calming down enough to think maybe Andy wasn't a complete sociopath when he said, drawing the words out with uncertainty, "Maybe you should know, though."

"What?" I said.

He gave that pooch-lipped look again. "We at New Hope will always be there for you if you need us."

"If I need you?" I asked. "I need to start a retirement account more than I need anything at New Hope. I need a four-day work week and a two-month vacation, better strawberries at the discount grocery, and some vitamin B. I need a staph infection more than anything you're offering. So what I need the most is for you to go fuck yourself and paddle away. Preferably in the reverse order, because I don't want to see your nightly Lubriderm bacchanal."

Andy nodded deeply and smirked, maybe, I couldn't tell, as he lay down on his board. When he was five yards farther out, farther than any wave had broken all morning, the pudgy man lifted his stout arms toward the sky. He began a just-audible prayer. It involved the usual thanksgivings, the apologies—I tensed waiting for my name to appear in that roster, but it never came—and an appeal for waves. For big, beautiful, God-given waves, one especially for himself.

Andy finished praying and splashed his hands around in the water. Not ten minutes later a bigger set came toward us, at first just bands on the horizon, then growing into steep mounds approaching from the west.

I was too far inside; I'd be caught by it, for sure. Meanwhile, Andy was in the perfect position. He paddled for it, looking openly smug, deservedly rewarded by the God who at that very moment was letting who knows how many children die of exposure, of AIDS, of starvation and the violence of criminals, warlords, parents.

Andy stood when the wave began to lift him. It was going to break long and fast to the left, I could see. A section of the lip was ready to throw over in a wide barrel. He barely managed the hard drop. His bottom turn was sloppy and sapped his speed, so he pumped like a fool to make the first section. He shouted, like the Southern Baptist preacher he always wanted to be, "*Jay-sus!*"

It was a perfect wave, and this asshole, feet spread too far apart in a kind of yoga warrior pose, trying to turn like his legs were stuck in cement, went and wasted the gift he'd asked for.

Sammy Ray Gans had continued on at New Hope after I left. I didn't like coming into contact with my past. I didn't like anything that would return who I was to the view of who I am. But if anyone could tell me where to find Sammy, it was Andy. He'd said New Hope would always be there for me. Maybe this counted.

I called my old church as soon as I got home from Jimbo's, still feeling wired and jangly from my conversation with Shaw. To my disbelief, the main line was the phone number I still knew by heart.

"I'm surprised," Andy said when I got him on the line. "Surprised but happy to hear from you." I didn't buy it and bit my tongue. I told him I wanted to get in touch with Sammy.

"Sammy stopped coming here a few years ago," Andy said. "Why are you trying to find him?"

I wasn't going to tell him the truth, so instead I said, "Maybe seeing you made me want to dust the skeletons out of my closet."

He made a strange, throaty sound. I didn't know what to make of it. Then he said, "The only things I've heard aren't good."

"Maybe I heard Sammy's in a bad place, too," I said, "and I wanted to try to help the guy out. I mean, he was part of my team." I'd meant to sound dry, but as I said the words they sounded genuine. A lump of feeling wedged in my throat like a cancer, but the emotional chemo switched on as automatic as breathing to keep it from metastasizing.

Andy replied without the usual shit-eating veneer to his words. "I can understand that," he said. There was a long silence. "I'm not sure you want to find him, though."

I asked why.

"After he stopped showing up, I met him a few times. Tried to counsel him back onto a path of righteousness. But he was a mess. And he didn't want help. He made that very, very clear." His voice brushed against a few raw notes, and he cleared his throat. "And you know as well as I do how little you can do for someone who makes that choice."

It bothered him that he hadn't been able to help. It should, but hearing it wasn't what I expected. "Sure," I said. "I'd like to find him anyway. He was a friend."

"Look. I can't—" Andy said in something of a whisper. "Ah, give me a minute." He put me on hold abruptly and returned a couple minutes later, now all business. He read out the last address they had for Sammy, and it was a Ramona address. It matched Shaw's imprecise directions to the general area where the parties were. Then Andy said he had to go and hung up without offering to lead us in some trite closing prayer, even though our halting conversation had led us across what I'd considered an incommensurable divide—had left me considering this weak *selah*.

13.

I SLEPT RESTLESSLY THAT NIGHT. WHEN I WASN'T SLEEPING I RAN THROUGH Shaw's tale and tried to puzzle out exactly what kind of trouble Cindy was in—or Emily or whoever that flesh-and-blood person who'd been at my house was. That she was in trouble I didn't doubt. Why I should take it upon myself to find and help her I didn't question. I wasn't thinking about Mike, wasn't thinking about Aracely, wasn't thinking about anything, if I could help it, but I couldn't help myself from wanting to know where Cindy had gone.

When I woke in the morning, my arms were tense and sore like I'd been building a cinder-block wall all night. I made and drank a pot of coffee, fried some bacon and eggs, stuffed them into a tortilla, and drove out looking for Sammy. I knew I shouldn't go alone but there was no one to go with, so I did.

The drive to Ramona took about an hour. The highway ran through the landlocked towns along the 78 freeway. Inland California all looked the same to me, a boring repetition of stucco, strip malls, industrial complexes, and master-planned communities behind stone-faced walls in which the price of each home could buy a county in most parts of America. I didn't enjoy coming this far east. I liked the blue of the ocean, the bullshit of beach people. Inland California may as well have been Missouri, as far as I was concerned, and I planned to have a long, happy life of never visiting Missouri.

After a switch to the 15 and a trek down a side road, I was on a long thread of two-lane highway that would take you all the way to the Anza-Borrego Desert, if your interests ran toward dry places, pedophiles, elderly retirees with no income, or the flower bloom that turned out, for three weeks a year, a few colors on that martian craterscape. Threading through two mountains, my ears popped and I passed a ranch-style sign for something called the Lemurian Fellowship, oddballs among oddballs. Then I came to my turn and followed a winding road through half-burned-out oak and sycamore groves and horse corrals. These gave out onto an isolated trailer-park community. Then the landscape turned drier, and the houses were farther and farther apart, until there were moments that, past one place and before the next, none were in sight. I felt good and spooked and alone.

I passed a little tin-roofed place with a mailbox numbered 3779 and knew Sammy's was next, though I couldn't see it yet. I felt anxious, jumpy, and a little paranoid. It had been a long time, and everything about this felt wrong—but something kept me going.

On a rogue impulse, I pulled my truck off the road and parked it. I got out and locked the shell of the truck. Inside, the inland heat was melting the wax off my surfboard. The gravel ground beneath my feet as I picked my way through desiccated coyote bush. A quarter of a mile under the summer sun left me feeling like a Death Valley cowboy. My throat was an arid ridge even weeds knew better than to grow on. Maybe if I were wearing a Mexican poncho, maybe if it covered some iron plating tied around my torso, maybe if I were stanching the flow of saliva from my mouth with the stub of a cigar, maybe then I would have thought I was in the right place, doing the right thing. As it stood, I felt outlandish. But I was doing it. I kept walking. Somewhere in the hydroelectric dam of my basal ganglia, someone was throwing switches, opening sluices. It wasn't me. I never felt less like me. But it wasn't anyone else.

I crested a ridge and looked down upon a small house with red roof tiles baking in the sun. The house was at the end of a long dirt driveway. Taken together from above, the house and driveway made the shape of an easy-strike match. The house was a two- or three-bedroom. Off the back was a concrete slab bordered with potted plants. To one side was an inflatable teal kiddie pool with vapor rising from it and probably three rattlesnakes drowning in the stew. On the far side of the house was a detached garage with a green Tercel parked out front. Assuming the car was Sammy's and that Sammy wasn't just using but manufacturing again, maybe there wasn't room for the car in the garage. Maybe it was full of chemicals and beakers and barrels. I didn't know. I didn't know just about anything. And since I didn't know, I figured I'd wait and watch awhile. There'd been too many stories in the news about cops raiding meth labs only to find a tweaked-out Butch Cassidy and the Sundance Kid ready to shoot things out.

I knew Sammy when he'd cleaned up the first time. He used to slick back his hair and button his flannels all the way up and open folding chairs for the parishioners streaming in, used to sing loudly and terribly along to the worship songs, tears on his face—used to convince teenage boys in the full flush of hormonal disaster to hug their fathers, cook for their mothers, and pray on their knees every morning just by his testimony of a life where those things had been impossible, shared once a year on the stage before the whole church and more often for the smaller youth groups and summer retreats.

He was a sweet guy. But nobody's all sweet, and time is a caustic agent, stripping away sugar to unveil the bitter core.

After squatting in the pucker bushes for long enough to give my thigh muscles a good burn, a person came around from the front of the house. Even at this distance, I could tell it was him. Sammy was unusually tall, with spidery limbs protruding from a red Hawaiian shirt and blue running shorts. He wore M-frame glasses, just like he'd always done; they were the optical protection of choice among dedicated athletes, he used to say. In one hand he held a watering can, and he shuffled from pot to pot, pouring a bit on each plant.

After making the rounds, Sammy went inside through a back screen door. Okay, I said to myself. Okay. I picked my way back toward the road and then headed up the dusty driveway to the house. No going back. He might have already seen me.

The house could have been any tract home in the area built in the last thirty years, except it was missing its chromatically varied doppelgängers running in rows on either side of it and there were two gas-flame lamps installed by the front door. In the bright daylight I couldn't see the flames, just a ghostly movement. It was a strange touch.

I knocked hard, three times, on the door. My mind moved to a place like prayer. It was unsettling to be there, familiar in a bad way, like returning to the bridge you almost fell from and then slipping on a stone. The nerves in my arms and legs prickled to life, ready to move—ready to hit something or run away from it. It was the feeling I'd had trying to back out of the machine shop the night Mike was killed, I realized, only now it was too late to retreat. The door opened and Sammy's face appeared, sunburned and crimson over the muted red of his Hawaiian shirt.

For a man nearing forty, his skin was acne ridden and greasy. His eyes flicked, taking in different parts of me. I began to see myself as he would see me: with longer and grayer hair, the dry and worn skin of a man fifteen years older than the one he was trying to connect me with. Time is the final act of a tragedy that never ends: in Sammy's mind it created this gaping, vibrating negative space out of the last fifteen years of my life; in mine it let me guess what-ifs about this friend before me, who he might have been if I had done otherwise.

The summer before I'd left the church, Sammy had been my assistant on a summer retreat to Lake Shasta with over a hundred teenagers. He'd run his own small group, took them out for boat rides, made sure the boys stayed away from the girls, that the girls stayed away from two-pieces—all the important things. But it was the last night, when I was giving my final talk from the deck of a houseboat to a group of kids on the beach, that came to mind now: how full and magnanimous I'd felt, tan and healthy after a week in the summer sun, telling these young people, "In Jesus, change is possible—profound, life-changing, life-giving change, if only you hand over the reins to *His* will instead of your own." Then I looked over at Sammy, who beamed and nodded yes, yes, yes, like he would never stop. Now we both had, and change had come regardless, and undisguised.

I was starting to feel a dull, desolate tug of regret—at coming here, and for more, I'm sure—when Sammy smiled. His thin lips parted to reveal a set of immaculate, shimmering white teeth: perfect teeth, pristine teeth, the kind of smile you can't help smiling back into on a face that would cause a dermatologist a spiritual crisis. Then he reached out with those Erector Set arms and took me into an embrace that I was unprepared for. Maybe I leaned into that hug more than I should have, given the circumstances, but I did. I hugged Sammy like the old friend he was, like I had done with the lost kid I'd first known.

"It's so good to see you, man!" he said. "Oh, fuck, I can't even tell you. It's so, so good." Sammy made an odd, satisfied sound as he squeezed me harder and then let me go. "Jesus Christ, man. Oh"—pointing to the sky apologetically—"sorry, you know me. Come in. Come in, man."

I followed him, and my eyes strained to let more light in. The blinds were all drawn, and the air conditioner droned in the vents. "Shit, man," Sammy said, "let me get you a drink. Coke? Water? Beer? What do you want?"

"Water would be great. Thanks."

While he was in the kitchen, I looked around. It dismayed me to see that the living room was much like my own. The TV was a little bigger. There was a framed poster of Captain Planet on one wall captioned THE POWER IS YOURS! The main difference was the houseplants. They were everywhere. Ferns, aloes, cacti, succulents of all shapes and colors, philodendrons. On shelves, on small tables, on the floor. The only one that didn't look healthy was the peace lily.

I thought about what Shaw had said. This didn't look like a place where raging, drug-fueled parties were thrown. It looked like a place to play a geriatric round of pinochle. Cindy had said her last place was a dump, and this was that. But I couldn't see her living here. Not with Sammy. Sammy, I could remember more clearly now, had always been emotionally needy and unshy about asking for attention and sympathy, and Cindy didn't seem like the type to cater to that. Maybe this was all a misunderstanding—just me crossing wires, having life kick the legs out from under me, and Shaw being confused about who he'd talked to on the beach that day, which would explain him calling her by another name.

But still I was standing in a strange house in Ramona about to chat with one of the men I most associated with my life before, my god-and-fellowship life, and I didn't have any choice but to let what was going to happen, happen, now that I was here.

Sammy came back with a glass of water in one hand and a glass of soda in the other. He handed over the clear one and motioned to the couch. I sat. Sammy stayed standing, taking turns holding each leaf of a ficus between his fingers, gingerly turning them over to examine their undersides.

"It's good to see you, Sammy," I said. "Nice house you've got out here all by yourself."

"Yeah, it's good, it's nice," Sammy said. "But fuck, man. You. *You*. I can't believe it's *you*. In the flesh."

"For the most part."

"Yeah, I know. We're not who we used to be. Maybe a little less or a little more than we used to be. I don't know, but I've been thinking about that. The more or the less, you know?"

"Me," I said and slapped myself on the gut, "more. You, I don't know. You don't look too different."

Sammy walked over to another plant, a Christmas cactus on a side table by the window, and checked its leaves. "Yeah, man, you don't know. You don't know." For a minute he seemed absorbed by the plant, and his face twisted inwardly and his lips moved without sound. "And some things just never change. No matter what." Then he looked at me and asked, "Why are you here?"

I looked down at my water glass. "I don't really know," I said. Sammy left the cactus and folded his arms, staring at me. It was a look I'd never seen on him before, a penetrating, intimidating posture, his chin set and pointed right at me. I could hear his teeth grinding. It sounded like the rubber seals on the shark tank about to give way.

"I ran into Andy," I said, looking for a way to ease the tension. "Saw him surfing, and he mentioned you. And it had been a long time. So I thought I'd come say hello." He kept the same posture, like he was waiting for me to continue. "That's it, Sammy." But I prattled on like a stammering child: "I guess I'm getting old and sentimental. Maybe I'm just thinking too much these days. I don't know." Sammy was motionless for another minute, and then he broke away to examine the soil of an orchid in full bloom, pale yellow with a pink center.

"Yeah, you don't know." Sammy laughed to himself bitterly. "Shit. I don't know, but you. *You.* You don't know? That's something. If you talked to Andy, maybe you *do* know, you know?"

"He just told me where I could find you."

"Yeah, well, you found me. Things aren't exactly great. I'm not ungrateful, you know, for what I've got. You know, ungrateful to"—Sammy pointed to the ceiling—"but it's been different, I'll say that. *Different.*"

"That's all Andy really said," I lied. "That you could use a familiar face."

"If it were only that, Mark," Sammy said. "Marky Mark! Here in my living room, I can't fucking—but yeah, if it were only that. That's the simple part. Stupid simple. I run up some debts, play the wrong horses at Del Mar, step on the wrong toes, and so I go and do what I can do." He looked at me then, just for a minute—and it was the first real eye contact we'd made, and there was the old Sammy, the neglected boy, the young man who couldn't help himself, the unofficial mascot of every teenage retreat and summer camp I'd led.

"I won't lie to you, Marky Mark. I don't even get lying anymore. It's just a waste." Sammy paused and stared at the ceiling. He closed his eyes and his lips moved silently. "But yeah," he said, "I started helping people get what they were looking for, if you know what I mean. And of course you know what I mean."

"Sammy," I said. His name was out of my mouth before I knew it, and it sounded bitter, personal, disappointed. Like a father. Sammy looked like a struck dog. I tried to cover the anger I felt, how much I must have still cared.

"Goddamn, shit, sorry, fuck, I know. I *know*," Sammy said. "I do this fucking stuff, I just do it, man. It's like someone makes me, and I can't say 'no' or 'fuck off,' but I can say, 'You're a bad person, Sammy Ray Gans, you're a waste of space, piece of shit, shit for brains.' That's all I get to do, for whatever godforsaken reason. That's the only role I get to play—fucking color commentary on the sinful point guard."

He was visibly upset, worked up. His skin, already inflamed from sun and acne, grew more purple than red, and white flecks gathered at the corners of his mouth. "Shit, man," he said, running his hands through his pale crew cut and sending up flakes of dandruff that looked like tiny alert flares in the dim, raking light of his living room. "I wish you'd come around, back then, and set me straight about me. You were always good at that. You were the *thing*, man. You made it happen. But hey, I got my wheel loose and ended up rolling all the fuck over the place, so now I'm here." I started to speak, but he kept on. It was like he hadn't spoken since the last time I saw him. "Shit, though, I'm glad you're here. Seeing your face, man. It's like getting sprayed with a fire hose."

"That's a good thing?" I asked.

"That's a good thing, man. A *good*. For damn certain."

He smiled at me broadly, and then something gave out in him. He sat down cross-legged on the carpet and began to weep. It wasn't like the tears he'd shed during worship. They weren't beatific, weren't symbols of joy after hardship, weren't anything anyone could take inspiration from. They were pitiful and plain.

I didn't move or say anything. I was sitting on the couch with one ankle propped up on the other knee like this was the goddamn *Oprah Winfrey Show*, feeling like the asshole I'd be if I were on there, and still I couldn't get any part of me to budge. Finally, I managed to say, "I'm sorry, Sam."

His lower lip hung loose, his jaw slack, a line of spit reaching down to connect with a hibiscus on his shirtfront. He looked at me. "No, man, it's not your fault. You had your own fucking downward spiral. It's too bad we didn't do it at the same time. It would have been fun to have your company heading to rock bottom. Especially *you*. But," he said, pooling snot in one sleeve of his shirt, "don't get the wrong idea. I never turned my back on God. Couldn't do that, never got that bad. So that's where maybe you're more fucked up than me."

"Yeah, maybe," I said, looking to pacify. But he gave me an apologetic look and said he was sorry for being a jerk, so I'd done a poor job hiding what I thought of his suggestion.

"I don't mean to be like this," Sammy said. "Things have just been a little emotional lately."

"A little emotional," I said. "I can see." Maybe I couldn't help myself either, because I added: "You know, maybe figuring things out gets a little simpler when you don't have plague hanging over your head and fire looming under your feet every moment." Whatever I'd intended, which must have mostly been a mislocated impulse to protect myself, it did get Sammy to stop crying. He laughed derisively and gave me a long, leering sort of stare. "Maybe it's just me," I added.

"Just you," he muttered, and started laughing again. He laughed for a while to himself, deliriously, with it rising into a little apex when he seemed to think of a new, humorous facet to what he was perceiving in me. I could imagine well enough what these little peaks were—he, as wracked and ruined as he was, preaching to his lapsed preacher being first among them. Then he stopped the laughing and I could hear his teeth grind again. "What'd Andy tell you about me?"

"Not much," I said. "But I met this other guy, this kid at the beach, and he knew you, too. He said he'd come to some parties out here with you that were better than *Fantasia* on acid."

"Part of business," Sammy said coolly, no trace in his voice of the weeping that had welled up in him only a few minutes before. "Have to make certain people happy, you know—gotta serve somebody."

"Sure," I said, not wanting to take that bait. "He also mentioned seeing a girl out here, a girl I'm trying to find."

Sammy raised an eyebrow—more properly he raised one half of a unibrow—a gesture that, due to his sickly skin, came off looking more grotesque than anything else. "We're *all* trying to find a girl, man. Trying, trying. Except the fags, I guess."

"Not like that," I said. I took a swallow of water. It was lukewarm and had a sedimentary taste. "I'm worried about this one."

"What a hero."

I winced. "Not like that either," I said. "But the kid at the beach said you guys were friends, he thought."

"You pretend you're different," Sammy said with a snide condescension that irritated me, "but God—you're still doing it."

"Doing what, exactly?"

He stood and wiped his hands on his shorts, leaving streaks on the nylon. Still seated, I felt constricted and emasculated, like a schoolkid roughed up before he can untangle himself from his wraparound desk.

"How long are you going to try to save this one, Haines?" he said bitterly. "A couple months? A few years? When's the expiration date? Because there *is* an expiration date. You've got a formula buried in your funky, twisted brain for calculating it, for figuring out when you've gotten enough out of it. And then one day it goes bad, and it's time to find some more freshly wounded bird."

An angry calm came over me, that placid clarity of rage. What did this tweaker know, even if most of those jabs had made contact with tender points? This was insult by horoscope, and he already knew I was a Pisces. Of course some of those would land. But that wasn't why I'd come. Sammy wasn't why either. I tried to stay focused on that. "Believe whatever the fuck you want, Sammy," I said, "but I never meant anyone—I never meant you—any harm."

"No," he said, sucking on his teeth and appraising me in a way that abraded like sandpaper. "This isn't about belief, man, and it's not about harm. But like usual it's about you. Why didn't you call after you quit the church? I called you. I left messages. I'd done the addiction thing before. I wanted to help." His anger faded into a tender tone that took me unsuspecting. The concern of it, the earnestness of his wish to have done some good for me back then. That hurt some—hurt a dusty corner of the cold, charred meat I called my heart. I tried to will the feeling out of that deadened muscle, but it didn't work. "I would have done that, Haines," he said. "Maybe that would have been a good thing for me, too."

My limbic system shuddered as I tried to shake it loose from its connection to my brain. "I couldn't do it," I said. "I could make my choices, but I was a leader of the church. I wasn't going to lead you or anyone else down the way I was going."

That's what I said, but in my mind I was back in the hospital, wearing pajamas with drawstrings removed, taking messages from the receptionist and depositing them directly in the garbage. I was sitting with Dr. Khan, in much the same way I was sitting here but with the tongues of my shoes flayed open, laceless. He was worried that I had no recollection of my suicide attempt. The only trace of it in my memory was a big, redacted blank with a single image hovering in the middle: Aracely, in her frilled pajama shorts, placing the phone in its cradle. The pills I'd swallowed could only account for so much memory loss and none of my sudden atheism, which the doctor questioned. I explained how the absence of God was the same as the feeling of absence I had in the first year after my sister's death, of there being a chance when the phone rang of it being Ellen. Ellen, beyond where I could reach her, beyond where I could help, or anyone could. What I didn't tell Dr. Khan was that it wasn't just her. Everyone had slipped beyond my reach. Gabby, Aracely, Sammy, too—all too far to be helped by any of my weak, selfish, useless grasping. I didn't tell that to Sammy either, but that was why I'd never called him back. His help wouldn't have been any help at all. It was contingent on God, and I didn't want it.

"I couldn't call, Sammy," I said. "I just couldn't."

Sammy folded his arms. I studied the coffee table, the mold growing under the bevels of glass where it slotted into varnished pine. How much later I don't know he touched my shoulder, and I started.

"Jesus Christ—sorry," he said. "Don't cry, man. I just get going. I can't help myself." I didn't think I was crying, but I felt my face: he was right. "Just forget about it, okay? I'm just a fucking asshole."

Forgetting is what I do best. "We're all fucking assholes," I said, erasing the feelings that had overcome me and replacing them with bitterness and distance.

"The girl," I said to change the subject. "The one I'm looking for, that the kid at the beach said you were friends with. She told me her name was Cindy but he thought her name was Emily. Tallish. Short black hair. You know her?"

Sammy studied me, his face held together by surface tension like a framed and hung puzzle, with its secret impulse to fall and return to pieces. His eyelids began twitching. "Oh, yeah. Emily. She lived here awhile," he said breezily while his hands fidgeted with his shirt, always resettling it farther back on his shoulders. "She was a cool girl."

"How long ago?"

"Maybe a year. Maybe two," he said. "She needed a place to crash, so she helped out around the house. A woman's touch. You know. Drifted in with a few kids who were working with me and asked if she could stay." He turned to study the base of a fern, dipping his hand into the soil and rubbing the moist earth between his fingers. He was making me nervous. For an instant, I thought the plant was where he hid his firearms, but I dismissed it as me getting overheated, an overactive imagination. I waited. Sometimes silence is the best way to get more information, being present and silent and paying attention. Another of my old tricks.

"Seriously," Sammy said as if I'd accused him, "that's all there is to it. She was going with one of my boys awhile, and then she left. Maybe about a year ago, I guess. Said she was going to Seattle, God knows why—said she wanted to live somewhere with lots of rain. The opposite of a desert, she said."

I nodded. It sounded like her, and she had drifted out to Oceanside, where I found her trying to hitch a ride north. But Shaw had seen her a few months ago, here, and Sammy was lying. I just didn't know why he was doing it, or how to get at it.

"You haven't heard from her since then?"

"Nope. Nothing. So long. Thanks for all the shoes."

"Did she have any other plans?"

"Not that she told me," Sammy said, "but that's like having heart-to-hearts with your housekeeper, you know? Doesn't work that way, really."

"Your place does look like it's hurting for some TLC."

What was I doing? I didn't know what else to say, or what I'd hoped to find out by coming here anyway. Did I want the truth of Emily—I guess that was her name—the truth of her time with Sammy, if he had taken advantage of her in the way Shaw said? Was I trying to make sure that her leaving wasn't my fault? All I'd accomplished was making my insides feel raw.

Then there was a thump from the back of the house and a woman's voice cursing.

Sammy stared through me. He looked stern, apprehensive. I didn't move while we both waited for another sound. It was quiet for a moment. Then came a voice: "Sammy, can you get me some ice?"

It was Cindy's voice, or Emily's—whatever her real name was, for whatever good knowing names does, though not knowing my grandson's had certainly tweaked me enough. Sammy stopped seeing the wall behind my head and locked onto my eyes. I tried not to let on that I recognized the voice, but for all I knew my hair had gone white and a bolt of lightning had reached down into my skull.

"One sec," Sammy called to her, without taking his eyes from me.

"Sammy," I said, and there was that tone of paternal disappointment again.

"Look, man," he said with the sudden command of a military officer and the diction of a teenager. "It's complicated. It's not your thing, and it's complicated. But you need to trust that I'm not being a bad person and go."

I felt able to stand and did. Once vertical, though, my legs went liquid. It was the fear, but it was also the fear that kept me talking, the need to keep moving in some form or another or else collapse. I took one step toward him and said, "I can't—"

He moved toward me and jabbed one of his bony palms into my chest, holding me at a distance. "Just go, Marky Mark. Just fucking go." His fingers pressed into my chest, almost tenderly, and then gave a small push. I let myself stumble back a step.

From the back of the house came her voice again, all incomprehension. "Did you hear me? What's going on?" Sammy whispered to me under his breath, "Just go, just go, just go." Then, from the hallway, from out of the ether like breath on the water, there was Emily. She wore the same yellow shirt as the day I met her and gray sweatpants rolled over on themselves at the waistband. She was rubbing a spot on her elbow, and when she saw me she stopped dead.

"Oh," she said. Her eyes were red, blissed out, bleary. All the vital theatricality in her demeanor was gone, replaced by sordid dreariness, an exhausted presence. Darkness shadowed the undersides of her eyes. Besides the red spot where she rubbed her elbow, her skin was dry and pale, bone-like.

Then Sammy was pacing toward her. She raised her arms like she was expecting to get hit. My anger rose in me, sidestepping my brain and going straight to my muscles, and I started after him. Sammy laid his hand on the small of her back, pointed down the hallway, and hectored her like the bad parent of an unruly child, "Stay in the back, like I fucking said. This is personal, so mind your own goddamn business." Emily looked between us with confusion etched on her face, though for a moment I thought I caught a flicker of something else beneath it.

"But I know that guy. Haines, what are you doing here?"

Before I could answer, Sammy was pushing her down the hallway. I was two steps behind him. He shut her in a back bedroom and surprised me with how fast he turned and had my throat in his hand. By the pinched esophagus he marched me back down the hallway. The shift in direction made it hard for me to get leverage, and I stumbled backward, choking. He got me into the living room. The backs of my knees caught the coffee table and I went over, onto the ground.

Sammy stood over me. His face was beaming and twisted with rage, but his voice was as cool as aloe when he said, "You're going to leave now." I struggled to breathe. It burned worse than a lungful of cigar smoke. "Reunion time is over. You've gotta get back to your life. And I got mine, and she has hers, and we're all going back to that."

My voice returned but came out dry and bitter, like the taste of raw sage. "I thought you said you didn't get lying."

"Fuck you, Haines," he said quickly. "You're good at leaving. Go where your gifts lead you. That was always your advice. I'm following it. So just leave and forget all about this."

I didn't like getting pegged so squarely by a tweaker. I scrambled to stand up and hit him. By the time I got to my feet, Sammy had a decent-sized pistol in his hand—from where I don't know, a houseplant, maybe—and pointed it at my chest. My anger soured.

I imagined the hole, not psychological this time but physical, being ripped through the center of my body. I thought of poor, dead Mike, damn dead Mike.

"I'm not going to shoot you, Haines. But I work with people who will. That's not a threat. That's just part of the lay of the land. The topiary, man. You need to forget about me, forget you ever came here. Forget Emily, too. She's better off if you do."

"What I heard was you were whoring her out," I said, despite the feeling of ice and bile running through the muscles affixing skull to jaw.

"You don't know the fuck of it, man," he said, voice rageful and showing no sign of cracks. His pistol hand lifted, and I found myself jumping, turning, hollering, holding my arms out as if I might catch the bullet he was thinking of sending my way. It never came, but somehow I ended up back on the floor. The gun barrel cut the air, occasionally making the hollow note of a beach bum's Corona bottle. "It all gets so complicated. You wouldn't understand. I don't fucking understand, most of the time. It all gets too huge and complicated. But I know you like it simple, so let's keep it simple, man. Get the fuck out of here. Don't call the cops or tell anyone about any of this. That's the only way you get to keep up your full calendar of surf sessions and breakfast burritos, my friend."

"Friend," I said.

"This is my way of looking out for you. Get up. Get out. It's more than you did for me. Don't die because of this. It's not worth it. We both know which way you'd go, and it isn't up."

We stayed like that for a while: me on the ground, bruised, breathing raggedly; him holding the gun pointed toward my body without his own betraying hesitation or doubt. I couldn't see any good way of calculating worth in this moment. I couldn't see any way forward other than leaving.

"Okay," I said. "I'm going." I got to my feet slowly, keeping my hands raised. It's strange to think how naturally this came to me, down to the slight stoop, the slow steps, the seething resentment.

As I backed my way toward the door, Sammy said, "I mean what I said."

I reached behind me and opened the door. The dry desert air hit my neck and cooled in the sweat. A deep shiver crawled down my spine. I felt like an ice cube cracking in a hot whiskey that someone had puked in. "I don't doubt it," I said.

Sammy lowered the gun a couple inches and made a nodding motion with the barrel to shoo me down the driveway. "Bullshit, Haines. You doubt everything."

Outside now, the sound of the gas flames in the lamps whipped like tiny flags in the wind. He watched me backpedal all the way to the street. Then he shut the door. At that point, I turned and walked like a semiprimate should.

The fear was fading. If he was going to shoot me at this point, it was my time.

Maybe that was bravado talking. Maybe it was a good way of reorienting myself, a new context for an old habit. When I was in high school, my sister, Ellen, had tried to help me deal with the hell of being seen by other teenage people by focusing on God—that it was God who determined my worth. She said I had nothing to be ashamed of or to apologize for if it was acceptable in the sight of God. I tried it, walking to classes or across the quad, a vertical band of illumination spotlighting me in the sight of the absolute, the living beings around me cast into the shadows of outer darkness. It stuck so much that it wasn't until Ellen died that I ever approached a full consideration of another's thoughts, the weight of them—and that their judgment of me might be important and necessary.

The comfort of that beam of light, of being perceived by a single, omnipotent gaze, that's what having Sammy's gun trained on me felt like. It took everything else off the table. And the ghost of that being in the sky, that's who I must have been imagining when I told myself it was perhaps my time to go—that there was some out-of-time deciding force instead of all this very mundane, capricious mess making—that there's a time to go, and not just going.

As I walked down the street, it was quiet save the sound of lizards in the brush and the coos of hidden quail. It was so quiet I heard the click of Sammy's front-door dead bolt. I listened for more, for voices, for a fight, but nothing came.

Emily was here. She didn't look like she was being held against her will, but she didn't look good. Addiction could be its own kind of incarceration. And I didn't like the way she flinched when Sammy came at her, though I had to admit—my phrase of choice again—that he hadn't, in fact, struck her. Maybe this is right where she wants to be, I thought. And who was I to her when it came down to it? A random encounter, a short-term leg up, an obliging mark she'd tried to use. What of it? Plenty of people choose and rechoose abusive, destructive relationships every day. Who was I to get in the way of another's rock-bottom living room? Shaw's story could have been just that—a story, one where he'd get to rescue her, take her back to his bedroom at his mom's house, a tube sock full of the mess of wishful thinking.

But Sammy. Sammy was the problem. He said people would come after me, would kill me, if I said anything. Maybe it was just his drug operation he was trying to protect, or theirs, or maybe it had something to do with Emily, too. Or maybe he was just afraid that Emily could expose him. I didn't know. How could I have known? How could I know anything? It might have been only an empty threat, a bid for me to leave his girlfriend alone, a girl who, sober, wouldn't have given him a glance if he were on fire. I needed to think, but the adrenaline kept thoughts short and circular. The possibilities presented and re-presented themselves like shuffled flash cards of what to be afraid of—an endless, circular solitaire.

A car passed at high speed, and I realized I'd been dead to the world, walking slowly, staring at my shoes. I looked up. A short way ahead was my truck, parked among the pucker bushes. Another car came over the hill, doing maybe seventy-five on the two-lane road. It was a police cruiser. Then there was a third, and a fourth. They left me in a fine dusting of pulverized granite. A fifth came over the hill, partially off-road, and almost swiped my truck. This one braked hard and came to a stop next to me. The glare on the windows was flinty and opaque. I peered harder until the doors opened and two young men pointed their two young guns at me.

One shouted for me to put my hands on my head. I did. The other came around and knocked me roughly to the ground. He cuffed my hands behind my back, high enough that it felt like my shoulder blades would burst through the skin. Gravel ground my cheek and nose. From this vantage, I almost imagined I was out on some kind of barren prairie, and I wondered why I'd come to this strange place and how many rainbows I'd have to hurdle to get back to my real, monochromatic life. If someone had been offering, I would have clicked my heels and taken a drink right there.

14.

A COP GAVE ME A BOTTLE OF WATER ONCE THEY HAD ME IN A CELL AT THE Ramona Substation. I guessed they hadn't gotten the running kind yet and looked forward to taking advantage of a bedpan. I asked for a cup of coffee, and a blond cop brought me one. When I asked him if they'd also picked up the girl, he gave a sweet, dumb look and said, "What girl?"

The coffee settled my nerves, and when an hour or two later they brought me some food and told me to get comfortable, I knew I'd be there for the night. No one would tell me why, though I could guess a few versions of the story they were writing.

The coffee, though, let me sleep. In the morning, before breakfast, a tall Samoan, half-bald and solidly built, walked me down to an interrogation room and let me sit awhile longer. The floor only had six dozen deep gouges in it. I know. I counted. That's a bunch of rough interrogations, I imagined, or one shitty cleaning service.

I would have counted other things in the room, but that's all there was. I was trying to keep things slow. I knew what would happen if it went the other way. Under the circumstances, I assumed it would go the other way. There was a weird calm, though, on the other side of normal. It was like me and coffee, a counterintuitive reaction from a challenged central nervous system. I was in an interrogation room, had been arrested, had been threatened by a kid I used to evangelize with. The terms were different suddenly, and I didn't know what to expect, so there was nothing to be prepared for. What else was there to do but wait?

Two detectives came in eventually. One was the big Samoan, the other a white guy with unusually long and fulsome hair for a cop. He introduced himself. "I'm Detective Lawrence," he said, "and this is Mose Tuitele." His accent straddled midwestern reserve and southern gentility, though he pronounced the voluminous vowels of the Samoan name easily and well.

"Look," I said. "I haven't done anything wrong. You guys can't hold me like this."

Tuitele lowered his solid frame into a chair in the corner and gave his partner a half smile. Lawrence folded his arms and remained standing. "Mr. Haines, you're right in some ways and not in others," he said. His cadence was that of a long-suffering history teacher. "You haven't broken any laws, that's true. And we aren't going to suggest you did." This made him laugh, silently, to himself. "We don't work like that. But there are a lot of gaps here. I'm always trying to understand people. That's the part of this job I enjoy the most. So help me understand how a man like you ends up walking away from a man like Samuel Gans, someone with a history of dealing drugs, after getting into an altercation with him?"

I found myself holding up my hands. It was something a guilty person would do, I realized, and put them on my knees. "He was a friend from a past life. We'd been out of touch. An acquaintance told me he'd fallen on hard times, so I thought I should check up on him. That's all it was. And a mistake, obviously."

"Past life?" Tuitele said. "You don't mean *past life* past life, like you and him used to feed grapes to Cleopatra together?"

"No. Not that," I said. "I just mean that we knew each other when we were younger, a long time ago."

Tuitele laughed and balanced a notebook on one knee to write something down. In his hand, the pencil looked like a sewing needle. "We get all kinds," he said. "Never assume, you understand? I had to ask."

Lawrence was giving his partner an inscrutable look, but Tuitele never met it. "Now that we've established that beyond a doubt, another question," Lawrence said. "It's less than a week ago that you were interviewed regarding the death of a Michael Padilla. I understand he was also your friend. I spoke to Detective Harper with the Carlsbad PD. He gave me the full background. But it *is* noteworthy, to be at the scene of a murder and then a few days later get picked up on the premises of a raided drug house, where you'd gotten into some kind of confrontation."

I began to respond, the maw of the events he invoked opening up gaping holes of negative space inside me, but Lawrence kept on, raising his voice gently to show he wasn't ready to cede the floor to me: "We're not saying you've done anything wrong. I'm not suggesting that, sir. But these are questionable circumstances. The facts, when placed together in this manner, are suggestive." He rubbed his lips, muddling through those suggestive possibilities, I guessed, or at least making a show of it to give me time to do the same. But I knew where I stood. "Would you care to elaborate on anything that this should be suggestive of? Anything we might need to know about?"

"Just that my luck seems to be working against me," I said.

"And you've been feeling well?" Lawrence asked.

"My coworker got killed and I was just roughed up by a tweaker, so I've been a little more maudlin than usual. But sure, just fine."

"In a larger sense, though. You've been stable? It's been a long time since your last arrest for drunk in public—about ten years, it seems. Have you been drinking?"

That was as far as I wanted this to go. I stood, roughly knocking the chair away behind me; it left a new set of gouges in the floor, I noticed. Didn't take much. "No. And I haven't done anything wrong, and you two can pull whatever you want out of my record, but it doesn't change that. If you're trying to scare me or insult me or whatever, I want to get a lawyer. I've been clean and sober for nine years running, not hurting a fly. This is all a little too much." Lawrence had poked the flopping, thirsty fish always splashing around my insides, and it made me angry—angry, looking back, because of how much that feeling of thirst had crept back around, how the brick wall I thought I'd built was full of doors and secret passageways and framed over a forgotten aquifer.

"Please, Mr. Haines," Lawrence said in a conciliatory tone. "This isn't an interrogation, and like I said, we don't think you did anything." He gave a quick glance to Tuitele, eyes communicating something. "This is just a helpful conversation. Helpful for us. Have a seat, please."

Without looking up from his notepad, Tuitele asked brusquely, "What about the sexy stuff? Was that a part of your and Gans's past life?"

The question took me by surprise, didn't fully compute at first. It allowed me to overtake my overheating brain, which had started to get away from me. I knew I shouldn't let that happen. This wasn't the moment to get out of control.

Lawrence sighed. "That was going to be our next topic of conversation, but I guess we can go there now." He pulled the chair back to the table and held it out for me. I took a seat. The more I watched Tuitele, the more I was sure he was drawing and not writing in his notebook.

"In the past or present," Lawrence continued, "is there anything you can tell us about Mr. Gans's sexual appetites?" By the way he asked, I could tell something about the question made him uncomfortable.

All I could think of was what Shaw had told me. "I'd heard some rumors," I said. "About some things that were maybe not consensual or maybe drug related. But yeah, it sounded like he had them. Today was the first time I'd seen him in fifteen, sixteen years. I'm not the expert. What did the girl say? She's known him more recently."

The two cops exchanged looks. Tuitele drew a sharp vertical line on his notepad, grimaced, and asked, "What team was he playing for? Any unusual things ring his bell?"

"Excuse me? If you're asking me if Sammy is gay, I wouldn't know. He never said as much to me. But I was his pastor, so why would he."

"Pastor, eh? That's surprising," Tuitele said.

"It was a long time ago," I said, and then a moment later: "I think he had some kind of relationship going with the girl—Cindy or Emily or whatever her name is. She'd be able to give you more information about all this, I imagine."

Tuitele said, "Right." I don't know if it was to himself or directed at his partner. Lawrence rubbed his flat chin and narrowed his eyes, a cliché of a thinking face if I ever saw one. But he must have been thinking sincerely. Abruptly he said, "Excuse me a moment, please," and left the room.

Tuitele didn't even glance up. Whatever he was drawing must have been a *Mona Lisa*, to judge by the attention he gave it. We sat in silence a good long while.

"Any idea what your partner is up to?" I asked.

"Of course, man."

"But you're not going to tell me."

"You've got the right idea there."

I tried to stay silent, but the sound of his pencil scratching itself to oblivion against that paper irritated me. I felt like I was the lead, wearing away. "You're both not from around here, are you?"

He laughed a little. "Who would want to be from around here?"

He had a point, but still I said, "I'm sure some people."

"If I was from around here, I wouldn't be a cop." He glanced at me, briefly, squinting one eye my way with a cool, cetacean intelligence. "I'd be a surfboard-riding burrito maker and a part-time improv comedian, doing a healthy web-design-slash-pot-growing business on the side. It tells you something's odd about a place when most of its cops are outsiders." He went back to his drawing with a heave of his body that suggested he'd given his final word on the subject—on any subject. I went back to waiting.

I didn't like any of this. I didn't like being questioned, didn't like how it forced me to admit how little I knew of Sammy—even when we knew each other. If they wanted to know what he was afraid of when he was seventeen, what he asked for prayer about, how many times a week on average he committed the sin of self-pollution against his better intentions, I could dig all that out from somewhere in my brain. I could tell them that Sammy had been desperate for approval, for the love of an authority figure, but how he had a self-destructive streak that kept him thinking he always had something to apologize for. He couldn't see love unless it was contingent on miraculous and undeserved forgiveness. If he wasn't looking for that, he didn't know what he was looking for. But all that was the polish on the piano, the public presentation he found acceptable in our confession-based environment. How the wires were strung, what gauge, and the kind of tension by which they were made straight—I didn't know that, had never known that, not with him, not with anyone. Confession usually pulled up well short of the deeper truth.

I don't know how long it was until Lawrence came back, but it felt interminable. Then he walked in hurriedly, like he was an obstetrician late for the birth of a child. "Sorry for the delay. Things always take longer than you think."

He sat in the chair across from me. The three of us made the points of a right-angled triangle. It was all a little Pythagorean, this distancing between us, too mathematical. The cops exchanged looks. Tuitele sighed and nodded, then Lawrence faced me.

"Let me give you a little background. I was just speaking with the Oceanside PD, who have searched your house." I must have colored. Lawrence knew it was coming because he used his sweetest voice to say, "A warrant was issued, you can see it if you like, but nothing was found. And"—he tried a smile here to see if it would soothe me—"I have their assurance nothing has been too disturbed. No one's flipping mattresses or kicking over bookcases."

I didn't smile, didn't laugh. I felt a numbness in my jaw like I'd been struck by a brick. A big black cloud of thoughtless, helpless rage bloomed in my brain. I recalled waking up in the machine shop's silent, dusty office. I didn't say anything because there wasn't anything to say, but it was the second time in a week I'd been considered a suspect, and that idea of me felt lodged, like a blade, between two ribs—the point pressed against but not yet puncturing my heart.

"We had to look," Lawrence said apologetically. "We didn't think we'd find anything, and we didn't. But at Gans's residence we found materials of a disturbing and illegal nature."

My first thought was a meth lab in the garage, but Tuitele interjected: "Porno shit. Stuff'd make you sick for a week and look into hiding your kids until they become adults."

Lawrence cleared his throat. "Mose." He never looked away from me, which I took as a sign that he was still watching for a suspicious response despite what he was saying. "But yes. There was a laptop in the garage with what looks like underage pornography, animal snuff, other things. So you see, what with your relationship to Gans having, at one point, involved youth activities, we had to take any possible connections seriously."

"To me," I said. "Connections to me. To see if I was involved in it, too." Tuitele was right. I did feel sick.

"Yes," Lawrence said, almost timidly. "Right." He seemed to lose his train of thought studying me. "Can I get you a glass of water or a cup of coffee? This may be a lot to take in, I know."

In the rising heat of my mental circuitry, I knew what my brain wanted. Instead, I took the coffee, and Lawrence left to get it.

"Wasn't anything to find at your house, right?" Tuitele said from his corner. "You look a little green."

I said of course there wasn't, that this was just overwhelming. I was nauseated. My thoughts were moving more quickly than I could keep up with. All there was—all there was were boxes of letters and books, journals, notes of my discussions of other people's private struggles, the crazy writings and drawings of a man in the midst of recovery, some in a child's hand but somehow made by my oversized, clumsy adult one. All this secret life, mine and that of others. It had all been sifted through like it was nothing, nothing because it hadn't pointed to outright crime. Crimes that Sammy was involved in or interested in. Crimes that may have involved Emily and who knows how many other kids.

Tuitele nodded. "That was my sense. Lawrence, he likes to check all the corners. Good for him, right?"

"Right," I said, feeling out of breath.

"Waste of my damn time, though," he said, not unkindly, "and now yours."

The door opened and Lawrence returned. He gave me a paper cup of coffee. I willed myself to bring it to my mouth slowly, to sip instead of guzzle. But the way it burned my tongue, the way it hit my gut and immediately made my nerves snap to attention, it took the edge off. And it was good coffee. He must have skipped the prisoners' scaly pot and gone to the staff break room for it.

"Hey," Lawrence said, slapping me on one shoulder in a friendly way that made me want to pop him in the eye. "Your house was clean. I only made it to the 'due diligence' chapter in my police playbook. And that takes time, hence why you're still here." He sat across from me again. "Gans is claiming that the laptop we found was someone else's, and he'd never used it. Not likely, but possible. It doesn't show prints, but we've got the computer forensics guys checking it. Between that and the bit of weed we found, we can hold him for a little while until we figure it out. But there's another part of the picture we're trying to put together, some things we found in the house."

"Like what?" The dark cloud evaporated and my vision attenuated to a clear focus on Lawrence's pale blue eyes. This was important. This was about Emily.

"Hm, there was also a good amount of, let's say, novelty sex items—devices, harnesses, that kind of thing—in one of the back rooms. On its own, I'd be blushing but not alarmed. But with the other business, well . . . And twice now you've mentioned a girl. Who is it you're talking about?"

I said, "When I first met her she told me her name was Cindy Liu. Someone else told me her real name was Emily. I don't know what to call her, but maybe she gave you her actual name."

Lawrence hummed uncertainly through his teeth. "How would she have told us? Did she file a report?"

"No," I said, not understanding. "The girl. At the house." Tuitele's pencil stopped moving. I looked between the two of them, and both shook their heads.

“She was there right before you guys showed up,” I said. “I saw her.”

“There was no girl,” Tuitele said. “You outside. Gans inside. A computer full of some sick shit. Too many goddamn plants. That’s it.”

“She was there,” I said. “I saw her, right before—” I remembered Sammy’s threat, too late when it came to talking about Emily but enough to stop me from saying anything about the gun he used to push me out the door. “Right before I left. Where could she have gone?”

Lawrence furrowed his brows, but his expression didn’t show any concern, any urgency. “Okay,” he said. “What did you say her name was?”

“Cindy Liu or Emily. They’re both made-up names for all I know, though.”

“And you’re sure you saw her in Mr. Gans’s house?”

I’m a skeptical person, but I couldn’t entertain this kind of doubt. I let it settle on me a moment anyway: Was I sure she was there? Don’t be a damn fool, I told myself. Of course she was. We spoke. I watched Sammy chase her back toward the bedroom. Sometimes obsessive self-scrutiny makes a person disbelieve what he knows in his bones—puts the whole world behind a glaze of glass, a microscopist’s remove. I didn’t have time—Emily didn’t have time—for distance, for contemplation.

“With my own two eyes,” I told Lawrence.

The two detectives conducted a wordless conversation before me, a long communicative stare passing between them. Finally, Tuitele looked at me: “We turned that house upside down. You two were the only living souls around there. When you kept saying something about a girl, I assumed someone had told you about the woman who called in the anonymous tip.”

"No," I said with an urge to rise, to walk out the door and go scour Sammy's house myself. "She was there. Where the hell could she vanish to? You guys need to get someone over there. Sammy had been angry with her. She was supposed to stay in the back, he said, and he was angry—maybe you missed something. Maybe she's still there. Maybe—"

"Don't get panicked yet," Lawrence said chidingly. I didn't realize I was until he said so. My consciousness slid back into a familiar notch, the one just a little above and to the left of my body. For a minute or two I'd been in it.

Lawrence continued: "We'll get some people back over there right away. Maybe she was hiding somewhere we missed. Maybe she left the property before we arrived. I'm going to have someone come in and get you processed and out of here. Sorry for all the trouble." Lawrence nodded in a genteel way, and then both men stood and made to leave.

"Wait," I said. "How can I follow up? How can I find out what's happened to her?"

Lawrence paused with one hand on the door and made a noise halfway between a laugh and a sigh. "That's not really how it works. Don't worry. We'll do everything we can do."

"But," I said weakly. "I'm worried about her."

"You her mom?" Tuitele asked. "Her dad?"

I thought of Aracely, among the pine trees in Oregon that couldn't be more different from the desert I was in, hating me while tending to her year-old son. "No," I said.

"No," Tuitele said. "There are limits."

A feeling of panic gripped me unreasonably. It was the panic of being tied up on your back in the bottom of a canoe as it coursed down a river, no sense of where you were going or what dangers were in store, only the occasional tree blotting out your view of the sky—

every splash or jolt a surprise and a premonition of the waterfall to come, the one lurking in your mind. It was the distilled panic of time itself.

"If only—"

"Mr. Haines," Lawrence said, measuring his words as if cutting exquisite Italian tile. "Your concern is . . . well intentioned, it seems." He glanced away a moment and then looked me straight in the eye, hard enough that he appeared in my mind as if spotlit, his surroundings dimming. "But I imagine you have your own concerns that need attention. Let us do our job. Tend to yours."

They left me sitting there, wondering what my job, what my concerns truly were. It seemed like they knew I'd been fired. Maybe they knew about the incident at the office. They clearly knew about my past, the things the old me had done—at least those committed to official record, etched in partiality on the edifice of institutional history. And my concern for Emily: it was true, I wasn't her parent, wasn't even her friend. What was I to any of these people? A cipher, a drunk, a potential smut peddler, an accomplice. I'd had so many people think so many things of me in the last week my head hurt. Screw them, I thought. Screw all of them.

The first blond cop came back in and asked me to follow him, I had some forms to fill out. I said, "No," just to refuse something.

"Come on," he said meekly, "I'm trying to get you out of here as quick as I can." He looked so pathetic, I gave in and followed him. There was something left in me that tended outward, as much as I wanted it gone. I just didn't know where it was leading yet.

15.

THE BLOND COP LAUGHED WHEN I ASKED HIM WHO WOULD GIVE ME A ride back to my truck. I waited a long time for a cab. They don't do cabs in Ramona. The ride cost me forty-five bucks. The driver was a short guy, maybe sixty years old. He tried chatting me up at first, but I didn't want to hear the sad story of why he couldn't retire and would die behind the wheel of this thing, or how he'd screwed over too many people and then got screwed out of his retirement, how he'd gotten what was coming. Either way, I didn't want to know. When I stepped out and paid him, he put what I thought was a few bucks' change in my hand.

"No," I said, "that's for you."

"I'm not giving you money," he said, his voice like a kindergarten teacher's. "I want to give you something more valuable."

I looked at what I held. It was one of those Baptist comic strips. The first panel featured a lovingly drawn young woman the artist had probably nicknamed Slutty Suzy. A few panels later, she was dead and burning in eternal hellfire. Normally I laughed at this kind of stuff, but it wasn't funny today. I threw it on the ground and asked the guy for my tip back.

"Do not store up for yourself treasures on earth," he said, "where moths and rust destroy, and where thieves break in and steal." Then he drove away. I waved him off with a one-handed here's-the-church-here's-the-steeple.

My truck was still on the side of the road. The shell had been obviously jimmied open, but the surfboard was inside, oozing wax onto the corrugated metal. I stood there, thinking a minute, not really thinking, waiting. It was as silent as only a desert can be silent. I had a few empty, shimmering thoughts about Emily, where she was or wasn't. I pushed those away. When I opened the truck door, a lizard skittered across the hood and nearly gave me a heart attack.

I tried driving over to look at Sammy's place, but the police were back there and I didn't want to seem like a nuisance or a nutjob. A couple hours later, I pulled into my own driveway. I'd stopped for food and more coffee. My hips and spine ached from sleeping on the jailhouse cot. My nerves were worn out, and everything in me felt heavy with loss and lethargy. I'd fallen asleep only once on the drive and was desperate to have another go at it.

As I walked up the driveway, though, a puny car horn honked behind me. It sounded like a quail, but it startled me anyway. I turned and saw a Civic parked across the street, white under a veil of gray, sooty dust. An arm stuck out the window and waved, but shadow cut across the person waving. I'd never seen the car before. I walked over. Halfway across the street Esmeralda's voice reached me:

"Where have you been, Haines? I've been waiting for thirty minutes. We're going to be late."

If you had asked me the week before, I would have said Esme

was just another person I worked with—someone with whom, because of forced proximity and regular contact, I knew how to trade an occasional joke or quick chat, like shells for corn. She'd never been to my house. We didn't get together on weekends. At most, we had a few years of regular bullshitting on company time between us, her, Mike, and me. Nothing more. That's what I thought and what I'd wanted. I was like Pinocchio; I didn't want any strings on me, even the most tenuous threads—incidental cobwebs picked up moving from hiding place to hiding place on Displeasure Island.

"Esme," I said. "Hi. Late for what?"

"Oh, honey," she said in a patronizing way that, surprisingly, I didn't exactly mind. "The funeral is today. It starts at four. I left you messages. We're going together. Didn't you get them?"

Gravity has a limit. It's based on relative mass and distance, the accretion of material and the resistance of physical matter to compression. I was at mine, dark and low. The thought of Mike couldn't add any weight. "I've been out of the office, so to speak," I told Esme. "I'm sorry. Look, maybe you should go ahead. I—"

Esme reached across and popped open the passenger door. She gave me the look a mother gives a trenchant child. "I know this is hard for you," she said, "but you have to go. All you need to do is get in. I'll take care of the rest."

A dense fog of emotion upwelled in me and, it seemed, a kind of relief. It was just neural triggers, stimulus converted to somatic response, a looping circuit no better than the Clapper's—that's what I told myself.

I cleared my throat, blinked away something like the premonition of tears. "My clothes."

"It's specifically casual," Esme said. "They don't want the black suits and veils."

I sighed. "Don't expect too much from me," I said, going around and lowering myself—and then lowering myself some more—to fit into the Civic.

"It's okay," she said, patting my knee in a way that made every inch of my skin stretch toward sleep. "I never do." She let a brief, bright laugh escape. "It's why I like you. You make me feel better about myself."

I buckled in, and she pulled away from the curb. The car was clean and smelled like vanilla. A sun-curled cardboard tree swung from the rearview mirror. In one of the cup holders was a *lux perpetua* candle inscribed with the image of the Maria Dolorosa, the Virgin Mother pierced through the heart by a sword.

"So, asshole, why didn't you call me back?" She put the car in third gear, changed lanes, and looked at me in one fluid motion. Her hair was down. It was the first time I'd seen it that way: a curt black bob that she kept tucked behind the ears.

"I haven't been home," I told her.

Concern covered her face like a shadow. "Where have you been?"

"To be honest, I'd rather not rehearse it."

She made a quiet clucking sound against the roof of her mouth in steady time. "Just tell me if I need to be worrying about you."

We were on the freeway, heading south. A bank of idiotic ice plant sucking down moisture gave way to a long view across the Agua Hedionda Lagoon on both sides of the highway. To the east, Jet Skis did circles in water made choppy from their play. To the west, a fog was coming in off the ocean, slipping beneath the wooden trestle. A pod of brown pelicans moved silently across the mingled fresh- and seawater. The last one dragged a foot on the surface of the lagoon as it vanished into the low clouds coming in. I found myself thinking about the idea of God's breath on the water. What a ridiculous way for all this mess to come into existence. Bring on the cosmic Breathalyzer.

"No, Esme," I said. "I'm the same as ever."

"Good," she said, touching me again, this time with an elbow on my arm, "I think. Then stop sitting on your ass and start worrying about me."

We spent the rest of the drive talking about her. She was still struggling with Mike's death. Every shift she worked was filled with panic that the next call she'd get would be the worst news. She didn't think she'd make it much longer, was thinking of moving, even; she had a sister in Chino who would let her live there while she studied for an RN, maybe. I listened, asked questions, kept her talking. It meant I had to say less.

We pulled into the funeral home, out past the McClellan-Palomar Airport in East Carlsbad. It was one anonymous building among a series of boxy gray nondescript buildings in a new industrial complex under construction. More of the same was going up across the street. The neighboring building was a box manufacturer. The irony of it filled me with a nasty, mean dread. This was the dismal place where we would honor Mike.

Others were arriving, too. Most were wearing floral shirts and dresses, shorts, sandals. Esme's jean skirt and polo shirt weren't too far above the dress code. There was milling. Everyone wore sunglasses. A few even shook my hand, said it was good to see me. I thought up a few sarcastic responses, things Mike might have found funny, but the vinyl lettering on the front door—CREMATION SERVICES INTERNATIONAL—stopped me short.

We stepped inside. In the entryway was a poorly printed sign taped to a microphone stand pointing to the bathrooms. Nearby a young woman—no, she was a girl, maybe thirteen—was dressed better than any of us, and beaming. She had a name tag on her black blazer that told us her name was Erika and that she always, always, under any circumstances, made the dot over the *i* with a smiley face.

She handed me a flyer and bounced a little, with the hint of a curtsy, the way girls sometimes do when they've conducted themselves well in an adult moment. I looked at the flyer, saw Mike's fat and happy face looking up at me, and stuffed the thing in my pocket.

When Esme saw me blinking at everything, she walked ahead, giving me something to follow. The next room could have housed industrial machinery, but the floor had been carpeted an awful brick color, and the walls were mauve. White wooden folding chairs were arranged in a semicircle, maybe a hundred of them. Half the seats were occupied, and another forty or fifty people milled around outside the seating. I couldn't believe the turnout. It wasn't that I didn't think Mike was probably a decent guy or had friends. It's just that I'd officiated funerals for plenty of decent guys. Most weren't as well attended as this.

Around the room were blown-up photographs of Mike on easels: with his wife, a heavy woman as tall as he was and with as big of a smile; wearing a straw hat and waist-deep in water, fishing in a lagoon; grinning in a reflective vest and directing traffic someplace. Seeing him without a uniform on was almost like looking at another person. A stranger who reminded me of a coworker who had passed away. But none of them was the Merchant Marine who'd slept his way around the world, blowing a cool chunk of his paychecks on it—none was the guy who called me a cocksucker the night he died, not quite.

In taking everything in, I lost track of Esme. I turned a few times, trying to spot her. Being alone in that room was unsettling, a reminder of another person who had died: me. Some vestigial preacher in me kept thinking it was about time to call all these people to their chairs—that it was time for me to begin the service. If I'd let that little voice take the lead, what would my sermon have been? Look around you, I would have said. None of us are making it out alive. No consolation. Enjoy the cheese tray.

It wasn't something my sister would have approved of. It wasn't something that would have occurred to me to say back then, no part of the scripts of language I kept my old self fed on—all ephedrine and Crystal Light and rice cakes. Even when we were kids, Ellen would get me on my knees in the backyard, praying her words of prayer, one at a time. Her words were always better than mine. The way they lit up her face, her clear blue eyes, made her glow like neon in the miracle of true belief. Too true. She was my big sister—my icebreaker through the Arctic sheet of youth.

It took a minute, but I spotted Esme in a corner, talking with a couple who—thin, fit, tall, white toothed, and exuding generosity of spirit—were the picture of the picture of health, the high-contrast, overexposed, third-generation Xerox of success. It seemed tacky here. They could have dialed it back a notch, I thought, out of respect for the dead and grieving.

I walked over slowly, keeping some distance so as to avoid any introductions. Luckily, she cut off her conversation with the couple as I approached. They peeled away, looking for someone else to inspire a sense of inferiority in. Esme turned. She smiled a patient, steady smile at me, with a touch of a mocking smirk at what she saw. I've heard Pentecostals talk about being slain in the spirit. Her look slew me in a harder-to-reach place: that minute, hidden nexus where spirit and body are comingled. I was slain in her kind regard.

"Hi, Esme," I said. "Hi."

"Sorry," she said. "You started wandering, and I needed to say hello to some people."

"It's okay. I'm okay." Looking at her eased my agitation, and I stared, couldn't or didn't want to stop. She looked away, and it felt like something had been pulled from out of me.

"They're friends from church. They lead a group I'm part of." She tucked her hair behind her ears and scanned the room.

"Oh, right," I said. "This is at God's Gym?"

She bumped herself into me. "Stop. They're nice people. The group meets at their house. It's like a Bible study group."

"A bicep study group? If you're trying to entice me to join, I'll wait until they start to focus on other body parts."

"You're very clever," Esme said. "Don't be annoying." She gave my arm a squeeze. "Besides, if anyone needs a bicep study group . . ." She started pulling me. "Let's sit down."

We took seats near the back of the room. The din of the place was something else. The bare walls made it an echo chamber. Esme and I didn't try to talk. She read the funeral program. I looked around and felt out people's soft spots—their weaknesses, their points of hypocrisy and failure. There was no shortage of options: People-pleaser. Attention-grabber. False piety. False humility. Disguised vanity. Power hungry. Self-absorbed. Sex absorbed. It's wonderful how many looks of frank sexual appraisal you can catch at a funeral, if you're watching.

Then the din subsided and the lurkers sat. Everyone turned toward the front. That's what I'd been avoiding, was one of the things I was avoiding. Our semicircle of attention focused on a small, wooden platform, cloaked in cloth. On either side were ceramic pots holding tall, vaguely tropical plants—birds-of-paradise, cattails, hibiscus. They were like living candles at a pagan altar, rehabilitated from yesterday's discards in the alley behind a La Quinta hotel. On one side of the platform was a simple oak podium with a microphone protruding from it. In the center of the platform, on a small table on a white linen runner embroidered in blue, was a black marble urn with a gold band at its waist—was Mike Padilla, or what remained of him.

As I studied the urn, the room quieted in a way that made me wonder if it was in my head. My thoughts grew loud and dark and full of death, inexistence. There were ashes in there, ashes only—ashes that would be spread, scattered, absorbed, broken down, bonded, reconstituted. Nothing of the guy would take part in any of that, and I knew it. The end didn't look like an urn and a hundred close friends in attendance, not for him. The end was watching his blood mingle with metal shavings and dust in the corner of a shitty fabrication shop, at a job he never cared about once. The end was cheap and unexpected and without grace, and I knew that, too.

A man walked up to the podium, and I realized the silence wasn't just in my head. The service was beginning. The man beginning it was Tom Gustafsson.

He wore the same smug smile he used on me right before I was escorted from the security office. Unlike many of the people here, he wore crisp slacks and a wide-collared dress shirt, sleeves rolled up in an apparently haphazard way, like he'd spontaneously grabbed a shovel at an Earth Day tree planting just outside.

"Hello, everyone," he said evenly but with an undeniable hint of ebullience. "I wish we were coming together under better circumstances, but here we are." On his face, sobriety looked slapstick. There was too much pleasure in his eyes—all the time, I imagined, so damn pleased to have been born who he was instead of any of us. The only crack in the brickwork was his habit of sucking in his cheeks a little between words, cheating out those cheekbones. He must have wished they were a little more prominent.

Esme placed her hand on my back. I hadn't realized I was leaning forward, arms braced on my knees. She mouthed, "Are you okay?"

She hadn't seen my firing. Maybe she didn't know who Gustafsson was. I didn't want to upset her, wasn't going to cause a scene here. I nodded and sat back, folding my arms casually. But it became clear with every word the man spoke: his was the voice of Screwtape that I'd carried in my head for years. A voice that wasn't gravelly or grave, not snide or twisted, just a clear, confident, everyday voice saying everyday words that were a little off in their ring, hollowed out, rotted from within, infected, as they mentored his young demon in the art of temptation. Screwtape's voice, I could see through its representative standing before me, was the voice of American success.

"I didn't know Michael Padilla," Gustafsson said after a heavy, theatrical pause. "And I want to turn things over to those who did. But very briefly, I wanted to thank the people at Cremation Services International for donating their services and this space, especially Matt and Harry Hadrys, Carolina at Floral Creations for the beautiful flowers, and the kind folks at the Carlsbad Café on Palomar Airport Road for the refreshments. I appreciate their generosity in this trying time, and not just because I'm their landlord."

He waited while there was a polite round of applause, light and relief-desperate laughter. His eyes scanned the crowd without a shade of insecurity. Insecurity was how I existed—constant doubt being the way to feel out where I actually stood—and people who lacked it made me wonder. He looked in my direction, and I had a momentary impulse to hide and a simultaneous idea that he'd heard my thoughts. But he kept sweeping the room with his eyes. Then he looked down ceremoniously before lifting his head and speaking again.

"This is an unmistakable tragedy. There's no way around that. All I want to suggest is that we shouldn't forget to be heartened by the ways in which, during hard times, the community comes to our aid." He looked at a person in the front row pointedly. It was the tall woman from the photographs. She was wearing a summer dress made of white linen. "Darcy," he said. "Please accept our condolences and our support in this trying time." I watched her daub at her eyes and nod. Then Gustafsson was walking back down the aisle, head bowed in a humility I had no faith in.

Another man stepped up from a seat in the front, a shortish guy with a yarmulke-sized bald spot and a goatee. I heard a click from the back of the room and turned to see Gustafsson stepping through the double doors. He wasn't even bothering to stick around. I wondered if he thought this was a professional obligation, or if it was the nice bit of necessary PR it seemed to be.

The next guy introduced himself as the pastor of a church that had some arrangement of words like "new," "love," "song," "peace," and "community" in the name. The order wasn't fixed, didn't matter—Evangelical Scrabble. This person at least knew Mike. He talked about meeting him years before, about Mike's service at the church, guiding traffic in the parking lot, cooking a whole goat on the men's retreats to the Borrego Desert. He had a funny story about seasoning a stew with wild sage that turned out to be something else, something that made their tongues numb. I missed most of the details because I was thinking about Gustafsson, wishing I hadn't seen his ugly face, how I wanted to see his kidneys sold on the black market. Those kinds of distracting things.

When the man finished the story, he laughed once and then began crying. That brought me back to the present. He made an honest and hard transition to talking about the loss of a person in terms of scripture. It was a struggle, but he kept on. At least he spoke with an awareness of how far short a few Bible verses come.

Of the funeral services I'd led, I had lacked that awareness at all of them save Ellen's. She was the real exegete anyway. I was the one who was good with people, with standing up in front of a crowd, with marshaling them toward a single and supposedly worthwhile purpose. If I was stuck on a verse, I always called her. But I couldn't call her after she was dead, and prayer didn't offer much hope when I knew the eternal consequence of a suicide, and turning to the Bible seemed like a mistake when the person who knew its words—their spirit and their letter—better than I ever would had killed herself out of a hidden doubt. She had to know: was God there, or not. This dire impatience not to believe or to maintain in doubt, but to know, without question, the truth of eternity had bloomed in her heart like a secret spring—one she'd known would be endangered if shared, even with me. Some doctors suggested different pathologies, after the fact. A deficiency in the brain. An obsessive-compulsive need for certainty. Suicidal ideation masked by intelligence and a disordered desire for divine communion.

The wish for certainty was a wish for death. I saw that. So that's what I gave up: God, certainty, control, a hold on everything I loved. The only way I'd stayed alive was by running in the opposite direction of knowledge. I found life more livable in disbelief, uncertainty, ambivalence, and doubt. Even in death, Ellen was my teacher, helping me find new words.

I watched this pastor wrestling his doubt at the podium, the way he'd surely wrestled it before and would again. What allowed him to go on in his way? And what about my self sent me down mine?

Then I stared at the urn. The white marbling in its black stone made it appear full of inexplicably large distances. If I looked hard into it, it would only go on and on. I knew that. Spaces between the atoms that formed molecules. Spaces between the protons and electrons that formed atoms. Quarks within, more empty space between. This was how I saw death. I'd never fully understood someone being gone, how something that had been was now nothing. But Mike wasn't sitting on a cloud or living as a beetle in Korea either. Neither was Ellen. So the best my brain could do was imagine them being infinitely far away, always moving beyond me, out of sight.

The harsh buzz of an instrument cable being inserted into a live amp jolted me out of my head. A young woman with a guitar was preparing to sing. I knew it wasn't Emily, but that's who I saw when I looked at her. The short hair, staccato with ocean salt. Her changeable face, the theatrics of her poses, the careful way she kept herself a secret within herself. Mike was beyond me, but Emily I could reach. It was Emily who was vanished, first from my house and then from Sammy's, but not from the world—not as far as I knew. Wherever she was, there was a gravity pulling from that place. I decided I should let it.

16.

WHEN THE SERVICE ENDED, ESME PLACED HER HAND ON MY KNEE. "I'M going to give my condolences. Do you want to meet me outside?"

Did I want to sneak out? Yes, I did. Facing Darcy, whom I had never met, keeping my head up to see her; saying a few words that meant next to nothing—no part of me wanted to do those things. And Esme's maternal touch was there, giving me an out. But it wasn't really a choice, I knew. I wouldn't take it and said instead, "Come on then, let's go."

There was a receiving line proceeding toward the widow, like an inverse wedding. The two people in front of me, early thirties maybe, were speaking to each other quietly, but I could hear the woman complaining about the tacky choice of flowers and see the man strain not to let his laughter register on his face in a way that Mike's wife could notice from afar. I looked at the picture of Mike in a reflective vest, directing traffic with a smile couched in unreasonable cheeks. I suspected he'd made a few lewd jokes using the two neon sticks in his hands, despite everything his pastor had said about him. But at the end of the day, I'd known so little about this man—and despite that, he was one of the closest human contacts I had in my life. Too close, it turned out. Not far enough away to keep all possibility of pain or obligation at bay.

And then we were at the front of the line. Darcy was still sitting in a chair. She looked like she wouldn't get up until the end of time. Her face was wet, and the blonde hair that hung nearest to her eyes was damp and darkened, clotting thickly, unlike the golden sheen spilling down her shoulders and over her bright white dress. The dress made her look like a bride, almost.

Esme held out her hand. Darcy didn't seem to see it, but her hand raised as if moved by something other than will. The two hands gripped each other. "You don't really know me," Esme began. "But Mike, I worked with Mike." Neither Darcy nor Esme had let go; their hands were still holding.

I noticed that Darcy was looking at some spot below Esme's face. Every time Mike's name vibrated the air, she glanced at the urn holding her husband. It was a word that had become unfathomable now, I knew: with a depth that couldn't be plumbed, all the deep and dark pressure of a life lived sent permanently pastward.

"He was a beautiful man," Esme said, "in so many ways." Something about calling him beautiful sent a shudder through Darcy, and the semidry tracks of tears on her face surged. She sucked air through the scrim of mucus and grief in her throat. It was like watching a person in a shipwreck movie come up for breath among miles and miles of waves—the sight of no one, only debris, no hope, none coming. There's terror, and then there is that.

Esme let go, Darcy's hand fell, and something in my stomach yawed. It wasn't about Mike, not exactly, not entirely. It was coming to this precipice of grief again, the memory of my own having lost none of its awful prospect for all I'd done to avoid it. What it felt like. Where it led. No good.

But Esme had let go so as only to hold Darcy's shoulder. They looked at each other. I couldn't see her face, but Esme's shoulders were crying. I had a moment to catch my unruly mind. Then Esme was stepping away, and Darcy looked to me. No doubt she saw my weak face, my pocketed hands, my unwilling body—the next piece of debris that wouldn't float her.

17.

MY EYES REVOLTED AGAINST THE LIGHT WHEN WE STEPPED FROM THE funeral home—that pure California sunshine, redoubled by white stucco and concrete. It made me feel seasick. Maybe it was the exhaustion. I could feel the jailhouse cot I'd slept on in each spasm of my back. The thwacking of a hundred sandals around me wasn't helping.

This casualness was wrong, all this was wrong, and I wished I were in a black suit, black tie, black polished shoes. It would be a better container for whatever I was feeling. That's all form is anyway—a way to give shape or structure to feeling. It's where California had gone wrong, something the Jesus Freak churches of the 1970s that California spawned had taken into absurdity. Their Christianity's shape was the absence of shape. It fit itself to the life it found, like a parasite. It attached itself to the longhairs but was still feeding off the self-help ethos of the early twentieth century and the morality of the 1950s, before it began to bleed off the business culture of the 1980s and then late '90s, the sprawl and comfort of our architecture and lifestyle, the self-empowerment centered on pleasure and influence, the range of your spiritual Rolodex. Like Hollywood stars, its most steadfast ethic was to act light in spirit, free of worry, convinced of the beneficence of tomorrow. It was ridiculous. Tomorrow is coming for us. And not to hand us an award.

People milled about the concrete pad in front of the funeral home, chatting, smiling wistfully, crying tastefully. Esme dug around in her purse. Plastic objects clacked. She pulled out sunglasses and slipped them on. With her swollen eyes now hidden, she was a different person. Even her posture changed. "You have time to grab some dinner?" she asked. Her voice was lighter, a little flirtatious even. We could be anywhere, any two people—anywhere but where we were.

But my mind was on other things. "Do you have a cell phone?"

"Of course. You don't?"

I told her the same thing I told everyone: that they'd rot my testicles off. "Can I borrow yours a minute?"

"Sure," she said. There was more clacking of plastic, and then Esme produced the phone from her purse. I walked with it to the side of the building and called Gabby. It was all I'd been thinking about doing as I stood before Darcy, failing to express any sentiment of comfort. Even in her grief her face was patient, as if tolerantly aware of how below the task I was.

Gabby answered with a skeptical edge to her voice. "Hello?"

"Gabby, hey. It's Mark."

"Where are you? Already milking the long distance at a new job?"

I had to laugh. "No, not a work number. Maybe soon. Then I'll call all the time on the boss's dime." I tried to laugh again, but it sounded terrible, an embarrassing betrayal of how I felt. "No, I'm just at Mike's funeral. I, uh . . ."

There was something I'd wanted to say. Now that I was talking to Gabby, I didn't know what it was.

"Oh, I see," she said. "I'm sorry. Did everything go okay? Are you okay?"

"Of course," I said. "Of course. I didn't call to talk about me."

She hummed skeptically. "Then what were you calling about?"

"I can't remember."

"Then you must have been calling to tell me about your early-onset dementia. It's the only thing that makes sense."

I didn't trust myself to force a laugh again. I didn't know what kind of yelp or sob would come out in its place. So I just said, "Hm," and then we were quiet a time.

"Well," Gabby said eventually, "if you were calling to check in on me, I'm great. Love my job, love my apartment, love my yoga instructor—let me tell you, that man is flexible. And strong. His legs, my God. It's a dream."

"Oh, I was going to ask about you, I was."

"Sure you were, Mark. Sure you were."

"No, really. Are you okay? I think that's why I wanted to call."

"Right," she said sarcastically. "If that's the case, then something really *is* wrong. But okay, I'm fine. Really. Aracely hasn't changed her mind, though, to get that out of the way."

"I didn't figure she would have." There was a long pause while the blankness in my mind slowly developed into more blankness. "How," I said, "are you liking being a grandmother?"

I listened to her breathe for a couple seconds. "Are you really asking? Or is this the setup to one of your mean punch lines?"

It was a true-enough thing for her to say that it didn't even hurt, I think—not much. "I really want to know."

"It's incredible," she said. "He's a beautiful boy, and Aracely is a beautiful mother. Exhausting, too, though I still can't get enough of them. Which isn't to say that he's the only handful. Aracely's, well . . . She's a kid herself, and everything has changed. And the father situation . . ." I braced for some new accusation, deservingly. "It's hard for me to accept that she doesn't know who it is. Jared was a loser, but she loved him, and maybe it would have been better if he'd actually been the one."

"Good," I said. "I mean, I'm glad it's good for you, and I'm glad Aracely has you there." Again, I ran out of things to say. Then I knew: I'd been feeling the feeling of wanting to help. It was Emily I thought I could help, but I'd called Gabby instead, some wire getting crossed between the two.

"You okay?" she asked.

"Yeah. Look, I need to go. Sorry to bother you."

"Aracely hasn't changed her mind," she edged in before I hung up, "but do you want to pass on anything to her?"

I thought about it as long as I could, before I felt overwhelmed and my mind flatlined. "No," I said finally, "I've passed on enough." Some vestige of all that funereal grief rose up in my face. "I have to go. Talk to you soon, Gabby."

Next I dialed information and got the Ramona Substation. I tried to get Detective Lawrence, but he was out. I asked for Tuitele next, and the dispatcher put me through.

"Yes?" he asked, already bored.

"Hi, Detective. This is Mark Haines—the person you, uh, interrogated this morning." This sentence coming out of my mouth should have felt more odd than it did. "They must all blur together."

"Yeah, I remember. Want us to have another crack?"

"No, I'm good," I said. "Look, I know what you said, but I had to see if you found Emily back at the house."

"Same line," he said. "We don't talk about it, not with you. Unless you're a relative or with the FBI, there's no reason for me to say a word."

"I don't need details. Just a yes or no. Did you find her?" My blood pressure was rising, and I could feel my brain getting ahead of me. I tried visualizing its wet, pulpy mass—to see myself forcing this convulsive goop back into my skull. "Christ."

"Don't get angry, man. That won't help at all."

"I'm sorry, but it's just—"

"And don't get the wrong idea. Apologizing won't help either, and I'll mail the box of cookies back COD."

"Look," I said, forcing air into my body like I was an engine. "Maybe you don't have kids, but I had a daughter. I have one, I mean, but she's grown. This girl, I was looking out for her, trying to. And if I don't know what happened to her, it's like I'm letting down another daughter. She's not my kid, but it's like that. I'm not asking for much. I'm going to lose it here if I don't know. Help me keep from going nuts."

"Nuts, right," Tuitele said. "I know you know about nuts."

I figured they'd read about me, but knowing was different. The shame I felt was deep and fresh, a kind of shame I didn't think I was capable of anymore. And I knew this compulsion to know about Emily, the intensity of it, was questionable, was unlike myself—was like Ellen, in fact, and what had driven her to kill herself. They knew about nuts, but they didn't know the half of it. "If you're going that route—"

"Don't get me wrong," he said. "I know nuts. My brother got into some fucked situations, didn't make it out. Never found him. My parents stopped being the same people like that." He snapped loud enough the phone receiver picked it up. "So, yeah. I get it."

"Then please."

There was only breathing on the line. When he spoke again, Tuitele was nearly whispering. "There was no one there. You said maybe her name was Emily, and in the garbage we found some mail with the name Emily Hsu on it. H-s-u." The words caused a strange refocusing to occur in my mind, as if the name—her actual name, it seemed—

exerted a gravitational pull on all the detritus of my thinking about her. "That name matches a missing persons report from a few years back. At the time she was listed as a runaway, and there wasn't too much follow-up after the initial report."

I felt like I was taking a risk speaking, that all this would somehow be retracted. But I asked if there was more.

"That's all I can say. We're going to see if the parents can identify her in any of the photos, the ones we found with all the kinky shit. But we have to be careful about that. So far forensics is showing that the files hadn't been accessed in some time. The laptop never connected to the internet through Gans's ISP, none of his fingerprints on the thing, so besides it being in his garage there isn't much to link it to him. No other tangible sign of, you know, *that* kind of thing, or drug dealing either. He says he has a couple girlfriends who come in and out, so right now we're stuck with the idea that somehow she ran away again, between the time you saw her and when we showed up."

"That's a good sense for timing, don't you think?"

"Tip came from somewhere else, anonymous. Wasn't her."

"But where would she go out there? It's the middle of nowhere."

"That's the question," he said with the first edge of annoyed resignation in his voice. "That's the question. But Gans's bail was set at thirty grand, and he's posted."

The thought of Sammy being free gave me pause. His threat hovered in the back of my mind, compounded by Emily—her name was Emily—being out there somewhere, too. I was scared for her, a little for myself, but knowing these things had settled my anxiety. "Thank you," I said to Tuitele.

"No way," he said, his voice rolling back up to full volume. "Fuck off, never gonna happen. Don't call here anymore. Let us do our fucking job. Your job now is to check the papers. That's where you get your news. Got it?"

"Right. Got it."

"I've got fucking work to do. Have a good life, old man." He hung up. I couldn't help but feel there was a genuine element to the over-performance. Maybe I just didn't like being called an old man, but that was my problem.

I stepped out from the side of the building into the dispersing crowd. I was woozy, disoriented. The way they looked at me asked questions, and their presence snapped my emotions back into position. Even in a moment like that, the things I felt could be modulated, as if musically, by the imagined attention of others.

Esme was standing near a massive, nearly empty planter with a single six-inch square of beach grass positioned in its center, statement landscaping that uses invasive plants because they're cheaper than Mexican hot sauce. With her glasses on, Esme looked glamorous, in a way—a ridiculous thing to say about a middle-aged woman in a jean skirt and white polo shirt, I guess. But she ran her fingers through her hair and pushed it behind her ears and was unordinary. Her life made me feel my exhaustion.

"Ready to hit the road?" I asked.

"Dinner?"

"Not today. Sometime soon, I promise."

She looked at me skeptically.

"Honestly. Pick another day, any day. But I need some sleep."

"I'm the one driving, and you aren't going home until you've had some dinner." She shook her head. "Don't pretend like you know what you need."

18.

WHEN ESME DROPPED ME OFF, I THANKED HER FOR COMING FOR ME. I meant it. The dusk was doing its thing and everything was going gray. Gray house, gray tree, gray something, gray something else—the things mattered less and less. She said to call soon. I told her I would.

I walked up the driveway, unlocked the front door, and went inside. A flick of a switch, and there was everything that was supposed to define me, to give me a sense of meaning and self and history: a couple rooms, a beige fridge, a secondhand couch, books and magazines worth less than the paper they were printed on. I turned off the lights, sending it all back into darkness, and went down the hallway to the bedroom. Never has a word so entirely described the contents of what it denotes, bed and room. There wasn't even a frame. I undressed and pulled a sheet over my body.

There's a kind of exhaustion that sleep doesn't resolve. That's the kind of exhausted I was. My mind loped in lazy circles, kicking up stray thoughts; my thoughts were carousel horses carrying riders who came into my field of vision only momentarily and were accompanied by horrendous music: Emily, Sammy, Mike, Ellen, Gabby, Aracely, the "Macarena." I knew from the first that I wouldn't be getting any sleep, but I lay there an hour anyway, helpless against the feeling of helplessness.

Then I got up, made coffee, and started pacing the house, from kitchen to bedroom, thinking about Emily. Emily Hsu. A runaway or something worse. What else did I know? I went into my office, which I hadn't used in over fifteen years, and dug out a sun-bleached yellow legal pad from behind the desk to start writing. She didn't have a relationship with her parents, she'd said, and didn't want one. Had a falling-out with religion, or at least the Christianity she'd grown up with. She said she'd had a falling-out at the last place she'd lived, too, and that must have been Sammy's. But after she left my house, she'd turned up there again. Had she chosen to go back? If there was any truth to what the goiter-headed kid, Shaw, told me, choosing that life didn't make sense. Maybe Shaw didn't understand what was going on. Or maybe there was a fix that needed maintaining, and that was enough of a lure. She'd shown plenty of signs of being an addict when she stayed with me, and she was high when I saw her at Sammy's place. Was that how Sammy kept her around for so long? I didn't know, and my list choked out around there, without enough oxygen. I just didn't know her. Not well enough.

I looked around the office. The space felt like an indictment to do a kind of work I found useless, worse than useless, but still familiar. On the bookshelf, the red, blue, and green spines of the three-volume set of William Jurgens's *Faith of the Early Fathers* were unmistakable. Out of the blackness of another man's memories floated up a phrase in one of those books, from one of Augustine's sermons: "How could you have consented when you did not exist? But He who made you without your consent does not justify you without your consent. He made you without your knowledge but He does not justify you without your willing it." It sat in my brain like a fat, white, guilt-ridden Buddha.

Canaan Hills. The words were tethered to an image of a crucified Jew, strung up next to two naked criminals in the grassy knoll at the center of an Anglophilic roundabout in a California housing development, the kind that spun endless minor variations on the same three stucco homes. Canaan Hills was the name of the church Emily had gone to as a child. I knew that, remembered that. I didn't know how to find her parents or her friends, but I knew churches, and a glance at the clock showed it was, even now, Sunday morning. I could start there.

On the way I stopped off in Encinitas. There was the beginning of a Santa Ana kicking up dust, making the palm fronds snap in the wind like kites. Encinitas was too clean for my taste. Here trees stayed trimmed. Lawns were manicured, pedicured, seaweed wrapped, dipped in nutrient-rich mud baths. The asphalt looked as if it were scrubbed by hand. During the day, people waved at one another, especially if they'd never met. It was too much. Even the sun was warmer and purer, the kind of sun that wouldn't dream of giving you cancer. It had been a long time since I'd made this stop, and part of me wondered if the house I was looking for would be vanished: burned down in an electrical fire, torn down by a hobo developer with squatter's rights.

But no, it was there. The paint on the wrought-iron fence bubbled in places, looking like it would split if touched. Whole bars were bare, showing rust and black. The house itself looked only a little better. It was small by the neighborhood's standards, only one story. It had off-center cross-gabled front eaves that corresponded to the three-paned window of a reading nook below. A stone chimney lifted itself to the lowest possible height demanded by smoke. The patio furniture was mildewed, and the fabric of the folded-up canvas umbrella was crumbling to dust. I had sat under that umbrella, telling Ellen about this girl I'd met, Gabby. She'd grabbed my hands, said she could see it in my eyes that this one was the one—always certain, seemingly inexhaustible and permanent, fixed—and sealing my faith in that feeling, too, with her faith. Unlike this house or the sun's destruction of this red umbrella with light, only light. The red front door, though, looked as immaculate as hellfire, even if its brass hardware had tarnished. I unlocked the door with a key on my key ring and went inside.

Because of the neighboring eight-bedroom quasi-Swiss mess—it could have been an adult-scale stage set from It's a Small World and was probably designed by pointing at the illustration on an imported bar of chocolate—no sunlight made it inside until the afternoon. The living room was less alive and more in a vegetative state, dim and still. The air was thick, like fog in a low valley, and full of dust. I'd stopped paying for the biyearly housekeeping too long ago. Beneath the scent of dust and the general staleness, the smell of lilac and lavender persisted: the smell of my mother, a smell that couldn't be cleaned out of the place.

It was important to keep moving. I got out of the living room, past the floral-print couch and the cabinet of pie birds and miniature cottages, and headed down the hallway. The first bedroom had been mine, and I went in.

After Ellen's death, I'd avoided coming here as much as I could. Right away, my parents, in their grief, had decided to get out of this house, get out of the state, and were going to move to Arizona. I had taken to finding bottom like a born skin diver—hell on my heels and profoundly underwater and alone, having quit the church and alienated myself from my wife—but I hadn't yet realized it wouldn't be as comfortable as I believed. They needed me to go through my stuff, but I put it off and put it off. I was angry at the idea of them selling the house, which they never brought themselves to do before passing away, one after the other, in the red-state desert, of perfectly, stupidly natural causes. But eventually I had come to the house drunk and stripped the walls of my old room, tearing down the stapled-up pictures of Shaun Tomson and Tom Curren pulled from surfing magazines, the handwritten Bible verses, the pictures of old friends at camps where we'd all had so much fun, had grown so much in the Lord, had ogled girls, had water-skied. I threw it all away, leaving a bare room of white walls in which there were hundreds of tiny black holes. That was growth: the accumulation of marks, divots, punctures. The bed still had the same green bedspread on it.

I'd come for clothes but not the ones in my old closet. Everything there was earth-toned plaid and two sizes too small. Back in the hallway I passed a closed door and went into my parents' old room. The brass bedposts were still bright, if dusty, and the lavender bedding still vibrant enough to show off the small white flowers printed on it. I worked at not noticing things and went straight to the closet. A couple old, strange blouses, a couple shoeboxes, and a vinyl suit bag. I took that, laid it on the bed, and unzipped it. The coat and pants were a charcoal flannel. I slunk the white dress shirt off its hanger and onto my arms. It was a little loose, but not by much. Then I put on the pants, tucked in the shirt, tried on the coat. They were all a decent fit. Decent enough was the best I ever hoped for anyway.

This is what I'd been wanting to wear at Mike's funeral. It would do for today. I stepped before the mirror above my mother's dresser. The clothes looked fine. The man wearing them needed a shave. The man wearing them looked like a man to be feared, to be respected; a man to be pitied; a man to look up to and in some ways love. The man wearing it looked like my father.

I felt something on my face. In the mirror I saw they were tears—saw them with a dull objectivity. The suit. It was what he wore to her funeral. His little girl, alive for thirty years and then, in a moment, never to live again. My father didn't speak at the service, but his face betrayed what he knew, what suicide meant, his stoic and steadfast acceptance of that meaning. Everyone shook his hand. There were words but none of condolence. How could you console a father for his daughter's eternal separation and damnation? How could a father be anything but what he was? He couldn't. Then he'd taken all his beautiful, tailored clothes to the desert and left this one suit by the sea.

I went back to the closet for the brogued-leather saddle shoes that matched the suit. They made a satisfying click on the hardwood. When I stepped back onto the plush carpet in the hallway, something had changed. It was the atmosphere, and not just the high, dry lightness of the Santa Ana. On the left side of the hall was the open door to the bedroom. On the right, there was a Virgin of Guadalupe made from snipped, bent, and painted soda-can aluminum. Pepsi swooshes were visible on the backside of the fluted metal. But that wasn't what stopped me. A few steps past it was the closed door. Ellen's room.

I walked up to it, put my hand against the wood. I listened. There was no sound, nothing. But still I'd had some expectation, my ear had bent to listen. My mind divided on itself. A lower half was searching out memories of being a boy, standing here and asking through the hollow core whether she'd come ride bikes, the way it would open on some new and surprising configuration of her passion of the day—a massive diorama of local wildlife, a chessboard and Dover edition of *The Game of Chess*, a self-constructed wooden dollhouse with miniature furniture, a scribbled-in, dog-eared copy of the NIV Bible—and how easily she would leave it behind to lead me out into the neighborhood, down to the tide pools at Moonlight State Beach, up to the train tracks to shout at the commuter train. The higher part of my mind kicked at the lower one, trying to keep it down, threw some elbows. The part that was left, which was me, we waited it out to see who'd win. While we waited, my hand moved to grip the knob. I wondered what its goal was. The bickering parts of my mind both paused with their hands on each other's throats, turned, watched.

The knob rotated a centimeter, then hitched. Locked, from the inside. From all sides I felt relief. My hand retreated to a pocket, and I retreated to the front door with a feeling of abandonment. But who abandoned whom I couldn't say.

19.

BEFORE HEADING TO CANAAN HILLS, I STOPPED AT THE 7-ELEVEN AND USED the pay phone to call 411. They connected me, and then a lie about a mono outbreak in the teen ministry got me straight to Andy at my old church.

He answered curtly and directly, like he was a disaster relief dispatcher. "What's this about a mono outbreak?"

"Sorry, Andy," I said. "No kissing epidemic, at least nothing more than the usual one. Take the keys out of the nukes."

"Haines," he said, and I was a little proud that he recognized my voice so immediately. "It's nearly eight thirty and I have a lot to do to get ready for the first service. Don't call me like this."

"It's just that I'm chomping at the bit a little," I said. "Since I got Sammy's address from you, I've been arrested and interrogated. Forgive me for giving you a little heart attack. You love to forgive anyway. Hit me with it."

"You've what? What happened? Sammy didn't—"

"Thanks for not asking what I'd done to deserve it."

"Look, I don't know. . . . But if you need to call someone—"

"No, but I do need to know what happened to make you boot Sammy."

There was a pregnant pause, though I doubted a divine conception was behind it. This was more the guilty silence after an old-fashioned premarital fucking. "I can't," Andy said finally. "It's a confidentiality thing."

"You have an obligation. This is important."

"Really, I can't. Everyone's around. I can try to call you later."

"There's no later. The guy's a lunatic, and now there's a girl missing, too. I need—" some part of my voice broke on that word and I dropped it into a lower gear to keep going. "I need to know what happened."

The line was silent again. I wondered if he'd gone and hung up on me, cut me loose like he'd cut Sammy loose—which, I had to admit, was what I'd done, too. But then his voice came back, quieter: "Call me in five minutes. Here's my cell."

He gave me the number and hung up. When enough time had passed, I called it.

"This is going to be fast," he said. "I've got people showing up."

"I don't care about the speed. Just tell me what happened."

Andy's story was short but to the point: After I'd left, Sammy had hung in there for a while. Then something happened—the gambling debt, but Andy didn't know that—and he got back into drugs. By that time, Sammy had long aged out of the teen ministry as a member but had continued on as a volunteer middle manager, helping out small groups, coming on camping retreats. The kids liked him. Andy knew he was struggling, but he kept him on. There was too much to do, the church was growing. So he counseled Sammy privately. Sammy led him to believe the problem was his own addiction. With God's help, Andy thought he'd be able to turn him around. But he didn't see what was happening with this pack of popular teenagers, the boys who spent most weekends in the desert near Ocotillo Wells racing dirt bikes. A lot of the church families were into off-roading, and because these kids were good at it and were boys being boys, their behavior tended to get overlooked. Andy had been having trouble with them already, catching them making racist jokes, getting heavily petted by their girlfriends, stuffing wads of chewing tobacco in their cheeks during services. But then he found one with a bag full of OxyContin and Valium. Sammy was the source, and the dirt-bike kids were selling. Just as they'd convinced themselves that blow jobs and anal sex weren't sin, half the teen group had dabbled in these prescription drugs, sure it was categorically different from cocaine or heroin—the special, youthful pleasures of basking in one of God's technicalities.

"That it happened under my nose breaks my heart every day," Andy said. "I've got a kid who's gone to rehab twice now, never would have touched the stuff if it weren't for this. But—"

"But the kicker," I said, "is you cleaned it up quietly. Booted Sammy, kept the reason private—between a pastor and a parishioner. Maybe you kicked the little desert rat dealers out, too, maybe you didn't."

"I got them help. Help is better than isolation. Maybe that isn't something you'd understand."

"Maybe not," I said. "But maybe they aren't all that much better either."

Andy didn't say anything.

"The important thing," I said, "is that you saved your ass, saved the church's ass."

"If only you understood—"

"Believe me, I do," I said. "I wish I didn't."

There was a long silence. Then Andy said, "I should go."

I told him he left off a four-letter verb and a self-reflexive pronoun.

Still, I had some impulse to thank him, before he hung up, an impulse I ignored. I forgave myself the omission and weighed everything he'd said. Emily hadn't gone to church there, but she was a churchgoer. Sammy was a churchgoer, too, and somehow he had found her. Maybe he'd used several churches, made a network of them. Maybe Sammy and Emily just enjoyed a little pre–prayer circle pill popping. I called 411 again, gave the name Canaan Hills, got the address.

It was a little under an hour down the highway to Loma Portal, where Canaan Hills was located. By the time I arrived, I assumed I'd missed the morning service. The parking lot said otherwise. It was four square blocks of blinding windshields and eye-piercing casual wear on people threading their way to the main buildings. At least they were walking, unlike the packs standing around for a shuttle ride to the main compound. I scanned these people for any wearing hats with two big black ears but came up empty. There were plenty of traffic directors in reflective vests, though, and the blown-up photo of Mike was never far from my mind.

The buildings everyone funneled toward were simple, oversized industrial warehouses. Boxy, with a splash of adobe and teal paint in a nod to local culture and architectural history that waved more like a middle finger. Thin palms grew in freestanding wooden planters. The compound had the scale and style of a shopping center, one of those outlet malls you find between here and any place that matters. The sky was blue-white and endless, reeking of salt air and financial health. Everything terrestrial I could see stank of cheap development and high rents.

I parked as far back as I could and picked my way through the lot. I smiled at every face that smiled at me, which was every face, and turned away before any could start a conversation. They knew I was new. Despite the sheer volume of people here, somehow they knew. It made me feel paranoid, until I remembered the suit I wore. In contrast to all that conforming casualness, I must have stood out like a boner in board shorts—which, as it turned out, was the attire of half the men attending the service.

When I got in among the buildings, there were people heading in every direction: going in, coming out, milling, meandering. It wasn't clear where the service was going to be. I followed one of those young families, the father with a full-sleeve arm tattoo and a watch the size of a bull rider's belt buckle, the mother in blue-checked capris and red cat-eye glasses with matching lipstick, a couple little boys trying to push each other into wooden planters. In each of those planters was a little flag, encouraging us to visit the nursery that had donated them.

Like I was their third, much older, and overdressed son, I followed this family through a set of tinted glass doors that could have led right into the batting cages, it was such a generic set of buildings. The father held the door for his wife, for his kids, and then he waved me through, too. His sweet smile looked like it was hurting his face as I passed; if the meek were to inherit the earth, he was going to meek the fuck out of it. Inside, I had a dread-tinged expectation of finding Mike making music from a handful of batting-cage tokens.

Instead, there was a low counter with a swinging barn door on one side. A middle-aged woman in a black T-shirt and tight, rhinestoned jeans worked the counter with two teenage girls. Behind them I saw not the red steel of pitching machines nor the altar of any kind of worship. In place of these were foam pyramids, tiny tables with rainbow-colored chairs, tubs of LEGOs and wooden blocks and plastic ponies. I was lost.

I watched the mother I'd followed sign a couple names onto a sheet. Her husband stood the two boys up on the counter. They were three and five years old, I would guess. Then the rhinestoned woman peeled two bar code stickers from the sign-in sheets and slapped one on each kid's back up between the shoulder blades. Mom got a little rectangle of buzzing plastic, the kind you get waiting for a table at the restaurants I don't go to. The father put the kids on the ground and pushed them through the barn door, saying goodbye, have fun. The kids showed a lot of faith, for kids. Their parents disappeared from view, and the kids didn't cry, didn't despair of seeing them again. Rookie mistake.

The woman behind the counter smiled at me and looked around my knees for a toddler. "Can I help you this morning?" she said.

Her eyes had that eager sweetness I remembered with a little fondness. Some people served because they thought they should. Others did it because it made them look good or helped them make friends. Some because the overwhelming, incessant weight of guilt and shame was temporarily lifted by setting up some banquet tables or bringing the fruit salad. This woman, who seemingly did it for love and in joy, was one of the kind who throws herself into it, probably most of her waking hours, in order to avoid the lulls, times when she would have to contend with herself, that unfaithful companion she'd never gotten to know. I liked those people. There was something manic but honest about them.

"I think I'm in the wrong place," I said. "It's my first time here. Where do I go for the service?"

The woman was delighted. She seemed to leap, maybe just a little. "First-timer!" The two teenage girls working with her smiled at me like I'd just told them about rescuing a one-legged puppy named Jackhammer. People love a newcomer. It means a potential notch on their belt of saved souls. I'd known people who went as far as to estimate—not vaguely but with actual arabic numerals—the number of readers the Bible they'd donated to a faraway mission might have reached.

"You've come to the right place, let me tell you," the woman said. She went on to tell me much more than that. Why she loved it. All the ways you could get involved and be a part of things, the groups, the retreats, the service projects. Then she came to her dissertation on the options for viewing the service. It was no simple thing. I could go to the main sanctuary and see it live, though they were probably already full up. Then there were the other options where the sermon was projected onto a screen in the front of the room, piped in from the main sanctuary. Each venue had a different style of worship and decor: Heritage Hall was hymns, Pastimes old-timey music, Jitters coffee-house-style pop, the Verge a kind of grungy alternative thing, as she put it, not at all what I would enjoy, she was sure. Musically, it sounded like choosing between options in the thrift store bargain bin.

"You look like a Jitters type," she said. "It's a little classy there but very hip, too, if you know what I mean." I was sure she didn't know what she meant. Of the options, the Verge sounded like the one Emily would have chosen, so I asked for directions there. Then I couldn't help asking, "What are those bar codes for?"

"Oh, these?" She laughed in a modest, gee-whiz kind of way, playing with the sign-in sheet. "We have so many kids, and folks go to so many different places around here. If a little kid is just *inconsolable*, we just scan him with this gizmo"—she waved a handheld grocery store scanner—"and a little number goes up on a screen in each of the venues, and these little jobbies start vibrating. Then Mom or Dad can come take care of things, without us having to interrupt the message. Works like a charm, as funny as it sounds."

"Funny, right," I said. I thought I'd suggest that the bar codes were the mark of the beast, the fake ID these kids needed to consume the wine of God's fury. But I wasn't here to poke at these people and draw attention to myself. "Well, thanks for the directions."

"And thank you for coming to check us out today. I hope the Lord provides you what you're looking for."

"Right. I'm not picky. Anyone with a pulse will do."

Her face darkened, but then I saw in her eyes how she chalked it up to a slip of the tongue and forgave it. "Have a good day!" She waved goodbye with one of those stationary, finger-folding waves like you give to a little baby.

I found my way over to the Verge. It was hard to find, since it was in an industrial building that looked identical to every other, if not for the big sign that said THE VERGE in a graffiti-on-brick style that might have threatened the street cred of Vanilla Ice at one time. I imagined the middle-aged white guy scrolling through fonts on his computer and the delight on his face when he found that one.

The entrance was a rolled-up steel cargo door. Next to it was a red pop-up canopy, three tables under it. The first table had big brown coffee dispensers, labeled MEXICAN (LIGHT), FRENCH ROAST (DARK), and JITTER-FREE (DECAF). That was cute. The small pyramid of Starbucks cups rocked every time a person opened a spigot. On the second table were two three-tiered pastry racks, piled high with croissants, Danishes, and muffins. The third table was devoted to Krispy Kreme donuts, all GENEROUSLY PROVIDED BY, as the sign told anyone who could still read through the caffeine-and-sugar-induced glaucoma.

The real coup, I could see, was how all this worked together. Free child care for the small ones. An hour of peace with a big cup of your favorite corporate coffee and a deluxe machine-produced pastry. It was church as "me" time. A little pampering for the soul. And to gauge by the way everyone chatted with one another, and all the adult ministries and Bible groups the woman in the nursery had told me about, it was the promise of not being alone. That's what religion had always promised. God was there, could hear you. But that on its own wouldn't fill seats. A clean way to plug into an instant community, threaded between all this suburban and cultural sprawl, would. An easy way to belong, to stop wondering why you were a freak.

This wasn't a church. This was a logistically complicated machine, sure, a gearbox of belief like a Vatican City with a dress code of halter tops and flip-flops and the kind of you've-had-one-you've-had-them-all style that makes chain restaurants such a success. Like Olive Garden, it seemed to say: When You're Here, You're Family.® Unlimited and unleavened breadsticks. Special venues and groups for the older kids, just when the parents are worried about the kind of company they keep. To hear how Andy handled things with Sammy, though, this wasn't the safe harbor they were hoping for. Not when the machine works needed protecting.

I couldn't process this place as a church, but my pastoral brain—like some reptile lumbering awake in my basal ganglia, sniffing the air for lost souls—saw the function. It was ease and it was numbers and the dream of critical mass: the fission of believers across a hundred-mile radius through a cultural symmetry between church and Chili's. That's what was left if you took God out of it, and I wasn't seeing any of Him yet.

My own church had been only a smaller version of this. I had to admit, by force of habit, that seeing it grow to this scale would have felt like success—like providence and an ordination of my chosen vocation, a whisper from the boozy, stale breath of God Himself brushing against my cheek. Even having a comparatively small congregation—about eight hundred before I left—had affected me enough to give my claims of humility the ring of pride. My every move and gesture became a carrot or a stick to my faithful and those teetering on the edge. How could you not feel that power, when the imagined stakes are eternal and irrevocable? And then to reach a level like this place. It would be impossible. I would have become impossible. Ellen had seen it happening in me and counseled me otherwise by talking about Job. How little her voice mattered by then, flattered as I was with my own and its reach—I couldn't handle the thought, later, that there was a sign already present, a crease of worry or an unsteadiness in her eyes, something I missed—and how much less it would have mattered here.

"Sit with me," she had said, patting a spot of sand at Moonlight State Beach. We always saved our most serious conversations for the edge of the ocean; it's where I told her I was becoming a father.

"I can see it, the way you're getting lost in your own thoughts." She was in her oversized Biola University sweater, where she'd gone back to school for a master's, home for the summer. I remember the bags under her eyes, which I chalked up to a college social life and study schedule. "Look at the waves," she said. "Do you have power over them? Only God. Some days it's calm. Other days, the ocean rages. The ocean nourishes us, gives us food. We enjoy it and find it beautiful. And people drown in it, boats sink, lives are ruined—good people, some of them, blameless. Don't forget Job. Don't forget it was God who gave Satan permission to go back and forth on the earth, taking away everything good Job had. God who told Abraham to take Isaac to the mountain. Keep your heart pure. Do what you do best. If only two people show up. Or no one. Keep doing it, because it's the right thing to do—the only thing you *can* do."

"What about you?" I wish I would have said. Only later did I realize how much she was talking about herself, with the only code she was comfortable expressing it in. In pain, obsessed with her own kind of purity of heart, and no acceptable form in which she could share that bitter love or the dark place it was leading her. "Why is light given to those in misery, and life to the bitter of soul," Job lamented, "to those who long for death that does not come, who search for it more than for hidden treasure. . . . Why is life given to a man whose way is hidden?"

But instead I only agreed with her. She was right. It didn't change my heart. Being right never does. Even if you can descend from a storm and claim to have marked out the foundations of the earth with a cosmic Stanley tape measure as the opening gambit of your long-winded abuser's defense. Even if an all-knowing God can't comprehend the irony of asking the man He'd tortured, whose family He'd killed, for no reason other than to test his loyalty, "Would you condemn me to justify yourself?"

20.

BEFORE I WENT IN TO THE SERVICE, I TOOK A CUP OF COFFEE AND THEN slapped the top of the donation jar with a palmful of invisible coins, making the change in the bottom jangle like they'd just picked up a few friends.

Two young women in white cardigans and different-colored pencil skirts handed me a bulletin and a program when I tried to enter the Verge. The one in yellow asked, "Do you need to borrow a Bible? I see you don't have one today. And we have pencils if you want to take notes." She motioned to a table with both items in abundance.

"No, thanks," I said, pointing to my head. "Pornographic memory."

What was I doing? It was a good question. I would have asked myself it, if I could only catch my brain, but that impulsive mess had gotten ahead of me again. The girl smiled primly. She looked like a Renaissance Madonna, a beautiful girl child patiently holding on to the squalling, horrifically ugly babe that would save the world by developing a talent for sustaining puncture wounds before Criss Angel dominated the scene.

“Bad joke,” I said. “First time here. Thought I should try to be edgier, verge-ier, you know.” I was puttering worse than a do-it-yourselfer in a Home Depot. “Just ignore me.”

The other girl touched my elbow lightly and laughed like the remark’s off-color meaning had just come to her. “We can take a joke here. We’re not *that* kind of place.” Her directness and game-show announcer’s rounded syllables surprised me. She knew I was new, too. That I was a potential mark on her celestial scorecard. I mumbled thanks and moved into the dimly lit, cavernous space of the Verge.

As upon entering a cathedral, I was aware of the capacity of the space—but the comparisons ended there. The room was very large and very dark. The ceiling was twenty feet above me, all exposed air-conditioning vents and black spray paint. The floor was slick concrete. The stage at front, lit by a baroquely professional lighting rig attached to the ceiling, bustled with musicians plugging in cables, trying to look casual, telling jokes, rubbing shoulders. There were about two hundred folding chairs set up and maybe half that number of people chatting aimlessly. They were loud. It felt like a large dive bar. There was moody, melody-deficient background music. At the rear of the room a bearded guy did Reiki over a mixing board the size of a dining room table. Like the sign outside, the walls had been painted to look like brick and were covered in graffiti with X-TIAN and 4 YHWH, which I nearly mistook for a freeway designation. I got the impression they were about to stage a low-budget high-school rendition of *Rent* with all the homosexuality expurgated, which meant doing a staged reading of half the credits and then bowing.

I took a seat in the back row, as far over as I could. I thought I’d be able to keep a few seats empty around me. Soon, though, every chair was full, and helpers from the shadows had set up another fifteen rows behind me. In the end, there were people standing in the aisles, fumbling with the tough choices one is faced with when trying to hold a Bible, a coffee, and a donut in only two hands. I read the program over and over again until the service began, intent on avoiding any conversation. To read about it, the place didn't sound so bad. There were outreach and after-school programs, a building project in Tijuana, some poor kid with leukemia who didn't have insurance, a letter from her mother expressing gratitude. On paper, I could deal with a church like this.

Soon enough the lights dimmed and I looked up. I hoped the trailers before the feature film would be good. While I laughed about this in my head, a perfectly well-edited trailer for a women's retreat in the style of *Bridget Jones's Diary* played for three minutes on the screen that dropped down above the stage. Then there was one for a men's retreat in the desert that featured bros on four-wheelers holding rifles, and a behind-the-scenes featurette on a nutrition outreach program that served one of the poor Latino communities nearby. They had the structure right, the buoyant and sentimental ways commercials spoke to a certain set of stereotyped ideas: women needed gossipy companionship, men needed brotherly adventure, brown people needed charity. It told me something about how these people imagined themselves.

The videos ended. The screen rose and the stage lights came up. A woman with short, unnaturally red hair stepped onto the stage with a microphone. "Hello, and welcome!" she shouted. A cheer rose up from the crowd. It's an aw-shucks way to describe it, but it's the only way to describe that kind of reaction. Crowd noises are usually a mix of sounds—joy and aggression in a football stadium, hope and anger at a political rally, pleasure and rebellion at a concert, satisfaction and greed and desperation on *Oprah*—but this cheer was all cheer.

"We've got a great sermon for you today," the host said, "and the

Verge band has some kick-butt music, as usual. But first, a few announcements." She filled us in on the establishment of a seed church by some of their missionaries in St. Petersburg—all those cold Russkies and their cold, red orthodoxy, unfamiliar with a God who was relevant and interested in their lives but surely used to the feel of an invisible eye upon them at all times. One of their local contacts had fallen ill and I thought she was going to ask for money, but instead she asked for prayers. I saw pens moving around me, and a glance at the nearest person's program confirmed it: people were making a note to do so. Not everyone, but a good chunk of them. Then there were a few upcoming events to plug, a couple deprecating jokes about her husband (she was pregnant, and he was struggling with the emasculation of cleaning the litter box, vacuuming, etc.), and an invitation to put our hands together for the Verge band.

The background music we'd been listening to was an echoing chord strummed by one of the two gender-indeterminate guitarists with long hair and tight black pants, and now the chord was struck harder and the music came on fast and loud and polished: drums played by a man who was my age and wore a faded tie-dye shirt, bass plucked by a boy grazing the peach-fuzzy lip of puberty, and synth sounds from a young woman with a strong nose and a modesty panel under her V-neck. Everyone in the room stood up, so I did, too.

The singer wandered out slowly, carried by the warm, polished crescendo of this semi-rock-and-roll. She was thin and blonde, wearing white capris and a tight Ely shirt with the sleeves rolled up, the pearlescent buttons catching all the colored lights. Her eyes appeared to be closed, but she was able to step over cables and the legs of stands, so she must have been squinting. One hand was raised in adulation and the other grasped a tambourine. She just wandered for about twenty seconds or so, building drama, avoiding a stumble. Then she found the microphone, mumbled something unintelligible, and half the room lifted their hands up into the air. This I couldn't do. It was bad enough inhaling so many warring deodorant scents. If I lifted my arms, I might pass out cold.

Lyrics were projected on a screen behind the band. The singer called out the first couple words to each verse before she sang them. So I would read "Light of the World, You stepped down into darkness," and then she would say breathlessly into the microphone, "Light of the world," before belting the line out. It made for a staccato, neurotic effect. Most of the people around me sang along. Some swayed, reaching up. Nearby, a group of teenage girls sung gaudy harmonies around the melody. When the singer wasn't singing, she played her tambourine like it was a Stradivarius. Every time it made contact with her other palm, she raised her eyes in praise of the miracle of its jingle-jangle.

The chorus described God as "lovely," which seemed like calling Vladimir Putin a sweetie pie. Later the song sputtered in circles for a solid two minutes—including an extended a cappella break—of everyone chanting, "I'll never know how much it cost to see my sin upon that cross." Despite myself, there was something stirring when the instruments and amplifiers died away and we were awash in the mistuned, arrhythmic singing of three hundred strangers. The voices moved in a sloppy unison, like the surface of a choppy sea. The sound called out some sympathetic response through my nervous system—the sound moved me.

Of course it did. The music was a kind of tumbled-and-polished rock that was either bursting out in a manipulatively cathartic chorus or was swelling toward one. It was graduation-day rock, greeting-card rock. The music was stirring people up, sure, and I couldn't be entirely immune. It was the same kind of music that got them emotional during a Volkswagen commercial. They were moved and ready to make a purchase. I tried moving my mouth along, just to fit in, but it felt too silly to stomach.

I tried to imagine Emily here. Had she been one of those vain, harmonizing girls? Didn't seem likely, but I couldn't say it was impossible. She sounded like she'd been a true believer, though. How had she gone from that to the person standing on the street near Angelo's? She'd said she began to see through the bullshit. It was hard to see how she could have missed it in the first place. But something must have precipitated the realization for her.

The song ended, and then the band played a couple more. The singer jutted her hips forward and rocked them side to side with the music. Above her low jeans and below the hem of her shirt a band of skin glowed blue in the stage lights. Her calves were toned where they emerged from her pant legs. She did quick, strange dances, and her breasts moved under her plaid shirt. I had a series of unclean thoughts. I wondered how many prayer requests went through this machine that asked for forgiveness over what they'd imagined doing to the bandleader.

At some point the lyric of choice became "I am captivated by Your love." The kind of love that holds a person captive is an abusive one, and it made me think of Sammy. Was Emily there against her will, or had she chosen to go back? Maybe it was just for the drugs. Or had he taken her back, was she important to what he was doing? It seemed possible, too. Shaw's story still loomed in the back of my mind.

My nearmost neighbors were hollering their hearts out, wanting a love that subjugates. That's a need that doesn't always lead to God. I could almost remember what it felt like to be young and credulous, happily obedient to God's will. But God's will, it turned out, was other people's will, traced through the traditions I was a part of, my church, my culture, my parents, my friends. I was obedient to my idea of God, which was still obedience to myself. And my self was stupid. Still is, but was especially so then. I'd learned to distrust every desire and impulse for that reason. But there was some vestige, something lingering on the edge of memory, of how good it felt to believe everything I did was for the imagined pleasure of someone else.

Finally, the music ended. The crowd took their seats again. The projector showing the last set of lyrics flickered and was replaced by a video of a man walking around. He was making incidental comments to the crowd. The stage was bright and airy, dominated by a massive white cross flanked by potted plants. The man was late fifties, early sixties, gray bearded, but his hair was longish and combed back like a Brylcreemed surfer from the early 1960s. He wore a pale blue Hawaiian shirt and off-white slacks. At the bottom of the screen, in a five o'clock news-style ticker, his name was spelled out: PASTOR EDDIE.

". . . that's what you would think, but only time will tell," he was saying to someone in the front rows of the sanctuary. Then he looked up at the crowd: "Welcome, everyone, on this glorious morning. It's good to be here with you, whether you're right here with me or you're joining us at one of our video venues. Today we're digging further into our series 'What's Love Got to Do with It,' but before we begin, join me in asking the Lord—and not Tina Turner—to guide us through this teaching."

He led a short prayer. Then the sermon was off. Pastor Eddie could speak. His tone was casual, approachable. He illustrated tricky bits of verse with long, contemporary narratives. Miriam's envy of Aaron was like some characters from a reality show I didn't watch that ended in a lucrative, short-term marriage. In his telling, the speech of biblical characters usually began with "So God says, 'Dude, what are you thinking?'" and "Pharaoh says, 'Hey, that's not cool.'" Occasionally he girded a point with a discussion of a word's translation and original meaning, the clinch move for intellectual high ground. Everything was so damn explicable, which was most of the problem. There wasn't anything his baritone voice couldn't clarify, no mystery it couldn't plumb like sonar in the black depths of the deep sea. It strained into the saccharine when he made direct appeals, which seemed to fall in three categories: be kind, be more responsible for yourself, support the church.

Envy and pride were the themes of the day, solvable with a four-point plan. I plugged my ears and Eddie looked like he could be leading a "Rich Dad, Poor Dad" seminar through The Learning Annex. The goal was inverted, but the methods were identical and offered a path as similarly simple and within anyone's control. Eddie beamed the radiant, healthful benevolence of someone with a foolproof investment plan to share.

Every time the story involved a warning against sin, he rattled off a list of possibilities like a sommelier offering the wine selection. These lists were never off the cuff. His list focused heavily on sexual immorality, pride, and obedience. Shame came from the first two, a salve for self-hatred from the third, and seats would fill through the combination. No one got through a week without at least an unchaste thought, if not some unchaste action, so it always made sense to lead with that. It got everyone thinking about their lustful, untrustworthy bodies—it was never "them," always "their bodies," that fallen, fleshy host for the "real me." It was a little like the guy who hits his wife every six weeks and spends the other forty-one days promising her he doesn't even know who that violent person is. It's how we preserve our best view of ourselves: good, but occasionally possessed by demons or the flesh or some other impurity from the outside.

That was before Eddie turned toward the camera and made a ten-minute direct appeal to those who were new, those who had not yet committed to Christ. He encouraged us to give God the steering wheel of our lives. I felt a pang of conviction in the projected eyes of this man speaking directly to me, even though I knew his street magic. I could only imagine what someone a little more receptive, a little more vulnerable, felt. Relinquishing control, abdicating responsibility, trusting someone else's plan or even believing that there was a plan—who wouldn't want that? And it was all as much for the regular churchgoer, too: a reminder that at any moment, any person may need only a slight nudge to commit themselves to Christ—and it could be you who does it, or your support of this church, and then *you* pass go, *you* collect $200.

Eddie asked us to join him in a prayer. It hit all the sappy beats about realizing you're a fuckup, wanting to trust Him with your fucked-up life and put it to His inscrutable, fucked-up purposes, but with less hot sauce on the language. Pastor Eddie's tone was modulated carefully. His pacing was perfect. It was freighted like a well-rehearsed poetry reading but conveyed wide-eyed admiration and the joyful release of responsibility for oneself. He'd done this prayer before, that much was clear, though to an unpracticed ear it could almost sound spontaneous—which was good, because those unpracticed ears were supposed to be repeating the words with their unpracticed mouths like they were the outpouring of spontaneous devotion—not just an extension of the worship service, another well-orchestrated choral event.

When he was done, he slipped in a footnote to the main thrust of the sermon, something about how nobody likes to talk about giving money but that's how the church survives, it's part of being an obedient believer. There it was again. Obedience. It made me want to stand up and shout out a swear word, chew gum and walk at the same time, look only one way when crossing a street. Something.

Eddie ended the sermon by saying goodbye to the people in the various video venues. "As usual," he said, "let the folks in Jitters get a five-minute head start to their cars, since they're going to be a little untrustworthy behind the wheel—unlike all the fine folks here in the sanctuary. And you wackos in the Verge, try not to frighten our friends in Heritage Hall on your way out, okay? No headbanging in communal areas, am I right? I kid, I kid. Have a blessed weekend, all. Thank you for coming."

The layers of projection, literal as well as social and emotional; the false subcultures of each venue; the superficial sense of belonging a person gained from one or the other. I thought back to the girl at the door and her clever response to my idiotic joke. Even it had the ring of rehearsal. You had to be careful, I remembered, when He is watching. But also she is watching, and her husband, and their kids, and your old youth pastor, and the AV guy, and the woman making the rounds, and the leaders of the Bible study teams, and the teenagers who seemed to be everywhere. It was a network, a funnel. All churches do it to some degree, but this was a higher order of scale, a more strictly formulated process. After an hour here, my soul felt as if it'd been under a tremendous torque. It wasn't God turning the ratchet. It was this immense social machine. That's what Hannah Trout, the small-group leader from my old church, knew when I'd confronted her, at a higher torsion by virtue of being a woman in a place that considered women equal but different, subject to scripture's ideas of order and the "complementarity" of the genders.

One of those androgynous guitar players struck a sudden chord, and I almost ducked. The worship music kicked into gear again.

But this is how I could see Emily here. The different versions I'd seen or heard about—the rough street kid, the decent person in need of a break, the knowing seductress, the cynic, the con, the ingenue, the believer and the ex-believer—they made sense in a person coming from a place like this, where everyone was watching and personality was a venue. That didn't leave enough room for a person to be or become, instead of act—no room to allow for deficiencies, fallibility, picking up and moving on with that awful, fallen self everyone is left with.

After more music and a prayer that I mouthed along to by doing cunnilingual ABCs, everyone wished each other peace and the show wrapped up. A young man held up a sign for men's retreat sign-ups. I headed toward the stage. The blonde with the tambourine was looping a length of microphone cable around her elbow. I said hello and told her she was a talented performer.

She said, "Thanks. I give it up to God, or at least I try to."

I tried not to think about her giving it up to anyone. Instead, I plied the first-timer angle again. "I'm new," I said, "and I was hoping there was some way I could introduce myself to Pastor Eddie. What a speaker. I enjoyed the living heck out of that service." I felt like I'd slipped out of time, wearing a suit and saying "heck"—a Ward Cleaver chatting up Monica and Chandler.

The tambourine player called to someone behind her: "Hey, Daniella. Your dad usually hangs around a bit after the service, yeah?"

The tall woman with the straight black hair and the modesty panel came forward from where she was folding up her keyboard stand. "Sure. Why?"

"This guy wants to talk to him."

The woman looked at me. Maybe the formality of my clothes caused her to fold her hands over her belly, a Victorian pose of ladyness, a living person holding herself in the marbled image of good womanhood. She could have stood on a sconce in a Catholic mission, but she had a pea-sized diamond on her ring finger, catching the blue off the overhead lights. "It just depends on how fast you are."

"Fast?" I asked.

"He usually gets stuck talking outside the main sanctuary for at least a while before heading back to his office."

"Hm, I'm fast but not that fast, and maybe catching him somewhere quieter is better. My friend Emily told me to come check this church out, and I'm glad I did. She asked me to say hello to Eddie for her, if I came."

There might have been a little meanness in my tone, a snide edge. I was feeling irritated with everything and everyone here. Even the shirt this woman wore, the neurosis of it: she must have liked how its low-cut V looked on her, but then another voice had reminded her to show no skin below the collarbone so as not to lead all these powerful men around her to lust after her secondary sexual characteristics against their wills. I didn't even need to ask if there were any female pastors here. But Daniella's face darkened. Her eyes narrowed. Her hair fell forward. She rocked and shifted one leg to a wider, more stable stance. Then the beatific glare returned to her eyes and the hands that were over her belly fell down but remained linked. The white gold of her ring looked cold and blue in the stage lights.

"Oh, really?" she said. "Emily who?"

For some reason I didn't answer, let the silence drag out. Daniella's eyes were troubled, reaching. Finally I said, "Emily McDaniels. Do you know her? She's in her seventies, maybe. She's my neighbor."

"No," she said, laughing a little, her eyes turning down in a snap, searching for something in the coiled cables around our feet. "It's a big place, as you can tell. It's hard to know everyone."

"Sure is," I said.

A new and businesslike tone crept into her voice—a cooler formality, more a concierge's than a daughter's, though what, in the end, did I know about the tone of daughters? "My father, though," she said. "He'll go to his office after saying goodbye to the people in the sanctuary. The building in back. It has a sign. He's usually available for an hour or two, if anyone wants to talk to him."

I thanked her. Daniella grimaced a smile and turned back to tearing down the band's instruments. As I walked away, I felt a lump rise up in my throat. It happened when I was angry. Was I angry at the falseness of this whole place? No, the lump wasn't there before. It had appeared with Daniella's reaction to the name Emily. It was something in my own memory, a recognition of disappointment, maybe. A name hoped for and denied. I thought of the way her hands, when she heard Emily's name, fell but stayed together.

21.

THROUGH A SEA OF POSTSERVICE CHATTER—BAKED IN A CLAY OVEN OF stucco, concrete, and midday summer sun so potent I swore I smelled cotton candy and the reek of the pig barn at the Del Mar Fair—I waded slowly to the far end of what could only be called a compound. Maybe I just liked the word *compound*, the Branch Davidian ring that had stuck to it. There I found the building I was looking for, CANAAN HILLS ADMINISTRATION in white vinyl lettering on its tinted door. I went in, toying with the last word, how a "minister" was buried in it.

In the offices the artifice dropped and the decor was all corporate. Cubicles. Cheap walls installed to make private offices. Doors cut into the walls. Names printed on the doors. The glossy leaves of hardy indoor plants. The feng shui of bland fries-and-Coke American power. There were a dozen or so people in there, working. I checked doors for Eddie's name, and while I walked the place I felt the radiation of each cubicle worker's welcoming smile on the back of my head. I caught a glimpse of one, the worst kind: the kind that would love me despite anything I might say or do. Screw it, I said to myself, and asked the *agape*-steeped accountant where I could find the pastor. The man pointed, and then his smile diminished a degree as he turned back to his work, the spreadsheets that failed to provide him an occasion to exhibit Jesus's sacrificial love of the living.

At the far end of the building was a door labeled EDDIE LAMBERT: HEAD PASTOR. I tried out different titles for myself. Good to meet you, Head Pastor, I'm Mark Haines: Hand Pastor, Past Pastor, Taco al Pastor, Dick Pastor—maybe that was me, the last one.

I knocked. Sometime during my visit to this place, I had decided on talking to Pastor Eddie. It wasn't intuition or insight leading me. As my knuckles rang against the hollow door, I knew I was being led by a grudge, looking to score a hit or two on a person I could have been, in a different life. It didn't have anything to do with Emily, not at the root. I didn't expect he would have ever heard of her, not in a place this large. Deep down, I just didn't like the guy and couldn't stand the thought of leaving here without him knowing it.

But I didn't know what I was going to say to Eddie, how I was going to approach him. Nothing. A big, beige nothing was all I had in my head—the color of stupidity, without expectation or hope. It was my brain again, doing its usual bit, getting ahead of itself, getting me up to my neck in my own messes. But even though it was my brain, it felt a little more like me this time. I wasn't sure if that was a good thing, to be on the same page as my malignant neurochemistry.

A man's voice inside said to come right in.

When I did, I was surprised to see that, compared to the man on the screen, the Eddie Lambert in front of me was larger. Mostly in the gut. It must have been the light in here, the way it deepened the folds and shadows in his Hawaiian shirt, puffed by a belly whose macabre independent life seemed to animate the white hibiscus flowers on that expanse of pale blue fabric. He smiled through his white beard, and his Santa Claus–ish smile lines crinkled into a show of welcome. "What can I do for you?" he asked. His voice was sweet and controlled, the sound of humble service, but direct, too, with its authority. There was something cutting against the tide in his humility—something like a demand.

I shut the door behind me. Lambert leaned back against his chair. I reminded myself why I was here, tried to put that reason at the forefront of my mind. Emily. She was somewhere. I needed to know where. Lambert might be able to help.

"I'm part of a team that is going through a batch of old missing persons reports," I said, stepping into the room and straightening my coat. "Due diligence, you know." My voice had picked up a little of Detective Lawrence's midwestern accent. Of course, Lawrence and Tuitele may have already been here themselves. That could be suspicious, but I'd already committed. Lambert watched me patiently, placidly, so I kept on. "When there's new evidence, we need to go back through the file and run through everything."

Lambert put his fingers together and rested them against the cushion of his mustache. He waited for me to continue, offering up no sign of recognition.

"She was a former parishioner of yours, I believe. I was wondering if I might have a few minutes of your time."

"Of course," he said quickly. "This is about Emily, I assume?" He casually pointed to the chair across from him. "Please, have a seat, Detective . . . ?"

He knew Emily. This was good. Still, a dark little tremor began to work its way up my legs, so I sat. Maybe I wasn't ruining everything, wasn't going to get myself into further trouble. Maybe I was even doing something right. A kind of elation came over me at feeling like I was on the right trail, the right path, which should have been a warning.

"Johnson," I said, sounding a little more confident and a lot more like Lawrence, whom I was impersonating in all but name. I sat in the chair, which was a full four inches shorter than Lambert's own, and suddenly felt like a kid at his first interview for a job at the soda shoppe. "Mark Johnson." The name rang falsely in my mind, sounding as make-believe as Bilbo Baggins. "This is in regard to Emily Hsu, yes."

"Why don't I call you Mark?" he said, and didn't pause for my assent. "As I'm sure you can tell, we keep things fairly casual around here." He paused in the space where someone might have laughed. I smiled and nodded and waited. If I took his lead and started calling him Eddie, it was only a few steps before he had me tearfully handing over the steering wheel of my life so he could drop the junker of me off with God in an act of spiritual valet parking—complimentary, but donation and tip recommended. I didn't want to trust this teenager with my keys, and besides, the less I said, the fewer chances I created for making an ass of myself.

"Mark, can I get you a cup of coffee or bottle of water?"

"No, thank you," I said.

"Well, Mark," he said, giving my repeated naming a mild hint of chastisement. "I wish you had made an appointment. I reserve this time after the service to speak with individuals of my congregation, anyone who may have something on their mind. It's an important part of what we are here, what we represent, and to be honest, it's the part of my week I look forward to most." He laughed a warm, Claus-ish laugh. The belly, it did what you'd expect, the obedient sack of shit.

"I'm sorry," I said, feeling foolish, as he wanted me to feel. "We can—"

"Don't be, it's fine. I make time for whatever comes up that is important, anything that can be of service. This seems to fit the bill." He had stood up while he was talking and walked around behind me to lock the door. "Mrs. Jenkins's questions about whether or not a Mongolian boy who never hears about Jesus will go to hell will have to wait for next week. We'll all survive, even the Mongol tyke."

I forced a laugh and wished Mrs. Jenkins might send the kid a laptop instead of another badly translated, graphic novel edition of the Bible.

"So," he said, with a weary smile that suggested the weight of the topic at hand. "Emily. Something new has turned up? Have you found her?"

"I'm not at liberty to say." Then, to make a show of concession and trust, I added: "We haven't found her, no."

Lambert must have decided that the fingers-pressed-to-his-lips look was too formal or menacing or apprehensive. He leaned back in his chair, arms on the armrests, his fingers looped around the plastic pads. "I see. Sad, that you haven't found her. But hopeful, too. I was afraid you were going to tell me she was, well . . . Regardless, it is sad for the Hsus. They've had such a hard time of it."

"I can only imagine." I'd thought about her parents, but only from Emily's point of view—not about what they were going through. Losing touch with their daughter. Years without contact. Years wondering if. Yes, it was sad. I knew something about that. Maybe Emily had her reasons, maybe they were monstrous assholes, but it was still sad. As a monstrous asshole of a parent, I knew that, too.

"Imagine? You've spoken with them already, I presume."

I felt the blunder as a rash of warmth in my face. "Not me," I said, hoping to cover it. "There are a few of us tasked to cases like this. One of my partners is interviewing them as we speak."

"Of course," said Lambert. "They're good people. Such good people. It's hardest for people like them to have a daughter like that."

"Like how?"

"A child born with a spirit of rebellion." He gestured as if laying a bad hand of cards down upon the desk. "I'm not saying she was the Damien child. She wasn't hopeless. We all bear our marks, which we must learn to transcend in order to find the Lord. But she fought her parents on everything from an early age, I recall. Very difficult girl. She grew into a very prideful young woman."

"Pride?"

He must have picked up on something in my tone. He responded quickly, with a defensive note in his voice. "Wouldn't you call abandoning her caring parents in the dead of night, without a word then or since, prideful? Leaving them to wonder where their only child had gone?"

His belief in family values was touching. "In my line of work," I said, "sometimes people have reasons." My line of work: ex-security guard, ex-pastor, ex-husband, ex-father, current impostor. I guess it wasn't a lie, technically speaking.

"No one is a perfect parent but God," Lambert said, "and I'm sure the Hsus aren't any different from the rest of us. But the slight would have to be great to justify that. To blow the ordinary failings of your parents out of proportion is, at root, a sin of pride. The sin of sins. The sin of loving yourself and your wounds over your obligations to other people, over the gift of laying your burdens down in Christ's hands."

My heart rate increased, my palms began to sweat, my hearing narrowed to pinprick, and my vision dulled on the periphery to form a tunnel between Lambert and me. In practical terms, it meant I knew exactly what kind of prick Lambert was and how I wanted to hurt him. I didn't like what he was saying, didn't like its condescension, didn't like my body's ignorant initial response to it—from the moment his words, those stupid spoken sounds, brushed up against my eardrums—as truth, as acute and personal judgment. A rush of ancient chemicals was triggering a series of fight-or-flight-related physiological responses throughout my sympathetic nervous system. Who we were fighting or fleeing from was complicated, but Lambert was the one in view. The little coward of higher reasoning kept me back, just.

When I spoke, Lawrence's accent had left me. Now I was asking the questions, doing the talking. "I've seen parents do things that would make leaving quietly the kindest thing she could have done."

"Not them," Lambert said, the tone of the dismayed wise man giving way to something with a little edge in it. "I've spent enough time with the Hsus to know that whatever slights she endured were minor."

I couldn't let this devolve. I hadn't expected Lambert to know Emily at all, but here he was pronouncing on her character. He might be able to give me some helpful insight, even if I had to read against his judgment. But I'd never find out if I started flinging my shit at him from word one.

"Tell me a bit about what she liked to do besides church," I said. "Hobbies, interests, things like that."

"Oh, that's hard to remember," he said. "It's been a long time, and I've had so many congregants between then and now. We were smaller then, this church, but still. It's hard to remember her before all this happened."

If he couldn't remember what color shoes she liked to wear or what kind of games she tended to enjoy most—if he couldn't point to the details of what her life was—then painting a picture of her as a young, fatefully doomed rebel archangel was monochromatic, done with wide, clumsy brushstrokes, the result of processing and abstraction and more about the painter than the subject. If Emily's sin of pride was her choice and terminal, then the boundary was as clear as Lambert's conscience. But only if there was still some conflict would he go out of his way to establish that so quickly.

This wasn't a man who was contradicted enough. He glided on the admiration of his parishioners. I knew because I'd been him. I'd said the same things, used the same lines. They allowed me to cultivate a relationship to the willing and disregard the rest, put them out of my sphere of obligation. The person who used their free will badly became the person I didn't have to worry about, didn't have to do anything for. I understood why it worked this way: it was an easy method for making a manageable list of who to care for and how. But it also kept help from some of those who needed it. It put a limit on who to love. It cut someone like my sister out of the fabric and pretended the hole was supposed to be there. So fuck limits.

"You can't remember anything in particular?" I asked, giving him one more chance.

"It all runs together a little at my age." He made an exasperated expression. "All I can recall are the usual girl things. Liked horses but didn't ride them. Nothing too particular, and there's a chance I'm mixing the horse thing up with other young girls from back then. You understand, I'm sure."

"Sure," I said. "Of course."

"She was a dreamy kid." For a heartbeat, I heard it as a comment on her looks, a suggestion of something sexual, and sure, it wouldn't be the first time a man of faith had broken that faith with a defenseless child. But he continued: "Daydreamer. Kept to herself. Very imaginative, always playacting something or another—high drama, lots of danger, that kind of thing." It all struck an odd note, that this is what he'd remember. He stared at me while he spoke, through me. It was unnerving. Then his eyebrows perked up. "Her prayer requests were landscapes."

"I'm sorry?" I said.

"Her prayer requests. We have cards you can write your requests for prayer on. People write down what they need help with, and there's a team that collects them and divides them among prayer groups, and they pray for others. I remember hers because they were covered in drawings. Landscapes. Lonely farmhouses, Alpine castles, beaches. Those kinds of things."

I made a face like I was mulling things over. I didn't know what any of this really told me about Emily, but the idea of having your prayers reviewed by a community of peers smacked of spiritual surveillance, the panopticon, or Mom in your sock drawer. Things change when you make them public. I couldn't imagine the careful editing and self-censorship of prayers as they were written across those cards, the limited and cultivated image of a person they would reflect, even when they made the motions of confession or revelation. In some sense, Emily's were probably more accurate than most.

Lambert's mind was going now, the flywheel of memory humming the tones of its etches, grooves, and gouges, his recollection gaining confidence. "She could draw quite well. And I do remember her as something of a reader. Her father, Stuart, used to complain about the fights they had getting her to leave the books at home when they came to church. Well, all except the one book, of course." He picked up a binder clip from his desk and opened and closed it. "Intelligent girl. It can be hard for those with an abundance of gifts," he said, with a hint of satisfaction in his face—like he could speak to that one from personal experience. "Unless those gifts are returned to God, they can lead a person into a shallow, small life. A life lived only for yourself. It's not how He meant us to live." The contentment on his face implied that he thought this a fate he'd narrowly avoided, though I still registered it, absurdly, as an accusation.

"And what about you?" I said, trying to shift him off-balance, to make this less about me, even though it had only been about me to me—which is to say, I was trying to find my own center of gravity. "You seem to have known her quite well, Mr. Lambert. Is that standard? Like you said, you have quite a few sheep passing through your gates."

He cleared his throat and paused before speaking. Was he thinking back on what he'd told people in the past? Was he squelching the memory of something else so it wouldn't pass as a shadow in the blood vessels of his face? I didn't know. I didn't know anything.

"It was a long time ago, by church standards," he said. "We were much smaller then—nothing like what you see here today. One building. A few hundred tight-knit parishioners. We had something special, but that was before it really boomed. And the Hsus were with us from very early on. Without Stuart and Adrianne, we might not be in the place to influence as many as we do." The man's blue eyes seemed to focus hard on my own. "Stuart was a leader in our elementary-age ministry, until Emily disappeared. I worked closely with him for several years. A lot of these memories come through him. After she was gone, he couldn't work with the kids anymore. A shame. So, yes. There have been many sheep. But we try to remember the part each played. We try very hard."

By the end of the speech, I almost believed he meant it. I'm sure he meant most of it. I'm sure he tried very hard. But there was something dangling, something left to worry, like a tendril of beef stuck between two teeth.

"And what was her part, then?"

He thought about it a moment, eyes never leaving mine. "A missed chance," he said. "Our failure."

I couldn't say where it was, but his face bore some trace of pain. Then he picked up the binder clip again, and the pain slipped back to wherever it was stored away. "A reminder of our limits and the unknowability of God's plans for us. Many things, I suppose. When Emily went missing, we took a collection, funded a private search through an agency. Groups took turns with Stuart and Adrianne, cooked them meals, kept them talking, not letting them give up hope, helping them keep their hope in God. I'm sure none of that is in your files," he said with the smug resignation of someone who nurses the idea of being marginalized, misunderstood.

I made no sign of acknowledgment except to feel my own anger sour into the usual self-resentment. This guy wasn't a monster, I thought. Just a dipshit. Not too unlike the rest of us. A bigger platform, sure, but that just made him a dipshit on a stage.

"At a certain point," he continued, "we had to help them come to terms with the fact that Emily had made a choice. That this was God's will, in giving us free will. We could choose anything, though He desired us to choose Him. She didn't. Even so, we wish we could have brought her back. If not to Him, then to *them*." He pressed his lips together into a tight, bitter impersonation of a smile.

"I'm sure you did," I said. "Do. And no one at the church has had any contact with her since? Especially more recently?"

"You would already know if we had," he said tersely. "We take this very seriously."

"I can tell," I said. I stood up and put my hand out to shake his. He couldn't do anything else for me, and I knew who I needed to see next. "Well, thank you for your time. And thank your daughter again for me. I happened to ask her for directions to your office, coming out of one of the venues with a band. Seems like a nice young woman."

Lambert's smile was warm, but his face had turned red. "Funny coincidence. She's an amazing person. She has a heart for giving and for leading our giving efforts that's just incredible."

"You must be proud," I said, thinking of Aracely, of what I'd say if someone told me they'd seen her. Nothing. I would say nothing, because I wouldn't know how to praise her, how even to lie in praising her.

"Very," he said with embarrassment. "Was any of this helpful?" He took my hand in his. He had the warm, fat, dry handshake of a religious man. My hand might as well have been a ten-year-old's, dwarfed, crushed, and sweaty in the knowing, confident grip of his own.

"Yes," I said, "everything that adds to our understanding is a help, even if it doesn't seem that way."

He nodded quietly. "And what department did you say you're with again?"

I took my hand back, the bones in it a little worse for wear. "County Sheriff's Department, Ramona Substation," I lied.

"Ramona?" he said. "Interesting. I know, you're not at liberty. That's okay." He put his hands on his hips, notched on the belt that ran low beneath his gut. "If there's anything else I can do for you, Detective Johnson—Mark Johnson, right?—be sure to be in touch. And if anything comes to me, I'll be sure to call you at the Ramona Substation."

I nodded, thanked him once more, and left. He was checking the details again. I knew it wouldn't be long until he spoke to someone with the police in Ramona. The hairs on my neck stood up, begged, jumped through hoops, as if he might reach out and grab me before I even left the building. Maybe Lawrence and Tuitele would connect Lambert's description of the cop impersonator to me, arrest me. Tuitele had said they knew crazy, and what did this look like if not nuts.

I glanced back and saw Lambert lingering in his doorway, talking to a woman who'd cornered the market on floral prints. I turned away.

Maybe it was my brain getting the better of me. Maybe it was the God-hungry hole in my mind, delighting over a few static misfires in the place where epiphany used to reveal itself gloriously, regularly, and in accordance with my father's faith—doing its best to make a great ball of meaning from all this. Maybe it was a plain, flour-and-water self-destructive streak. I wasn't spending time thinking about that, wasn't caught up in doubts about what mechanisms were at work, and that should have been the warning. But despite all this weight bearing down on me, despite the possibility that Lambert would go back into his office and call the Ramona Substation and get me arrested, I didn't feel wrong. I was on the right track.

So I stopped at the desk of the accountant for Christ and introduced myself.

"Good to meet you!" he said, beaming. "What can I do you for?"

"I'm with the police department," I said. "Just finished meeting with Pastor Lambert. He said I could ask you to pull up the address for Stuart and Adrianne Hsu in your database. H-s-u."

"Huh," the man said, leaning back in his chair. "I'm not sure why Eddie would ask me to do it."

"You got me," I said quickly, sternly, wanting to betray nothing. "But he said you'd be the guy. I'm running a little late, so any chance you can do it right now?"

"I'm not supposed to use the parishioner database," he said. "I manage our investments." He held his chin in one hand, mock shrewdly. "Besides, can't you look it up in some police database?"

"Right," I said, "and waste a whole day calling the twenty Stuart Hsus in the county."

"Oh, sure," he said. "But, I'm really not sure—"

"Look," I said, "he told me to talk to you." I pointed to Lambert, still chatting in his doorway. My gesture must have drawn his eye, because he looked over to us. My heart clenched. He smiled his bearded smile, and I waved. He waved back.

"See?" I told the manager of spiritual investments.

It took a minute, a couple clicks, and the guy had an address on a Post-it note for me. But he didn't seem to enjoy it, it wasn't the way he had greeted me when I came in. Maybe I'm grating. Maybe greetings are the best part of everything, before the everything that follows starts making claims on your time.

"Thanks," I said, taking the yellow note. "God bless Monsanto or whatever's in your portfolio."

I made for the door, picking between cubicles. There were so many of them, the cells of modern monks with voicemail and instant messaging. Then I heard a familiar voice. The words weren't clear, but the tone and timbre ran through my body like the first warm fingers of scotch massaging your insides—that tingling sense of an awful but sought-after beginning, the setting in motion of a lumbering, creaturous desire beyond yourself. Leaning over one of the cubicle walls, not twenty feet from me, laughing with Jesus's personal stockbroker rendered invisible by corkboard and cloth paneling, was the sleek form of Tom Gustafsson. He was laughing like a goddamn cocksucker is what I thought, those exact words, for some goddamn reason, an echo of Mike's from within my mind.

He was in jeans but wore a cuffed dress shirt, just like he had at the funeral. His fingers were in motion, illustrating what he was saying. There was a milder touch to him here. An affability, an ingratiating quality. He was a churchgoer. Of course he was. The rich find deserved providence easy to believe in, when so much of it has been bestowed upon them. But why this church, and why did I need to see his ugly face so often? He was a walking reminder of how I'd failed to help Mike and been fired from my job; how I'd failed to find another; failed to be a father, husband, brother, or son; failed to learn the name of my own grandson; failed to be anything but a simple, beautiful American failure.

Then came a nauseating wave of panic. Gustafsson could identify me. I was impersonating a police officer. I turned for the door and walked fast. Just as I went through it, Lambert's biggest, warmest voice caught up to me, and I paused to look back, half expecting him to be coming my way with armed guards or Hawaiian-shirted crusaders with BlackBerrys instead of broadswords.

But he was just offering a warm welcome to Gustafsson. The two shook hands, traded off squeezing each other's shoulders. Lambert was short by a couple inches, short in every sense of the word. His energy was streaked with nervousness, something I hadn't seen while he gave the sermon to two thousand nor when I was asking questions. It looked good on him. I wanted to see more of it.

Before either had a chance to look my way, I went out the door. So many of those happy parishioners were still milling around, drinking coffee, hoping to find someone they could offer some support to. Maybe at one point they'd had some doubts, had wanted something in a way that frightened themselves, saw the path before them as full of peril and pain. Not now. On every face there was the contentment of settling, the happiness of being in a warm bath of belonging. I'd resented them before. Now the resentment rose up as anger. I wondered who was fucking whose husband or wife, whose parent was dying somewhere, waiting for a visit that wouldn't come or, worse, a visit intent on winning a deathbed conversion. I hoped for disaster in their lives. I hoped their children would reveal themselves to be perverts, masochists, alcoholics, sadists, power mongers, depressives, atheists, abortionists, Buddhists, Mormons, spiritualists, nihilists. I wanted them to look more like me.

When I reached it, the parking lot was emptying. It smelled like gravel and exhaust and a little like Easter, too—it was one of those mornings. The odor of things greening.

Then a severely lifted truck with flared fenders and chrome exhaust pipe—the whole shit show—growled past, almost clipping my shoulder with its mirror and kicking gravel at my shins. My arm began to rise to give it the bird, but I stopped it. No extra attention. It drove away, and I noticed the sticker that dominated the tailgate: the emaciated, George Romero–inspired Jesus on the cross I'd seen before, on a different truck, down at the harbor the day my tires were deflated and I found the goiter-headed kid, Shaw.

This truck had a blue-and-white dirt bike tied down in the bed. Another one of those kids, ripe for someone like Sammy to get them into some earnest trouble. Or were the Hard Corps Rangers, as the sticker called them, Sammy's little ring of drug dealers themselves? At the beach I'd self-righteously assumed they were the ones who let the air out of my tires. Now I wondered in earnest.

As I pulled out of the parking lot, one of the reflector-vested attendants—my mind flashed again on Mike, then pushed the image of him away—was speaking with a security guard. The guard was wearing my old uniform, or one close enough. That Gustafsson went to church here was one thing. That he probably helped manage something of their finances was another. But it hadn't occurred to me that he was Lambert's landlord, that my old pal Watt handled their security.

It was for places like this that I got canned. If I'd been given a different assignment when I started, I could have been standing out here. I could have watched Emily drive to and from this church every Sunday. And even if I was a better security guard than I never pretended to be, I wouldn't have noticed her absence, wouldn't have been able to protect her from whatever was coming, however it came.

22.

IT WAS HEATING UP IN MISSION HILLS, AND I WAS LOST. BEING FROM Oceanside, I didn't get down to San Diego proper very often. I passed through two alternate realities while I got my bearings: the mock Spanish village of Old Town, promising a window into early San Diego and an opportunity to buy overpriced ponchos, *lucha libre* masks, and mass-produced Día de los Muertos dolls, and a park ornamented with decadent Victorian homes painted with such thick, flat colors I thought they were cardboard cutouts as I drove by.

Mission Hills was tucked above this and only marginally less unreal. Every other home was a restored and expanded Craftsman with all-native, drought-resistant landscaping and sprinklers running in the full summer sun. In contrast, the Porsche SUVs that littered the driveways looked like a tolerable excess, a concession to pleasure compared to all that supposedly thoughtful *Architectural Digest*–driven consumption. The other houses sat upon the foundations of old homes with squared, modern asses. Their walls were gray concrete, haphazardly stained strips of reclaimed wood, exposed steel trusses. They were dressed up with sans serif street numbers, maybe a crown of bluing copper cut to resemble a wave running across a balcony that extended over a ramp into the private underground garage. It wouldn't have been my first guess at where Emily was from, but I could see some resemblances now that I was here. Even the houses, minute by minute, lot by lot, didn't know who or what to be.

I was going slowly enough in my old truck to earn a dirty look from an elderly woman in skin-tight baby-blue velour, speed-walking with her Great Pyrenees. High, thin clouds blew in with the afternoon. I found the street I was looking for.

Driving a shitty truck with a mismatched shell wasn't a cop thing to do, so I parked around the corner and stepped out immediately. I needed to look like I had a purpose. Not for other people. For myself. Lambert might have already called the police. The office drone might have told him I'd gotten the Hsus' address, and maybe he'd called them, too. Maybe the police would be waiting for me here, bored with having to cuff another lunatic.

So I walked firmly. With the suit on, I felt like a black-and-white film detective coming home after a long day or like an Adventist missionary launching a seed church. There were lawn mowers running nearby, but I guessed that their operators were less Ward Cleaver and more Cesar Chavez. Ward was off getting some dermabrasion, was performing his *savasanas* after a steaming bout of Bikram yoga, was jerking off to absurd pornographies using organic hand creams.

I turned the corner and the road rose. The street was tree lined and the asphalt was cracked and scabbed over, slipping downhill in tectonic chunks. Power lines were going in and out of everything.

I turned over my plan. There wasn't anything to turn over. It was as if I'd said heads or tails and then flipped a marble. After seeing that church, where every need was anticipated and every outcome planned for and expected, maybe the lack of a plan wasn't a bad thing. That's what I told myself anyway.

So when the street number on the mailbox in front of me matched the number of the Hsus' house in my pocket, I started toward it without pausing to gather my thoughts. Stopping once would be stopping forever, and I didn't have that kind of time.

The stone walk curved toward the front door. The place was big and old, but not especially well kept. The roof was cedar shake. The walls were brown-painted board and batten. It wasn't elaborate or elegant, but it was large and nice, and there were intricate designs leaded into the tall front windows. The jacaranda in the front garden was enclosed by a rock planter. On either side of the tree were stone benches braced by rosebushes, backed by a trellis of sweet pea. There was too much time being put into this garden. It looked like a branch didn't have a chance to grow before it was trimmed. The only gaps in the presentation were the few purple flowers from the jacaranda that had fallen the previous night. They puckered on the ground, empty pouches.

I couldn't bring myself to use the brass knocker in the shape of a cherub, so the door reverberated with a dull, fleshy thump when I knocked. It was opened by a man in a maroon polo shirt. He was on the short side, with thin black hair. He said, "May I help you?" without the least trace of a smile, and I saw a hint of Emily in his cool, appraising eyes. In the moment he spoke, a single tarred smoker's tooth became visible, then vanished again behind pursed lips.

"Maybe," I said, glancing over his shoulder. The house was dim, shaded, but there didn't seem to be anyone waiting for me in there. "Did Eddie Lambert call you?" A cool bead of sweat ran down my side.

The man's face tightened at the name. "No. No, he hasn't. And why might he have a reason to call us? What's happened?"

"Nothing's happened," I said. "That's to say," I heard myself ramble, "he heard there was news about your daughter. He called me. I'm with Calvary Chapel. I'm a counselor. He thought you could use someone to talk to." So I wasn't a cop anymore. I wasn't sure I liked this new self any better, but maybe it was an easier angle to play.

"Why not someone from his own church?" the man asked, his voice calm but confused, with a touch of annoyance.

"I have some experience," I said, "with similar situations."

"Eddie is a thoughtful, selfless man," he said tonelessly. "What experience?"

"Oh," I said, now on the defensive. "Nothing exactly like what you're going through, of course. But I know what it's like. To wonder about someone you love. To not know." Some other self rose up into my face, stretching itself into the heat of my skin, running itself along the nerves of my fingers, reacquainting, filling me with feeling—a disembodied impression of Ellen. I answered it with bile in my stomach, making fists of my hands, tightening my throat. "I know how terrible it is," I said.

The man had been standing braced against the door frame with one arm. Now he let his posture sink. His shoulders dropped a few inches. Where he'd formerly thrust his chest forward two small breasts swelled against his shirt. His belly pressed against the maroon fabric. He looked down, at my feet, shod in my father's saddle shoes. It was like watching the will vacate a person.

"It was kind of Eddie to think of us," the man said in a softer, more suppliant voice, eyes moving across the stone walk—stopping, I knew, where they came upon an out-of-place bloom, a fallen twig. He paused, letting something pass. When his words returned, they were gently bitter, like he had a mouthful of pith and rind, the fruit having passed into his gullet a lifetime ago. "He is a generous man, Pastor Lambert. That is true. Very true. Tell him I said that, when you tell him we didn't need to speak with anyone. I'm sorry you've wasted your time, but I think you have."

"There hasn't been more news about Emily, has there?" His tone had sounded so final that I was suddenly afraid I'd missed the worst, irrevocable news. I was no good father. I barely deserved the name. But I knew how I'd be if Aracely had died, and I searched the man's body for signs of it on him.

The man's upper lip pulled back. The smoker's tooth appeared again. It bit into his lower lip.

"I'm sorry," I said. "It's none of my business."

"No," the man said. "It's fine. There hasn't been any news, and we've had enough years to acclimate ourselves to this."

From within the house came the sound of shuffling feet. A woman's voice called out. "Who are you talking to, Stuart?"

The woman appeared over Stuart's shoulder. She was taller. Her eyes were large and unmade-up, brown and friendly. She had a narrow mouth and full lips that were only beginning to show their age. Across the bridge of her nose and on her cheeks she wore a dusting of freckles beneath the grime of later sun damage. She looked so much like Emily it was hard to imagine being her husband, looking at her and seeing his missing child instead.

Her smile was weak, but unlike her husband's, at least it was a smile.

Stuart spoke to her but never took his eyes off me. "Eddie Lambert sent this man. He's a counselor. He thought we might want to talk to him."

The woman—Adrianne, Lambert had called her—said, in the same toneless way of her husband, "Pastor Lambert has always been a good friend to this family."

"I told him we wouldn't need the counseling," Stuart said. I waited, watching her.

"No, we don't. But thank you. Tell him we say thank you," she said.

I felt awful that I'd come here and intruded on their long-standing grief in this way. "Of course, of course. Though I imagine you'll see him before I do."

"Not likely," Stuart said. Adrianne's fingers tensed once around his shoulder.

"Oh, I'm sorry," I said, sensing a gap, an opportunity I couldn't resist. "I got the impression you and the Lamberts were friends."

"Well," Adrianne said, and left it at that. They watched me with eyes that said it was time to go. But I couldn't, not yet.

"I'm sorry again," I said, letting my posture break, letting them see the appearance of my guard going down. Then I switched to a more confidential tone—everything I used to do to encourage young Christians to confide their sins in me, for which I could hold them accountable. "Forgive my misunderstanding. I must have just gotten the impression that he knew Emily well, and in a church that size you don't get to know everyone. I made the leap to assuming you were all close. My mistake."

Stuart continued to chew on his lip. Adrianne looked at me but didn't give a sign that she saw what was there. "Our daughters," she said with careful enunciation, "were like sisters. Emily was at their house as much as at ours. She called him Uncle Eddie. Before, of course."

I nodded sympathetically while my brain collapsed in on itself, self-compressing toward a gravitational singularity under the weight of the revelation—not the bright, divinely sun-streaked kind I used to imagine myself having. "I see where his concern was coming from then."

Stuart spoke: "We aren't friends like that any longer." Who he blamed for that state of affairs was clear from his tone. I wanted to know why.

"Like I was saying to Stuart, I've dealt with some of this in my own life," I said. I left the statement open enough that they could say anything, really, to fill the silence—in the hope that they would at least keep talking.

Adrianne brought her husband's arm down from where it had been braced against the doorjamb. She twined her fingers in his. She looked at their hands and didn't look up again. "Forgive me, but is that everything?"

It wasn't, I wanted to say. But I didn't want to press these people too hard. They were hurting. I didn't want to add to their burden. If they could say anything to bring me closer to Emily, they would have already found her themselves. But they'd told me enough.

"Pardon the intrusion," I said sincerely, and made to leave. "It was well-intentioned."

"What isn't?" Adrianne said, and shut the door.

23.

LAMBERT HAD LIED TO ME. HE WAS OBSCURING HOW WELL HE'D KNOWN Emily, his daughter's best friend. There could only be so many reasons for doing that, and only one I was convinced by—the most common one committed by a man of God against a teen under his care. The blood boiled in my veins, became red clouds churning through my body, clouding my sight. My hands shook.

I drove around awhile, trying to find a pay phone. By the time I spotted one, I was in City Heights and ready to admit I should have a cell. Instead, I was on a hot paved corner by a carniceria running an old, emphysemic grill on the sidewalk. The Santa Ana wind whipped thick, dark clouds of smoke my way as I plugged some quarters into the machine and got connected to Canaan Hills. I was hot and tired, but that wasn't why I was light headed, reeling. The knowledge of Lambert's lie had settled and left me giddy and vengeful, the way the first good buzz of the day used to feel, lifting a grudge up to the height of self-righteous truth, transmuting a wound into a crosshairs, aligning the pins in the damaged tumbler lock of my brain into beatifically pissed-off clarity.

I asked the voice that answered on Canaan Hills' end to connect me with Daniella Lambert. The receptionist put me on hold to track her down. A few minutes later she—of course, she—was back: "She's out at the Barrio Logan service project site. I should have known. She's got something like this going on nearly every day of the week."

"Yeah," I said. "Real heart for giving. I heard."

"It takes that to run the outreach programs. What a gift, am I right?"

"Where in Barrio Logan is it?" I asked. "I'd like to chip in."

She told me, and I made the short drive across town.

Tucked in by the harbor, Barrio Logan had been passed off over the years, from the navy during the Second World War to the shipping industry to junkyards to cheap developers and slumlords. The neighborhood was tucked under San Diego's swinging dick of a bridge that slapped down right through the middle of the community and let visitors come right through to tony Coronado Island without having to slow down, look around. In the seventies, locals took over a lot under the bridge when the city reneged on a promise to build a park there. Since then, the residents had been building, piece by piece, Chicano Park, which ran almost the entire way down to the water. Every concrete pier that held up the bridge was painted over with murals, making the place look like a prehistoric monument done up in Technicolor, only these stones weren't aligned to some astrological calendar—only the forces of weight and gravity and our deep and abiding desire to get massive numbers of cars to where we want them, when we want them, and to charge a toll for the right, damn those who live in the shadow.

I parked on the road under the bridge and got out. The pier

propping up the on-ramp to the bridge overhead was painted with ¡VARRIO SÍ, YONKES NO! Below that was a scene of workers protesting before a factory—men, women, and children picketing while others in the background tore down a barbed-wire fence with a kind of double-minded pragmatism. On the next pier a purple-skinned goddess looked more ambivalent about the whole thing. I preferred the Aztec warrior with the eagle headdress. He looked like he knew what he was about, knew himself to be a predator with a good eye.

I'd thought it would take me a while to figure out where Canaan Hills was set up, what they were doing. But it wasn't hard, just a game of spot the white person. I've got a good eye, too. There were about ten within view from where I stood. But none of them were Daniella, so I walked deeper into the park. As I passed, the purple goddess seemed to note my clothes and roll her eyes. Another gabacho.

There were a few tables and ice chests set up under the shade of a Mayan-style kiosk made of the traditional poured concrete and Behr latex paint, red and green. A few of the church people walked the park with trash grabbers and plastic bags, mostly just wandering, since the park looked pretty clean. They would have been better off on almost any beach on a Saturday morning. The rest of them fanned out, returned to the tables, then fanned out again. I watched for a while, trying to figure out what they were doing.

Then one approached me and gave me a can of soda still dripping cooler water. He'd tied a little tag to the tab. The ink was smudged from the water, but I could still read it: A SMALL GIFT FROM US TO YOU TO SHOW GOD'S LOVE, NO STRINGS ATTACHED. —YOUR FRIENDS AT CANAAN HILLS.

There were always strings attached, I wanted to tell the teenage boy with the recessive chin who'd given it to me. Maybe especially when your proselytic tool of choice is the Coca-Cola Company suite of products or when the nod to local culture means offering the full rainbow of Fanta flavors. Still, I was thirsty, the orange soda hit the spot, and he hadn't asked to share any news, good or otherwise, with me. He just wandered back to base camp and reloaded, grinning like a fool doing good, which is just what most fools think they're doing.

I went close enough to see that Daniella wasn't at the tables. I turned around, scanning for her. Wearing the suit, I felt conspicuous, like I was here to assess the value of the land for a coming wave of mixed-use development, half luxury apartments and half frozen yogurt shops. So I kept moving, walking a few blocks down toward the water. This part of the park seemed to be reserved for a gathering of homeless people, which looked enough like an outdoor AA meeting that I thought about introducing myself for the free coffee.

Then I came back the other way. Still nothing. The operator at the church may have had it wrong, or maybe Daniella had already left. When I was past the Mayan kiosk again, thinking I might have to give up on finding Daniella today—thinking about what to do instead, since things like going home and waiting weren't options—a voice cut across the park. It was her.

"Hey. You lied."

I turned around. Daniella was standing on the wheelchair ramp of a brick building's side exit. She was just outside the shadow of the bridge, so the San Diego sunshine fell on her hard, like a house from the sky. She was put together but not done up, wearing a teal top with puffed sleeves, charcoal slacks, and modestly close-toed shoes so as not to tempt the foot fetishists. With her straight black hair, darker complexion, and strong nose, she looked enough like some of the women in the murals to belong here. She definitely didn't get her looks from her father. I hoped she didn't get much else from him either.

She walked toward me with an older man. The shadow of the

bridge touched her, starting at her feet and cutting upward, dividing her into graduating proportions of light and dark until it consumed her. She sent the man off to the kiosk with a whispered word and a wave.

I headed toward her. "Your dad lied," I said when we were close enough. "He didn't tell me you and Emily were best friends. Didn't tell me a lot of things, I suspect."

I wanted her on her heels, wanted to know the truth and quickly. But she just shook her head and smiled politely. "Doesn't surprise me. That's not exactly against the law, though. Unlike, say, impersonating a police officer."

That rung my bell, got everything humming. "It's not what—"

"I don't care," she said flatly. "I'm not worried about that. Why are you looking for her?" Her eyes didn't betray suspicion or malice. I don't know what they betrayed, but there was something that kept me searching them. For Daniella to know I wasn't a cop, Lambert had to know. For Lambert to know, he must have spoken with someone in the police department, maybe the Hsus, too. Maybe Gustafsson had seen me as I hightailed it. That was not good. It was, in fact, a very bad kind of bad. But whatever was happening out there, back at Canaan Hills or in Ramona or wherever, it didn't seem like Daniella wanted to be a part of it.

"I was trying to help her out," I said, choosing honesty. "Then she disappeared. I saw her a couple days ago, living with a drug dealer. Cops raided the place, but she disappeared on them, too. I'm worried about her. I need to know she's safe." Even saying that I needed to know was insufficient. It felt stronger than that, bigger, more compelling, beyond need or obligation or duty, under the pull of a firm and unbending kind of force.

She looked me up and down. I couldn't imagine how I appeared in her mind, what she made of this haggard middle-aged man wearing discards of an out-of-date suit in a park like this, holding one of the free sodas her people had brought here. She chewed her lip, seemed to catch herself doing it, then reset the line of her mouth. It reminded me of Emily. She had the same habit.

"I'll be right back," she said, and walked away without waiting for an answer. She flagged down a short, round woman with a page-boy haircut and spoke with her. I looked around for a trash can. Then something like guilt kicked in, and I searched for a recycle bin instead. Daniella came back a moment later, squinting against the dust kicked up by the Santa Ana, which had grown insistently gusty and unfurled its heat on us, like the door to the oven of the Anza-Borrego Desert had fallen open.

"Carina's going to keep an eye on things here for me," Daniella said. "Let's go someplace a little quieter. I think that'd be a good idea."

"Fine," I said.

"Follow me," she said, already walking and not bothering to check that I was behind her. She waved to a balding old man with a feather earring who scooped up cigarette butts fanned out around a trash can. The charred dots on the lid made it look like a ladybug. The man looked like a hippie burnout turned born-again, someone whose countercultural suspicion was probably turned now to the war against Christians in America and, in all likelihood, toward anyone who tried to restrain the lily-white hand of God that made greed good in the munificent free market. Time and perspective, two unrelenting, changeable assholes—but not without a sense of humor.

24.

DANIELLA DROVE US IN HER YELLOW-PAINTED OLD VOLVO STATION wagon down to the embarcadero. The air shimmered with dust, blown garbage, and sunlight reflected brilliantly off sea chop. We sat on a bench along the sidewalk, pinned between the glossy downtown skyline on one side and navy warships and Disney cruise liners on the other, both vessels at the ready to take some drunk pleasure-seekers to a third-world country for no good reason.

It had been a quiet drive. I'd been telling myself to let Daniella take the lead. She had something she wanted to say, something she wanted me to know. You could frighten away confession with a wrong word or glance, and she hadn't given any opening that I could, like the patient and prying pastor I'd been, press into.

Then we sat on the bench. The bright light and military hardware, the smell coming off the hot dog vendor's cart and the tables of hats for tourists embroidered with TOP GUN above the bill, it all left me sore, suddenly, sick to death of this entire place, this entire world, and the thought of someone like Lambert living contentedly within it. The idea of waiting disappeared into thin air, like all ideas do.

"Your father abused her, didn't he?" I said.

My muscles tensed as if, at her word, I could spring to action and tackle the guy here and now. It had been a feeling first but then a narrative so straight and narrow and sure I could have walked over the water on it: a paternal pastor figure with a teenage girl in his charge, someone vulnerable who could likely be controlled or kept quiet; that girl running away—from what, it seemed obvious—growing up into a troubled woman choosing the wrong men, the wrong drugs; that girl passing through Oceanside, trying to skip town, failing and falling back into old habit. The only thing it left out was where Emily could be now.

Daniella laughed. It was short and low, dragged through some emotional rocks she'd already been steering over, and it left me feeling off-balance. She glanced at me, for the first time showing anything other than composure in her features. Her eyelashes flashed, wet, in this goddamn California sun that seemed to flatten out any feeling. Then she looked up, trying to keep tears from spilling, and breathed a long, heavy breath. "If only it were that straightforward."

My throat was dry. The muscles running down my neck clenched. "What does that mean?"

"He made mistakes—"

"Mistakes? So you're going to defend him."

"No," she said, waving a hand dismissively. "He made mistakes, but not that kind of mistake. If that's what you think happened, you're wrong. And if I were going to defend him, I wouldn't have brought you here."

Not that kind of mistake. Some ghost train in my mind was still chugging toward that destination. It seemed logical, inevitable. But another part of me was thrown from those tracks, rolled in the dirt, came up now to make sense of the remaining options.

“Then tell me,” I said. “What did he do to her? Why do the Hsus hate him?”

She eyed me like I was a beetle on its back. “That’s . . . that’s not the point. They blame him—not for her running away, but for her never coming back. They’re the ones who toed the hard line, but they blame him for telling them to. But that doesn’t really have a lot to do with the trouble she’s in now.”

“So you’ve seen her? You’ve talked to her?”

Daniella shook her head, massaging her own fingers anxiously. “She showed up, about a year ago. I hadn’t seen or heard from her for a long time before that, and she was in a bad place. She wanted money.” Now Daniella turned to cracking each knuckle of each finger, methodically working from left to right. When she finished with that, she spun the engagement ring thoughtlessly. “She said she was going to make a big scene unless my dad gave her some money. She was high, but she said she needed it to get clean, that she wanted to use it to get away to someplace where she could start over. She told us . . . horrible things, about who she was living with, about what her life had become.”

A year ago was around the time I first met Emily at Angelo’s. Before or after, I couldn’t be sure. If she’d had cash, she wouldn’t have been trying to hitchhike, though.

“I’ve heard some things of my own about who she was living with,” I said.

“It’s awful,” she said tremulously. “She was completely hooked on pills. She showed me bruises he’d given her. He was . . . was forcing her to prostitute herself. Threatening her if she tried to leave. Locking her in the closet. Telling her no one would care if she disappeared off the face of the earth—and I know her, I could tell she believed it. Then promising to take care of her. That he was the only person who understood her. The only person who could protect her. But he was the one she needed protection from. He's a monster."

The man was Sammy. It had to be. There was enough of Shaw's story in this. And Sammy was free, maybe trying to find Emily right now, too. The description fit God, too—the first mover, the urtext.

"So your dad gave Emily the money?" I asked.

She nodded.

I whispered under my breath whatever curses came to mind, a long litany of them. Daniella couldn't hear; no one did. In the old world, a curse could strike someone dead in an instant—traveling to the other side of an Atlantic Ocean crossable only by sail. Those same curses, if heard by others, could have gotten me burned at the stake, once upon a time. Today I could borrow Daniella's cell phone, call anyone on the planet, and anything I said would lack the power words used to have.

"Why?" I asked. "Why didn't he try to help her? Really help her? Why didn't you?"

She gave me a blank look, a touch of confusion around the eyes. For a minute she seemed at a loss for words, but then she blinked and found them again. "That's not, well . . . Emily has her reasons for not wanting help from me. But I needed someone to know the truth about the man she was living with. Someone needs to do something about him."

"Why not you?"

She released her own fingers and pulled back her hair with both hands, gathering it in a ponytail and draping it over one shoulder. The wind began to pick it apart a strand at a time, causing these to flutter around her eyes. "Look. This isn't easy to explain, but it can't be me."

"Are you scared of your dad? Did he threaten you to stay quiet about the money?"

"Nothing like that. I mean, sure. He doesn't want anyone to know he saw Emily, but he's not a violent person."

"You know I saw her just a few days ago, right?"

"I don't—"

"And you know, not five minutes later when the police showed up at Sammy's, she wasn't anywhere to be found, right?"

There was a strange look of panic in Daniella's eyes. "No—"

"She could be under the floorboards, for all I know. And you think there's time? There isn't time. Not for this."

"I'm scared," Daniella said, not without a hint of anger beneath. "For her. But also because this is my life. I can't be the one to help her."

"Or won't," I said. "Because it might cost you."

"No, that isn't it," she said with a sigh, then pulled her posture upright. "Fine. She won't take help from me. We were in love. Before. On principle she would refuse anything I had any part in. And what you saw back there, at the park, that *is* my life. It's . . . it's the most important thing to me. And yes, that could disappear in a flash. It would be like I never existed."

She sniffled only once afterward—no crying, no sobs—but her posture slumped at the admission, which may as well have been murder for the way her shoulders sunk with shame. She stared hard at the harbor. The hot light seemed to dry whatever tears were in her eyes before they had a chance to spill. She didn't say anything for a long time. As far as I could tell, she wasn't looking anywhere in particular, but her eyes never moved from whatever fixed point they'd landed on, while her mind carried her back to who knew what moments.

Maybe she thought that what she'd said had said it all. I knew what she was getting at. To help Emily would be to risk having that knowledge become public. I knew how these California churches, so sun-glossy welcoming on the outside, were fed by a steady stream of westward-ho Baptists and Methodists, lapsed Catholics, fallen Mormons, and fed-up Episcopalians, warming their hands around the Christian talk radio campfire—people who made their positions against homosexuality not just known but a cornerstone of their homilies.

We'd done it—I'd done it, I had to admit—too. I'd preached it at youth-group sessions, kept it high in the list of my warnings against sex and the culture at large, which was marshaling itself against our so-called God's so-called just guidance. Homosexuality as sin was there when I spoke to a fine set of fourteen-year-olds from my small stage about love and sex and proper courtship, taking its place right after masturbation and before the warning that the couple who prays together lays together. I'd gone as far as to let the boys in youth-group sessions know that if they didn't masturbate, God would take care of that for them, meaning—shit, the things I said back then—they should wait for a juicy wet dream to spill their seed for them, a little sin-free squirt in their *Star Wars* bedspread. I knew well enough that they'd all been rubbing up against the couch cushions by then. For every person who admitted to dry humping her boyfriend, I knew there were another five or six who kept it a secret. Despite all the nods of agreement, all the innocent and approval-seeking smiles on faces just breaking with acne, bodies just gaining the scummy patina of adult bodies, I knew the sexual morality talk watered a shady fern of shame in every heart. This shame was good, I thought. It would keep them from straying out into the desert, would protect them from the oppressive heat of damnation.

In my mind, I was giving the same message to the kid balls deep in his dad's *Playboy* magazines as to the Tommy who dreamed of kissing Timmy. I thought these sins were the same, even as the sin of sex between two men or two women became the focus of our ire. It was just one of a thousand ways a person's genitals could lead them away from God's light, but it became the vessel for serving up the delicious pleasure of feeling like our way of life was under attack, when in reality we understood nothing about threat. With God's voice I'd condemned the behavior, without seeing that I was also condemning the desire. What is a person if not his desire? That had become the whole point of my life since I'd been kicked out of my bunk on rock bottom: to have no desires, to let it all go, to be nothing. The things I'd wanted, the things I'd been and done—I wanted to take it all back. Which is what I'd tried with that bottleful of pills. My sister had killed herself to know. I'd tried to kill myself to annihilate what I knew.

So I could fathom something of the shame Daniella was feeling. Maybe I didn't know it, but I could understand it. "What happened?" I asked. "So you guys were in love. Probably not kosher at Canaan Hills. But not the end of the world, right?" Even saying it, I knew from experience it wasn't true—that it could feel exactly like the end of the world.

"Hm?" she said, turning to find me sitting next to her, surprised, as if coming back from a faraway place. "No, it wasn't . . . It didn't end well. Being caught by your father, who is also your pastor. . . . There's no way that ends well."

"Did he hurt you? Her?"

"No." She brushed nonexistent crumbs from her lap and then held her knees. "*I* hurt her."

I nodded. This was the deeper shame, it seemed. I tried not to move. Even a stray gesture or glance would be a breach of the gentleness she seemed to need.

"It's not that interesting," she said, doing a poor job of keeping the tremor out of her voice. "He didn't get the cane, didn't send us away for reprogramming. He just told us to get dressed." She paused, remembering. "He came down on us pretty hard. He was angry—he was right to be angry, I think, too—I can see that now. At the time, I don't know. . . . It all just hurt. But he needed us to know that what we were doing was wrong in the eyes of God, would separate us from His love forever." Her tone didn't hint, the way it can, whether "His" was more "his," whether the love she might lose was God's or her father's, whether that was even a difference worth parsing. In my mind, I saw Lambert's grinning self-satisfied face—his fat lips, Brylcreemed hair, trim beard, eyes like Santa Claus's bastard-born child—turning his rage on these children.

"I knew he was right," she continued. "Emily fought it. She pulled away from me, from the youth group, until one morning her mom went to wake her up and she was gone."

"Where were her parents in all this? They didn't know what happened?"

Daniella shook her head. "We made my dad promise not to tell. But they had to know something had happened. Emily suddenly didn't have a best friend. Started slipping at school and church. I remember them coming to the house to talk to my dad about her, right toward the end. They'd found a boy in her room at two in the morning. They didn't know what to do."

"Show her whose rules she needed to abide, right?" I said, jabbing my finger up, pointing to the flat blue-violet sky, beyond it only a vacuum and dark matter and figments.

"Yes," she said. "Then she ran away. We all tried to find her. My dad more than anyone. It was a stressful time. He was trying to expand the church and move it to the location we're at now. But that didn't matter. This mattered to him."

But he had sent Emily down this road. I knew that much. His impersonation of God, his gift of shame. His influence over Daniella, over the Hsus, over the whole church at which Emily knew, irrevocably, she'd become unwelcome.

I started to say something, but she interrupted: "Look, it's fine. I don't need to know your thoughts. I've gone through my own process of grief, and study. I know my mind and heart about it, and more important, I know His heart."

There was no doubt about the pronoun this time, when there should have been at least a shadow of a doubt about everything she was saying.

"Through His holy Word, I know what God wants for me, and I'm at peace with it. What happened to me happens—happens a lot with young women, especially. You're figuring out love, and you're getting filled with these new desires, and you have this best friend, this person you share everything with, and it can get confused. It's not the worst thing. It's not unforgivable."

She sounded convincing, but I wasn't convinced. With enough fear and force of will, a person can build a structure in her mind that self-erects a foundation even in the murkier, subconscious floors below. But doing that doesn't eradicate the moles and earthworms and all the other sightless, subterranean beings nosing their way through the soil. It just pushes them deeper, spurs them to dig sideways and around. Sure, people experiment, have adolescent phases. But I didn't like what she was saying, the edge in her tone of voice, the rigidity of preconceived words: that what happened had happened to her—she had done nothing—but that what she'd been part of was not beyond the pale of God's forgiving and instructive hand, a hand that had pulled her back while it swatted Emily away.

"The man Emily is with now," Daniella said, "is something else entirely. And Emily is still out there. I know it. You know it. She needs to be protected from him."

But I was stuck on Lambert's choice, how he'd done it because having a gay daughter would hurt his plan to expand the multiplex—to get his face on more screens, to move more Hawaiian shirts than a

Tommy Bahama—a post–Chuck Smith version of the California dream.

"Your dad is no saint either," I said, enunciating slowly to keep my own feelings in check. She didn't respond, eyeing me blankly, so I pushed at it again: "He was afraid of what would happen to his church if someone found out he was a pastor with a lesbian daughter, is that it?"

"Maybe, but you're missing the point." Annoyance entered her voice. "Ultimately, spiritually and morally, I knew he was right, even if I struggled with it in my heart for a while. I left her stranded. She hasn't forgiven that, and I don't think she ever will. But I still want her to be safe, and to have a chance of a better life."

"And it has nothing to do with that," I said, pointing at the engagement ring she was rubbing at again like a diamond-encrusted worry stone.

She sighed, made a pained expression, looking briefly like the image of the Maria Dolorosa on Esme's candle. "Sure it does. When she showed up for the money, she saw I was engaged. I'm worried it opened up the wound all over again."

"And if anyone finds out about you helping her, maybe your story comes out, too. And maybe the fiancé balks. The support you get for this outreach, maybe people start to think it's misplaced. Who's going to give the Latino world a Coke if not you?"

She grimaced derisively. "Those are just a bonus because we have the volunteers and resources. There were another twenty people back there tutoring kids and college students, teaching reading and English, getting people plugged into social services. Only about a hundred combined hours of educational support for the community on a Sunday afternoon alone. But sure, the sodas are nice."

I hadn't asked for a promotional pamphlet. "God giveth diabetes, and God taketh it away with expensive prescription medications."

She scoffed. "I don't need you to understand what we stand for. That isn't why I'm talking to you. We're not of the world, but we work within it. Expecting someone from the outside to get it is like asking a fish to tell me about the feeling of flight."

"I get it more that you think," I said. "I'm a bit of a flying fish myself. I used to be a pastor. But I can tell you about growing some legs and evolving to walk on only two of them, too."

She had a cold directness when she spoke next, suggesting an analytical mind that wasn't going to let emotions goad it. That was deeply annoying. "Let's not get into your thoughts about *The Origin of Species*, okay? It's trite, it's beside the point, and it's not helping. Emily needs our help. I was hoping you could help her."

She rubbed at her temples, pulling the flesh around her eyes, revealing the raw red underlayer of flesh around the socket, then releasing it, a tricky tiny peep show of exposure and concealment. "The work you saw me doing back at the park, that work is the most important thing to me. One scandal can ruin a church. It would cancel out all the good we've done, and all the good I know we can still do. I can't lose that, on *behalf of those people*."

I knew what she said made a kind of sense, and maybe I could even admit that not everything she was doing was misguided, full of duplicitous intention, a surface veneer of help papered over the expanding sprawl of brick-and-mortar evangelization. But still I said, "Oh, I get it. Like father, like daughter."

She looked like she'd slap me. Then the hand just waved wind at my face, like she was shooing away a mosquito. "You're a real shit, you know?"

"Pretty sure Jesus cries at all the seven words you can't say on television."

"Jesus also knocked the money changers flat on their asses. I'm not standing up for my dad. I'm standing up for a community of people who've found real meaning. I'm standing up for a community of people committed to improving the quality of life in the whole border region, both sides of the fence. Maybe they sing songs to Jesus, and maybe you have a problem with that, but I'm not the grindstone for your old, dull ax. I'm a person who wants to help Emily. There's a monster out there who has been hurting her for years, and maybe he's doing it again right now. I can't help her myself, but that doesn't mean I'm not on Emily's side. I'm talking to you, for one." Her hands dropped into her lap and gripped each other, an echo of the gesture I'd seen after the church service. "I'm talking to you. Maybe that was a mistake. But I don't know where Emily is. Do you?"

"No."

"Right. So what we can do is make sure this guy—"

"Sammy."

Her words caught in her throat. "Who?"

"Sammy Ray Gans."

Now she studied me with a new kind of scrutiny, and it was the first time I'd really noticed how beautiful she was, oddly late for someone like me. It was a sign of something, not least of which how far ahead of me my brain had gotten, edging over a horizon of some kind. Her eyes were flecked with green. I could see why Emily would have swooned before this confluence of self-assurance and aesthetic good fortune.

"You know his name?" she asked.

"Flying fish," I said, pointing at my ugly mug. "He used to be one of my parishioners. His house is where I saw Emily two days ago. If everything you're telling me is true, if Emily would talk to the police or if you did—"

"I can't," she said, sounding remarkably firm on that point.

"You won't," I said. "Me telling a story won't do her any good. What do you expect me to do? Call the cops and say an anonymous person who says she knows Emily told me that Sammy was prostituting her out sometime in the past? But she won't talk to you. And I don't know where Emily is. And I have absolutely no evidence of any of this. They can't do a thing with that."

"But they could do something," she said, "with the stuff in his secret basement."

25.

DANIELLA SPELLED OUT EVERYTHING EMILY HAD TOLD HER. I MADE HER DO it twice. Under the floor of Sammy's garage was a secret room where drugs were stored, then sorted for distribution. It must have been well engineered for the detectives to have missed it, but Emily had sworn it was there. So Daniella's plan was a simple one: I get the police to find it, they find what they need to lock up Sammy for a long time. Then at least Emily would be a little safer, wherever she was.

"If she finds out he's in prison," Daniella was saying as we drove back to Chicano Park, "maybe she'll come out from wherever she's hiding. Maybe someone can get her the help she needs. But at least she'll be free of that." The last word was ambiguous, but I knew what it suggested.

"Right," I said. I wasn't satisfied. She'd told me a lot of things, and I was still sifting through them all in my mind. This plan was only a little drop of good in a sea of sorrow and abuse. Sammy had taken advantage of Emily, but she'd been taken advantage of long before that. Daniella had jettisoned her to stay in someone's imaginary good graces. Lambert was willing to take a few spiritual swings at a child, maybe because he truly believed it was God's will, but he was also willing to pay off the child, now grown up, and to lie to the police, which could only have reflected his own.

It was all in the service of expanding his pastoral plantation. I knew how those conversations worked, had been part of enough of them. The hoi polloi's five bucks in a collection basket would never add up. He was courting the big donors, the ones who could write the real checks. Since the 1950s, big business had been using the pulpit of purse strings to push a message on US churches, drawing a fat, shiny halo around individual liberty, hard work, and family values. The enemy? Communists, New Deal socialists, regulations, taxes—threats to the established order or at least to that order's ability to make products by whatever means necessary and keep us all aligned to the true Good of purchasing our way into progress. The individual was the only person in whom a conversion by God's grace was possible and through whose prosperity we could see a sign of God's approval. The state and any collective other than the church was considered a red pagan lure. Christian CEOs were apostles, sworn in to their self-appointed roles with one hand on the Bible and the other on *Think and Grow Rich*, and the checks they could write to fund churches were the letters of Paul to the Corinthians: a guide and, when withheld, a warning.

Protestants were predisposed to its libertarian message, especially the more evangelical churches that were hungry for coin. A new generation of believers rose up in wealth and privilege, or the certified potential for it, supposedly of one nation, supposedly under God—or at least since 1954, when it was added to the Pledge of Allegiance on a wave funded by the same corporations. They would use their largesse and spiritual wisdom to fund a new great awakening, one aligned with what they wanted to see, with what had made them paragons of success: self-help seminars and Ayn Rand fairy tales. It was still writ large in the style and substance of Canaan Hills.

But if anyone could make it—either in business or into Jesus's private booth in the celestial supper club—then finding enemies to rally the troops was harder. The communists were losing the Cold War, America was ascending. Red scares weren't frightening, weren't filling seats the way they used to. Who would they have turned on, if the gay rights movement wasn't ascendant, too? And who am I to deny that I was one of "them," who saw gays' emergence into public American life as a threat to our own? AIDS lent a providential touch. Men loving men or women loving women was as optional as being poor, and so the disease became a sign of God's opinion on the subject.

Even for leaders who disagreed, if your church took another position on the matter, you took yourself out of the running for the big donations. I wasn't better about any of this. We did nothing, right as AIDS was working its tragedy through the gay community, except draw our line in the sand and sign it "Love, Jesus." The donors lined up.

Our church still fed the homeless, sure. But we assumed they were there and we weren't because of things we were responsible for. They had been weak, susceptible to Satan's whispers, while we'd plugged up our ears and hummed, "Na-na-na." For gays and lesbians, we said we loved the sinner and hated the sin. We said our Christian way of life was under attack, that we wouldn't let them dictate our children's definitions of love and marriage. In truth, we needed to feel under attack, and we loved to hate the sin—loved it until it made us sick with pleasure, loved it so deeply we couldn't be bothered to parse the difference between sinner and sin on the chance that, somewhere in that difficult accounting, we might lose the object of our disgust—the thing that made us feel attacked, that gave us a sense of purpose clearer than love—and tumble into confusion ourselves.

Then I became a drunk, spent my own time sleeping on the street, got used to a bit of confusion. Everything looked different from the other side. For the first time I thought I was actually seeing what was in front of me, and not through this screen of gleeful certainty about the underpinnings of the world's workings, a screen that is actually a diagram on an opaque background—a diagram that, when seen from the right distance, is based in the golden proportions of a goddamn smiley face.

It was a framework certainly flourishing at Canaan Hills. They had clearly courted the big patrons. Gustafsson was one of them. The size of that church, the Tony Robbins–style polish on its presentation—all the rough theological corners sanded down and padded for the toddlers' delicate foreheads—made it clear he wasn't the only one. In my anger, I kept seeing Lambert's face more than the others. Among the others, though, surely was my own.

Daniella hit the turn signal. Over the tick-tick, she asked if I minded a quick stop. "I look like a mess," she said, craning to study her face in the rearview mirror.

I said it was no problem, I had nowhere I needed to be.

We parked at a Circle K. She went inside at the same time as a family entered the adjacent check cashing place, the biker guy coming out holding the door like a true gentleman.

I was going to confront Lambert. One moment I knew nothing, and the next I knew that, knew it with every dumb, collaborative, self-replicating cell in my unreasonable and unnecessary body. I'd forgotten what real knowledge felt like. My eyes were open. I was clear like running water, and as certain about where I was going next. I was capable, omnipotent.

I glanced through the plate glass of the Circle K's front window. No Daniella yet. I popped open her glove box and flipped through the papers. There were old receipts, printouts from maintenance records. I thought I'd found what I was looking for, but it was an apartment rental agreement—the future love nest in San Clemente, it seemed, home sweet home on Elena Lane—and Lambert wasn't a cosigner. But then I came to the proof of insurance card, and it showed Daniella as being under her father's plan. It listed his home address. I tore a piece from one of the maintenance records and wrote the address down, checking that Daniella wasn't coming as I scribbled. Then I forced everything back in and closed the compartment. I'd need to wait, but not long now.

A moment later Daniella emerged. Her freshly brushed hair was blown asunder again by the Santa Anas. But she'd washed her face, put on a new coat of makeup. She looked refreshed, ready to save the world, and able to.

"Ready to go?" she said as she dropped into the driver's seat.

Me, the passenger, I said, "Already gone."

26.

NEXT THING I KNEW I WAS HIDING ON A HILLSIDE BLANKETED WITH WILD mustard, crouching down in the yellow and green of everyone's favorite invasive species as it rocked in the hot, dry wind.

I hadn't blacked out. I wasn't having an episode, or a stroke, or a little bout of spirit possession. But I'd been so lost in my own mind, unselfconscious of its mechanics and unaware of any reason to apply doubt, that I wasn't really there when Daniella and I parted at Chicano Park and when I drove to Lambert's neighborhood. Each made only a fleeting impression in my memory. It should have been more of a concern, but I had only one, blotting out everything else in my field of vision.

Across from me, undeniably, was Lambert's house, a gaudily modest five-bedroom Colonial on a spacious lot on Mount Helix. Of course Mount Helix was where Lambert had settled himself. The high property values were one thing, and the towering views over the plebeian tract homes and strip malls were another. But the massive white cross on the peak of the mountain, just a short way above his home, was the clincher. When I was a Christian, these monumental crucifixes didn't register. They were background noise, unremarkable. Now they seemed aggressive. It was hard not to see a shadow of their original purpose in them, hard not to imagine pierced and rotting corpses affixed to each. These were meant as a warning to the living, a little parable of who had the power and who did not. The ghost corpses were Jesus's now, not those of Roman criminals, but the crosses were still putting the public on notice: you're on Christian land now, and we don't fuck around.

The crucifix on Mount Helix had the added benefit of being on government land. This being San Diego, the government saw no problem with that, which had led to years of controversy and ACLU legal action. It ended not with the cross being removed but with the government parklands being handed over to a private foundation. So this couldn't have been a more fitting place for Lambert to live than if he'd built the mountain himself—a folksy Christian pharaoh's crucifix-tipped Prince Albert of a phallic pyramid.

Daniella's yellow Volvo was out front. That was why I'd driven past and parked a few streets down, where the road curved around and down the mountain. I'd taken off my father's jacket and tie, as hike ready as I could get. Climbing up a hillside in shirtsleeves and slick-bottomed leather shoes was rough going, and I kept slipping down. Each step ground loudly on the rocky soil, meaning I was about as stealthy as a maraca player. I couldn't help thinking of creeping up on Sammy's house, seeing him watering his plants in the blasted-out Ramona heat. I was making a habit of this. But I wasn't ready to go cold turkey either.

I don't know how long I waited in the bushes. I didn't have anything to mark the time by. I wasn't even exactly sure what I was waiting for. But eventually the garage door opened, and an SUV backed out. Daniella was in the passenger seat now. The older woman driving was clearly her mother. They had the same black hair, but the mother had deep, Italian eyes, angular features, and bright makeup. Going to pick out bridal veils, maybe, or the pure white sheet with a slit in it that would serve as the bridal lingerie and a clear canvas for virginity consummated.

I waited another two minutes, in case a forgotten chastity belt brought them back to the house. They stayed gone. I picked my way out of the mustard, jumped the low wooden fence onto the asphalt, and walked across the street.

The driveway gave out onto a peony-bordered front walk of pink-stained concrete. If treacle could be a pathway, this was it. The front door was red with a silver knocker in the shape of a fish. I knocked. Then I pounded the fish's ignorant little head against the plate a few times. It felt good, so I kept doing it, cracking its dull metal skull again and again, waiting for it to multiply to feed the five thousand or for its prehistoric face to devolve a few more generations.

The fish pulled away from my hand when the door wrenched open. I heard Lambert before I saw him, his muffled voice crankily saying, "What, what, what?" Then his face was there, and he registered mine.

"I'm more interested in how," I said, stepping up onto his imported tile floor. I took his shirt in my hands. I gave it one big jerk, pulling in more fabric, and then began walking him backward.

He scrambled to keep his legs under himself. I wasn't really seeing the house, only potential tripping hazards, options. The hallway went through a living room and past a kitchen. It was bright with natural light, airy and white walled, relaxed, like he'd been expecting the photographer from *San Diego Home/Garden*.

I tripped on a rug. To correct for it, I pushed against Lambert, making him fumble backward faster. It wasn't enough to help me regain my balance, so I let go of him to catch myself on the kitchen island. The granite countertop caught me in the gut instead, and the air sucked out of my lungs.

Lambert seemed to get his heels under himself for one, two steps, just far enough that when he fell, he fell ass first into the sliding glass door to the backyard. The single sheet of safety glass erupted in a spider's web of fissures, flexed under his weight, and then crumbled into a thousand individual pieces as his body passed through. The sound the pieces made on the concrete was like an enormous crystal chandelier caught in a sharp, brief cross-breeze. Lambert made a different sound: half-dropped sandbag and half-rutting sea lion.

I picked myself up and wheezed a couple thin breaths of air into my lungs. Then I stepped out the hole where the door had been. Lambert was just turning onto his side. There were spots of red on the back of his pale shirt, points where the safety glass had only been so safe. None looked too bad. He wasn't mortally injured. So I rolled him back into the position of a stuck turtle and knelt over him. He didn't say anything, but his mouth opened and closed like the fish he was descended from, probably only one generation back on his father's side. His dull, scared eyes watched mine, read my face like holy writ for a clue about my intentions. I liked the feeling, liked his fear and trembling.

"What is it you want?" he asked, trying to hide the quaver in his voice.

"Still the wrong question," I said, feeling the words slur out of my mouth. My head swirled from lost oxygen, adrenaline, and exertion—from rage, self-hatred, disordered brain chemistry. "How. How could you do what you did to Emily? How do you go on living with yourself?"

He understood right away. Still, a man of God is a creature of hope. He tried quirking his eyes, contorting his mouth into an uncomprehending grimace. "I don't—"

I watched calmly but without understanding as my hand pulled back from his face. My fist had opened up a grisly split in one of his fat lips. The expression on his face changed. He knew why I was here now, wasn't going to pretend.

"You lied," I said, then lost my balance and braced myself by planting one arm on his chest. He let out an *oof*. "You lied to me. You lied to her. You told her God thought she was wrong, was worthy of hell for who she was. And you *used* her."

"You don't understand," he said quickly. The act of speaking seemed to steady him further. The regret or sadness that tugged on his features vanished when he spoke. The pain of the cuts on his back didn't register in his voice. He was a good actor, a professional preacher, face muscles that could bench three-hundred and open a beer bottle with nothing but a dimple. Speaking was his way of control, his lifeblood. I didn't want to let him have it, kept taking it away.

"I understand perfectly. If you showed any weakness, any soft stance on the big issues, the guys who could save you with the financial ones would back out. Guys like Gustafsson. Right?"

"The Bible is clear—"

"You and I both know the Bible is as clear as a brick. We're not talking about the Bible. We're talking about Emily. A person you shunned. Emily, who's out there right now, hiding from a drug dealer, from someone who has abused and taken advantage of her. Emily, who you paid to disappear again." Lambert started to yammer something, but I plowed on. "Don't interrupt me. And stop lying to me. You don't even need to explain how you could have done it. I know how. You're a coward. Greedy. Proud. Thinking you're the rooster when you're just the chickenshit. So you throw a few shekels at your problem to make her—*her*—go away."

I took my arm off his breadbasket and stood up. It felt like every ounce of blood coursing through me had pooled in my eyes, stewed in the late afternoon heat, and was now pouring back into all the parts of my cold, mechanical body.

Lambert had been holding his head up while I spoke. Now he let it fall, thudding against the concrete. He closed his eyes, groaned, then opened them again. "I'm sure you've never made a hard decision in your life—an impossible decision," he said. He wasn't looking at me. He was looking straight up. The setting sun stained the sky, dust and smog ridden, stirred up by the wind and heat. There were a few insubstantial high clouds passing westward. I wondered if Lambert was hoping a bearded face, pale and not too unlike his own, was looking down from that cloud—was listening, watching. "I had confessed it to God, worked out my atonement. Then she came back. I saw how low the Lord had brought her."

"No editorializing," I said.

He pressed his eyes hard with his fingers. I wished he were using pins. "She wanted money. She said it was for rehab. I meet people all the time who are ready to turn over a new leaf, and she didn't sound like them. She wasn't hungry and glad to be hungry, the way they are. But I didn't see another way, so I gave her the money."

Everything seemed to darken a degree. It wasn't the sun's recession. It was me, my mind, something in my devices of perception. A visual depression. Something to match what I was seeing, what I was hearing, how I felt. "You could have helped her," I said. "Why couldn't you get her set up with her parents again?"

"I couldn't," he said, now looking away, off to a corner of his yard. He didn't say anything for a while. His body spasmed against itself, like he might lose his composure. But he regained it, depressingly. "You don't understand. I had seen—God showed it to me—that I could help hundreds, thousands, with Canaan Hills. It was my purpose on this earth. I owed it to those people. But she could have stopped it all. I couldn't do that to the others and to those I can still do good for. I couldn't throw it away."

"You should have," I said, shifting in such a way that I knew my body wanted to kick him in the side. His must have registered the slight movement because he groaned and grimaced, curling up on himself like a bug on hot concrete. I stopped short. I was proud of my restraint, my belated mercy.

"God would have wanted you to throw all that away to take care of that one girl," I said. "I hope that's what haunts you on your deathbed." He flinched again, seeming to think I was about to make that day today. I let him think about it a long time, then added, "Whenever that day comes."

I began to walk away, studying the pattern of broken glass at my feet. Immediately I was aware of some shape or order in it, but the pattern kept slipping away into my peripheral vision, refusing to be seen or given sense.

He pulled himself up. His feet ground glass into the concrete. The thin, high screech was like a car's brakes about to go out. "That's it?" he asked.

I stopped and looked at him hard. He was frightened, relieved, confused, guilt ridden. As he should be, as I'd wanted him to be. "That's it," I said. "I wanted you to know you weren't the only one who knew what you'd done. I know. And I'm not the type to think of you as a vessel for God's work."

Now I felt cold in my fingertips and hands. This inner chill was at war with the heat still lingering from the day's Santa Ana, and it left me uneasy, nauseated. I started walking again. It was then I looked up and saw him, framed in broken glass still clinging to the door frame: a boy, ten years old or so. Frozen, eyes darting from his father to me. The plastic dinosaur he held clattered to the ground as we made eye contact.

My stomach yawed, pitched over an edge. His hair was cut short, front plastered up with gel. His skin was a shade darker than his father's, but his eyes were Lambert's. He stood perfectly still, afraid to move and break his witness. I gave him as much room as I could as I stepped through the broken sliding glass door. As I did, I wobbled sideways and my shoulder shook loose a few more pieces of crumbled glass. A little blood began to leech through my dress shirt. Not enough to think twice about.

A vice cinched down around my temples. There was seawater up to my nose. I felt like I was drowning, like I was drunk. This time, I walked through the house and saw it. Clean and comfortable. At the ready for family movie night or a glass of wine with old friends. Cherry-scented candles in fucking alcoves. I went out the front door, closed it behind me, and walked across the street, into the mustard, and down the hill. I retched once then, at the base of a Cleveland sage. The scents mixed and made me feel worse. Feeling worse felt good.

I stood, unmoving, for a long time. The sun was setting in the west, catching the weeds and dust with its hot, orange light. Long shadows trailed from the coyote bushes. Clouds of gnats buzzed in the pollen haze. Dusk was falling, making everything go fuzzy and soft. All of it was being lost prematurely, in the dark, to places where human eyes couldn't manage. How had it gotten so late? How had these days gone past as they had? What days? I wondered. How many? I couldn't enumerate the answer, didn't know—the last nine or nine thousand?—and what did it matter anyway since those days were gone, part of all the oblivion.

So I walked on until I reached my truck. Then I drove slowly, with shaking hands, down the road that ran along the eastern side of

Mount Helix. I saw, in my mind more than with my eyes, how that crucifix above me lay down its long shadow on the neighborhoods below. Even its shadow, though, would disappear in the darker, more encompassing one of the mountain itself. As I drove, this larger shadow cast itself upon my truck, stretched out across the valley, and would settle over all of us as night, until the earth made another turn. Even my faith in that fact of rotation was unsettled. I doubted the dawn.

27.

IT WAS A LONG, DARK DRIVE BACK NORTH ON THE HIGHWAY. THE REST OF humanity and I streamed along with our headlights on, like we knew where we were going.

The road kept threatening to run in reverse on me, the way patterns at high speed can. I kept thinking about Lambert, and his kid watching. I felt my brain clawing at some black box of redacted memories, the ones of when I must have decided I'd had enough and swallowed a palmful of pills. When I was drunk enough and depressed enough to forget that Aracely was in the house. There was only that one moment I could see, the only one my brain had decided to keep around: my little girl, ruffles on her cotton pajama shorts, legs tucked up to her body, placing the phone back in the cradle. While I was wheeled away and the world wheeled into blackness again. I could only guess the rest, rely on secondhand reports, no memories of my own to go on.

That day hadn't been the only time I'd considered suicide. I knew that much. The possibility had bubbled up into my brain often enough after Ellen had done it. She had made the unthinkable more than only thinkable for herself, and so how could I not think it, too. And then there was this: that either God existed and my sister's soul was burning, damned; or Ellen was simply gone, and God was an illusion. For the longest time I was forced to sift myself between those two impossible weights. Alcohol lubricated the process, made it easier. The love of my family made it worse. Gabby's love meant worry over my eternal salvation. Not Ellen's—I was alone with hers, which for the others was already foreclosed and final. Then I drank myself insensible one night, and whoever of me was left wasn't afraid and wasn't beholden to anyone. Even then, before I realized belief was lost to me, I'd turned to death and not God. But death failed me, too. Gabby had found me on the couch early that morning. She thought I was only passed out, and she went to the neighbor's, a member of her small group, asking what she could possibly do—what she *should* do. The pills made me sick, the way they are intended to. Aracely must have heard me in the bathroom. She woke in her bed, walked her little body down the hall, and found me, deranged and semiconscious, and made the call that was all I could remember. And still I ran away from them and their concern—from her and Gabby, my parents, anyone who knew me—resented it, pushed it away. Any kind of love.

What had Gabby said to me when I spoke to her the night Mike was killed? That I was everything bad Aracely was afraid she was capable of. This was why: not only the attempt to end myself, but everything on either side. The drunken rages. The disappearances for days. The instability. The swift dismissal of God. And then, even after I was sober, the inability to want anything other than to be left alone, unasked for, unrequired. It was who I was, who was left. There had been nothing to do but live with that. Impossible. But there wasn't another choice.

A glowing, angled arrow appeared in the sky on the horizon—

the sign for In-N-Out, as good a symbol as I could hope for, which meant I was back in Oceanside. I got off the freeway and headed for home. I would do what Daniella had asked me to do. Get Sammy arrested. It's what he'd always needed, what he'd gotten from church at one point in his life. In the morning I'd call Tuitele and Lawrence. All I wanted was a little sleep first. I hadn't slept in days except for a half drowse here or there or a few hours on a jailhouse cot.

It felt good to be driving up Ditmar Street, off the freeway and in a familiar neighborhood, one that made sense to me. I knew who lived in these houses. Not personally, but I thought I understood. I swung the truck into my own driveway and stepped out. The clack of my dress shoes on the concrete made my heart jump; during the drive I'd forgotten I was wearing my father's clothes. As I walked up the driveway, there was a shiver buried in my spine from the sound of this tap dance on the concrete. Maybe it was the memory of my father's wood-heeled click, coat slung over one arm, on the way to the front door. Now I made my way to mine. I'd left the coat in the car. It could wait until the morning, too.

The bougainvillea scratched at the front window in the dry wind. It felt like the branches were scratching at the insides of my eyes. I pushed my key into the front-door lock. Instead of metal biting against metal, the entire door pushed in, opening onto a blue-dark living room.

The darkness quavered as I wondered what was inside and why my door was open. I was more bummed out than keyed up. I felt more depressed than angry. I hadn't expected it, but I did not feel surprised.

I snaked one hand in, flicked the light switch, and jumped back. For a few moments, I flattened myself against the garage door. No one emerged. No gunshots rang out. All was quiet. I went back and listened at the door. No sound, no movement. I kicked it open and jumped into the bougainvillea. The paranoia building in my brain smelled off, like old meat, like religion, and I didn't like it. I told myself that I must have just not shut the thing all the way. At least it was late enough that not many neighbors would have seen me run away from my own front door.

Still, I was afraid to step into my living room and stay there. It took resolve, and when I did, the room wasn't recognizable, not in the way I expected. I saw my *National Geographics*, but instead of being on the bookshelf, they were piled loosely on the ground with the bookshelf resting on top of them. The TV was on its side, on the carpet. Balls of stuffing from the couch cushions were drifting around the room in the cross-breeze like small, weightless rabbits. It looked like a crackhead had used my place for a DIY Build-A-Bear Workshop.

Sammy. Or whomever Sammy reported to. That's who had done this. His warning rang in my ears as if he'd just said it: leave Emily alone, or else the people he worked for would kill me. I looked in the kitchen. The fridge door was open and my carefully accumulated selection of condiments was shattered on the ground. The coffeepot, my closest friend, hadn't survived either. I checked the bedroom next. The bed was still made, and for a moment I was stupidly hopeful, though of what I couldn't say. Then I smelled the piss. The bed was soaking in it. The bathroom mirror was shattered, making an incomplete mosaic of bullshit on the floor.

In my office, someone had taken the time to pull my old theology books from the closet. They looked exhausted, half-opened and in loose piles, having humped one another all over the floor. Was this how a criminal sent a message? It seemed so unfocused and haphazard. Still, fear and adrenaline flushed through the rusted-out septic leech lines of my system.

Then, from out front, I heard car doors shutting. My body locked up and became one giant ear. There was the sound of steps on pavement. Whoever did this had been waiting for me. I knew it in a single flash, like a sudden convert under the hand of the televangelist. And now they were coming in.

I didn't stop to think. Instead, I ran. First to the kitchen, yanking on the sliding door and wondering why it wouldn't open. Then I remembered to flick the stupid little mechanical latch. I stepped out into the yard and shut the door, gently, soundlessly, and listened again. There was a party a few blocks over, sending a bass line my way. The traffic noise was steady, easily relegated to background noise. I didn't hear anything else.

Time was what I needed. Time to think and get the police after Sammy. If his people were after me, that wouldn't necessarily solve my problem, but if they were after me, then they were certainly after Emily. I couldn't just knock on the neighbors' door and ask to use their phone, dragging the Rosas into this mess, too. From the dark yard, the view of my well-lighted house through the windows could have been of any regular suburban home. Of course, in my head "regular suburban home" suggested a small but content middle-class family, which was something my own home had never known—was, in fact, an endangered species except as an idea, the gray wolf of American life.

Then I stepped onto the desiccated corpse of a palm tree I'd let die years ago and jumped the wooden fence into my neighbors' yard. It was strange to stand on the Rosas' grass, in the dark and uninvited. I'd always envied their white hammock, bolted to the trellis posts. In the dark there was less to envy. I tried to climb the fence opposite the one I shared with them, but there was nothing to get a foothold on. In a little garden patch was a two-foot-tall gnome with a pervert's grin and his finger pointed toward the sky. I grabbed him by the neck, set him by the fence. His oblong hat was just enough of a step to get me over.

With every fence I crossed, each new yard became a little less strange to enter. Then I reached the end of the block. From there, I skulked along the black-and-orange streets until I came to Pacific Coast Highway. There was still a lot of traffic, and I felt like a fool waiting for the crosswalk signal—a fool who'd get shot in the back because he stopped, midescape, to obey traffic law.

When the light turned, I ran with my head down and kept running. A hooker smoking in the red-and-green neon light of the Dolphin Hotel's inverted L sign shouted at me, "Slow down, baby. Enjoy yourself."

For that moment only, it still felt good to be home. Everything else was panic and fear.

28.

I WAS WINDED WHEN I REACHED OCEANSIDE STATION A COUPLE BLOCKS farther down. It wasn't really a station. It was a small cinder-block office, some automated ticket machines, a few awnings, and six shitters. There was a Burger King and a few refrigerated boxes that would give you a candy bar or a soda for a handful of quarters. The birds-of-paradise, oversaturated in the lamplight, were huddled in clumps and cowering. A homeless guy sitting on a planter fumbled furiously with what I hoped was his zipper. People used to meet in train stations, have lunch or a drink at them, flirt with counter girls, run away with alluring women and mysterious men. But you can't get a smile from a machine, and besides the scattered waiting passengers, the most mysterious man appeared to be perfectly content with himself.

The timetable showed a southbound Metrolink coming in twenty minutes. I lined up, bought a ticket from the machine, and was content to be surrounded by so much human indifference.

I paced while I waited, keeping an eye on every person in the area. It was a quiet night. Most of the business commuters had come and gone. I was left with some scattered gothic teenagers, a few domestics ending late shifts, a couple more homeless people, and a few wandering Burger King wrappers.

The sound of the ocean, only a few blocks away, was loud, a solid booming rumble every couple minutes. The waves had to be big. The surf report had been my most important news source for so long, and now a tropical storm must have come up in the south while I was distracted. Distracted by other people, their bullshit business, their nonsense. I tried to tell myself that, but I knew it wasn't true. I'd been distracted for just about my whole miserable life.

Then there was a bang. I spun around, already expecting to have a new orifice in a part of my body that didn't need one. A maintenance worker picked up the heavy domed trash can lid he'd dropped and put it back where it belonged.

Soon the train was grinding its brakes from the direction of San Clemente. When it stopped, I climbed in and took a seat on the short mezzanine level at the end of the car. Tucked in one corner, I had a view of who would come up the stairs from the lower level or down them from above. If I needed to, I could run in the opposite direction, never forgetting my security guard instincts. A vagabond of an old woman snored in the seat across the aisle. Soon we were moving again, skimming through neighborhoods, voyeurs gazing into the backs of houses bright like lanterns in the dark. These were where those normal families lived, in their normal houses, little places worth maybe a million dollars, even though they backed onto the tracks. Just single-family places, you know, in safe neighborhoods. A good value.

Vagabond grandma woke up and began searching through her bag. "Old goal, old goal, old goal," she said. I was being chased, possibly about to be murdered, for poking my nose into some kind of trouble, all because I'd been friendly with some hitchhiking lesbian Christian. The idea of me being the crazier of the two of us in this train car helped me hold it together. Then the woman hooted victoriously and pulled out an enormous bag of pretzels, Rold Golds. At least she knew what she wanted.

The train rolled across the trestle over the Agua Hedionda Lagoon, the same one I'd seen going to Mike's funeral with Esme. That was yesterday, in the daylight, with fog rolling in. It looked different in the clear, dark night. It felt like a decade had passed. Some hormone pulsed through my body. I didn't care which. Someone was trying to kill me. And Emily: I had assumed she'd left my place by choice, but now it seemed like she'd been taken. They knew where I lived. Sammy said I'd die if I did anything to help her, so she was important to him. She'd been seen at the beach with me, around Oceanside.

I would be fine at my parents' old house, at least long enough that the police could locate Sammy. There should have been a sense of strangeness to all this—there having been men at my house, tearing it apart, waiting to tear me apart, going into hiding—but I felt none of it. I was focused on what to do, clear on what that was. I had an absurd faith in the next step.

It was around midnight when I got off in Encinitas. The wind whipped hot on my sweaty neck like dog's breath, if the dog and I were in a microwave set to ten. The 7-Eleven wasn't more than a block out of my way, and I stopped there. Because of the time of night and its proximity to a dive bar, which I'd frequented in earlier days, there were fake ID–bearing brosephs fucking around out front. Best I could tell they were taking turns punching one another in the dick. I tried to ignore them, plugged some money in the phone, and got through to the Ramona Substation. When I asked the dispatcher if she could put me through to either Tuitele or Lawrence, she told me it was my lucky night.

"Why?"

"Street racer caused a three-car accident on the 67. Two fatalities. Tuitele's here."

"That doesn't make me feel lucky," I said.

"Tell that to the baby in the back seat of one of the vehicles. Not a scratch. Hold, I'll put you through."

My cup of grief was full, and I tried to put the thought of this fresh tragedy out of my mind. Thankfully, it didn't take long for Tuitele to pick up.

"Can I help you?" he said in a tone that clearly meant he'd rather do anything else.

"This is Mark Haines," I said.

"Oh, really," he said. The tone had changed. He was listening in a different way, like he'd been expecting to hear from me. I wasn't sure that was a good thing. "That's interesting. You know what else is interesting? Finding out that you're running around town pretending to be one of us. I told you to let us do our job. That doesn't mean *do* our job. If you need to know, my job right now involves making some unpleasant next-of-kin calls and treating a toasted white kid who had a little too much fun in his dropped Chevy Cavalier with more dignity than I'd like. So finding out some drunk old-timer seems to have forgotten impersonating a cop is a crime, that's not something I really want to deal with."

I didn't need to check any guilt or anger or resentment. That should have been a bad sign—the lack of fear or sense of consequences, the missing typical self-protection and self-hatred. "Beside the point," I said. "There's something you need to know."

"Wrong," he said. "There's something *you* need to know. You're looking pretty suspicious from where we sit. So why don't you tell me how you were involved in Michael Padilla's death. Why don't you tell me how long you've been in business with Sam Gans. Because those are the only things I want to hear."

He hadn't included assaulting a pastor in his own home. That was good, at least for now. It would take only so long, though, for a line to reach that dot, too. "That's not what I have to say, but I don't think you're going to be disappointed."

Tuitele didn't say anything for a moment. At first I thought he was debating taking the bait and changing topic, but no. They were tracing the call, probably. He just needed to stall for time. Time was what I didn't have, so I spoke up unrequested: "You need to go back to Sammy's house, to his garage. Start digging around. He's got a secret room under the floor, and that's where he runs the drug operation from."

"Oh, yeah?" Tuitele sounded happy to mock the lead I'd given them. "And you know this because you've got a key to it, too? Were you behind the camera on that video of the chick in the bikini smashing a dog's head with a brick? You manage the archive of kiddie porn?"

"No. I didn't have anything to do with the drugs or that laptop. And I didn't have anything to do with Mike. But promise me you'll have someone look at the garage. I don't know exactly where the entrance is, but it's hidden in that garage."

"Only if you promise to stay right where you are until one of our guys comes to pick you up. We need to talk to you some more."

"Sorry, now's no good," I said, and hung up. The change hidden in the pay phone jingled. They'd probably finished tracing the call anyway, so I left. Behind me, four young men held their injured dicks in front of the 7-Eleven, laughing like it was a good thing. People needed something better to do with themselves. People probably included me.

29.

WHEN I LET MYSELF INSIDE MY PARENTS' HOUSE, THE LILAC AND LAVENDER scent wrecked me, completely, for a split second. Then I walked my body like a pet zombie to the bed and fell onto the blankets. The smell left me worse than wrecked there, but I was too tired to care. Unfortunately, I was too starved for calories to sleep, and my brain did some diabetic laps thinking about Emily and about Sammy. How I'd come into each of their lives. How we had churches between us.

That was one way Emily could end up with someone like Sammy. His little crew of miscreants at my old soul-stomping grounds were church kids. A lot of those kids were tourists, attending different services around the county like they were putting together a religious Zagat guide. It wasn't hard to imagine Emily, a little younger, angry and blasphemous, ending up with them, ending up with Sammy. Their way of speaking and thinking would have been familiar, even if the words and deeds had different ends.

My head was thrumming, all thin atmosphere where I'd expected something breathable. My skin grew cold and fishlike with chilled, anxious sweat. Outside it was still dark. The clock showed a little after two in the morning, so I got up and tried to drink some tap water. Nothing came out.

On my way back to the bedroom, I stopped in front of Ellen's door. What would she make of all this? I didn't know—and if I didn't know, I didn't want to guess. Most of my childhood I'd spent trying to guess what she was thinking, mimic and hem my way into her thoughts and world. There's a strip of film somewhere, of a diving contest at the lake my parents would take us to each summer: Ellen makes up dive—a wounded swan, the Thinker, the false belly flop—then I, creatively, do the same one, and do it worse. Even in play, at tennis courts and shopping malls, in the music she sent home from college—she was the shadow I felt safe in. Then I stepped out at a certain point, made my own shadow, didn't run from it. I wondered less and less about what she would think, and then, before I even realized it, she was gone, never to darken my door again. Then I tried that same vanishing act, and again I couldn't live up to her example.

Her life had taken a couple rough turns, those last years. A fiancé had broken things off. Then she switched churches, then again. Said she was looking for the right fit. She was looking for an ideal impossible to find on earth. But every time I talked to her, it was the same unshakable Ellen, so I didn't worry—didn't think I had the need to, and I was too busy anyway. The last time I saw her, we got coffee and talked about my money problems. Then we saw a forgettable action movie—my choice—and said see you later with a quick wave. I didn't know. So many things I didn't know. The drinking started then, the anger at my family. It only took a year to disassemble my life, brick by brick.

I paced the hallway awhile to clear my head. That didn't work. I fitfully read one of my father's old business books, which was better. The principles in them were so clear, the steps to success so linear, almost unavoidable, that they had a narcotic effect. That the steps were unsuitable for most and impossible for the rest, I knew. These books were more like comics, or any Harrison Ford film: in them even the most outlandish was claimed as an attainable possibility. Who wouldn't want that? After an hour or so, I sure as hell didn't. But it had killed a bit more time at least.

And it got me thinking about Gustafsson. These books were bibles to a man like that, but he seemed to have his nose in the capital *B* one, too. I didn't know if his name was on the deed to Canaan Hills, filled with its spirit of consumption and comfort, but his name was high up on their donor wall, and his heavy hand was in their books. He probably owned my house, somehow, without me knowing it. I didn't like how he connected Emily to me, too—indirectly, sure, but his presence drew a circle from the place where Emily lost her faith to the fabrication shop where Mike lost his life.

But Gustafsson wasn't the problem, I tried to remind myself. Or at least he was the problem in a larger, more universal sense only. I was on the run from Sammy. I was trying to protect Emily from Sammy. I hoped that what Daniella had told me was true. If the police didn't find a basement full of drugs, if Sammy didn't get locked up, I didn't like imagining what that would mean. The room had to be well camouflaged if the cops hadn't seen it the first time.

Then I remembered going into the machine shop, the night Mike was killed. There were people there, shuffling around in the dark. They were moving heavy machinery. The sound of it was earsplitting, but the detective who questioned me said nothing had been stolen. Whatever they'd moved had been put back. Maybe it was just a new iteration of paranoia, but I couldn't explain it away as hunger or exhaustion: maybe there was a similar kind of hidden bunker or compartment in the shop, one that those supposed burglars used for a very different kind of job. Maybe something had been taken, just not anything the shop owner would have missed. I couldn't shake the thought. If anything, it became only more insistent, more committed.

The hunger and exhaustion had me thinking strangely. I had to admit that as a possibility, as is my way, but I couldn't believe it. I couldn't sleep, but I could resolve the other problem. I walked the few blocks to the corner market. The offshore wind of the Santa Ana was increasing in speed, obliterating any drop of humidity, whipping up a helium head rush in my brain. The streetlamps were on, and the sodium light caught all the dirt in the air. Palm fronds crackled like sails. I threaded through parked cars, windows glinting dimly orange with the grime of baked-on salt air.

At the store I bought eggs, butter, bread, and coffee. Back at the house, I dug out the old camping gear from the garage. I set up the propane stove on the kitchen table, boiled a pot of water, and made three quarts of cowboy coffee. Then I set a pan on the stove and melted butter on it. Sweet cream overwhelmed the floral, motherly smells of the house. I fried two eggs. With no toaster, I used a couple forks to dangle two slices of bread over the burner and then buttered them.

I ate the food and drank two cups of coffee while standing at the kitchen window. Everything out there was unknowable, black shapes on black, except for how I could draw on my memories to make a map of the space, a ghost image: the love seat on the patio, the detached garage at the back of the property, the gravel pathways in the miniature rose garden, gone to seed now but not as I saw it, trimmed and lush and brilliant with color. I wasn't hungry anymore, and the idea of checking out the machine shop hadn't lost any of its pull. It was connected to everything else. I'd need to make another call, not to the cops this time. Esme knew the situation with Mike and how I was a little off the rails, and she was the night dispatch for the security firm. I called her instead.

I opened the garage door by hand. There was a little light coming from the alley, not much, and I heard the rats scurrying. Inside was my mother's 1965 Chevy Nova, dull and dusty. But the keys were still on a hook by the door, and I reattached the battery terminals. Of course, there wasn't any juice to turn over the engine. But the alley had a good slope, so I put the car in neutral, got it rolling out of the garage, and was able to push-start it before I hit the city street. The Nova ran rough, on some old and no doubt sedimentary gas, I'm sure. But it would get me around for a while, and that's all I cared about.

In the middle of the night, the red marble accents on North County Security's exterior looked like massive, geometric scabs. The building was in a quiet corner of industrial zoning, and the closest streetlamp was out, so I could wait in the shadows. An unmarked back door opened. Esme paused, hair pulled back again, silhouetted against the bright interior. I could see her where she stood in the light, but by standing in the light, she couldn't see me here in the shadows. There was some kind of metaphor in that, but I wasn't thinking in metaphors—these thoughts were becoming purer than metaphors.

"Mark?" she called in a whisper.

"Over here."

She walked quickly, her sneakers sucking up mud in some overwatered grass. But she slowed down when she got near me and kept some objective distance between us. She held the ring of keys in one hand, but she was making a point of not passing them over.

"I want you to tell me again," she said firmly, "while I can look at you."

"Esme," I said, sighing. Even as far apart as we were, the vanilla scent of whatever was in her hair made me ache. But everything ached, and aches didn't matter, and Esme's worry didn't matter, her concern about what I was doing with myself, doing to myself. None of that mattered. "I already told you—"

"Seeing you now," she interrupted, "I'm not sure you're alright. I don't want to be a part of you doing something stupid. Something stupider than what you normally do anyway."

"It's what I said before." The story I'd come up with rolled off the tongue easily enough. "I can't sleep. I keep thinking of Mike, keep seeing what happened to him. I was right there but I didn't see it, and I keep trying to picture it. To picture what I would have done."

Here's where I turned on the showmanship. A little less breath, bringing my voice down into more of a chest tone, inserting the right pauses—in the key of overwhelming but barely repressed emotion. Then I could secure myself from her doubt through a jab of guilt-inducing accusation: "You weren't there. You don't know. You have no idea how . . . what this . . . what this did, or what this has done. To me." Now it was time to hang my head, turn, look away, take a few breaths.

"I don't expect it to make a whole hell of a lot of sense," I continued, steadier now but still threatening to give out, "but I just need to see the place. The place where he died. Only having memories to go back to is driving me crazy. And you know Watt wouldn't let me anywhere near the complex."

Esme pursed her lips and appraised me. "This is a mistake," she said. For a moment I thought I'd misread her. "Your doing this. I don't think it'll give you what you want. But it's important to you, I see, so let's give it a chance." She passed me the key ring. The warmth of her fingertips brushing against my palm was brief and then gone. The weight of the keys was cold and familiar and lasting.

She took a step toward me, and I started away from her, just slightly. She was going to hug me, I saw, but she'd read my quick retreat and let that go. "I've already notified the on-duty guys that the owner has someone doing some early a.m. work. You should be good, but don't tell them who you are. On second thought, don't talk to them at all. If Watt finds out—"

"I know," I said. "I don't want to make your life harder." Even that tasted as thin and flavorless as communion bread on my tongue, as empty of any human or spiritual content beyond a few bland carbohydrates.

She rubbed the back of her neck and sighed, looking at me so kindly I almost felt it. "A little harder isn't a bad thing, if it helps you. I'm not expecting life to go so easy on me. But I'd like to avoid going on unemployment. So don't get caught."

"It will help," I said. "More than you could know."

"I hope so," she said. "Even if I'm not counting on it."

30.

AT CARLSBAD PALMS NORTH, I STEPPED OUT OF THE CAR AND THE WIND HIT me hard. I'd been sweating, I discovered—sweating obscenely. My shirt clung to my back and, despite the heat of the air, was as cold as cast iron.

I was in the same lot where the ambulance had been parked, where that detective told me Mike had been killed. Maybe even the same spot. I couldn't remember for sure. I remembered the glaring morning sun and how basically my injuries were tended to. I heard the detective's voice: *This whole shit show doesn't get up and running for a piddly B&E.* But seeing where everything was, where everyone had been, that was harder for some reason. The sweat and the wind got a rattle working in my jawbone.

I wasn't sweating because I was afraid of getting caught. In all likelihood, this was the safest place for me outside of a padded cell. It was because of Mike. Returning here meant seeing the place where his life ended—not "his life," as if he still existed and his life were one of a number of things he could possess and misplace, but where *he* ended. He hadn't been on my mind while I drove, but the idea of him must have been in it: worrying the synaptic gaps, drifting among the clefts' chemical dark matter—an invisible, ineradicable presence in the dead air. Something in my lie to Esme must have been like most lies: ashamed truth peeking out from under the bedsheet.

I'd parked close to the machine shop. No guards appeared while I walked across the lot. Some memory lingered right below the surface, of walking around similar lots and abandoned streets, at similarly ungodly hours, only run through with the sour tang of inebriation and a kind of dark wish for some evil or accident to reach out from the shadows and claim me—claim me so I wouldn't have to. I couldn't fully perceive the memories, but they cast a piss-yellow wash over how I felt everything.

My hand was shaking when I got the right key into the lock. Maybe it was the sweat and the wind. Then I went inside, shut the door, and found the light switch. The reception desk was as spartan as I remembered it, a simple plywood and paint barrier between the public and the guys doing the work. Behind that was the office where I'd spent the night against my will. There was a new door to replace the one they'd busted up getting me free. The carpet had a few new stains on it, ones I didn't remember sleeping on. A fresh calendar—this month featuring a pinup housewife with grocery bags in her hands and panties around her ankles—hung above a computer so old that it might as well have been a typewriter duct-taped to an oscilloscope. I was wading in a strange kind of nostalgia.

I went through a heavier door into the shop itself. A moment of fumbling in the half-light coming through the window in the door and I found the light switch. The space was arrayed just as I'd remembered it. A couple bays with lifts to hoist up Harleys to a more reasonable working height. The tool chests, workbenches, and heavy machinery all looked flat and dull and lifeless in the cold blue fluorescents that dangled by chains from the ceiling. They were swinging slightly, shifting the shadows back and forth, making me feel shipbound and unsteady.

I got down on my hands and knees to inch around the space like a worm, one square foot at a time. The floor was filthy. There were dust bunnies and metal shavings, pieces of food and stray hairs. I worked slowly, clearing piled-up dust and debris around each piece of equipment or table leg, feeling for openings in the concrete floor. It took a long time, but it slowed my mind down, cooled my body. At least until I got a screw wedged into the fat of my knee and I took a little pent-up something out on a box of drill bits. Then I had to collect the bits from where they'd scattered around the shop. I did that on two legs, like a human at least.

Finally I worked around to the corner where a couple trash cans were lined up against the wall. I'd been avoiding the spot. I'd hoped to find what I was looking for before I reached it. Now I couldn't. This was where Mike's body had fallen, after the bullet opened a hole in the muscle of his heart. This place, one week ago. Mike, who loved his wife, fucked his way across Southeast Asia, served his church, hated his job, but liked to waste time with me and call me a cocksucker while we hit robot pitches in the batting cages. Here I was, and here he was not. None of these were mysteries I was going to solve.

It was only a corner: a slab of concrete where two walls happened to meet. I pulled the trash cans out of the way and got back on all fours. I ran my hands along the floor, sweeping for dust and debris with my fingers, searching for a seam or hinge. Instead, my fingertips felt what I told myself was the charge of static electricity. But something of belief was still alive in me. Some wish for it. Hidden within this fragile, scattered excuse of a self, it had bided its time—this something beyond the desperate hunger not to die, which racked a body's worth of stupid, selfish cells into working together. God didn't exist; Jesus was at best a decent but long-decomposed person; all that remained of my sister and parents were components of their bodies' molecules, long-since broken down and rebonded in new forms, attached to new bodies. These were irrefutable truths. Yet my hand on this cold concrete reached for some trace of Mike. It reached so hard it felt that trace and began, through mute physiological signals, trying to communicate this to my conscious mind. And my mind, fool that it was, began to hear them. The hairs on my arms rose. That static charge settled into a premonitory tingle in the back of my neck. Nausea gave my insides a once-over.

I pulled my hand away. The concrete was smooth. Its pattern of stains was inscrutable, but like the urn into which Mike's remains had been poured, the floor suggested a wide, interior space, like a child's marble seen up close. It was a trick. It was an illusion caused by the meeting of visual phenomena and errors in my brain's evolution to process them. It was the influence of unconscious desires on mutable powers of perception. But knowing it was a trick didn't make it feel any less like truth.

About a foot away, there was a small chip in the polished concrete that was unreflective. I felt it with my finger, wanting a sense of what a break in this continuous surface felt like, a way to recognize it by touch. The concrete at the bottom of the quarter-inch chip was darker than the rest. There was too much shadow to be sure, but it appeared to be stained a coppery brown-red. I was sure this was Mike's blood—long dried, near fossilized, but missed by the mop in every cleaning of the spot—even if I had no way of knowing. Knowing didn't matter. I knew it another way.

Was I taking this as some kind of sign? If I did, it was a difficult one, but it woke up my eyes. I began moving things around, anything on casters first: the tool chest, the shop vacuum, the stools. I dragged the worktable away from the wall. When I leaned into the mill, which was old and made of heavy blue-gray steel in the shape of a massive KitchenAid mixer, the sound it made was loud and deep, run through with a piercing screech. Then the tone of the screeching began to rise in pitch, to become more resonant.

After I'd shifted it a foot and a half, I stopped and got down on the ground. I'd exposed a length of the concrete joint that ran wall to wall beneath the mill. I tried to hook my fingernails in the joint, but there wasn't anything to get purchase on, no way to pull. I shifted to a new spot, tried again, failed again. But there was something different in how the two spots felt. I wasn't sure what it was at first. They looked identical: polished concrete, steel gray with little flecks of white in the mix.

I moved back to the first spot and felt around. It wasn't as cold. That was the difference. Everywhere else, the floor had acted like a heat sink in reverse, storing the chill from the heavy air-conditioning that ran during the day. The AC was shut off at night, and the Santa Anas brought warmth into the shop through thin cracks around the corrugated-steel roll-up door at the back. Most of the floor retained the day's cold. When I felt the seam where the mill had been, it was warmer.

Maybe the mill's base had insulated it from the cold air during the daytime, I told myself, as I shifted the mill a few more feet over. I picked at the joint some more, to no avail. I tried pounding on it instead. Nothing. Then I stomped with the wooden heel of my father's shoe, and the floor sank almost imperceptibly. There was a muffled warble, the hollow bump of metal depressing somewhere beneath.

I should have been self-righteously pleased. Instead, I felt like I was going to throw up.

They must have left that part out of the Bible, how a person would react to the hoped-for but impossible thing to come to pass, for what might be delusion to be confirmed as truth. Mary Magdalene had witnessed this person nailed to a cross and impaled, consigned His cold body to a cave without hope of ever seeing it with gelatinous, earthly eyes again. Then outside the sepulchre, she heard Jesus sayeth her name, and He appeared before her. She responded, "Rabboni," but the authors tactfully avoided describing how she vomited up her breakfast in the same breath. Which would explain why Jesus said, "Touch me not, for I am not yet ascended to my Father," wanting to be in reasonably puke-free garments for that paternal reunion. Think of poor Thomas, who needed to touch before he would believe—and then reached into that wound and felt those resurrected intestines.

When I'd stomped on the spot, I had seen a ghostly image of a rectangle, thin depressions in the concrete for three of the sides and the joint as the fourth. I felt along these. The three sides weren't concrete at all. They were covered in a thin material painted to look like concrete. I could peel it up with a fingernail along its outer edges, but I couldn't pull it back completely.

I needed a crowbar, so I searched the worktable for one. Because I needed one, one was there. That was how I was thinking.

With the crowbar wedged into the seam, I leaned into it with my full weight. The bar flexed, but the floor resisted. I leaned harder. There was a thunderous, mechanical crunch, and then I was falling backward.

From on my side, I looked over, and there it was: an entrance. A square hole in the floor. The three-by-four-foot covering lay on the ground where I'd pulled it free of its supports. For so long I'd felt like I was close to something that kept eluding me. Now I was here. Elusion wasn't the base fact of life itself, like I'd long held, and it fell onto the heap behind me with the other myths and fantasies, friends and acquaintances, discarded selves upon selves.

I crawled over to the opening. The uppermost part was framed in metal, giving way to a tidy hole through the sediment and rock below. A hydraulic arm, ripped from its mount on the covering, groped out into the open air. Just visible inside the opening was a ladder bolted to the inner wall. It proceeded down into the pitch black. There was nothing to do but climb in, no other option and so no room for debate or second-guessing.

I took each step slowly, making sure my footing was solid. My heart was so high in my throat I could feel it humping my brain stem. The machine shop disappeared above me, except for the cat's pupil of the fluorescent tube that hung directly over the hatch. I went farther down into the darker and darker inner recess. After descending about ten or twelve feet, my foot found ground. My eyes struggled to adjust, reaching out for scraps of light and the features of things. Even though I could only see vaguely in the gray-black, I could tell this space was long, if not especially wide—more a passageway, it seemed, than a basement.

The light from aboveground helped while my pupils widened their apertures. The walls nearest to me were bare compressed earth. Wood-and-steel framing girded them every few feet. A small steel cook's table was pressed against one wall. Running along the other, disappearing into the blackness, was eight-foot-tall commercial kitchen shelving, baker's racks. The place felt like a dungeon for prep cooks.

But the shelves I could see weren't piled high with produce. Instead, on each were stacks of vacuum-sealed bags, and each bag's contents were a different pastel shade. I picked one up. It was full of pale yellow pills, a four-digit number scrawled on the bag in black ink. I'd never won a jelly-bean-counting game in my life, and it was too late to hope my luck would change, but there had to be at least two hundred pills in the bag I held, about twenty or thirty bags on each shelf. All the bags were numbered the same way.

None of the pills were marked in a way that would allow me to confirm what they were, but they had to be prescription narcotics, the popular ones like OxyContin, Vicodin, benzodiazepine. I'd heard Sammy had gotten away from the dirtier drugs, but if he was pushing something—like he'd done with the kids at my old church—it would be those kind. This place was connected to the one in Sammy's garage. They were part of a network, a means to distribute them to the right small dealers, something.

For a while now it had felt like I was possessed by a new kind of sight, which was an old kind, in which everything radiated with interconnectedness—shafts of light only I could perceive slicing the air in every which direction. They were overlapping, though, and impossible to trace, like a single page that has been printed on over and over again. There was something buried in there, I knew, even if the fundamental message was obscured. Now it was as if those layered golden lines of interconnection had parted, and I could clearly see a few of the important ones: the line running from here out to Ramona, the ones connecting Emily to Sammy, and Sammy to Mike. It made the world feel small and me feel the other way. I moved along the baker's racks, pulling down random bags to study them closer. It got darker and darker the farther back I went, but I didn't notice that much. If anything, this room had become the radiant center of the newly visible world. A world that had nothing to do with my eyes, or the world.

After about twenty-five feet, I reached the back wall. Not a passageway, it turned out. The bare earth was roughly chiseled away and hard as stone. I couldn't imagine how difficult it would have been to build this, or what the value of these bags were on the street, but I wasn't thinking about difficulty or value. I was thinking about how I'd slipped through the surface of this secret. I was the only one who knew this was here besides the people whose work depended on it. I was the only one who knew this was what Mike died for—to ensure this value could be preserved and actualized, to make sure this system could continue. The anger I felt was different from the one I'd grown used to, the one I'd depended on. That anger had been low and mean, targeted and physical, even if it came out only in words. This one had a measure of glory in it. It wasn't godly or metaphysical, but still it was filled with a kind of mad righteousness over the disclosure of a new, hidden layer of the world's wickedness. There's power in that kind of awareness—too much—and it left me floating, disembodied. It would have taken a Mack truck to knock me off my center of gravity.

Along the ceiling I noticed the lightbulbs: six of them in pairs with insulated wire running between them. I hadn't seen a switch, but it didn't mean there wasn't one. I started to look at the same moment I heard a voice say "Jesus."

I thought it was in my head, the usual rendition of the word halfway between gratitude and the disgust at something disgraceful, disclosed. Then came a sound, a thin clanking from down the corridor. Hairs did something credulous and stupid on my neck.

The voice had sounded too young and dumb to be in my head. At the end of the room, the light from the open hatch flickered. Angular fluorescent patches moved along the floors and walls. Metal snapped into place, and the entire room went dark.

I was frozen in place. A statue facing the slow, approaching arc of a sledgehammer would have been more responsive. Overhead, through layers of earth and concrete, something heavy was being moved. The mill. It was being dragged back over the hatch, rumbling. I couldn't see, but I'd been facing the right direction when things went dark, and I had enough memory of the space, so I ran with my arms out. I hit the ladder hard, didn't stop to consider the pain, and climbed. I climbed fast and tried to push open the panel that had been dropped back into the opening. It shifted an inch or two, but then something forced it down again. I banged on it. I shouted. I cursed. I begged a little. The only answer was the muffled grinding of the mill's feet as they were dragged over the hatch. Then silence. It was so perfectly quiet. The silence filled the darkness, and the darkness filled the silence. Then the terror rose up.

31.

NOTHING. I WAS ADRIFT IN NOTHING. NOTHING TO SEE. NOTHING TO DO. Nothing to hear, except my own breathing and whispered profanity. It was cold. I was scared and small again. It wasn't long before I began to shiver, and then my teeth made a sound, too. The click of enamel on enamel. Vibrations in tense jaw muscles sounded like a boat's hull groaning in rough seas. I'd like to say I exhausted myself shouting for help, banging on the underside of the hatch for hours, but it seemed well insulated down here and I'd already been exhausted for days. It wasn't long before I gave up.

I sat on the floor at the far end of the room, back against the wet-smelling earth, though it was dry to the touch. The smell seemed to grow stronger as time dragged by. Such a living, rich smell. Where seeds might sprout, if there had been a little sunlight. A smell you might bask in lying facedown in the grass on a spring afternoon. Wanting that grass, that yellow warmth on my back—it tore at my insides, pulled at them from above. I let it, didn't try to suffocate the desire with bare hands or bitter thought. I didn't kill it, but I didn't give it any hope either. I let it crawl like a bug across my lens. The autofocus never rendered it more clearly than a fuzz ball with buried desire and random volition, until the thing decided to fly away and find some other place to shit.

I started talking to myself, as much to figure out what to do as to keep those more abstract thoughts at bay. Someone had found out what I was doing. Then he'd closed me in this place. There wasn't anything else to know, but I had some guesses. He—whoever he was, but I pictured one of Andy's shouting surfers—would leave me here until he figured out what to do. Or he would leave me down here until dehydration did the job. It wouldn't even take that long. My best bet was that he'd barricaded me in so he could call Sammy. No one else would let me go. No one else would leave me to chance.

The weight of exhaustion settled into my bones, but my bones refused to settle on the cold concrete floor. If I lay on my stomach, my ribs and hips and knees ached. On my back it was my shoulders and spine. On my side, the ache moved deeper, into the joints of my arms and legs, arrested in unnatural positions. The best I could do was lean against the wall, one elbow propped on a knee and that hand holding my head. There was nothing to do but wait, it seemed, so the science of getting comfortable had been a worthwhile distraction.

I tried to sleep, to force sleep on myself. Anything to pass the time between this waiting and whatever would come. Anything to quiet this neurochemistry evolved and hardwired for activity, for industry. But I was too exhausted, too uncomfortable—and, though I was trying to overlook it, there was a fire inside that was burning, far enough down to cast wild, elongated shadows on the backs of my unseeing eyes. It wasn't just that I knew about this place, knew something about the operation that made use of it. It was that I had the ability to expose it, to end it. I still had a kind of power, once poured down the sink by a person who'd sworn off the stuff but burbling back up from the septic system.

It was this that kept my mind moving in slow circles, like a shark: sniffing out the Jesus Freak kids, whether they were the same ones who found a way to rationalize dealing drugs, putting a bullet in Mike, burying me in here; Lambert, ladling dyed Karo syrup masquerading as blood of the lamb, overserving himself; Emily, raised on the same; Sammy, still believing it was transubstantial blood but unable to change his shameful ways. Each had believed themselves the recipient of unmerited but sanctifying love, one that bestowed a simple, delusional self-confidence that had nothing to do with who they were, what they'd done. These churches were nothing if not a venue for proving that each member deserved to be accepted, loved, trusted—without doubt. Sermons in compact words, none over three syllables, all accompanied by easy pictures. You can't build a community on a message of scathing and endless self-scrutiny, on bottomless skepticism of each person's goodness and motivations, or doubt about the ultimate meaning of the workings of the world and its evils. You can't even build much of a self on that, and I'd been trying long enough to know. But when that love turns on you, it turns hard. Sammy knew that, in a way. I bet Emily knew that, too.

Places like Lambert's liked to talk about the mysteries of the faith, the doctrines beyond human comprehension: that God made something from nothing; that the Bible is divinely ordained but written by men; that God is one and three, and also the union of man and God in the corporeal form of Jesus; that God is omnipotent and omnipresent but allows us and the devil to make such a fucking mess of everything. But these mysteries are recited as prompts for a response of "Wow!" or "Beautiful!" or "Isn't He amazing?" Dumbstruck, overawed, and then quickly moving on with the unthinking smile and shrug of the satisfied and the saved, for whom mystery is about as humbling as the Grand Canyon printed on a poster about hard work.

Emily had been inducted into a different kind of mystery of the faith when the man she looked up to turned on her, told her with certainty that an all-powerful God had created her to be an abomination in His sight. Her life itself became the mystery, not something she could explain or share, not with anyone she knew from her life then. That's what shame did, the real undiluted stuff. After you'd been singled out by it—pushed, stumbling, onto the stage while the crowd laughs and points—it was safer to hide, even from yourself. I didn't know the details, but that had to be how she ended up with Sammy. She must have felt something familiar there, even if it was never articulated, and so traced a circle that ran from her life through my own past life in the church.

This circle enveloped Mike, too, and his church—a place I couldn't imagine as being too different from the others. Between the guy they eulogized at the funeral and the one I knew, it was hard to see Mike as a single and whole person, but I could picture the God he envisioned: one of those masculine, laissez-faire, free-will, no-bullshit, ain't-no-queer, suck-it-up gods, made in the image of the collective American unconsciousness's bourbon-breathed Southern Baptist grandfather. The kind of God who'd call you a cocksucker Himself. If God was a man, and the man people imagined was one of these kind of men, then something was wrong with men.

Gustafsson was the kind of man people based gods on, the worst kind. His financial form of prayer could part the American seas, and he, too, was part of this. He was at Mike's funeral service, at Canaan Hills, and his name was on the deed to the land I sat buried within. His threat to find another security firm moved Watt to fire me; his charitable support meant people like Lambert follow the bouncing ball to whatever tune he requested for their moral karaoke. A not-so-invisible hand, with exceptionally managed cuticles, and calluses formed only by his weekends at the rock climbing gym, among the other wealthy hedonists, as much from the ropes as from the hand jobs in the sauna after.

What was I doing, thinking like this? It was only a desire to make the irony perfect, the kind of irony we've come to expect: that the man using his wealth to combat the scourge of homosexuality was covering his own unpalatable lusts. There's a poetry to completion, to a total understanding, that's difficult to resist. It has a meter all its own, making it easy to memorize and easier still to dance to, right off a goddamn cliff. Still, the more I thought, the more it seemed like Gustafsson was important, that he was the innermost sharp-toothed gear, connected to the driveshaft, around which the wider gears turned.

32.

THE GROUND WAS TOO COLD. IT LEFT ME SORE AND SHAKING, SO I started pacing, sweating—my body desperate to make itself useful while the gray matter spun its stories. By the ladder, I listened awhile. Maybe I could catch that voice again, could hear him discussing options, making calls. But no. Nothing. Silence.

This underground room: Gustafsson had to know about it. This wasn't a little false vent where a person could stash an ounce of weed. It wouldn't be simple or cheap to build, and impossible to do so without someone noticing. I'd heard a story about Mexican drug cartels digging border tunnels near San Diego with forced labor, making the captives sleep on-site, threatening to kill their families if they left in the middle of the job. When the tunnel was done, they were all taken to a ditch and shot anyway. Secrets want to stay secret, have helpful friends. Instead of Sammy's face appearing when that hatch opened, I wondered if I'd see Gustafsson's smug grin instead.

Hours must have passed—how many I didn't know—and I was stewing in paranoid sweat, fuming and on the edge of a sleep I couldn't resist but also couldn't reach. Eventually my mind began to cool back down. There wasn't a damn thing I could do with any of these thoughts. The hatch would open, or it wouldn't, without any input from my pathetic self.

And what was I doing anyway? Trying to help a girl I barely knew. It was uncomfortable, how comfortable all this was, how familiar. There was something happening out there, and I was one of only a few who truly understood—was in all likelihood the only person who could do something about it. My mind was blind and blinking into the harsh spotlight of self-importance. I used to feel like that all the time. I'd been running from the feeling for years, only to end up right back in the thick of it.

Everything except for giving up was out of my control, so I decided to get good at giving up. I tried to clear my mind, focus on the present, let the exhaustion do its work. I was back with the blackness and blank walls of thought. Even the smell of the earth faded. How quickly our senses integrate the new into the expected and thus unperceived. Most of the world streams by like that. Dark matter.

Let it, I told myself. Let even what I could perceive—the dampness in the air, the sound of my breath, the aches in my joints, the way gravity flattened my muscles and skin against the pebbled earth—let it all melt when it struck me, like snowflakes hitting a sun-warmed road. Let none of it stick. If I could manage that, I knew, I might get out of this alive. And by alive, I wasn't thinking bodily, and certainly not in spirit. No: I wouldn't have named it, but to get out alive was to make it to the end without excess suffering—without suffering and fear causing me to abandon all the hard-won lessons of my life that had led to this moment. No one would find my corpse with nails ripped off, wild claw marks on the ceiling. No one would see, despite all evidence pointing to the futility of it, that I had acted so desperately, so outside rationality and sense. No one would see that, in the end, I had tried.

33.

BUT THE MIND HAS TROUBLE WITH DARKNESS. OUR BRAINS WILL SEE EVEN if there's nothing to see and will hear even if there's nothing to hear. When the senses can't forage, they farm.

The forms harvested from my memory were vague at first, amorphous, shapeless. Then it seemed like there was a faint light shining through a fog-heavy morning, and there was a horse nickering in the dimness. I remembered that day, just one in ten thousand normal days. The air was cold on my face, but there were blasts of heat coming from the car's vents. It smelled like cut grass and dry oak and the sweet, cakey aroma of fresh donuts warmly greasing a paper bag. A Styrofoam cup of coffee squeaked in my hand comfortably. Aracely, still in yellow-footed pajamas, was sitting in the passenger seat, her hair a debutante's day-after rat's nest. She was eating a sugar twist, a carton of milk held between her plum-sized knees. "Where are the horses?" she was asking, and I knew I'd tell her we'd be able to see them soon, when the sun came up and the fog burned off—knew because I'd lived this, had taken her some mornings to the racetrack to watch the jockeys do warm-ups so Gabby could sleep in. I tried to detach myself from the memory, to see it more dispassionately, to let it dissipate like the fog. But in the dark my recollection of the morning only became more insistent, and I beat my hands against the cold metal of the ladder, trying to shake it from my head.

Then, as unbidden as it had come, the memory was gone. There was a bitter flavor in the pit of my stomach. It was no use entertaining the past. Not here. Not now. But in the boredom and stillness that I couldn't avoid, my mind had other plans. Out of nowhere I remembered being a child in a twin bed, in a dark room. I was sitting up, sobbing. My mother came in to change the pillow, which I'd thrown up on. Then she wiped my face with the satin-lined sleeve of her robe. It felt so smooth. She eased me back down on the cool cloth of the fresh pillowcase and rubbed my back, pulled up my shirt to run her nails along my skin, which was feverish and prickled where her nails dragged.

I hadn't thought about that in decades. It was simple, I told myself: I'm in the dark, I'm scared. It's association, a wire connecting two parts of the cognitive machine separated by forty-some years. I tried to shut my eyes, to block these passing memories. But then they'd snap open onto nothing different from when they were closed—it felt like I'd lost the ability to blink—and a fresh recollection whispering in the dark.

I was failing at giving up. How like me, to fail even at that—to be trapped in a hole in the ground, facing what in all likelihood were the last however many hours of my life and using them to berate myself as a failure. I couldn't stop myself. Aboveground, there was always something I could find to direct my ire at. Now there was me and only me, who was failing at giving up, at resigning himself to this, but who had been trying to give up for half his life—trying, trying. And now, too, I was failing—when I was so close—to help Emily.

My bladder started to hurt. That gave me something to focus on.

First it was almost enjoyable, a little distracting game to see what position I could put my body in to relieve the pressure the most. Then all of them hurt about the same. I should have just pissed, but then I got stubborn about seeing how long I could wait. I walked the twenty-five feet of my human-sized ant farm, hopping when necessary to keep things under control. Then I remembered hearing about a woman who died during some talk radio challenge, holding her urine so long her own body turned toxic. If I was going to die down here, I didn't want it to be for such an asinine—or is it more urinine?—reason. The acrid stench filled my limited pocket of air so powerfully that the black seemed to become almost green.

Air. That was something I hadn't considered. I went to the far end of the chamber and climbed the ladder, feeling with my fingertips around the edges of the hatch. I sniffed, trying to catch a fresher scent. Nothing on all counts. This room was only so big, with no ventilation I'd seen, and the hatch appeared to make an airtight seal.

They wouldn't have to wait for terminal dehydration to set in. I'd just pass out, and then my body, starved of oxygen, would expire after one final exhalation. If they waited long enough, maybe they'd find me shriveled but preserved like those Japanese monks who mummified themselves alive at the end of their lives, eating bark and drinking lacquer and chanting away in a sealed tomb until their hearts gave out. But they'd done it to reach a new spiritual plateau, to become bodhisattvas who would later help others reach enlightenment. I'd do it only because I was stupid and stuck.

I climbed back down the ladder. Was my heart pounding more than it should have been, considering the climb wasn't exactly a workout? Maybe it was just the anxiety at the thought, the prospect. Or maybe it was my body already working overtime to pull oxygen from this thinning air. I closed my eyes, tried to calm down. I wanted my heart rate to drop, but I couldn't get a handle on it. I knew adrenaline and epinephrine and cortisol were ramping up my system now, these new inputs triggering the physiology of panic. This would cause me to breathe more heavily, which would burn up my limited oxygen. I had no way to know how long this air would stay breathable—how long until this unseen, life-sustaining ether would turn, as invisibly as so many things had, to poison.

I sat on the cook's table. Sitting was good, I reasoned. It didn't use much oxygen. But it didn't feel right. I couldn't sit still. It was like I had vertigo in my limbs. It felt better to be standing—on my feet, able to move.

I held my forehead with both hands. Brains weren't falling out my nose yet. That seemed like a good sign. Pulling on my hair helped. The pain seemed to focus my body and mind, at least for a moment, creating little flashes of light in my mind's eye. It reminded me: before I was sealed in, I'd seen lightbulbs along the ceiling. I'd been sitting here in the dark for however many hours, and there were lightbulbs in the goddamn ceiling. They couldn't give me air, but if I could see, maybe I'd find something that could help me get out of here. I would take anything, from a radio to a pipe bomb.

In my mind, I ran through everything I'd seen in this chamber: The small table, nothing under it. The rows of racks, polished chrome bars that framed bags of pastel and chalk white. Nothing else on the shelves that I could recall—just the drugs and nearby the table for sorting them. I'd walked the length of this room, checking the shelves fairly well. Then I'd looked back, and that's when I heard the sound and the room went dark. I'd never seen a light switch, but I could feel my way around.

It was good to think in these terms. I'd have to be systematic. I would start at the ladder, work my hands up the wall as far as I could reach, down to the floor, too, then move six inches to the left. I could travel the whole room along the wall that way, like a spider.

My hands felt numb, tingling, while I felt around the ladder mounts, behind the rungs, and along all four sides of the tunneled earth as it approached the false shop-floor opening itself. Maybe it was nerves. Maybe it was a sign of oxygen deprivation. And besides, I reminded myself, this problem didn't tell me anything new—it only bumped the timeline up a few notches. It was part of what was coming no matter what, part of what would pass. By the time it passed, if I hadn't found my way out, I wouldn't even be there to feel it or to mourn it. No one would, really. Not Gabby, even. Not Aracely. They'd done their mourning for me. Whether I lived or died, in the end, wasn't of any great significance.

I pictured Esme at Mike's funeral while I fumbled up and down the wall adjacent to the ladder, feeling around the wood and steel supports that kept this place from caving in on itself. We weren't all that close, but still Esme would mourn. I couldn't pretend she wouldn't. I knew how she would do it: how she'd attend whatever there was to attend, would see about helping where help was needed, would cry when it was time to cry, would console when there was someone to be consoled. And I'd be the reason—or her memory of me would be the reason. I couldn't be the reason for anything after I was gone, anything that was properly me having collapsed into dead neurons, into ash and dust.

I didn't know what to make of that prospect. For a moment I witnessed it coldly, from behind the two-way glass, while I searched for the switch around the cook's table and, having failed to find anything, began to inch my way down the length of bare wall. My death was a plain fact, as meaningful as a mussel being picked off a pier by a gull. But my memory, my ghost, would put Esme through pain—a pain I could see clearly because of Mike's death. As much as I might doubt it, how could my death not hurt Gabby or Aracely, too? Still, though I wanted to defer it, though I preferred to spare them that unnecessary suffering, I refused to let myself, even then, see it as any great loss.

My body, however, had other ideas. The longer I searched and didn't find a switch, the tighter my chest felt, and the harder it was to get a full breath into the clenched fists of my lungs. Then a brilliant pain burst out from my heart. It refracted along my ribs, flickering in thin, nail's-point tendrils like searing light on the rushing water of a river mouth. My body ran cold, and those tendrils turned icy, painfully so, while my heart tried to collapse in on itself, go nuclear or form a white dwarf from a red giant or something else cosmically catastrophic. Yellow-orange shapes began to warble and agitate in my vision. I felt dizzy and hungry and sick, so I sat back down. It had begun: my body was starving for air.

34.

KNOWING THE WEIGHT OF THE CONCRETE AND THE MILL ATOP IT, THERE was no way I could muscle the hatch open from below. Still, I found myself running back to the ladder, clutching the rungs clumsily, relying on a hooked elbow a couple times to manage the climb through the suffocating tightness in my chest.

Blood seemed to be pouring into my eyeballs, sloshing red in my view of the dark surroundings. I pressed my ear to the metal underside of the hatch, stretching out my hearing with all the effort I could manage. I tried to believe I could hear something, someone, on the other side. But no, there was nothing.

That wasn't true. I had silence, darkness, solitude. I had no one I could call to, no one there to hear me. And I had this pain now, like my chest would cave in on itself in order to bury the weak and struggling muscle for good, my body the soldier diving onto its own grenade. These things would keep me company.

I climbed back down and sat with my back to the ladder—woozy, rushing, thirsty. My fingers and toes were cold. My limbs felt fat and heavy with chilled and thinly watery blood, while everything beneath my ribs combusted. This was my body, sending up flares, putting on a somatic light show to get me to recognize what was happening. I got the message, but it didn't know that and I couldn't tell it, so my body kept running through the routine again, again, marshaled by an invisible theatrical producer who still believed there was some way to get this number right. This was survival, my brain getting ahead of me in the most complete and terrorized way.

I focused on slowing my breathing. My gut cinched hard, and I felt a pungent craving for whiskey. I knew immediately I'd been living with this craving for a while now, could recognize the raw lines it scored on all other feelings. It had been sawing away somewhere down below, muffled by the business of the last week but giving it all its anxious, desperate edge.

The baker's racks loomed in the dark, and I thought about what mystery compounds were engineered and synthesized into those pills. They wouldn't help, but help wasn't what I craved then. Help was what I'd been trying to give. This desire was about something different from help. I wasn't thinking about a few pills, a temporary palliative. I was thinking about a few handfuls and an end to this—the pain and all the rest.

The idea tugged at me. It would be clean. I'd go on my own terms. The fear and despair would take over soon enough, and I'd be helpless at that point, a passive witness to whatever desperate things I would do with the end of my life—animal instinct forcing one last pathetic fight against the unchangeable and unmovable. Ellen had possessed the courage to do it, once she'd chosen that path out of interminable not-knowing—not knowing if God was real, if the book she'd been raised to live by was worth the price of ink and onionskin. She chose that over knowing what it would do to us, what it would do to me. It wasn't fair to her to think like this, I knew. She was mentally ill, she was terribly depressed—had lived with it, in secret, for a long time—she couldn't have known the consequences, she was out of her own control. But I had never let that go, never forgiven it, and never would. I would be angry with her until they burned my remains. My ashes would cause steam to rise up from where they were poured into the ocean. The ashes of an angry man.

But the anger got me thinking about something other than eating a pile of unnamed pills, so I let the anger come. I let it get me to my feet. I went back to where I left off feeling the earth, the wood, the steel—feeling for the light switch. The farther down I went, the more the grip on my heart seemed to tighten, the colder my hands felt.

Lambert deserved this anger; Sammy deserved it; Andy at my old church deserved it; Gustafsson deserved it. I deserved it, more than ever. I'd picked Emily up, sure. I'd offered to drive her to Portland, a little closer to Seattle. But I didn't tell her my trip was more a figment, that it had been sabotaged from the start by my own inability to have a relationship with my daughter, and she had to see my eyes, where they darted. I was just another man who couldn't see past his own interest in her, an interest about six inches long on average. I hadn't used her, but I would have if given enough time and opportunity.

But I wasn't trying to find her to ask her to forgive me. She shouldn't forgive any of us. Forgiveness was the hangover the entire Western world, Christian or not, couldn't shake. God had come up with this scheme to forgive us our sins through Jesus's planned-for and ordained murder—which made it a Trinitarian filicide/suicide/ghostbusting all to undo the damage of sins that He Himself had demarcated, sins that He had created us to desire or be susceptible to—or He would have if He and Jesus both weren't the mirrored white space on a few hundred pages of scriptural invention. But in our injunctions on how to live, the beneficence and power—and the obligation—of forgiveness had soldiered on, forever reanimating like a moral zombie. It had become neutered of metaphysical power, sure—practicalized, psychologized, turned into that slippery move of me forgiving you because I hope it will make me feel better. But it was still the forgiver's call, the forgiver's moral charity and well-being with which we were concerned.

I didn't want to explain myself to Emily. She didn't need Lambert and Daniella and her parents to explain the machinations that had pushed them to treat her in the ways they had. Accounting for that was beside the point. But I wanted her to know that I was sorry for the part I played.

Running my hand along the edge of one support, I snagged a split in the wood and felt it pierce deeply into the fat of my finger pad. I spat out a few *fuck*s and *shit*s and *motherfucker*s, felt the blood running across my puffed, numb hand, hit the wall again and again and again until some specific pain bloomed—warm, at least, while it hurt—in my palm. The general pain issuing from my chest caused my lips to curl back in a grimace so wide my skull could have slipped out between them.

My anger turned back on me. The panic and fear Emily had shown when I'd picked her up asleep on the patio that night—that wasn't about me. That was about other men. What I'd done was nothing compared to what Sammy had done, nothing compared to how Lambert had hurt her. I hadn't *done* anything at all, and still I'd made myself the center of her tragedy—made my thoughts the core of what had hurt her, and that was a shameful, selfish thing, done by a shame-filled, thought-policing person. It was all because I'd had a desire. For years, my desires hadn't extended much further than burritos and a couple hours in the ocean. Then she showed up, I had one passing paroxysm of lust-care-loneliness, and it led me here, like a Christian even to the end, even without God.

God and the entire host of heavenly attendants were all still floating in the formaldehyde of my brain. They were dead, but some part of me thought they were watching nonetheless—not gone but near infinitely far away. I hadn't known it, but there it was. Even so, I didn't feel a need to explain to them what I'd done. I didn't need to be told that they understood, that I could be accepted despite it—always despite. If there was some near-dead wish of mine still bloating in that brine, it was that I wanted an apology. Something I'd never get. I wanted to hear their regret at how much was fucked in the world's founding, how much was fucked in my own. I wanted them sorry for what they'd made.

My hands moved more quickly now, fumbling over the chiseled earth and the wall supports, leaving streaks of my blood I pictured but couldn't see. A switch had to be somewhere in this hellhole. They couldn't have it up in the shop; it'd be a giveaway. The air was thinning in my head. I knew I was threatening to collapse—that part of me wanted its forced calm, its cold comfort.

An apology from my own fleshy, fumbling, faithful father would have sufficed. An apology by proxy. But he'd never given one while he was alive and was offering up nothing as one of my numerous dead. They all owed me as much. Ellen, for abandoning me to replace her faith with fact. My father, for so quietly accepting her fate. My mother, for following him. They had all gone away, left me. Leaving is what people do. As soon as a person arrives, they promise to go. But all these people had left, and none had apologized for the abandoning.

Even Gabby: she hadn't died, but when my faith gave out, it was a divide just as eternal that separated us. She had held fast to the spiritual terms by which I could cross it—terms I couldn't live with, terms I pushed at to discover who she loved more. The discovery of being second best only sent me further away, set me up—I saw it clearly then—to work out how unlovable I could become.

I didn't blame Gabby for leaving, for taking Aracely. But I wondered if she ever wanted to say she was sorry they had gone, even if she couldn't see having done it any other way. I wondered if she had any idea what it would have meant to me. I hadn't.

It felt like days, though it must have only been minutes, before I reached the back wall. It was as empty of what I was looking for as everything else I'd touched. Now I was at the far end of the racks of bagged drugs, feeling behind the cheap, chrome-plated bars for that small protrusion of plastic that, at this point, was only the difference between me dying in the dark or dying in the light. Which was no difference at all.

The first bag I found, I tore a hole in. I shook a few pills into my shaking, senseless hand, got them into my mouth. They stuck to my tongue dryly. Not enough to kill me. Just enough to kill some of this pain, until I was killed by other things.

Aracely never needed to forgive me. She was the one who deserved an apology. I could see that now, could picture doing it, but my self-defeating attempts to reach out to her over the years stunk of the opposite. Now I wouldn't get the chance. She'd never know she didn't need to forgive me—that I didn't want her to forgive me—that I needed her not to forgive me. I wanted her to hear, in my own voice, how deeply, how fully I knew I'd done wrong by her.

But I was taking this voice with me, it seemed, into the pit. Then I would be one of the dead, too, and I would have left her, in the tidal surge of fetishized and therapeutic forgiveness, feeling like she'd withheld her mercy past when she could change her mind—that she'd never find catharsis in giving it to me, never find peace because she'd held on to her anger and disappointment for too long. Then I'd become a ghost lesson, teaching her something I didn't want her to learn.

Her memory of me would do this to her, for the rest of her life, even if I was dead for what was left of it. She'd keep wishing she could press her forgiveness into my hands, like a small, wrapped package, and I—handless, bodiless, being-less—could never take it. I was so furious at the thought I barely felt the pain in my chest anymore. Or, if anything, the pain had become so total, so extensive throughout my body, that it became another constant I could disregard.

Forgiveness wasn't what I needed, I wanted to tell her. It wasn't where anything like salvation persisted. No: it was in apology, and in blind chance, time's erasures, human grace.

The pills on my tongue: I spat them out. The taste of stale flour lingered, pale and bitter. I leaned against the wall, holding my face. My palms were wet. Thrombotic shapes swam across my vision in puce and amber. The lurching of my heart and the pain racking my body terrorized my mind. I told my whole body to go fuck itself. There had to be something I could do. I couldn't leave Aracely like this—couldn't leave her with yet another awful inheritance.

I inched my way along the rack, slowly and painfully, using the bars for support. The grip on my heart tightened, and panic rose up like bile in the back of my throat. I was losing whatever thin sense of control I'd found. Maybe the bad air was pooling at this end of the room. Maybe all the air had gone bad. I was breathing harder, but my throat felt constricted. The thin air that reached my lungs had a parched, unleavened taste. Drunken spins seized my proprioceptors, unstabilized the floor beneath me. The backs of my knees sweated, and the joints unlocked. I tried to steady myself on the rack, but I couldn't grab it with my fat, stupid hands.

I got one arm hooked around an upright, just in time for the air to vacate my skull. The rack wasn't bolted to the wall, so the whole thing came down on me. I'd failed, even briefly, to break the descent.

35.

WARM AIR WAS BLOWING ON MY FACE, GENTLY. I'M FINE, I REALIZED.

I was lying on a couch. The windows were open. A breeze billowed the flower-patterned curtains Gabby had made herself, blowing them into the living room on one side and causing them to flap out the window on the other. I could see the curtains as if I were now on the street, looking up. They waved like a botanical flag from the apartment complex—a warning from that vantage, and where I was cold—and then I was back on my sun-warmed couch. The ashtray on the end table was empty and clean, there for my father's occasional visits to "his favorite" and only grandchild.

There was singing. In the back room there was singing. It was Gabby. Her warm, low voice. I couldn't place the song, couldn't identify the words. I wanted two things: to stay still on this couch and listen as I drifted back to sleep, and to go back to that room and watch Gabby sing, to hear the words. The room. It was Aracely's room. She was singing to Aracely. I wanted to see her, too. I'd been wanting to see her for a long time. But I couldn't move. The cushions had curled and re-formed around my back and shoulders. I couldn't get myself to leave them. I couldn't leave the blanketing light that came through the window. It felt so perfect, to be warm and wombed on a soft couch in this living room.

The singing stopped. There was an indefinable sound, and then came laughter. Aracely's laugh. Not her genuine laugh but the stage one she'd picked up somewhere. The one she used when she knew, already, that she was supposed to laugh. It was loud and harsh and sweetly cartoonish.

I would see her if I could get up. I couldn't get up, and then I did.

The U-shaped apartment kitchen shone hazily in the sun pouring through the dirty skylight. It had stained-oak cabinets, antique white tile counters. I turned back to the couch I'd slept on—the hand-me-down, a great-aunt's, the pale blue monster. On the living room shelves were all the books. Out and in view. I could see them, remembered how often I pulled them down, not even to read them but just to touch on that set of ideas, then another, to bring them back to mind through these blocky artifacts—the bookmarks, too, each signaling a particular place or time: a train ticket, a brown leaf, the torn corner of *Los Angeles Times* newsprint; and the people who bought me some, turned me on to others, taught me how to read still more—but I remembered, too, painfully, that I'd stacked them in a closet, in a different house, and how they'd remained there in the dark into a new millennium.

But no, I didn't live in that house. I lived in this house. Apartment. The singing had begun again. I followed my footsteps on the path I'd known so well, the path I knew and was learning to know, was knowing. The one from this living room back to my daughter's bedroom. In this apartment. On the second story. Our second apartment on the second story, that's what Gabby had taken to calling it; the first was the cramped studio near the seminary. On the wall were pictures, eight matted into a single frame: a wedding photograph, Gabby in lace and tulle, me in a brown suit and cummerbund; Gabby, pregnant and waist deep in the sea; Aracely in her first bath; my father shaking my hand at the seminary graduation ceremony; my mother holding Aracely in her rocking chair, in the house I'd grown up in; Ellen and me in camp chairs, laughing around a fire; two images of Gabby's parents, people who had loved me and whom I had loved but who were so completely gone from my life that it was like I'd never known them at all. So many of them were gone. But they weren't. The picture with Ellen was taken only a year ago, only twenty-two years ago.

The singing. It had stopped again. I waited for the stage laugh, but none came.

I started to run. The hallway was only a few feet, but it took so long—forever—like I was a born-again Zeno running in a river of Californian light. The hallway seemed to stretch and darken, became lined by metal racks, and then it was my hallway again. What had been or was my hallway. Then, abruptly, I was standing at Aracely's door. I was looking in.

There was nothing to see. It was pitch black, dead black. Not dark. Something less than dark. I reached inside for a switch. There wasn't even a wall. Inside was nothing. Inside wasn't.

Where had Aracely gone? Gabby? I'd heard them. Calling from where, if not here? I could have called back, but I didn't. I came to them. I tried to come, but it took too long—I took too long. There was nothing here. The room hadn't been for such a long time. This apartment didn't exist anymore either, even if the rooms still stood. Those people and the people in the photographs—vanished, too. Even the ones who were still alive. The ones I knew then, those people were long since departed. Everything worth reaching lived in the past. There was no getting there. They weren't outside existence, waiting; they'd become nothing within it. Everything worth going back to was gone.

I couldn't get past that. The longer I couldn't get past it, the angrier I grew. Time taught me I couldn't hold on to a thing. Memory wouldn't let me abandon the wish. So the person I was, the person that was left—I bore the weight, being crushed while still reaching out, still hoping for one more moment of feeling, one more impression, on the tip of my finger, of those wished-for, long-gone people. Pulled forward by desire, drifting backward in resignation, groping blindly and blindingly, seeing every chance only when it was too late to take it.

Then I stepped forward into the room—into the absence where the room had been. The blackness enveloped me, held me, became me. For a long time I was nothing. That isn't right. I wasn't. There was only nothingness, of which I was somehow a part. There wasn't a self to sense it, a body to feel it, a memory to compare it with, a mind to articulate it, time to pass through it. Only me unfolding like undone origami into the flat page of nothingness.

36.

THE ONLY INDEPENDENT, ORIGINAL THOUGHT IS DARKNESS, SILENCE. AS soon as a light is cast or a sound is made, there is recognition and imitation and mistake, and you're made dependent on everything that came before, everything around.

The first light came out of the darkness. It was a want: I wanted to be alive. I had been nothing. There was nothing to be content with in being nothing, nothing to resist. But then I wanted this. From within that nothingness, I could feel the muscles of my eyelids contract, release, contract, release. What I saw made no change. My world went from black to black, but I could feel this movement. I could register what it meant. I'd wanted to be alive, and I was. Other sensations returned. Cold concrete against my face. The smell of dust and wet earth, piss. Pains in my back, in one wrist and a finger. Weight pressing down on me—the metal rack and bags of prescription drugs.

I tried to lift myself, but my muscles were weak. The pain in my heart was gone, replaced by a deep, physical exhaustion and a postnauseous hunger in the pit of my stomach. I pushed up again, couldn't get out from under the racks, fell back.

Then I saw the second light. It was at the end of the corridor, a thin shaft of blue-white. It came from above, made a square on the floor at the base of the ladder. It caught and reflected off the metal table, the chrome shelving, each coming toward me as new lights, a few hundred now, now more. The hatch was open. Air was coming in. My head was muzzy and I couldn't hear well, but I tried to listen for voices. There was nothing.

"Hello," I tried shouting. It came out like a disgruntled purr. "Hey. Whoever the fuck you are, I don't care," I said, louder now. "Just come get me out of here."

It was quiet. I wondered if I was deluded, hallucinating on a better present instead of getting subsumed in all that past. Then a single voice, one that sounded young and eager to hide the fact, said from somewhere above, "And who the fuck are you?"

"Nobody," I said. I think I meant it. "I'm stuck is who I am, under these racks. I must have passed out."

Some murmurs of a conversation aboveground reached me. So there were at least two people here. Someone laughed. I didn't like that sound. It was edgy, anxious. I tried to shimmy out from under the rack, but I was so exhausted I thought I might pass out again.

A head lowered down from the hatch, along with a hand holding a flashlight. It beamed into the backs of my eyes, blinding me. When it clicked off, the face was gone again. I hadn't gotten a good look, but it was safe to assume these guys weren't the police, and they weren't a couple machinists surprised to find a hole in the floor of their shop. These were people who knew why this place existed.

The first person to start down the ladder was wearing flip-flops. The night Mike died, one of the people I'd seen in the shop wore them, too. I was scared, but, without recourse, the fear burned off like a marine layer.

I waited while he slapped his way down the ladder. He reached the floor and wound his arm behind the first baker's rack, reaching as far as he could, and then every second bulb along the ceiling lit up.

My eyes sizzled back to the optical nerve for a second time. I blinked against the pain and protective tears, wanting to see again as quickly as possible. I wasn't sure what this guy's next move would be, or what I could do about it, but I didn't want to be rubbing my eyes like a tired baby when it came.

But he was just standing at the end of the room, watching me. He had on blue shorts and a white V-neck shirt. A flannel shirt was tied over half his face like an oversized bandit's handkerchief. He couldn't have been more than twenty years old. A damn kid.

The second person stepped onto the top rung of the ladder. I wondered if it would be Gustafsson, in one of his tailored suits. I wanted it to be. Or, if not him, then Sammy, grinning and acne scarred and inconsolable. I didn't have much hope in either case, but I wanted it to be one of them. My brain hungered after the closure either of their faces would represent, while the rest of me hoped there was just some way to make it out of this alive.

But it was another kid, a youngish guy by the clothes. He wore a short-sleeved button-up and oversized sneakers. To hide his face, he'd put on one of the welding masks from the machine shop. He climbed down and stood next to his pal, and they both looked down the chamber to me. Only the one in the welding mask was intimidating, tilting his static metal face to scrutinize me like a sentient but cold-hearted automaton.

The kid in flip-flops nudged the other one, tried to press something into his hands. The one in the welding mask shook his head. Flip-flops tried again, and this time his pal took whatever it was and whispered to the kid to fuck off. Then they walked my way. You could see them puffing themselves up as they got closer, until they almost looked like a unit—seasoned, familiar with this kind of confrontation.

The one in the welding mask came within a few feet of me and knelt down. What he held was a pistol, low, in his right hand. It wasn't a surprise, but my heart stuttered. There was a lump in my throat.

"How'd you get in here?" he asked. He sounded a bit more like an adult than his pal. Maybe he could grow a beatnik beard under that mask, if he let the fuzz on his face metastasize long enough and did a pubic hair transplant. I wondered if I should tell him that and get this over with. Then, sick to death of my mind's habits, I wondered if I really was that much of a fucking moron and tried a different tack.

"I'm pals with Ed, the guy who owns the shop," I said. "I came in to borrow some shit last night. Started moving stuff around and came across this. Then while I'm down here, someone shuts me in. I don't even know how long I've been down here."

"Yeah," said the kid in sandals. "You tripped the alarm." The other guy didn't react, didn't move.

"Sure, but look," I said, "I don't know what any of this is, and I don't—"

"Come on, you know it's drugs," said the sandal kid unhelpfully. "For real?"

"I don't care what it is," I said, trying to salvage this attempt to give them a way to let me go. "I just want to get out of here. I won't say anything to anyone. I don't have anything to say. It's none of my business. I smoke a little grass. I'm not one to judge. I shouldn't have been here in the first place."

The older one tilted his head to one side. A reflection of the burning bulb overhead shifted across the dull black of the mask's single rectangular lens. His voice ventriloquized through the welding mask, sounding colder, flatter, darker. "Eh," he said noncommittally. "Not sure that works for us."

Maybe feigning a little fear and trembling would tug at their heartstrings, I thought. "I'm pretty sure I almost died," I said, trying to let the fear come through in my voice. But it got stuck somewhere farther down, while the actor in me had to ham it up for the desired effect. "I think that hatch is airtight. I started running out of oxygen—I think that's why I passed out. Being this close to kicking the bucket is enough to scare me straight, I promise."

The sandal kid whined, "Shit." He punched his friend in the shoulder like I wasn't even there. "I didn't even think about that."

The older one didn't move. "It's fine," he said.

"No, man. No, it's not fine." Nervous energy poured off the sandal kid. He started rubbing his hands together like a doctor before the surgery. "Not after what happened."

"It's fine. Let it go."

The kid in sandals paced, bobbing his upper body slightly. He was threatening to revert to a prior, more birdlike form—skittish—and fly away. I knew I was seeing something that was as revealing, but of something different. "I should have called you sooner," he said.

"Let it fucking go," the older kid said louder now, turning from me to glare at his pal.

After what happened, he'd said. This was the person. This nervous fucking kid flopping around in sandals who didn't want to be the one to hold the gun. He was the person who'd killed Mike. But he didn't seem like a killer. He sounded doubtful, conflicted, a little shrill. There was hesitation and anxiety in how he handled himself, and fear and remorse. It was strange to glean a sense of his spirit through only a few minutes of presence, a few phrases, and to be convinced of his crime from them—a coming-together of convictions.

"You're the one," I said to him, without forethought. It had to be said, it seemed, and so I'd said it. If I'd wheedled or lied my way out of this, it would have only been to save my own skin, and I wasn't sure it was worth that.

"What?" he asked. "What are you talking about?"

"You. In that shop up there," I said, pointing above our heads. "You know what I'm talking about."

The kid backed away. His face crumpled, like a page of notes balled up and ready to be discarded. "You don't know what you're talking about, man."

"You shot him in the heart," I said, more firmly now. "You put a bullet in Mike Padilla's heart. Maybe your friend rolled him into the corner, maybe you did that. I don't know. But you're the one."

"Don't talk," the kid said, retreating farther back in the chamber. His friend in the welding mask still knelt on his heels a few feet from me, watching the exchange like it was between a mouse and a lizard and he was a boy with a magnifying glass on a hot day. He'd be paring his fingernails like an indifferent God, if God only had fingernails and this kid wasn't a filthy animal who couldn't give two shits about hygiene. "Shut your fucking mouth, man. If you don't—"

"What?" I said, glad to be feeling this anger again, like I was home, if home was a piss-drunk, blackout rage. "What are you going to do? That you weren't already going to do?" There wasn't a way these guys would allow me to live. Still, it was odd to call out Mike's killer when I was the one trapped and vulnerable—odd but exalting. If death was coming for me, I could at least hail it on its approach. "If I don't shut up you'll what? Why pussyfoot? Get it over with."

"Stop," the kid said, his voice cracking. "I can't listen to this. Jeff, I can't—this isn't what I signed up for."

Jeff, of the welding mask, muttered, "Fuck me." Then he walked over and clubbed the sandal kid with the butt of his gun, cracked him right in the ear. The kid cried out and bled red on his white shirt. At least I knew he wasn't a Dodgers fan.

"Go back to your fucking corner," Jeff said, pointing toward the ladder.

The sandal kid did as he was told. As he slunk off into his corner, he muttered to himself. He didn't seem mad at Jeff for coldcocking him. He was mad at himself.

Then Jeff walked back over to me. He passed the gun from one hand to the other, to reorient it from the pistol-whip grip he'd just used to the more traditional one. Then he passed it back to his right hand, with the business end pointed my way.

The ruse was up. No sense hiding behind, well, anything. The lies weren't working, and we were past lying now. "Where's Sammy?" I asked. "He's your boss, right? I've known Sammy since before you were a sperm going for a swim. Get him down here. Let me talk to him."

Jeff shook his head. "I don't know any Sammy." I could hear his breath hitting the inside of his mask, could almost taste the humid reek he must be rebreathing in there. He was close enough I could see a design on his shirt over the breast: a skull in a Nazi helmet, biting into a crucifix. Above it were a few words: HARD CORPS RANGERS.

"Sam Gans," I said. "Sammy Ray Gans. He's got a place just like this under the floor of his garage. He's part of how you guys get this stuff moved around. All you Hard Corps Rangers guys are part of it, right? I know. Youth-group kids, dirt bikers. The lifted trucks. And Gustafsson, he's behind all this, too—Tom Gustafsson. He knows me. He'll want to talk to me."

Jeff didn't move, didn't say anything for a minute. I felt myself hope—felt that skyward swoop in the chest—and hated it. I knew viscerally what that feeling had represented, what it had always represented to me: prelude to suffering, a sign of overdue and imminent readjustment to reality.

Then Jeff laughed bitterly, cut it short, and said, "I don't know anyone like that." My chest became my chest again, just a cage to keep a few pounds of organic slop from falling on the pavement. “These things,” Jeff said, pointing to the skull on his shirt, “are on fucking T-shirts you can buy anywhere. I drive a Hyundai, and you don’t know shit about how the world works.”

The sandal kid was groaning down by the ladder, and I was lost. “But, Sammy,” I said. “He’s got something just like this place.”

Jeff took a step closer. “Like I said, I don’t know any Sammy. Now shut the fuck up about it.” I tried to scramble out from under the rack again. I felt a little stronger now, could feel it rocking a bit as I moved. Jeff raised the gun. I pictured an invisible tube of potentially disrupted air that ran from the barrel to my head, then through it. “Don’t do that,” he said, sounding disappointed. “Dawn patrol working stiffs are going to be coming around the complex pretty soon. I don’t want to shoot you. Too risky. Someone might hear. I don’t really want to deal with cleaning you up either. But I can deal with it, if I need to.”

I stopped. My eyes had closed without me realizing I was doing it.

“No, I think we’ll close you back in,” Jeff said. “Help me out and scream a bit after we’re done, so I can make sure the sound doesn’t get through. Never has before. We come back in a week. Not that it’ll really matter to you.”

I’d wanted to be alive. Now it looked like my life was going to be taken away again. I’d never consented to being born, but I couldn’t consent to this. Not now. Not with what I needed Aracely to know.

“You can’t,” I said stupidly. “I’ve got a kid. There are people . . .” Even then, I couldn’t bring myself to say that there were people who needed me.

Jeff crouched and waved the gun toward the pills on the ground. “Want a little mercy before I go? Make the swim for the big light a little more peaceful,” he said, getting off on the whole situation.

“Not that kind,” I said. Maybe when it was my choice I’d come close, but there wasn’t anything I wanted from this kid, mercy included. "Go fuck yourself, you goddamn monster." I spat at his face, slick smearing across the mask's lens.

He took off the mask like a slo-mo catcher looking for a pop-up foul ball. It turned out he did have a couple days of patchy beard under there, a narrow and recessive jaw, a smudged nose, beady eyes. He didn't look like a monster. His wasn't the face of evil. It was the face of a kid I might have counseled, talking him through his parents' divorce and how inscrutable God's plans for us can be. An angry kid, not that different from me.

But he wasn't that church kid. He wasn't telling me his secrets. I wasn't being paid to turn them toward adhering him to the faith. I had failed Emily, and I was going to fail to reach Aracely. The sandal kid might have killed Mike, but what good was knowing that? The reasons were nonsense and going down with me in this smuggler's den they were turning into a tomb.

Jeff made a clicking sound with his mouth and left the mask on the floor. He stood and walked away slowly, self-consciously.

I started tearing myself out from under the fallen rack. My muscles felt like they'd been chewed up, but I found I could push with my legs. While I inched out, Jeff reached the sandal kid, who'd been holding his ear and watching us like a struck dog. Jeff pointed up and pushed him toward the ladder. Before he followed, he reached behind the first rack and flicked the switch, sending most of the room back into shadow. Then he climbed up in the column of light coming from above: the shit ascension of a motherfucker.

I was still only partway free. I knew what that meant. Before I could get to my feet, get to the ladder, get out—before any of that, they would have this place closed up. I didn't have a chance.

Then came the sound of scuffing metal while they settled the hatch back in place. Planes of light snuck through the cracks, flickering, before the seal was complete. Then I was back in full dark.

I didn't want it. I could have jumped out of my own body just to escape it if there'd been anything of a self to leave the body in the first place. Instead, I hit my head against the floor a few times. I was glad for a little sharp hurt, for the flash of pain so bright and red that I could see, for a moment, every time my forehead made contact.

I listened for the sound of the mill being moved back over the hatch. It was quiet. I must have been far enough down even that sound was muffled to nonexistent. The thought left me shaking. I took a deep breath and shouted a few curses. It didn't help much. I thought about the finite number of breaths left in this room and took another deep breath. I did it again. Fuck this air, I decided, taking big, luminous breaths, flooding my system with this oxygen until I was on the edge of hyperventilating. It was a clean kind of panic, and my face welled like it was a single, giant eyeball without a lid.

Then there was a sound. It was the mill finally being moved. No, it sounded different. It started and stopped. The pitch of it shifted as the noise vibrated through a few feet of earth and concrete. A moment later the hatch opened roughly. Light returned, that small shaft at the far end of the room. Tears came to my eyes—not tears only. Sobbing, I stared at this light, not knowing if it meant these kids were coming back to shoot me or if they didn't have the heart to let me die, not knowing if I was saved or lost—having no way of knowing what this light meant and not caring because it had returned. It had returned, when I thought it was gone for good.

Then something dropped down the column of light. It was about the size of a bar of wax. When it hit the ground, there was a new light—brilliant and immediate, like the flash of revelation, the illumination of conversion. With this flash came an explosive rush of sound, which hit my head like the seafloor after a bad drop, and a cloud of inwardly illuminated smoke that left me gasping for breath.

37.

THERE'S NO SUCH THING AS THE REVELATION THE PROPHETS DESCRIBE—the voice in the burning bush, the angel in the parted clouds, the sudden clarity of vision and purpose. Revelations are a slow build, the dull and time-consuming development of feelings, convictions, and prejudices. The other kind are a magician's reveal, reserved for the conversion of the actor in the Christian Broadcasting Network crowd.

Mine was followed by an aggressive greeting from some SWAT officers and then another good seat in the back of an ambulance. I had spots in my vision from the flash grenade, and its fumes in the enclosed space left me feeling woozy. Other than that, and nearly being murdered, I was fine.

I guess I wasn't all fine. I was cuffed to the gurney and driven to the hospital. There I got bad, wet hamburgers and Pedialyte. Whenever a nurse came in or out, I could see a cop stationed in the hallway.

After a couple hours of watching QVC like it was alien communication, I was interrupted by the detective who spoke to me after Mike's murder—Harper, the one who did some moonlighting as the

L.L.Bean centerfold. He seemed like an alien, too, or at least like he was two-dimensional and behind glass. I faintly heard his questions, foggily gave my answers. How had I gotten involved with Sammy? How long had I been part of this distribution operation? To what extent was I an accomplice to Mike's murder? I didn't feel unmoored by being considered a suspect again. None of this felt real. I did. Some of the darkness of the bunker hadn't left me—some of what I'd seen in the dark but had passed unnoticed in the light.

I explained how I'd found Sammy again, how I'd learned what he was doing. I told him how I'd called Tuitele about the bunker, and how I'd started to wonder if there was one in the machine shop. I left out Daniella, left out Emily. If the idea was to keep Emily safe, nothing I'd learned about the two of them would help in the hands of the cops. Emily didn't want to be found. I could respect that. And I'd assaulted Lambert in his home. I wanted to say someone else had, some past self, not me, but they were all me, and the scope of how far ahead of myself I'd gotten mortified me worse than Junípero Serra burning himself with candles, whipping himself with spiked chains, pounding his chest with stone—and still he'd felt justified in treating Indians as little more than slaves, showed who knows how many the enlightened way to an early grave, and found his name enshrined not only among the saints as the apostle of California but as a freeway exit in San Juan Capistrano. I'd settle for two days' sleep.

Harper listened, asked more questions, wrote on his notepad.

"Thank you guys for finding me," I said when it looked like we were done.

"Thank the night dispatch for security. She called it in, said you'd gone missing after poking around there. We were keeping an eye on the place, thinking you might show back up."

So I owed Esme another thank-you. And an apology—of course, an apology. She'd been so scared after Mike died. She must have thought the same thing had happened to me. To Harper, I just nodded and tried not to cry too visibly. I'd rate myself a five out of ten on that count.

"The doctors want to keep you overnight," he said, looking away politely. "You don't have a choice about that. Checking yourself out isn't an option—or you'd just trade this bed for one of ours. Someone will be back in the morning to talk about what happens next."

I nodded and inhaled to keep a few nasal drips where they belonged. He just watched me for a minute. Trying to suss out my motivations—my guilts or regrets or fears—from a few facial tics and eye movements. Then he said, "Thank you for your cooperation today," and left with a nearly imperceptible bow, like a waiter who'd finished taking the order.

He'd probably waited his way through the police academy, couldn't shake the customer service habit. I fell asleep considering the possibility of him slinging shrimp cocktails at the crab shack—not to cut him down or laugh at his expense, but because it reminded me: he wasn't a bad guy, and there was more to him than I could see.

I was woken by the sound of someone clearing his throat. Dimly, through the sleep-grime coating my eyeballs, I saw Tuitele filling the chair by the bed.

I sat up slowly. I felt weak and well rested, like a geriatric cat. Tuitele wore a light blue collared shirt, sunglasses in the pocket. He was busy resettling himself in the uncomfortably small pine-framed chair. On the other side of the room, Lawrence, in a tan suit, pulled back the curtains and looked out the window at the crenellated roof of the children's hospital across the way. It was nestled in another sprawling complex of low rectangular buildings, this one full of medical specialists and imaging centers.

"Hm," I said. "This isn't a good sign."

Tuitele shifted from leaning on one arm to the other. The chair creaked in its joints. His heavy-lidded eyes watched me guardedly. "You should know by now," he said, "that there are worse signs."

Lawrence turned from the window. His face was a little more readable, though I couldn't fully trust the polite smile of a midwesterner. He walked slowly to the side of the bed. "Sorry to wake you, Mr. Haines," he said with his hint of a drawl, which only partly hid the fact that he wasn't sorry. "We thought you'd be up by noon. But we all have better things to do than sit around and watch you sleep." Then he sighed and changed his tone. "I'm surprised we're talking to you again so soon, Mr. Haines."

"Get in line," I said. "It's been one surprise after another."

That wasn't exactly right. As absurd as all these events had been, I'd been running toward them—seeking these days or something close enough. That I'd found them was the surprise, but only in retrospect, and only because of my deeper need for disappointment's comforting smack to the face. "Did you catch the kids who tried to kill me?" I asked. "They're the ones who killed Mike Padilla."

Lawrence waved his hand in a gesture of so-so. "We got two young men at the shop. One's dug in, swearing he doesn't know anything. We'll work on him. The other's confessed. We've got to go back through evidence, make sure it's all solid."

It was strange to hear about confession in this sense. Not in confidence, like the kind I used to hear, the confessor intent on relieving the burden of sin by asking for Jesus's intercessionary heavy lifting. This was public confession, entered into the civic record, part of calculating the line between reasonable and unreasonable doubts. Each offered an incomplete truth. Truth could never be fully shucked from its hiding place, only carved out, little pieces at a time.

"What did he confess?" I asked.

"Moving the drugs," said Tuitele. "Shooting Padilla. You surprised them, the night you walked into the shop. Getting ready for a big drop. Padilla was more aggressive in his confrontation, it seems, and the kid panicked. Says it was an accident—that he was just trying to threaten Padilla, who was coming at him. Still, he doesn't deny it was his finger on the trigger."

Knowing this only left me feeling sunken and bitter, like my eyeballs were about to fall back into my cranium and float in the soup. A bad decision, a bad decision, panic, death, guilt, forced remorse. That was the story of this kid now, the story of Mike's end. It wasn't a good story—too much accident, no evil cause and effect, no Manichaean black and white—the kind where morality only gets a brief, greased grip on a person as they're torn out of their own life by the riptide. But as someone who'd once built a life around perfectly formed stories, I could accept this one as the truth of his—ragged, incomplete, unexemplary. Getting to the bottom of it wasn't something anyone could do.

I must have looked glum. Tuitele punched me in the shoulder with something like a smile on his face. "Hey, bonus is while we were there, some bikers came by and then tried to keep cruising like they were out for a Sunday drive. They had some interesting stuff in their saddlebags, and in the false gas tanks and exhaust pipes, too. Some organized *Easy Rider* shit. Maybe it doesn't mean so much to you, but we might be starting to figure out how these drugs are making their way across the border and around the county. Not bad for an unemployed security guard."

I didn't smile. Later I would read in the paper about a border tunnel task force that would find an entrance in the floor of another motorcycle machine shop. This one was in Otay Mesa. You could throw rocks from the roof over the fence between the United States and Mexico. The hatch led not just to a room but to a full tunnel, dug twenty feet down and lined with a set of small-gauge rails to run drugs from one side to the other. They'd been using moving trucks to move the stuff on the US side, but those had been getting seized. The new scheme used a running stream of modified motorcycles. Moving the drugs in smaller batches minimized the risk, allowing them to be sent to probably a dozen or more distribution points around Southern California—places like Sammy's house or the machine shop in Carlsbad.

Having a part in any of this was never my plan. No plan had deliberately gotten me involved in it either. But still, these coincidences—how the drug smuggling intersected with Sammy, how Sammy had used Emily, how Emily led back to Lambert, and Lambert to Gustafsson—they got my mental flywheel humming, the way they had in the bunker. The velocity was lower this time, though, like my hand was dragging on its surface, the way it does on the face of a wave as I slowed my speed.

"What about Sammy's house?" I asked tentatively, knowing it was crazy—that some part of my rotten noodle still believed these thin connections were a bridge strong enough to step out on. The cops finding a smuggling operation was a little taste, and I could sense how my brain started jonesing for the buzz of epiphany. Apophany was more likely, a longing for links in a chain where there was only a series of unexpected collisions within a finite, closed system. But the knowledge could only do so much to stop me. "Is this stuff part of Sammy's operation?"

Lawrence pursed his lips. "We're not ready to make that leap yet," he said with a slight defensive edge, picking up the hint of desperation in my tone. "We found a hidden storeroom in his garage, like you reported. With the amount of drugs inside, Gans is in custody and won't be out of it for a good long while. And none of your prints were in the place, so good news for you, too."

That they'd found the garage gave my nervous system a warm surge, got it rubbing up against its own little pleasure centers. It certified some of the conspiracy I'd worked up. In my chest I felt a wave of certainty, though I was present enough in my mind to call it what it had to be: wishful thinking. Still, I couldn't entirely give it up. I was like the older kid who's pretty sure Santa Claus doesn't exist but won't commit because of the prospect of lost presents.

"The kids you arrested—are they connected to him?" The one in the welding mask had sworn he didn't know Sammy. "Sammy had done something at my old church, after I was gone, and gotten some of the youth-group kids dealing prescription drugs for him. These kids looked like the type, and Emily was in a church like that, too, and"—I heard myself saying it, though I was already regretting it—"Tom Gustafsson, he owns that church, and he owns Carlsbad Palms North." I stopped myself there, before I tried to connect all these dots for them in Sharpie ink and made a bigger fool of myself.

Tuitele grimaced frankly. Lawrence didn't look away this time.

"Gustafsson was advised about the situation," he said curtly. "But he's aboveboard as far as we know. He doesn't need a side job running illicit drugs. He's richer than the pope. I have no reason to believe the young men we have in custody had any interaction with Mr. Gans, let alone Gustafsson, and their religious affiliation has so far been irrelevant to our investigation. When it comes down to it, San Diego is a small town." He lowered his gaze. "Too small, in point of fact, for you to run around pretending to be a cop."

My skin flushed with shame—shame at tipping my paranoid hand, shame at being found out.

Lawrence smiled at my body's response. "That settles it was you, I suppose. I wouldn't recommend pretending it wasn't. After all this, if your only crime is getting a little overzealous, I think a slap on the wrist could be arranged on the impersonation charge.

Only a misdemeanor anyway. Maybe some community service would be good for you, eh? Obviously, you shouldn't make a habit of interrogating pastors while pretending to be us. But we know you were just trying to find the girl."

The thrum of anxiety that ran through me made the light in the room seem to dim and waver. "Have you? Found her, I mean?"

"No," Tuitele said flatly. "Her prints were all over Gans's storage room. She was involved down there, though he isn't saying how—isn't copping to more than a short-term hookup. We'll see."

"You should know, though," Lawrence said, "that Ed Lambert, the pastor, he asked us to go easy on you. Said he could tell from talking to you that the deception was well intentioned, that you were trying to help someone they all care about. Call me old school, but I tend to defer to the wisdom of gray-haired, godly men."

I wanted to call him something other than old school for making that kind of mistake. But if Lambert said to go easy on me, and it was only about pretending to be a cop, then he hadn't told them how I'd stormed into his house and roughed him up. He probably hadn't filled them in on giving Emily some cash from the collection baskets either. He was an hour away, doing whatever the fuck he was doing, and yet here he was, somehow, still making a deal, bargaining with me. One secret for another.

I could refuse it. Maybe he'd press charges. Maybe it meant I'd get to add an assault rap to my record. But it would also mean pulling Daniella into this. Maybe her sweet little marriage would go poof when the story came out. She didn't have anyone looking out for her either. Even though she'd gone one way and Emily the other, she was still trying to help her friend. As much as I would have loved to be the cause behind some bad press for Lambert and his church, I didn't want to hurt Daniella any more than she'd already been hurt. And if Emily was going to reach out to anyone after the dust settled, it wasn't going to be the cops, and it wasn't going to be me. It would be Daniella again. Still, I wanted Lambert to sting. I didn't want to let him off the hook—not easily, not at all.

"Don't look so green," Tuitele said warmly. "You're okay. A little probation, a little community service. Maybe some counseling on the California taxpayer's dime. Then you're golden. You can take a new lease out on life, man. A good idea, since you were pretty damn close to breaking your old one down in that bunker—breaking it several times over."

Lawrence interjected: "I don't know if he really—"

"I'd want to know," Tuitele replied. They watched each other a minute, and then Lawrence nodded, relenting.

Tuitele turned back to me with relish. "You were about this close," he said, holding his hands two inches apart, "to burning your damn self alive."

"Excuse me?" I felt a few fingers of bile creep up my throat. It wasn't exactly a bad feeling. I was pretty sure I'd almost asphyxiated, that I'd somewhat narrowly dodged getting shot. But fire wasn't anywhere in that grim laundry list. "Is that supposed to be some kind of metaphor?" I asked.

Tuitele shook his head. He was smirking like a Halloween pumpkin carved by a kid with vertigo. "There were two sets of lights in that little bunker. Two switches, back behind the first row of shelves. The second switch would turn on the lights, every other bulb in the place. The other set of bulbs had been cut open with an acetylene torch, filled with gasoline, and then sealed up with putty. If you'd found the first switch and flipped it—boom."

My father had prayed, until the day he died, that the fire of God would rekindle in me. This was different, but of a kind. Just knowing I'd made it through a needle's eye with my own demise all around it disturbed the comfort I'd felt since getting to the hospital. Several needles' eyes, a needle factory's worth. I opened my mouth, but nothing came out. I hadn't liked being in the dark, the idea of dying blind and thirsty like a lost gopher. Going out in a gas bomb in an enclosed space wasn't a better option. And I'd been looking for the switch. If I hadn't passed out—not from lack of oxygen, a doctor would tell me, and much more likely from a panic attack, hyperventilation—I would have found them eventually. That would have been a kind of poetic completion to the story of me. I'd survived by nothing other than chance.

Lawrence motioned to Tuitele with his head, toward the door. Tuitele braced his hands on his knees and stood with a groan. Must have been a former football player, I guessed—had the size for it, and the aching joints.

"This is a lot to take in, I'm sure," Lawrence said to me. "Take a little time. Get some rest. You made it. Must have someone looking out for you."

"I don't know about that," I whispered before I found my voice. "More like dumb luck."

I wasn't the only one in this mess. No one had been looking out for them, not when it mattered. No one had been looking out for Emily, or Daniella, or even Sammy, who'd had a decent shot at making a clean life not all that long ago but was heading to jail, or the kid who'd shot Mike, or any of these kids—young, reckless kids. It left me furious, but I felt pathetic about it in my pale hospital gown, these baby-soft, overwashed bedclothes pulled up to my waist.

I hated that all this was true, and I hated how much of what I'd wanted to be true was false. But most of all I was filled with despair—after living it for how long?—over how I'd made a dogma of hate: hating myself, hating others; hating God, hating being without a god; hating the world, hating the lack of anything but the world.

38.

THE NOVA WAS STILL OUT AT THE INDUSTRIAL COMPLEX. THIS TIME I GOT A ride, in the back seat of Tuitele and Lawrence's cruiser. It had a steel-mesh cage between me and them. It wasn't the first time I'd ridden in that kind of seat, but I'd never done it sober. I hadn't realized how uncomfortable the seats were, hard and vinyl clad, cramped. Designed to pin and subjugate and then make it easy to clean up the shit and piss afterward with a fire hose. It had been someone's job to think that through. Or was that everyone's job? To think through, guard against, plan for, and attempt to control the actions of assholes? Most days that seemed true, today more than most. But it was a tall order. As I considered it, I felt sober in every sense. My thoughts moved like reptiles in the snow. The tension that had been building in my mind seemed to have passed now. Maybe I could get back to my old life.

Parking my mother's old Nova in the driveway of my house, though, I knew the old life had slipped the reins. To even get home, I'd had to ask Tuitele to use the cruiser to push the Nova fast enough to bump-start it. He'd done it, but he and Lawrence looked glad to be rid of me by the time the old motor got running—about as well as a heart undergoing cardiac arrest. Then I was stepping out in my driveway, still wearing my father's shirt and pants, which stunk of my own human grease and, under that, sagebrush. The wooden heels of the saddle shoes clacked on the concrete like they were daring me to Fred Astaire it up to my front door, taunting me with the impossibility of anything other than a collapse in the dead yellow grass. The house was the same as it ever was, on its slow decline into condemnation. The bougainvillea scratched against the window like a cat to be let out.

I didn't want to be there. I didn't want to deal with the wreckage inside. I didn't want to try to reorganize the chaos into a version of how my house had been before—before it had been ransacked, before Emily had stayed there—didn't want it back to any version of it I'd ever had. I wanted—could feel it floating throughout my mind like cirrostratus clouds, filtering all the available light—my old apartment, and all the life that came with it, as gone as it was and would remain. But the air was cool, coming from the west. There was a hint of a chill in it and a whiff of sea air, a relief after the hot, dinning wind of the Santa Ana and presaging the mild onslaught of fall and winter beyond that. That could be enough of a future, for now.

I'd started to walk up the driveway when a weak car horn sounded behind me. My heart scraped along my vertebrae, clacking like a frog-shaped guiro of dread. In my gut resounded a sick and unwanted sense of déjà vu—a feeling that everything I thought I was clear of wasn't clear of me. I stopped but couldn't bring myself to turn, to see what was coming. Then I heard her:

"Mark," a warm voice called.

It seemed to wrap around me on its route to my ears, and my body shuddered minutely with relief. I turned around to see Esme and her little white Civic across the street. She shut the car door and walked to where I stood. I knew I should say something, should fill the silence of that walk. But I just watched her—didn't think any thoughts about what I saw, but just saw her: Her black hair was down again, not glossy now but dry, with looping frizzes like the tracks in images of atoms colliding. She wore a simple gray hooded sweatshirt and white jeans. Her black sandals set off painted toenails, purple. She looked tired but relieved, bags under her eyes but no rush in her gait. She stopped a couple feet away and gave my sorry state a frank appraisal, coming in well under *Blue Book*.

"When I called the hospital, they told me you'd just checked out," she said. "They wouldn't let me see you yesterday. I was there. There was a policeman sitting by your door. How much trouble are you in?"

I shrugged. "None with them. That was all a mistake. So just my usual kind of trouble."

"Maybe a little more than you realize." Her smile was pained. Still, it was something of a smile. "I don't see any flowers in your hands. No box of chocolates. Can't imagine you've got a gift certificate for a massage in your back pocket. If you don't have a thank-you present for me, you'll be in more trouble than you know."

The laugh that came out of me could have been the first chuff before a bout of crying. "I know," I started, then got stuck. It took me a second to get going again, to find the right words. "I'm sorry for everything. I'm really, really sorry. You didn't need that. And I'm sorry for being, well, me. I'm working on it."

The pained look didn't leave her face, and the smile stiffened and then soured. Her eyes were squinting against something that wasn't coming from outside.

"As far as a thank-you present," I continued, "follow me and I'll see what I can find inside. At least some coffee first. And"—I felt my left frontal cortex buck against what I wanted to say, an aphasia of emotional disability, threatening to arrest the words in my mind—"my gratitude. Not just for the keys. For, ah . . . for all of it."

I turned away, I had to, and started walking up to the front door. I knew I was hiding from whatever was threatening to come through in her expression. I didn't think I was up for dealing with it face-to-face, not right now anyway. Without hearing her come up on me, I was surprised by her arms as they reached around my chest and held me from behind. I stopped, couldn't move. Her cheek pressed against my spine. The warmth of her body warmed around mine. She held me, and I was held. The last fight went out of me, and I thought tears would come then. But they didn't. Instead, I felt light, aloft. Borne by another's care. Adrift but in balance, like a balloon a few days after the party, not jerking on its string but not on the ground either, the little party ghost, floating room to room.

Then she let go and prodded me in the fat of my back. "Walk, mister. Into the house. I think I need that coffee."

I started to turn around to look at her, but she pushed me roughly on the back of the head.

"March," she said firmly. "You need a shower, too. Whew. I'll take care of the coffee." As we walked, I heard her sniffle. I couldn't see but could somehow sense, in my peripheral awareness, that she was wiping her eyes. "Then we'll see if any of that trouble's real trouble."

39.

BEFORE DAWN, I WAS AWAKE AND AT THE JETTY. THE SURF WAS LOW. Chest-high sets came in lazily every fifteen minutes. The morning fog was light. The moisture in the air left my skin clammy and chilled. The sound of the waves in the dark was thin and high and comforting.

While I was putting on my wetsuit in the lot, a beater of an old Jeep truck parked a few spots down. A ratty-haired teenager got out. He blew a couple loud shots of snot out his nose and started scraping the wax off his board. The grind of the wax comb against the fiberglass echoed off the cinder-block shitters and the moored sailboats in the harbor that were floating on the black ocean stained with streaks of orange lamplight. I walked past him and grunted on my way down to the shore. His smile was a toothy grimace, but he said, "Have a good one," and I told him to have one, too.

By the time my ankles hit the waves, I was far enough away from the lights that the sky and the ocean were the same black ink. My feet shimmered and disappeared into it, and my board buoyed against it, slapping gently like the hull of a boat against a passing wake. I paddled out, felt calmed by each dive under another gentle, broken gray-white wave that had been set to roiling into itself by the seafloor, unseen below. It was an easy paddle out.

Soon I was floating past the waves, in a dark that was different from the dark of the tunnel. Maybe there are two kinds: the dark we fear and the dark we rest in. And so it's the same with light. One warms us and gives us color and form, beauty, but the other gives us other people to see and lets us be seen—it exposes us to judgment and shame, without rest—and makes us hunger to know everything we see, and then even that which we can only infer or imagine. Here I was held in the dark as much as I had been held by Esme, tenderly and without reserve. In this kind of dark I felt able to contend with the world, to be content with myself. I wouldn't move to paddle, wouldn't catch a wave until the sun rose, and that would be just fine.

But before the sun could brighten up the view to the west, the ratty-haired kid was hooting his way along a couple swift, if small, right-handers. It was quiet enough I could hear his breathing, the respiratory sound of the wave breaking, the surprisingly soft splashing of his body falling back into the water when each wave was over. And then his laughter. He was laughing so hard. Maybe it sounded a little crazed—or, if not that, somehow impolite, like we should be respecting some unspoken rule of silence under these conditions. But that was my rule, my imposition, my law that I would hold against his actions, his joy. He was having such a good time. He paddled back out a dozen yards away from me, an easy distance even for an old man like me. Still, I left him alone.

At Angelo's I bought two breakfast burritos. The plan I had was to take them both back to the jetty, eat mine and leave the other on the rocks. Mike and I had never finished our round in the batting cages. I'd been thinking this whole time he owed me the breakfast, but maybe I was the one who would have lost. Maybe I owed him.

It was a way to close things out between us. A bunch of sentimental nonsense is what I mean to say, the idea that I owed him anything, that he—dead and gone—could register the debt as paid, that this was anything but an off-off-Broadway play with a cast of one and an audience who was the cast, a little theater to trick whatever emotional beast pacing restlessly inside me to slip its cage and wander into some other habitat. I could articulate all that, and still I couldn't tell you why the idea of doing it won out, but that didn't bug me much.

When I got to the jetty, the kid was still surfing under a clear, blue, morning sky. I watched him, remembering those kinds of mornings when you wouldn't come in until your arms were useless and you could barely stand from exhaustion and hunger. I ate my burrito. When he came in, I gave him the other one.

40.

WHILE I HAD BEEN GETTING LIGHT HEADED IN A BUNKER, GABBY LEFT A couple messages at the house. Our last conversation, when I'd called her after Mike's funeral, had been bugging her, and she wanted to check on me. I hadn't felt up to calling her back yet, but she caught me a few days after I got home, sleeping at six at night.

"I thought you might be dead," she said dryly when I answered. "You're usually more punctual about harassing me."

"Yeah," I said. That hollow flutter from being woken straight out of a deep sleep hadn't left my chest yet. It mingled with a dark humor about how close Gabby was to being on the nose. "I've been off my game. I'll try harder, I promise."

"Even the other day," Gabby said, still teasing aggressively. "You were acting so strangely. You didn't insult anyone in our family. You didn't insist on your rights. You're slipping."

Our family. That was a strange thing to hear her say. It hadn't been ours for a long time. It was theirs. Even the phrase "our family" felt more like a postwar ruin than anything you'd put faith in, like the church or a middle class. But a crumbled edifice was still a structure, and I had at least helped set some of the foundation stones, for better or worse.

"No yelling, no insults," I said. I needed a glass of water, three weeks' sleep, some Xanax. My voice broke off the words in weak, dry chunks. "I don't have it in me today. Really, I don't."

"Aw, but you sound terrible, and I've got you on the run. It's a rare opportunity."

"Sorry, I can't—"

"You sick? Or just scared?"

"Gabby. Please."

"Okay, okay, I'll stop. But you do sound bad. Really. Are you okay? Ignore the tone of how I say it. I can't help not taking you too seriously. But are you?"

I breathed heavily through my nose. "I doubt it," I said lightly, "but I'll manage." It was too difficult to explain everything that had happened. It was too hard even to know what it meant to me, though I could feel the meaning in my gut, clear and articulate as a fist. I thought of Gabby in her small home in Eugene. I thought of Aracely, my little girl, and her apartment, a crib next to the bed. I thought of my grandson, whose name I didn't know.

"Hey," Gabby said when I hadn't spoken in too long. "You still there?"

"Hm," I said. That was about all I could manage.

"Come up."

"Excuse me?"

"Come up," she said again, with less fear and anticipated regret in her voice. That was meaningful, too. "No promises about seeing Aracely. But come stay on my couch a few days. At least it'd get you out of the house for a while. You forget how well I know you, and I know this voice. Haven't heard it in a while, but I remember it. And

Eugene's nice right now. You might find it exceptionally difficult to shit on."

I closed my eyes. "You sure?" I asked.

"Of course not," she said, but her voice was easy on me in a way I hadn't heard for years.

We agreed that I'd come up in a few weeks. There were a handful of things I needed to take care of around the house. A broken back window. Some stains on the carpet I'd pretend to try to remove by buying some caustic product and never applying it. I put the Nova back in the garage at my parents' house and had a real estate agent meet me there.

By then I'd put off leaving long enough. There was one stop I needed to make along the way, but I'd been dragging my feet. I had reasons to wait, wanted to give her some time. But eventually I was out of reasons and out of time to kill. I packed the truck and headed north on the 405.

After the arid expanse of the Camp Pendleton Marine Base, where all three of the nation's best and a few thousand other guys reenacted Normandy Beach invasions every fourth weekend, I pulled off the freeway in San Clemente. There were some regular buildings in the town, like the liquor store, but mostly I drove past mock Spanish Colonials built in the 1920s and '30s and then the more recent and palatial ones from when we really hated Mexicans but wanted to pretend to live like españoles in prerevolutionary New Spain, down to the complexion of the household staff. Eventually I came to the hard-luck, mid-century shoebox on Elena Lane that had been subdivided, probably using cardboard and duct tape, into two apartments. I parked a few dozen yards down to wait with a view of the driveway.

Waiting was easy now—no rush for anything, no push or pull

forward. I wasn't looking for something to get pissed off about, wasn't looking for that little adrenaline high of unrighteous indignation—any kind of distracting buzz at all. The last year had been a relapse, even if I'd never had a drink. I was back at meetings, a day or two a week, after years of swearing them off. Alcoholics, like pastors maybe, are never recovered but always recovering. It was a grim truth, and I didn't like it. I hadn't fallen into spraying crowds with holy water and preaching the end times, but something of that wretched and retching way of thinking had drifted in like an algae bloom in my brain. Now I was past it, waiting in the still water for whatever would come—no predictions, bitter or metaphysical, and no great hopes, but no certainty about their impossibility either. To wait around in my truck for a while was tedious in a way I could live with, was nothing.

The tedium evaporated like a marine layer when I saw her.

Emily's hair was blonde now, pasted down with some kind of product, but of course it was her. She was carrying a blue foam surfboard, a seven-footer by the looks of it. She wore knee-length trunks, olive green, and a white rash guard. She stopped at the curb to check her pockets and looked down the street. I thought about ducking but didn't, and she didn't see me anyway. She wasn't looking for me. She didn't know I was still looking for her.

I let her walk away a full five minutes. Then I got out and walked after her. I knew her destination anyway. She wasn't taking that board to catch a bus. It was only a few curving, downhill blocks before I passed the Beachcomber Motel and could see the pier below, silhouetted and looking like a zipper in the denim of the ocean. Emily was walking down the stairs to go under the train tracks. I waited on the bluff to see if she'd emerge on the other side and go north or south. She went north, disappearing in the shadow.

I followed under the tracks, where the puddles might be seawater or piss or both—the smell was all the same, putrid and sour but familiar in a way I liked. She was out in the water, so I sat in the sand and watched. The waves were knee-high, and she was, as she'd called it when I took her surfing before, getting hassled, if not surfing. She was still finding her legs, falling mostly before she stood up. That was partly the fault of the waves. They didn't have enough push, and the board would founder, underpowered. But she was paddling more confidently, was seeing how to get around the break, get over or through waves. And even from this distance, I could see she was finding out that it could be fun.

By the time she rode into the thin, sandy gloss that squeegeed itself against the shore, the sun was low in the sky. It was a perfect kind of post-tourist and pre-autumn evening to be down here, all the blast and idiocy of the summer fading in memory. She wrapped the leash around the tail of the board and walked up the beach, a classic California profile in nearly full shadow, her features existing only in a burnished, golden shade, like the saints on Renaissance altarpieces that seemed to be inwardly self-illuminated. But Emily couldn't be the surfer girl the Beach Boys sang about, the girl half the young (and not so young) men around her lusted for, laughing through evenings at bonfires and ukulele sing-alongs. That was just her darkened profile, a corresponding outline. And if she was in shadow, my face was catching the light, and she was coming my way.

"Emily," I called.

If she was startled, she didn't let it show. She brought her free hand up to wipe some salt water away from her eyes and blinked at me a few times. Then she laughed and shook her head, saying something quietly to herself, and walked over to me.

"Shaka," I said, waving my hand with thumb and pinkie out like it was a faulty flip phone.

"Oh, fuck off," she said, standing only a couple feet from me now. Her expression was stern.

"You're getting better," I said, motioning toward the waves.

"I'm getting shit," she said, not taking her eyes from me for a second. "Maybe a tan."

"It's something."

"Speaking of shit, you're looking . . . well." It wasn't untrue, and the way she said it wasn't unkind. I'd probably lost some weight since the last time I saw her, wasn't shaving. I was still so exhausted my face felt numb most times, and my jaw ached. It had been over a year since we first met, but I looked like I'd aged five.

"You are what you eat," I said.

That made her laugh, but it was bitter and she cut it short. "God damn it. I shouldn't have gone to Angelo's that day. I'd have been better off at Denny's."

"Not likely," I said. "The geriatric Oceanside Chamber of Commerce surf team goes there for Grand Slams and games of waitress grab-ass. One of them would have lent the wrong kind of hand."

She rolled her eyes, and her smile puckered like a jacaranda bloom a day after it'd fallen to the sidewalk. "Fine. I should have gone to the grocery store and bought myself a bag of salad, is that what I should have done?"

"I don't regret getting you a burger."

Her laugh was dismissive. "Maybe you should. Anyway. Sorry I fucked up your house."

After the bunker and the hospital, once the paranoia and wish for meaning had faded, I could see there were enough clues that my ransacked house wasn't done by Sammy's people sending me a message. It wasn't even clear if Sammy had people; it was more likely that he was someone else's person, a tool in its own compartment in the toolbox. But someone had wanted me to think he did. Someone wanted me motivated to get Sammy locked up.

"Figured that was you," I said. "No apology needed. Nothing

there, nothing to fuck up, I mean. Only took a couple hours and some air freshener to put it to rights. The bed was maybe a little too far."

"Maybe. But doing the fridge was fun."

"My poor Tapatío."

She smirked and looked down the beach in either direction, a trickle of water running from her hair down her cheek.

"No one else is here," I assured her. "I haven't told anyone."

"Then what do you want?"

It was a fair question. I'd been thinking about this since the hospital. I never told the cops about Lambert giving Emily the money or how he'd lied about seeing her so recently. I'd wanted to ruin whatever he had, but when Tuitele told me to take out a new lease on life, I remembered finding the rental agreement in Daniella's car. It had a San Clemente address, Elena Lane, Daniella's name and signature in the right spots. It hadn't meant anything at the time, but Elena stuck because of Ellen, my sister. Then, in the hospital, I saw it: Daniella claimed her life was the work she did at Canaan Hills and in the community around the border. She was getting married, doubling down on that whole life, the antithesis of the one she might have had if she and Emily had been united in their response to Lambert—a life that would be hard to live from a tiny apartment in San Clemente, an hour and a half away without traffic. The rental couldn't have been for her new abode of marital bliss. I'd at least read those signs well.

And Emily had admitted to ransacking my house, likely figuring that if I thought Sammy was sending me a message, I'd have more of a fire lit under me. She'd read my signs well, too. At the end of the day, it got Sammy locked up. Emily was safer, living quietly up here. So what was it I wanted?

"To see you," I said. "Just to see you."

Emily laughed dismissively. Her nose creased at the bridge, and though I couldn't see them from where I sat, I pictured the freckles that ran across her face, saw how they related to the ones on her mother's face. "So you're going to tell me," she said scornfully, "that under all that you're just another sentimental asshole?"

"Maybe," I said. "Probably not. I just needed to see with my own eyes that you weren't gone for good. That you hadn't just up and vanished."

"I don't know, man. That seems like bullshit to me," she said, shaking her head. "You don't want to know what was happening with Sammy? Why I was in Oceanside that day? What's happening now? You're good at playing quiet, but I bet you're looking to meddle some more. It's the dad in you."

I took a breath and let it out. "I doubt it," I said. "I was never much of a dad. And I could ask you a bunch of questions, but what would I get? The whole story? I don't think so. Even if we spent the whole day talking, I wouldn't know it all. I've got a decent sense, though. I can make some solid guesses, and maybe it's better to leave it at that. San Diego's a small town, and the evangelical scene is even smaller. After Lambert broke your heart, I can see how you would fall in with some people who'd eventually lead you to Sammy."

She nodded confidently, but she wouldn't meet my eyes now. "Sure, close enough."

"Fine. Then you get hooked on whatever Sammy was selling. You start doing what you need to do. Maybe you trade sex for room and board. Maybe not."

"Eh, not," she said. "Sammy's a big, stupid baby. He can barely look at his own dick, let alone get a girl to do much with his or anyone's. He's really not good at much of anything. I'm organized, can think ahead, keep track of things. I helped him get organized."

"So everything I heard, from that kid Shaw and from Daniella, the forced prostitution, or at least using sex for—"

"That was my own shit," she said. A wash of stale pain passed over her face, and she looked away, fixing her features to glare into the setting sun for a moment.

"Fine," I said. I knew something of what she was feeling, that hard blade a person can wield against oneself. It was sharp, and unbreakable, and knew exactly which tender places to pierce, exactly how to maximize the pain it could render from the flesh and more than flesh. But I knew enough about what I didn't know, too, and how foreign her life was from mine.

"Then maybe you figured you'd had enough," I said, "or felt backed into a corner. Maybe you just couldn't shake your feelings for Daniella. You'd buried them deep, but they kept growing anyway, without water or light. You had to see, now that you were both adults, if there was something still there. So you left Sammy and tried her. But I talked to Daniella. I got a good sense of her take on what happened between you, and she was engaged, so you got hurt all over again."

Now Emily set her board down next to me and sat on it. She curled her toes again and again in the sand and looked out at the piddly waves that had crossed half an ocean to do their next to nothing against the shore and then recede. She kneaded one palm with the other hand's fingers, and I thought about the cartoon she'd left on my patio—the ad for fate line plastic surgery. They weren't her hands she'd drawn, I saw now. They were Daniella's. A joke, a wish, something more complex.

"So then you figure it's a good time to leave town," I said, quieter now that she was next to me. "Maybe you end up having a little too much fun first. Some habits are hard to kick, and you'd talked a good chunk of change out of Lambert." She scoffed under her breath but not in a way to stop me. "Somehow your money's gone before you can split. Maybe you never really wanted to get to the Space Needle."

She smiled thinly. "I just don't look good in flannel."

"Sure," I said, glancing at her. "Maybe that." She was rubbing her knees where they'd been scuffed red by the wax on her board. She was beautiful, and beside me, but I felt nothing but an aching tenderness for her now. No, I had to admit, even then some of the attraction that had mingled with paternal affection still lingered. Nothing goes away completely. But some things can fade for so long they might as well have, and others you're just too tired to be ashamed of, when you know they're too weak to act.

"I thought I could start a new life," she said. "But then none of them sounded good. No version seemed worth the hassle."

"So then back to Sammy's?"

She nodded, pursing her lips. "That wasn't worth it either." She picked up a small blade of kelp with one dangling bulb and fidgeted with it. "But I couldn't think of where else to go, and I couldn't keep staying with you. I could see the way you were looking at me. I knew where that was going. The way every other one had gone."

My heart stuttered a beat, and I felt pierced, accused. It was true, of course. It was no use hiding from the fact. There was a new kind of pressure inside me. A dislocated sense of shame, like fog, settled over everything. She was right, and that was all. I'd tried to help, but still I was there, part of the lineup of figures that fit what she'd learned to expect from men. Maybe only a shadow of it, among the longer shadows cast by those others. I hated feeling on the hook for it. But on the hook was where I needed to be, like a fish, and always.

"I'm sorry," I said. "If I did or said anything—if I could have said or done anything different, so that you would have stayed. So that I could have helped you."

"Forget it," she said firmly, popping the kelp bulb between her fingers and tearing it from the blade. "You were low grade, compared to . . . you know. But I couldn't handle the halfway, the not-knowing—"

"The decent enough."

"Right." She threw the blade of kelp, which caught in the early evening breeze and landed a couple feet away in the sand. "At least I knew the way shit went down at Sammy's. I wasn't going to slip up and get the rug pulled out from under me."

"Unlike Lambert."

"You have no fucking idea."

There wasn't anything to say to that. We sat together in silence, or at least next to each other in it—it's hard to tell the difference. I would accept either.

"But still, for some reason Daniella started to help you," I said softly.

Emily laughed derisively. "I made her."

"Blackmail?" I asked, without thinking.

"Fuck you," she said, facing me. She held a fistful of sand—not to throw at me, I think. She'd just grabbed for something when the anger hit. I could understand that. "What Eddie did to me, what he's done to her? That's fucking blackmail. With the fate of your eternal soul as the price, for fuck's sake. I'm not like that."

I held my hands up defensively. "I didn't mean—"

"You meant what you meant. Don't get all fucking holy and judgmental on me."

"That's not what I'm doing. It just came out."

"Exactly," she said.

I tried to touch her shoulder but stopped myself when she flinched away. "I don't need to know," I said. "Like I said, I just want to know you're okay."

"Okay?" she said, voice rising, tears coming to the brinks of her eyelids but refusing to spill. "What does that even mean to someone like you? How do you define it? Is okay getting clean? Fine. I'm in a program here. I'm getting clean. Is okay never speaking to my parents again? Okay for me, but maybe not for a guy like you. I don't give a fuck. They made that bed. And what about mine? I get Daniella here with me a couple days a month. I'm getting what I always wanted, right? The other twenty-eight days a month she's off singing worship songs and planning her wedding. But she's thinking about me. She's thinking about my lips when she kisses his. I can fucking live with that. But does it fit your definition of okay? Because I never thought she would admit to feeling anything for me again. But she did. Dealing with those twenty-eight days a month? I can do that. That's okay. For me. And she can deal with it, too."

I regretted making her so mad. But I couldn't undo it, couldn't go back. All I could do was try to untangle it. It wasn't blackmail, but still I could sense there was some pleasure in there, in making Daniella's life harder, in hurting her by driving her to admit her love. "So when you say you made her, you meant . . ."

"I just kept showing up." Emily was speaking emphatically now. This was a narrative she'd been playing and refining in her mind often enough, running rehearsals at least twenty-eight days a month, a way of justifying herself. "I kept writing her letters after I went back to Sammy's. Kept pushing her. Kept reminding her of who she was, of what we'd felt. Maybe I just liked making things weird for her. She needed a little more weird. Then you, you fucking moron, you show up at Sammy's. But it was my chance, too. I'd been thinking about taking his money. I was the one handling the books anyway. I'd gotten the laptop ready, and when that didn't work, I could get Daniella to help me, and then you'd get Sammy locked up, and then I'd be free. I thought that was what I wanted. I hid out in the garage underground for a few days, until the cops cleared out. Then I went to Daniella, and something had changed. She'd changed."

"But she's only changing about as often as a full moon," I said.

She stared hard at the horizon, felt about that far away from me. "I'm not going to explain it. But who she is down there"—she pointed to the south, to San Diego and Canaan Hills—"is who she is, too, as much as when we're together in my apartment here. It's not supposed to be easy. It's supposed to be this hard. And she's reminding me of some things, too. I thought I'd be getting free after I left Sammy's, but freedom doesn't look the same now. We're not going to change our beliefs because of who we are. We aren't going to turn our backs on God like that."

"We?" Now I was starting to understand, when it was too late to wish I didn't. This was two-way ventriloquism, then: Emily had coaxed another voice out of Daniella, but now I was hearing Daniella's words come out of Emily's mouth. "You can't even go to the church. Who's the we?"

"Fine. Daniella. It's who she is. Can I change that? It's in her heart as much as I am. They're all part of the person who's helping me, the one who's looking out for me when no one else does. So fuck you if you think I'm the first person to do this to herself for love. That *is* love. Compromising yourself for someone more important than you. I'm ready to do that. Daniella is."

I looked at the people on the pier, couples and families and teenagers throwing french fries to the seagulls. It gave Emily what little privacy I could while she fought back her emotions. I heard her stifle a sound in her throat—a guttural, heart-wrenching sound. She didn't think anyone understood her. I don't think I got it all—who does?—but I got the gist. It wasn't all good, and it wasn't easy, but who was I to judge whether or not this ground would prove fertile, for now, maybe for longer. She was making a go of things in the only way that seemed available to her, in the only terms that were real as she understood them. Even if I wouldn't take that leap, she was convinced it was worth the risk. I hoped that willingness to place her heart in another's chest—the risk, if not the reward—

would be good for her, but I hoped, too, that her feet would find purchase and not air.

In the late light, a fisherman on the pier reeled in his line. A stingray squirmed in the open air among the pylons, water rushing from its back. "This is what you want?" I asked Emily, without looking at her yet.

"It's what I want now anyway," she said. Her voice was small, fragile, childlike, still a little petulant, a little lost.

"Then all I have to say is good luck." I stood, still looking out for a minute, letting my peripheral vision linger on the form of her next to me. "And go easy on yourself, if you can." Then I turned and held out my hand for her to shake. Goodbyes should be formal.

She grabbed my hand and pulled herself up instead, then held it past when she was on her feet. Her eyes were raw rimmed, her lips red and chewed. She lowered her head to watch me in that cautious, canine way she had. "For what it's worth," I said, "I was trying to help, too. It didn't go the way I wanted it to, and I don't think I did you much good. But I wanted to. And thank you for that."

She let go of my hand. A chilly onshore had come up, another premonition of fall. She folded her arms across her chest, and I felt how cold the rash guard must be growing. "I know, man," she said. "If it helps, I don't know if I could have made the jump if you hadn't shown up at Sammy's. Maybe you didn't mean to, but you gave me the push."

It was a kind thing to say, but I wasn't so sure. I nodded, though, feeling neither good nor bad about it. There was no way for me to know if any of this was good or bad for her—no way to know anything. But she wasn't being tossed around by other people, wasn't being hassled by her life. She knew how the swells came in, and from where. She knew the break, how it shaped the waves. She knew where she'd chosen to paddle out, and what wave she'd caught, even if there was time left for surprises in the unraveling. She was riding it, come hell or high water—had found the nerve, in fact, to paddle back out after the last one and ride it again.

Emily shivered and held herself tighter. Her smirk settled into a tight, wary grin.

"You're cold," I said finally. "Go have a hot shower. I'm going to stay down here a little longer, and then I'm out of your hair forever."

"What hair?" she said, running her fingers through the short, blonde strands. The water in them sprayed into the air, and I felt a few drops dash against my face and lips. My soul groaned, or the array of misfiring neurons that made up the respiration of my mind, what the Greeks called the *anime*, or breath, and what I called a goddamn diagnosable condition. Then she picked up the board and turned to go. With the board in one arm, her gait was functional and solid. Her hips chugged linearly, and the muscles across her back flexed every time the wind blew against the length of her board and threatened to turn her. She moved like she had a purpose and no room for wasted gestures, like the flirtatious ones she'd used on me in Angelo's.

She stopped a few yards away and turned back. "Hey," she called. "Give it a few weeks. Let things cool down a bit more. But then stop by. I still need to get you back for that hamburger."

I nodded solemnly, and she smiled. It was a dark smile, a mouthful of sadness framed by sarcasm. The setting sun was now full on her face. Her eyes were rose hued. The freckles on her damp cheeks showed like the dim stars you sometimes see at dawn, the ones that aren't stars but planets, reflecting. It was strange to see her mother in her face, her father, too, and to know how in the dark they'd remain. I wanted to ask about them, but it was too late and it would have done no good. I'd been wanting to ask if Aracely still carried anything good of me from her childhood. Probably not. Probably lost years ago. And this was Emily's darkness to dole out. The wind dragged at her board, causing her to twist at the waist. She let it pull, turned with it, and then was walking away again.

I sat back in the sand. My brain hummed wordlessly. Everything my eyes chanced on was rendered in sharp lines, vivid colors. The marbling swirls where the water thinned against the sand. The divots in this surface where sandpipers goose-stepped and dipped their beaks. The lamps on the pier flickering to life. Surfers bobbing in the break like otters. The old, wiry-haired woman in the Lycra sports bra and bicycle shorts doing some kind of earth goddess dance to the setting sun, for fuck's sake. I laughed. I was alive. That's what had filled my mind over these last days, cloud-like and blocking the light of all the usual nonsense of my passing, familiar life. And so was Emily. And that was good. Good enough.

The sand I sat on retained the day's heat, even as the air grew colder. It was almost time to leave. Gabby was expecting me. Maybe Aracely, maybe even my daughter's son. I didn't know. I hadn't brought myself to ask. It was better not to know. But even the prospect meant more than I could say. That there were people who expected something of me, and not only insignificant things, and not only hurt. The world could work a person over until he stopped asking anything of it. But the expectations in my power to meet, I would meet them. I would try. The drive was fifteen hours along dark highway. But on the other end, maybe by the next evening, three faces would be there for me to see: one who knew me well, one who'd needed me once, and one I would recognize without ever having seen it before.

The light went from bright to golden to orange. The sun sank behind the horizon. No mythic green flash, just there, there, there, and then not there. I waited for the blues to settle onto the surface of things. Then I got back on the road.

ACKNOWLEDGMENTS

I AM so grateful to so many people that this will inevitably be an incomplete list. But first, my warmest thanks to Tim Wojcik, my agent, for believing in this book and for invaluable encouragement and insights along the way. To Sofia Groopman for seeing something in Haines, and Mary Gaule for all kinds of editorial wisdom and guidance. And to everyone at Harper Perennial for the warm welcome, hard work, and enthusiasm. Thank you.

FOR TEACHERS, mentors, and guides who've helped me see this was possible and how: Terri Meier, Susan Pope, Galaxy Force writers in the late 1990s, Joshua Ferris, Michelle Latiolais, Michael Ryan, James McMichael, Alex Espinoza, Charmaine Craig, Tod Goldberg, Romayne Rubinas Dorsey, Samrat Upadhyay, Tony Ardizzone, Lydia Davis, Dan Chaon, and the much missed Don Belton, who pushed me to "work it" (and grow a bohemian goatee). Special thanks to Bob Bledsoe, for helping me into this novel, and for encouraging me to stay with it—I wouldn't have without your encouragement. Sending love and gratitude to fellow writers who've shared support and feedback over the years, including Michael Andreason, Jacob Angelo, Juan Aragon, Ramona Ausubel, Tina Bartolome, Bradley Bazzle, Devin Becker, Caroline Diggins, Jesus Duran, Michael Hartwell, Kurian Johnson, Deborah Kim, Jenny Liou, D.A. Lockhart, Nina Mamikunian, Leila Mansouri, Pablo Piñero-Stillman, Ashley Rutter, Andrés Sanabria, Rick Sims, Lana Spendl, Alexander Weinstein, and especially novel crew Catalina Bartlett, Aya Bassiouny, Nancy Coner, Rachel Lyon, Michael Manis, and Sana Younis.

I ALSO want to thank the many people who've shaped my thinking about life and the spirit in ways I'm grateful for, with an especial nod to: first and forever foremost my grandmother; Evan and Kyle Rosa; Devann Yata; and Richard Miller.

TO VERNON Ng, for love and intelligence and humor (well, sometimes), and for being a first reader for so many drafts and half-baked ideas.

I DEDICATE this book to my siblings and my parents: this isn't autobiography but you're in every page, and a part of everything I do. To Mark and Chris, for adopting me so fully into your family. And a shout-out to family all around: sisters-in-law, cousins, aunts, uncles, nieces, nephews, and a wonderful grandmother-in-law. And to Grandpa-dude: longtime light in all things.

TO NORA and Alice: I'm coming up from the shed soon. I love you *this* much.

TO LAUREN: I've been working on this book nearly as long as we've been married. For your patience, encouragement, insight, big-heartedness, wisdom, leadership, and love—for everything you make possible in this world, which for me is everything—I'm forever yours.

ABOUT THE AUTHOR

PATRICK COLEMAN'S writing has appeared in *Hobart, ZYZZYVA, Zócalo Public Square,* the *Black Warrior Review,* and *Utne Reader,* among others. His debut poetry collection, *Fire Season* (Tupelo Press), won the Berkshire Prize. Coleman also edited and contributed to *The Art of Music,* an exhibition catalog on the relationship between visual arts and music (Yale University Press with the San Diego Museum of Art). He earned an MFA from Indiana University and a BA from the University of California, Irvine. He lives in Ramona, California, and is the assistant director of the Arthur C. Clarke Center for Human Imagination at the University of California, San Diego.